CW00632100

# Heartsease

# Heartsease

ANN TURNER

Matador
9 Priory Business Park
Kibworth Beauchamp
Leicestershire LE8 0RX, UK
Tel: (+44) 116 279 2299
Fax: (+44) 116 279 2277
Email: books@troubador.co.uk
Web: www.troubador.co.uk/matador

ISBN 978 1783060 993

British Library Cataloguing in Publication Data.
A catalogue record for this book is available from the British Library.

Typeset in Aldine401 BT Roman by Troubador Publishing Ltd
Printed and bound in the UK by TJ International, Padstow, Cornwall

**Matador** is an imprint of Troubador Publishing Ltd

*This book is dedicated to Brian, John and Caroline for putting up with my incessant scribblings for years.*

# AUTHOR'S NOTE

The following people mentioned here have been a help to me during the process of the creation of Heartsease and they all deserve my thanks.

The church of Saint Nicholas featured in this book is an actual living church in Essex. I would like to thank the Reverend Diane Ricketts, vicar of Saint Nicholas in the parish of Laindon with Dunton for giving me permission to use the name and location of this fantastic 13th century church.

I would also like to thank Rosie Munro for her original ideas for the cover, Simon Cuckow for his help and Lara Eakins for her assistance.

# PREFACE

*It stands solid, glowering. The Tower built by command of the Conqueror. A fortress with a reputation so potent, the mention of its name strikes terror into the hearts of the bravest men in England. The ominous shadow it casts falls like a suffocating pall across the country. Those who enter the sinister, unyielding walls as living, breathing beings never taste freedom again. To be condemned to the Tower means certain death. The Tower does not care who it incarcerates. All you can expect is that swift ride on the flood tide. The Watergate would open out, like welcoming arms, ready to gather you to the breast; only this breast is not warm or soft. There would be pain, excruciating pain. Pain as stretched limbs tear mercilessly from sockets, pain as white-hot pokers blister skin. Flames lick your flesh as a kitten licks milk. Here the heartiest resolution would crumble; here there is no chivalry, no respect of rank or title. You die as you were born, in torment and blood. Your last awareness would be exquisite pain as the axe sliced through your neck. Your last sound heard were the crowds baying as hounds' bay at the trapped fox. Then finally, blessed escape from the nightmare.*

*Stay nobody; stay living a peaceful, tranquil life, away from corruption and greed. The coiling, snatching, grasping tendrils of doom from the Tower may not reach you if you stay true and honest. Stay nobody.*

# WINTER 1497

*Essex*

A nurse tucks her small charge into his warm, safe bed. The wilful child complains he does not want to sleep. He wants to play, wants to be disobedient.

'Master Robert, if you do not go to sleep, the axeman will come and take you away to the Tower,' the nurse warns. 'He will put you in his sack, carry you away and cut off your head. No one will ever see you again. Your parents and baby Mary will forget you.'

The boy pulls the counterpane up to his nose to hide, and he shuts his eyes tight, now willing himself to sleep. He is scared. No one escapes the axeman once he has taken you to the Tower, certainly not a small, insignificant, disobedient child.

# SPRING 1513

*Essex*

England on a spring afternoon was an exquisite place. Birds sang from the branches of trees that hung heavy with fragrant blossom, and bumbles hummed lazily around the garden, searching for early nectar.

Seated on a bench, Lady Margaret Hawke gazed languorously around this haven of tranquillity. Primroses had flowered, followed by the daffodils and now blue harebells were taking over. On a low wall nearby, an old tabby cat and a young, deaf white cat basked in the warm sunshine. On days like this, Margaret liked nothing better than to reflect upon her life.

She and her husband were proud of their son, Robert. He had entered court as a squire to a local knight, and had promoted himself enough to receive a position as an attendant in the king's household. The position held no title, but the men whose sway was paramount to the king surrounded Robert. On his rare visits home from court, he would amuse the family with hearsay, what woman had caught the king's eye, and then for how long she kept his attention. Who was visiting from Europe, and there was always scandal.

Margaret's daughter, Mary, was a girl of sixteen and soon to be married. The young man chosen for her was Henry Crawford. She was a substitute bride; the original had died suddenly of a fever. The match was advantageous for the Hawke family. Her husband Sir Anthony, had quickly stepped in and offered his daughter to the wealthy Crawford's son. The two young people were to meet for the first time this very day. Henry, it was rumoured, was conceited beyond his years, and had already gained a reputation for

3

womanising. The only use he would have for a wife would be to bear the next generation of Crawfords.

A voice calling brought Margaret back to the present; Mary was running across the lawn towards her, waving. Beside her ran a small dog, its tongue lolling out of the side of its mouth as it raced to keep up. Margaret raised a hand and waved back. Mary, her cheeks flushed, her hazel eyes sparkling, sat down with a flounce on the bench beside her mother. The dog leapt into her lap, tail wagging excitedly and she began to stroke it lovingly. She had inherited her mother's fair complexion, and her father's dark brown hair. Mary's hair fell in heavy tresses over her shoulders and an errant strand dangled over her eyes, which she absently brushed aside.

'Are we leaving soon?' she asked breathlessly. 'I don't want to be late, I need to give Henry a good impression of me,' Mary laughed, and sprang to her feet, tumbling the dog off her lap. She was so happy at the thought of marriage, Margaret thought. The gossip about Henry's indiscretions had not appeared to reach her ears. She was a naive child going out into the adult world. For now, let the girl enjoy these blithe moments. The world could be a pitiless place; would she discover that for herself eventually?

Margaret allowed herself to be pulled to her feet by her excited daughter. 'It is nearly time, Mary. Where is your father?'

'Oh, he's busy in his study; he should be here with us,' Mary complained, but all good humour was quickly restored and she began to dance around the bench. The tabby cat looked up lazily at the commotion. The deaf cat sensing the movements by her side also stirred. The dog raced over, yapping noisily at the cats, the tabby growled angrily and struck out with a paw, claws unsheathed, scratching the dog's nose. It turned and ran back to its mistress howling.

'Silly, Belle,' Mary chided, scooping the dog up. 'Come on, Mother.' She urged and danced towards the house. The two cats relaxed once again, now that the dog had learnt not to interrupt them.

Once inside, Mary, childlike, ran through the rooms to find her father, and brought him into the entrance hall, impatient to be away. Briefly, Margaret wondered whether her daughter was ready to be married. She had been raised on stories of courtly love, of chivalrous knights in gleaming armour, astride magnificent caparisoned white chargers, saving fair maidens locked in towers from fire-breathing dragons. She had been told of the legend of King Arthur, Queen Guinivere and Camelot. She was still very young for her age, would this match be good for her? It was to be good for the family, bringing wealth to them. She sighed; arrangements were almost finished, making the wedding unavoidable now. Whether the young couple were compatible or not did not matter. Few marriages started with love. Mary was fastening her cloak, chattering excitedly. Together, Margaret and Anthony pulled their cloaks over their shoulders and they made their way out to the courtyard and the waiting carriage.

Sir William and Lady Eleanor Crawford welcomed their guests warmly and offered wine to them when they had entered the lobby. Eleanor led the way into the solarium. William and Anthony followed behind talking business. The solarium radiated sociability and calm, Mary liked this room instantly; she could imagine herself in years to come as the Lady of the manor residing in here, holding court over the local villagers. A kind and gracious mistress, who was amenable and just in all matters.

'Markham is a happy place, my dear; you will like living here with us. Henry is looking forward to meeting you; he will be with us presently,' Eleanor said proudly.

'Our son had business to attend to in Bastelden,' William continued. He turned to Anthony and Margaret. 'Come; take some food while we wait.'

The parents talked while Mary sat in deferential, silence gazing out of the window at the gardens that spread out below and watching as birds flew past the windows. She was feeling apprehensive now, what would her intended think of her?

It was an hour later when she received her first glimpse of the man she was to marry. Henry Crawford, tall, blonde-haired and eyes the colour of the bluest cornflowers, strode into the solarium, still in his riding boots, cloak fastened across his chest. He looked flushed from riding. Eleanor beamed with maternal pride at her only child. Mary suddenly realised that she was staring open mouthed at him. He was so very handsome.

'Henry, what kept you? We have all been waiting.' Eleanor said. Henry took his mother's hand and lifted it to his lips, and then he bowed to his father.

'This is Sir Anthony and Lady Margaret Hawke, and their daughter, Mary.' William announced. Henry bowed low to Margaret and Anthony, and then turned to Mary who had now stood. He took her in his arms and kissed her lightly on her cheek.

'Madam, it is my pleasure to meet you finally. You are everything my parents described,' He said, but in spite of the honey words, there was little sentiment in them. Mary blushed and Eleanor sighed happily.

'Good, I knew you would like each other once you met. Henry, take Mary out into the garden for a walk, you must to get to know each other.'

Henry offered his arm to Mary, and escorted her from the solarium to the garden where the young couple sat at either end of a bench both staring ahead of themselves, neither knowing what to say, Mary felt reluctant to open the conversation. She was feeling awkward and immature being in Henry's presence. Eventually, he broke the silence.

'Both our parents want us married as soon as possible,' he said, still looking ahead. Mary turned to look at him.

'It is our duty to obey their wishes,' she replied. He faced her. Still there was no sign of a smile from those lips of his and his blue eyes were still impassive.

'Duty, yes,' he answered. Sitting back on the bench, he sighed wearily. 'Your duty is to be fertile and give me an heir,' he paused. 'Know this, Mary. I have no yearning to marry you.'

'Your father seems nice,' Mary said innocently, realising immediatly how childlike the words sounded.

Henry shrugged his shoulders.'He is frequently away on business, I see little of him. I lead my own life when he is home.'

'Do you have an ambition?' Mary asked. For the first time, a smile lit Henry's face, making him look even more extraordinarily handsome.

'I intend to shag as many women as I can and one day I shall become the Sheriff of Essex,' he grinned.

'The second part of that sounds impressive,' Mary accepted feebily, wounded by his remark. Henry looked at her with surprise.

'You didn't expect me to be a faithful husband, did you?' he responded in astonishment. Mary cast down her eyes.

'My father never looks at any other woman than my mother,' she replied quietly. Henry laughed aloud.

'My father is the same, the fool. They do not know what they are missing. I will introduce him to Nellie one day. She'll knock his balls off,' he laughed. Mary stood up, her face flushing with anger.

'Your manners do not match your appearance! Do not talk about our fathers that way,' she cried furiously, her voice tremulous with emotion. Henry pulled a face.

'Do I look as if I care? You will get use to my ways; I'm not changing them for anybody,' he retorted.

She gave a cry and ran off. The servant sent to chaperone the couple hurried behind. Henry watched her run away and made no effort to go after her. He had spent the morning with Nellie and her activities always left him exhausted.

Everyone saw Mary run back into the house; Margaret and Anthony were perturbed at their daughter's distressed state. Eleanor brushed their fears aside.

'A lovers' tiff no doubt. Marriage will be a big challenge for both young people. They will settle down once all the fuss is over,' she reassured, and took her husband's hand in her own. 'I was lucky to be chosen for him,' Eleanor purred happily.

'A toast to love, let it pass to our dear children,' William announced. Everyone agreed and drank more wine in celebration.

Back at Yardeley Chase, Mary attempted to slip to her room to be alone, but Margaret stopped her.

'You were upset earlier, what had Henry said to you?' she asked. Mary sat on the stairs and looked unhappily up at her mother.

'He doesn't want to marry me,' she explained. Margaret sat beside her daughter.

'Give it time. You both met for the first time today, you are both strangers to each other. Once you are wed, things will change for the better,' she assured as Anthony approached.

'When I first married your mother, I was reluctant too. You will be fine.' He guaranteed and they smiled fondly at each other. Mary felt comforted. Henry could have been behaving in that way because they were strangers. All would be better once the wedding was over.

The morning of the wedding dawned bright, full of sunshine and birdsong. Mary awoke tingling with excitement. Her maidservant, Lettie, had thrown open the shutters, letting the sunlight stream in, and was now filling a tub with hot water, sprinkled with rose petals and sweet, smelling herbs.

'Come, mistress, bathe and smell sweet for your husband,' she urged. With a giggle, Mary scrambled from bed, stripped off her nightshift, stepped into the steaming tub and sat back.

'Lettie, why have you never married?' she asked, as the maidservant poured a jug of water over Mary's hair.

Lettie shrugged her shoulders. 'I suppose no man ever came along. Anyway, I enjoy looking after you, mistress.'

'We are almost sisters you and I, Lettie,' Mary said, taking Lettie's hand and kissing it. Even though they had been companions since both were small girls, they were still mistress and servant, Lettie smiled and gently squeezed Mary's hand.

'Indeed we are, mistress. Now, get dried and into your wedding gown.'

The gown was white silk with long, narrow sleeves, embellished with pearls and intricate embroidery. A collar, edged in lace, sat high around Mary's neck. It opened at her throat to reveal a single pearl drop on a gold chain, a gift from her parents. Lettie sat the crescent-shaped, white silk band onto Mary's head and adjusted the veil so that it covered the young bride's face.

A carriage waited in the courtyard for Mary and her father. Someone had decorated the horses and carriage with white ribbons that fluttered in the breeze. Mary laughed, delighted. Anthony helped his daughter into the seat, and then climbed in beside her. The driver cracked his whip and the horses moved into action, pulling the carriage out of the courtyard for the journey to the church.

Mary looked out of the window at the church. Saint Nicholas was old and had seen many weddings in its long history. She sat back and thought of Robert; he had sent word from court that it was with regret he could not attend his sister's wedding. She adored her brother and was sad that he was not here today.

They pulled up at the base of the steps leading to the open door, and with her father's help, Mary stepped out into the sunshine. They ascended the wooden steps and then, turning to her father, Mary took a deep breath.

'Ready?' he asked. She took her father's arm and, wavering only for a brief moment, walked through the ancient porch and into the cool, dark interior of the church.

At the altar, Mary saw Henry standing facing away from her, looking, she imagined, at the golden plate and candlesticks on the altar, and her heart sank. Any groom would turn to see his new bride approaching. Only when she stood by Henry's side did he turn to look at her, dour faced. He acknowledged her with an incline of his head, then they both turned to face the priest, and the service began.

Mary, smiling, emerged from the church on the arm of her sullen husband. They would return to Markham where she would be mistress of the manor and, God willing, mother to his children.

'Wife, you will find that if you obey me in all I command, you'll not be displeased with married life,' Henry said quietly so as only Mary could hear.

'I am innocent in many ways, please be patient with me.'

'I expect you to be passive and obedient…you blush, I like that, it is sign of virginity. You grow scarlet. Then you are *Virgo intactia.'* Henry chuckled, he would enjoy teasing his little wife, and she would be easy bait to rebuke. The couple climbed into the carriage that had brought Mary to church. She looked out of the carriage window and waved. Henry just sat back, fractious with all the commotion. The carriage took the young couple back to Markham for the revels and bedding.

Mary tried to keep up with Henry's invariable circling of the hall, as he greeted family and friends, and drank excessively; he seemed unaware of her, and kept laughing and repeating in detail what he would do in bed that night with his little bride. Finally, she gave up and crept back to where her family sat. Margaret embraced her daughter, seeing the dismay on the girl's face.

'Don't worry, child, you will be fine by the morning.' She comforted, pushing a lock of Mary's hair from her forehead. Mary laughed uneasily, feeling an increasing dread about the rapidly approaching bedding. *Just keep thinking about the morning* Mary thought. The dreaded first night would then be over.

The women of both families came bustling around Mary, ready to usher her off to the bedchamber. Eleanor already had a great fondness for her new daughter-in-law and had sewn for Mary a skilfully decorated night shift, edged in lace. She was gracious in accepting such a lovely gift. With all the women leading her, Mary climbed the stairs. She glanced back at the great hall to see Henry whispering in a young woman's ear, causing her to giggle as his hand caressed her breast.

Candles softly lit the bedchamber, but Mary was aware only of the large bed with the counterpane turned down. The women had departed the room, chattering excitedly, leaving only the two mothers alone with her. She took off the wedding dress, corset, girdle and stockings, and then they helped her into her pristine nightshift.

'Sit, child, so I can brush your beautiful hair,' Eleanor urged, pulling Mary to a cushioned chair. Eleanor produced a large brush and began pulling it through her hair. Mary was not listening to the talking, all her thoughts focused on that moment when Henry would pull her to him, would he be forceful or tender? Should she lay there, passive and let him have his satisfaction, or act with passion. Margaret was scattering sweet, smelling herbs on the bed.

'To aid fertility and hasten conception,' she assured. Mary climbed into the bed. She sat there as the covers were smoothed down, and pillows plumped up. 'God speed, daughter,' Margaret said. Then she and Eleanor left, talking quietly together, gently shutting the door, leaving Mary alone, and sitting there, hands clasped in her lap. Now, she could not even think of what was about to occur, her mind was blank. She felt strangely serene. Her breathing was deep and rhythmic. Her heart beat steadily.

A burst of noise from the other side of the door brought Mary abruptly out of her tranquillity. There was the raucous sound of uproar, swearing and laughing. She heard furniture knocked into, and Henry's slurred voice above all others. The door burst open, and the men stumbled in, one falling on his face, cursing as he fell. All were laughing, Henry among them. He straightened up, and gave an overstated bow to his new wife, sitting alone in the big bed. Her eyes wide with alarm, her breath now rapid and shallow.

'Madam, I trust you are well and ready for tonight's sports,' he said seriously, taking a large swig of wine from a pewter goblet and then sniggered, the men did not even attempt to stifle their laughs. Mary nodded quickly. Henry turned to the others. 'Be gone, I want to be alone with my virgin.' There were protestations from the others, Henry laughed and pushed them from the room. 'This is my wedding night and I'll spend it alone with my wife, go now, and go!' He slammed the door shut, the men hammered and kicked on it shouting crude suggestions. 'By God's hooks go away!' he shouted at the door. There were more shouts of protest and encouragement for the night to come, and then silence. Henry turned to Mary, now looking anxious.

'I didn't think they would go, Henry,' she said quietly. He slowly unlaced his shirt, his eyes never leaving Mary's face.

'Would it have perturbed you if they had stayed to watch us?'

'Henry, what will happen is only to be shared between husband and wife.'

He snorted a laugh. 'It adds a certain something when sex is shared with others. You should try it some time.' He removed his shirt, sat on the bed alongside Mary, pulled her to him and kissed her firmly on the lips; he tasted of beer and wine. She gasped involuntarily and he smiled at her reaction. Standing up, he hurriedly undressed and she looked away. 'Are you ready for me, wife? Look at me, Mary.'

Mary looked up to see Henry standing naked before her, and she flushed with embarrasement. He grinned and indicated to his groin proudly. 'You see, I am ready for you.' He climbed in bed and began unlacing her nightshift then, losing patience with the silk ribbons, angrily tore the delicate material apart before harshly pushing himself onto his shocked bride.

The only sounds to break the silence in the room were the broad leather straps that supported the mattress creaking and the bridegroom panting in simultaneous unison.

Once finished, Henry gave a satisfied yawn, and fell back on to the pillow. Mary waited until she knew he was finally asleep before pulling the torn nightshift around her and curling up as near to the edge of the bed as she could, trembling with fright. She kept very still, fearing that any movement could wake him and the disgusting act would start again. Where was this courtly love? Where was the tender touch of her knight she had imagined? Nothing had prepared her for the pain she felt as he brutishly came into her. Eventually, miserably, she finally fell into an uneasy sleep.

# 2

Henry left his sleeping bride early, he had plans for the day, and a timid, trembling girl like Mary was not going to keep him from his schedule. He went to the kitchens where the cook and her assistants were already preparing the meals for the day. He helped himself to a plateful of cooked meat, tore a piece of bread, poured a flagon of beer, and sat at the kitchen table, ignoring the cook insisting she needed all the space on the table to work. He watched a young girl at a tub of hot water washing large copper bowls, humming a tune. Tendrils of loose hair seductively escaped from under her linen cap, and he looked at her hips swaying under her brown skirt. She must have been about thirteen years. *Old enough* he thought *for a good rut*. The way she swung those hips in such an enticing manner, Henry licked his lips in expectation, the girl was asking for it. Wiping his mouth on his sleeve, he left the remains of his meal on the table and approached her, kissing the nape of her neck, she dropped the bowl, startled.

'I'll bang you like a shit-house door in a storm,' he muttered, nipping her ear lobe. The girl looked round distressed by the crude remark and touched her ear, feeling a spot of blood. He slapped her buttocks hard as he left the kitchen. *Yes*, Henry thought to himself, *she is asking for it*.

He rode promptly to a neighbouring estate where he had an appointment to see the landowner about acquiring a new horse for his stables.

After, he rode into the nearby town of Bastelden and made his way towards the tavern where he kept his usual assignation with his flame-haired whore, Nellie. He felt the excitement rising in his body at the thought of that slut waiting for him. Of all the women he had known, and still knew, Nellie was the most thrilling.

He swung from his horse and, throwing the reins at a young boy, entered the tavern. From behind the counter, the innkeeper shouted a salutation and waved a hand at Henry, one of his most habitual patrons.

'Mister Crawford!' he called snapping a finger to one of the serving girls to fetch ale. 'Lubricate yourself before you greet Nell.'

Henry accepted the flagon of ale, dropping several coins on the counter in payment. His liaison with Nellie was not exclusive; he knew that, she entertained many men. A woman with such expertise like Nellie was popular.

As a girl, her widowed father had sent her out to earn their keep. She had quickly become pregnant, giving the infant away as soon as it had been born. When her father died, the lord that owned the village threw Nellie onto the streets, leaving her to fend for herself in the only way she knew how. At twenty-five years old, she was now at the peak of her profession, demanding high recompense for her services. In the corner of the room, a small, grubby girl with unkempt ginger hair, dressed in rags, sat nibbling on a dry piece of bread; she was Annie, one of Nellie's children. Henry barely noticed the child, as there were the sounds of footsteps treading on creaking stairs and a woman laughing. Henry looked up and saw Nellie descending, arm in arm with her client. She was laughing at something he was saying. At the door of the tavern, she kissed the man lightly on the lips and said farewell to him. The door closed, and she turned towards Henry and approached him with a smile on her face.

'Give me ale,' she said to the innkeeper, and on acceptance of the drink, swallowed it in two long gulps. Henry sat watching her, admiring her shapely form, from her plump breasts to her round hips. When Nellie had finished her drink, she turned to look at Henry. 'Waiting long, Harry boy?' she asked shaking her breasts at him.

'A while,' he replied.

'I hear you are now a married man, not even a whole day yet, why aren't you giving your wife a good shafting?'

'Nothing can keep me away from you, Nellie,' Henry said, making her gurgle with pleasure.

'That doesn't sound a promising future for the new Mrs Crawford, does it?'

'She'll give me sons.' Henry shrugged indifferently.

'Where do I fit in all this?' Nellie bit her lower lip and lent forward allowing Henry to see down her cleavage.

'You're my fun.'

Nellie raised her eyebrows and nodded in the direction of the stairs. She took Henry by the hand as her daughter, still crouched in the corner, watched with mild curiosity.

As the couple passed down the corridor, they heard the other prostitutes earning their living behind closed doors. Screams, laughter, even crying heard.

'Meg has a boy in her room.' Nellie thrust a thumb towards one of the closed doors that from behind, frenetic squeaking from a bed could be heard and a woman's voice curtly telling the client with her to slow down! 'It's his first time, poor bugger. Do you remember your first time, Harry boy?' Henry smiled and nodded, recalling that first sexual encounter.

It had been a warm autumn day, he had been no more than twelve years of age and the woman must have been thirty years older. She was one of the laundry women, and had lured Henry to a small room where large baskets holding fresh laundered sheets were stored. Behind the baskets, she had a warm nest ready for them. She had told Henry to lay on the plumped pillows and sheets and then straddled the boy. Even though he was not naive, her sexual expertise and the entire tawdry episode left a profound mark on his life. After they had concluded and Henry had returned to the house, the event was never spoke of again. The woman always gave him a knowing wink when she saw him, but never invited him back behind the baskets again.

'Hey! Come back to me, Harry!' Nellie called pushing Henry's arm. He snapped back to the present and the forthcoming sports.

An old bed dominated Nellie's room. A chest stood under the window, in that, she kept her treasures. Two chairs were the only other furniture in the room. Once the door shut behind them, she turned to Henry and smiled seductively. He was feeling that awareness again that only Nellie could provide. Unlacing her bodice, Nellie allowed her breasts to fall out into Henrys eager hands and he kissed them. Pushing his whore onto the bed, Henry threw himself onto her, they rolled in the sheets, laughing, and

15

shrieking until he could feel he was ready to burst with desire and lust for this incredible woman.

When he had taken her, Nellie threw herself down next to Henry and regained her breath, a smile spreading over her face. Henry was always most vigorous, he was a stimulating lover, and she revelled in his coarse behaviour.

Over the following months, Mary became accustomed to married life. Her husband would ignore her, speaking to her only when necessary. She was aware of his infidelity; apart from Nellie, several of the female servants at Markham had entertained him willingly or otherwise. He made no secret of reminding her that they showed more gratitude to him than she did, even the ones who were reluctant to be tumbled in the stables or the laundry rooms would thank him for bestowing his favours upon them. She would shrug her shoulders; the comments hurt her, the jibes to her own lack of passion wounded her. He would throw spiteful comments on her lack of conception, he bedded her every night, performed his duty thoroughly but there were no signs of any pregnancy. The fault was not with him, he had an illegitimate daughter. Mary found it easier to say nothing and pretend his cruel words did not matter.

It was a late one afternoon when Henry, weary but pleased with his day, rode back into the courtyard. He strode into the entrance hall, tossing his riding gloves and hat at a waiting servant, and entered the solarium where Mary was sitting by a window preparing a sheet of material for needlework. She looked up at Henry and her heart fluttered both with pleasure at seeing his handsome face, and trepidation of what his behaviour might be for the approaching night.

'How was your day, Henry?' she asked resolutely, trying to sound interested in his life. After taking a long swallow of ale, he turned to Mary.

'My day was good. I have purchased a filly for you. If you wish, you may ride her.' He saw the gratification in Mary's eyes at such a gift. 'What of your day?' He tried to make the question sound customary. Mary's chattering seemed to fade away into the distance, as Henry recalled how after the business came the pleasure of an afternoon spent with Nellie that had passed with much amusement.

'When we have dined, we'll take a walk in the evening air,' Henry unexpectedly said. He was thinking of taking Mary to a quiet arbour further down in the gardens, where he could get her alone, pull her skirts up, and hump her. Mary's image of a walk in the evening air was more amorous, ending with wonderful lovemaking.

Eleanor and William noticed how more comfortable Mary was that evening as they dined; even Henry seemed less sullen. Mary kept glancing towards the window, looking to see whether the weather was remaining fair for their evening stroll. She imagined that every evening she and Henry would walk in the garden and talk about the events of the day, so when he helped Mary from her chair, and led her away from the table, she had built a marvellous scene that was about to unfold.

In the evening air, the perfumed flowers wafted their fragrance around. Henry tucked Mary's hand into his arm and led her down stone steps to a lawn. As the couple strolled across the lawn, Mary relaxed, she talked a little, and Henry answered with brief monosyllabic words. They entered the arbour and he turned to Mary, taking both her hands in his.

'Wife, how much do you love me?' he inquired. Mary, startled by the question looked surprised.

'I know that I love you more than you love me, Henry,' she answered honestly.

'Tis true, but don't think I'm an absolute brute, I have strong desires.'

'That I don't know, you are my first, and will be my last,' Mary replied. He nodded, pleased with the response

'What would you do to please me, Mary?' he asked next. Mary went on her guard, she did not like where this conversation might lead. 'If I told you to do certain things, would you do them without question?'

She sat on a wooden bench; he sat beside her and began to rub her legs, pulling at her skirts, leaning towards her.

'Like what?' she asked fearfully, attempting to push his exploring hands away. Henry whispered a licentious proposition and Mary pulled back shaken and afraid. 'That is an unnatural act, never,' she recoiled. Quickly infuriated by the opposition, Henry threw his wife from the bench, face down onto the grass and fell on to her, pinning her to the ground, forcing her into submission. He pulled Mary around and slapped her hard across her face.

'Tell anybody of this, and you'll be very sorry. Understand. You are nothing. You are my chattel, my possession for me to use as I desire. You are lower than my hounds; you are lower than the worms my hounds shit on. You will obey me. You will obey me in everything I command of you,' he growled, pointing a finger into her face. Mary could not speak; she only nodded and lay there unmoving, watching as he left the arbour without a glance back. With her shoulders heaving from soundless sobbing, Mary crawled to the bench and sat on it, drawing her knees up to her chin. She could not think of anything, the incident had left her mind blank. She just sat there as tears unrelenting slid from her sad eyes, looking up through the branches at the sky, changing colour as the evening began to draw in, listening to the sounds of the night. She was trembling, not because of the coolness of the night air. She did not want to be alone with Henry anymore; he would misuse and debase her repeatedly.

Henry strode back to the house, his mind mulling over his conduct of the past hour. He had not planned to be so violent. He felt a sudden pang of guilt for his treatment of Mary, she did not warrant what he had forced her to do, and he halted, rubbing his chin thoughtfully. She had gone freely into the marriage, he had not. It had been a business transaction between their parents. It was a contract. She would have to accept his ways. He absently kicked at a stone and continued walking.

Hours later, Mary still sat on the bench in the arbour, she felt calmer now, her body had stopped hurting, but she could not bring herself to return indoors, preferring the tranquil night air and the sanctuary the darkness provided. She turned her head sharply at the sound of men's voices. Had Henry returned with others? Then she recognised one voice, that of her father-in-law. His tall form, followed by a servant, entered the arbour, both carrying burning torches. William looked astonished as his eyes set upon Mary.

'Dear God, child, what are you doing out here alone? Henry returned several hours since.' He sat alongside Mary who slid along the bench, away from him, fearing his contact. William handed his torch to the servant. 'Did Henry do anything to hurt you?' he asked cautiously. Mary looked away, tears welling up yet again. 'What did he do?'

'He did nothing,' she whispered. William scowled.

'Has he hurt you? Tell me, Mary.' she shook off William's hand as he placed it on her shoulder. He felt her trembling.

'You cannot stay here all night, come back home with me. Eleanor is waiting for you. Come now,' he urged. Mary knew he meant well, and slowly, she stood up, still not letting her face be seen. William gradually put an arm around her shoulders; she tensed first then felt safe in his kind embrace. Together, they returned to the house. As he had said, Eleanor was waiting in the lit entrance, concerned for her daughter-in-law's safe return. Lettie was hovering behind, peering over Eleanor's shoulders.

'Oh, my chicken, come here.' She threw out her arms to receive Mary seeing them appear from the dark. Mary let the pent up tears now surge freely, and she began to howl as though she would never stop as Eleanor gathered her in and cradled her there. William sent Lettie to find a blanket to cover Mary and to fetch warm wine and something to eat. Eleanor led Mary into the solarium with William following. They sat down together, Eleanor rocking back and forth with Mary in her arms until she finally ceased crying.

'Tell us what happened?' William said. Mary shook her head. 'Why do you not tell us?'

'We can help you if you tell us,' Eleanor urged. Once more, Mary shook her head.

'Nothing happened,' she lied, remembering Henry's forewarning if she spoke of the occurrence. William sighed. Mary appreciatively drank the wine offered, not realising until now how cold she had become, even though the wine made the abrasion on the side of her lip sting. She wanted to tell of the ill-treatment she had suffered at Henry's hands, but she did not want to face his rage when he found out that she had talked. 'We are still newlywed. Both of us have to adjust to each other's ways. We will be fine in time.' She looked into the faces of William and Eleanor. 'Honest we will.'

Seeing the bruising on her face and swollen lip, William and Eleanor exchanged glances; they were not convinced.

'I will speak with my son in the morning about that mark on your face. Why did he hit you?'

19

The chalice clattered to the floor. 'No!' Mary cried in distress. 'Please don't.' She dropped to her knees to pick up the broken pieces. 'We had a quarrel, a misunderstanding that is all. He said he would not strike me again.' The lie came quickly to her lips. William opened his mouth, but Eleanor shook her head towards him, without a sound warning him not to speak.

'If you wish, then I will not speak of this,' he conceded.

'Let me get you to your bed, it's late, and I am not as youthful as I use to be and need my sleep,' Eleanor said, attempting to lighten the atmosphere. Mary stiffened.

'I'll sleep with Lettie tonight,' she said hastily, and then seeing the apprehension on their faces. 'As you say, it's late, and I don't wish to disturb Henry,' she added.

'Come, mistress, we will pretend we are girls again,' Lettie said, helping Mary to her feet and leading her in the direction of the servants' sleeping accommodation. William and Eleanor watched the two young women leave the solarium.

'Henry has done something else besides strike her to make her this afraid to talk,' Eleanor observed.

'I think it's time he accompanied me on one of my trips abroad. He needs to learn the family trade so he can take over after I die,' William said.

'Don't talk like that; it'll not happen for years yet, God willing.'

William took Eleanor in his arms and they kissed passionately. He still loved her deeply after all the years they had spent together.

'Come to bed, if Henry and Mary cannot be happy, we can.' He took his wife by the hand and led her from the solarium, up the wide staircase to their bedchamber.

The morning dawned cloudy, threatening rain. William had left before sun-up; he was visiting a fellow merchant to arrange a forthcoming visit to Spain and a new contact with whom he would set up trading links. Mary was at the table; she felt famished and ate vigorously. Henry entered; instantaneously she tensed as he approached her and kissed her cheek, ignoring the bruising on the side of her face.

'Where did you sleep last night, Mary?' he asked.

'I retired late, so I slept with Lettie. I didn't want to disturb you,'

She replied without looking up. Henry sat beside her, and through a mouthful of bread, he spoke.

'About yesterday, I may have expected too much from you, after all, you are only young, with no understanding of man's desires.' He swallowed the bread. 'I expect your obligation towards me. Please me and you shall not fear me.'

'Yes, Henry.'

'Then we may get along cordially. My father wants to speak with me when he returns home. Did you reveal the events of last night?'

'No, I told them nothing, just like you said.'

He patted Mary's thigh and smiled at her, but there was no warmness behind the smile.

'See, already we are getting along.'

She just smiled weakly. Henry stood up and stretched.

'I'm visiting colleagues this day and will be out late myself. We shall continue this conversation privately later.'

The incessant rain prohibited the opportunity of walking in the gardens, so Mary spent the day with Eleanor and began to learn how to run a household, manage the servants and the accounts. As the day passed, Eleanor convinced herself that the difficulty of the previous evening had been resolved. She refused to believe that her son was capable of cruelty; he was a man of passion that was all.

Within an hour of each other, William and Henry arrived home late in the evening; both men locked themselves in William's private study to eat and to talk about the future. When they emerged, Henry looked surly; he threw an incensed glance at Mary, she felt an iciness run down her spine. William must have mentioned the episode at the arbour. She began to dread the approaching night when the couple retired to their chambers. Henry hardly spoke for the remainder of the evening, except to insist she accompanied him to bed.

Sitting on a chair in their chamber, Mary lowered her eyes while Henry paced the floor, drinking from a goblet.

'Do you know what my father and I talked about?' he asked loudly. Mary shook her head. 'No? He asked me why he found you sitting alone late at night, with your lip swollen.'

'What did you tell him?' Mary asked quietly.

'I said we argued over something irrelevant, but I do not think he believed me. What did you tell him and my mother?' he shouted angrily. She looked up, the tears once more welling in her eyes.

'Nothing, I told them nothing, just like you said.'

'Really,' Henry threw the empty goblet into the fire hearth. He crossed the chamber and hauled Mary to her feet. 'I don't believe you,' he spat. She cowered.

'I told them nothing, Henry,' she wept. He threw her onto the bed. She had no option but to yield again to his assault. She felt anger and revulsion growing with every jolt, every shaft of pain to her sore body. He stood up, regarding his wife disdainfully.

'You shall serve my every demand until I leave with my father for Spain.'

'Spain!' Mary echoed astonished. Henry glowered at his wife.

'Yes. Spain. I am to accompany my father on his trip there to meet some Spanish Don.' He turned to the door and slammed it shut as he departed. Now the moment was over Mary began to shake with emotion. She crawled into bed and lay there afraid of what Henry would from now on. Was there nothing he was incapable of doing to her?

They saw nothing of each other until the next evening.

For the following weeks while the preparations took place, Mary infrequently spoke to Henry. He avoided her throughout the day, but took his rage out on his wife every night. She was familiar to his conduct, knowing the sex would last for only a short time, prior to his rolling off and quickly falling asleep. She would just lie there, trying to isolate her mind from the painful torment. The one thought that kept her sanity was knowing that soon he would be leaving, and she would have peace during his absence.

The day of departure arrived. Henry rose early and threw her wrap at her.

'Get dressed. I want my parents to see you biding me farewell as a devoted wife.' He dressed and went to greet his father in the hall. William, dressed in his riding clothes, was prepared to leave. The two men would ride to London to meet with an associate; they would then sail to Bilbao. Mary descended the stairs and stood beside a maudlin Eleanor.

'Keep safe, my dearest, don't go looking for trouble,' she cooed, stroking her husband's hair. Kissing her, he smiled reassuringly.

'I'll return and I shall bring you gifts from Spain,' he and Eleanor turned to Mary and Henry. Mary took Henry's hand and kissed it lightly.

'Travel well, husband,' she said plainly, avoiding his gaze. He awkwardly kissed her lips.

'I shall. Remember, I will return and we'll be fine together,' he replied. Eleanor threw her arms around her son.

'Sweet Henry, be good and do as your father tells you. Please, do not act without contemplation,' she cried kissing his face. Henry disentangled himself, tutting intolerantly.

'Mother, I am a man, not a boy,' he complained. Eleanor wailed and dabbed at her eyes, she always detested these departures when her husband went away, and it was particularly agonising to see her son go as well. William took Mary in his arms.

'Keep well, look after yourself, child,' he said gently.

'I shall, thank you,' Mary replied.

'Come, Henry, we have a long expedition ahead of ourselves, no time to waste,' William cried, slapping his son on his back. He pulled his hat on and strode out of the hall with Henry following. Both men swung into their saddles. William pulled the hat from his head.

'We shall return before Christmas, Eleanor!' he cried, waving his hat gallantly at his wife, before bringing it back onto his head with a flourish. He then blew his wife a kiss, and wheeled his horse towards the gates. Henry gave a reluctant wave to Mary and rode out alongside his father with their entourage close behind. Eleanor was sobbing as she waved until both men had disappeared into the distance, then she turned to Mary.

'They are gone now, I will not be happy until I see them come back through these doors again. I worry about William when he is away.'

'He'll be safe,' Mary comforted.

'And you, only a bride for such a short time, separated from your husband.'

Mary shrugged and said nothing; she did not want to distress Eleanor more. It was to be a boon, to retire to bed with no fear of her husband's attentions. She could relax these next months.

# 3

Now that Henry was away, Mary felt more contented than she had done since arriving at Markham. She became aware that her monthly flow did not occur, and she felt nauseous most mornings, but paid little regard to this. In passing, she mentioned it to Eleanor casually. Her reaction was euphoric.

'You may be pregnant! We must get it confirmed, oh, what will Henry say when he returns and finds you carrying his child!' She commanded one of the servants to fetch the local midwife.

The midwife confirmed the pregnancy. Eleanor burst into tears and Mary laughed joyfully. She put her hands on her slim stomach and tried to picture herself large with child, and even holding her own newborn baby.

'I pray it'll be a boy, Henry wants sons,' Mary said plainly.

'Whatever it is, it'll be the most loved,' Eleanor crowed. 'You must write and tell your mother, she will be excited to know she is becoming a grandmother.'

Mary sat at a bureau, quill in hand, the paper lay blank before her.

*My Mother,*

*It is with a jubilant heart that I write to you today with the most amazing news.*

*I am with child. I have been unable to convey this news to my husband, as he is away in Spain. I would wish with all my heart that you attend me at my hour of confinement, and see your grandchild enter this world.*

*I remain your devoted and loving daughter,*
*Mary.*

She re-read the short letter. Mary had never been keen on writing letters, preferring to let others put quill to paper. The words were brief; she had said all that needed saying.

A servant rode to Yardeley Chase with the letter and returned with a communication from Margaret. She wished her daughter well, and sent regards to Eleanor.

Eleanor had turned into a bustling, clucking mother hen, professing she was proficient on everything to do with pregnancy and birth. Mary was contented to be swathed in blankets of love, knowing her mother-in-law meant well. The wise woman with cures visited Mary, now beset with continuous nausea.

'Drink this, my dear; it'll help stop the sickness.' She handed Mary a bottle of vile smelling liquid.

'What is it?' Mary asked sniffing its contents and grimacing, then putting the plug back in the bottleneck.

'Crushed bones soaked in apple cider vinegar,' the wise woman urged. Mary took a swallow.

'It's hideous,' she complained. The wise woman laughed.

'If it tastes hideous, it'll do you good.' She dug into the sack she always carried with her. 'Take this.' She thrust a package of dried leaves into Mary's hand.

'What's this?'

'Red raspberry leaves to be drunk as a hot infusion daily.' The wise woman patted Mary's arm. 'All my ladies have drunk this and most of them have borne healthy babies.'

A letter arrived from William. They were at Bankside, and by the time the letter arrived at Markham, they would be at sea with wool, grain and rye to take to Bilbao to trade with the Spanish Don for exotic spices and fabrics to trade back in London.

Mary did not miss Henry, she was sleeping better and her nausea was subsiding. She spent her days dreaming of her baby. What it would look like, would it be a boy? Henry had said his first-born must be a boy to carry on the Crawford name. He would be satisfied with her if she gave him a son. As she sat stitching garments for the baby to wear, she would talk quietly to it, already assuming it was a boy.

The hazy, lush summer days metamorphosed into a golden and warm autumn. Mary received a letter from Robert, still at court.

He congratulated his sister on her forthcoming confinement and wrote about the king's itinerant eye, the events going on at court, and all the scandal happening. His letters were always witty and entertaining. Her brother had a talent for making the most mundane occurrence at court sound exciting.

Another letter from William now arrived from Spain; he wrote to say that the Spanish Don was a genial host and lived in opulent grandeur in a hacienda that stood in the centre of a garden of flamboyantly coloured flowers and tall, graceful trees. It sounded like heaven, and for the first time since Henry had left, Mary began to wish she were with him to observe this vision of gorgeousness herself.

With the beginning of November, the final letter from William arrived. They had docked at Bankside. The party were to travel home via the Royal Court. Accompanying them on the passage was the Spanish Don. He wanted to visit the king and queen and present them with gifts from Spain. William was concluding business in London and after that they would all return to Markham.

Although Mary was very eager at the prospect of meeting the foreign visitor as he would liven up the place, she was anxious about Henry's return, and how he would behave towards her now she was growing big with their child. Surely, he would not beat her in this condition. He would not dare risk the well-being of his unborn son.

# 4

In the first week of December, the travellers arrived home with much clamour and celebration. Mary, now blooming in her pregnancy, stood beside Eleanor, who was wringing her hands fretfully as William and Henry galloped through the gates. Their Spanish guest was mounted on a magnificent, tall, black Andulusian stallion, riding beside them, his face concealed by a hat and a cloak pulled up to keep him warm in the colder English climate. William dismounted and swept Eleanor up in his arms as they whispered sweet words to each other. There would be a more intimate reunion later. Henry's jaw dropped when he saw Mary.

Unexpectedly, he leapt from his horse and pulled Mary to him. This was not the petulant Henry departing with his father. The kiss full on her lips was affectionate.

'Dear God, how many months until my son is born?' he cried, putting both gloved hands on Mary's swollen belly.

'April, Henry. He kicks me much these days, a very energetic boy,' she replied. Henry laughed exultantly. He turned to the Spaniard, still sitting on his horse, now leaning forward in the saddle.

'Look at my wife, look how beautiful she is,' he cried proudly. The Spaniard pulled his cloak down to expose his features.

'*Ella es lan Hermosa como cualquier senora en Espana,*' he said with a temperate low laugh. 'She is as beautiful as any lady from Spain,' he then translated. Mary looked at his face, and saw deep brown sparkling eyes, olive skin crinkled in a smile. Even though he was nearer in age to William, he was more dazzling and handsome than Henry. The Spaniard swung from the saddle in a distinct fluid movement and patted his horse's neck. William motioned him forward.

'Eleanor, Mary, let me introduce to you Don Rafael Perez,' he announced. Don Rafael bowed, and then took both Eleanor and Mary's hands, kissing them.

'Your husbands talk at every occasion about you,' he said, looking between the women as Eleanor giggled like a delighted girl. As for Henry talking non-stop about her, Mary did not believe him, but Don Rafael was so mesmerising, already she could excuse him everything.

'Come inside, it must be cold for you out here.' Eleanor tucked her hand into Don Rafael's arm and led him into the Hall. 'I have mulled wine and warm pies for you. You must be tired after your journey.'

'*Gracias*, Lady Eleanor,' he replied. Henry fell into step beside Mary.

'To my parents and Perez, we will look as though all is reconciled. Give me sons and all shall be well between us,' Henry said curtly and hurried forward to talk with his father. *Well*, Mary thought, *at least he has not changed*; more fool her to think he might have done.

That evening, there was a feast in Don Rafael's honour. Henry sat beside Mary and was attentive towards her. She played along with the pretence, not wanting to do anything that may cause harm to her unborn child.

'Don Rafael, tell us about your home and life?' Eleanor asked. Don Rafael dipped his finger in a bowl of scented water, cleared his throat, and then began to speak.

'I live in an unpretentious home just outside Bilbao with my second wife, Pilar. I have one daughter, Isabel, born of my first wife. God never granted us the gift of more children, but His will be done. Isabel now lives with relatives in Madrid. After her mother died, I knew I could not care for her myself. It was the best I could do for my daughter.' He sighed. 'I travel; around Spain and France I buy and I sell. My life is good, I think.'

'What about Spain, how different is it from England?' Mary then asked. Don Rafael smiled cordially at her; and Mary returned the smile, her cheeks flushing with pleasure. Henry noticed this, but remained unspoken.

'This is my first visit to your country. Even in winter it is warmer in Spain than here, which is something I have already noticed.'

'Bilbao is not on the coast as I had thought,' William said, trying to sound knowledgeable. 'We arrived in a small coastal town called Santurlzi. Then it is a ride to Bilbao and on to Don Rafael's home, which is remarkable.' There was genial laughter around the table. Mary was acutely aware that Don Rafael kept looking towards her, it gave her a thrill, and she wanted to return his gaze. His presence commanded awareness.

At the end of the evening, William showed Don Rafael to the chamber where he would sleep while he stayed with his guests. Mary was feeling exhausted, so Henry, still playing the compassionate husband, helped her to their bedchamber. Once the door closed, Henry turned on Mary.

'You were making cow eyes at him,' he pinned her arms to her side and shook her.

'He's a guest of the house; we must be agreeable towards him,' Mary replied, her voice wavering. 'And he is attractive to the eye.' As soon as the words slipped from between her lips, she knew it was a mistake. Cursing, Henry raised a hand to strike her. 'Your son! Your son!' she cried, cowering. A stinging slap to her face silenced her.

'You can't use my son to shield you forever,' he warned. 'Just keep your distance from that Spaniard. If I catch you so much as looking at him, I shall punish you so that you never forget.' He pushed Mary aside. 'I shall sleep elsewhere tonight.'

Mary could not believe what she was hearing. A wave of relief swept over her. For tonight, she was safe. He left the room slamming the door behind him.

During the night snow fell, and the morning dawned crisp, dazzling, and very cold. Don Rafael and William, along with Henry, strolled in the gardens, discussing business. Mary sat in the solarium watching the three men, but she could not keep her gaze from settling on Don Rafael. His presence excited her, in a way she could not understand. She tried to concentrate on her needlecraft, but found her eyes and mind turning to the attractive Spaniard. Every now and then, she heard laughter from the men; his was the deepest and most melodious.

'He is elegant,' Eleanor said quietly as she entered the room. 'I noticed you gazing at him yesterday.' Caught out, Mary blushed.

'Henry is jealous already,' she said, turning her gaze to Henry talking intently with his father. Eleanor looked out of the window at her son.

'Would he ever have reason to be?'

'No.' Mary sighed. 'Henry is my husband, I promised to honour and obey, and keep only unto him,' she said despondently, how lucky Don Rafael's wife was. He would not be cruel; he would treasure and love her. Both Mary and Eleanor continued to watch their men silently through the window.

Several days later, William and Henry were away on local business. Eleanor had gone to Saint Nicholas to help with preparations for the Christmas services. Mary remained behind to spend time as accustomed in the solarium. She sat on the long settle unable to concentrate on her sewing, and dozed in the warmth of the fire burning in the hearth. She abruptly awoke with a start, sensing someone else had entered the room. Looking over in the direction of the door, she saw Rafael standing, watching her. Mary went to lever herself out of the settle, but he signalled for her to remain seated. He came over and sat beside her, stretching his legs out towards the fire. After emitting a long sigh, he looked over to her and spoke.

'Your husband does not care for you, does he?'

'What do you mean?' Mary asked.

'He plays the devoted husband and fools everyone else. But I see through his deceit.' The Spaniard slid along the settle to be next to Mary. 'Your marriage is arranged?'

'It was, yes,' she replied gloomily. Rafael nodded with intent.

'So was my first marriage. I did not care for Manuela, or she for me. I recognise the signs.' He moved even closer, and leant towards her, so that Mary could feel his breath on the side of her face, smell his seductive fragrance of musk. Secretly, she delighted at his closeness. Nonetheless, respectability made her move slightly away. 'If you were *my* wife, I would never let you from my sight, you are very beautiful.' His lips lightly brushed her cheek, leaving her thrilled.

31

'I am big and awkward now.' Mary excused herself in an ineffectual endeavour to discourage him.

'I find you very attractive, particularly as you are *embarazad*,' he breathed, putting a hand on her belly. Mary stood up and tried to move away, now uneasy as to where this exchange could be leading. Rafael quickly stood up and held Mary in his arms, ignoring her struggling, as he attempted to kiss her. Deep down, she wanted to kiss him. He gave up trying to kiss her, and put both his hands on Mary's stomach. He leant over so that his face was close to her belly, and whispered Spanish words that she could not understand, but sounded beautiful. His hands felt blistering, and every hair on the back of her neck prickled and stood up. This man was so desirable. After kissing her stomach, Rafael straightened up, wrapped his arms around her and pushed himself against Mary in a second attempt to kiss her. His hands explored her body, pulling at the laces of her bodice, and then hoisting up the materials of her skirts and squeezing her exposed buttocks, pulling her nearer, his lips kissing her bare shoulders, her neck, her breasts, and groaning with ecstacy. She gasped with desire, it would be so easy to give in, let him continue and take her there and then, in the solarium. She could say it was rape, she could say he forcabily took her against her will. He was stronger than she was, and in her condition too! He would be ostracised for the violation of a pregnant woman. These and a dozen more excuses tumbled into her mind. Any excuse allowing him to have her. Suddenly, a small harsh voice entered her head.

*You carry your husbands' child,* it said. *Whatever Henry does to you, you are his wife, his property.* Mary struggled away from Rafael, shaking her head.

'No, no, I can't,' she said, her voice quivering, and dashing tears from her face. Rafael looked bewildered.

'Why? You desire me, I know it, and I crave you, no one would know,' he said. 'I must have you.'

'I just can't. This is happening all too quick for me,' Mary said backing away, hastily retying the laces, pulling her dress back into shape, leaving Rafael standing alone in the centre of the floor. 'Just keep away from me please, I cannot stand to be alone with you.' She pleaded, and then turning, escaped the solarium, a hand over her mouth to avoid Rafael hearing her sobs. He took several steps to the doorway.

'You have a husband who does not deserve you, Maria!' he called down the gallery as Mary ran to her room to cry for hours in desolation. That evening, she excused herself, saying she felt unwell. In reality, she could not bring herself to be sitting near either Henry or Rafael.

For the rest of Rafael's stay, she would not be in any room alone with him, or permit herself to look into his face. Desperately, secretly, she fantasised about being with him. He had said she was beautiful, he said he desired her. Henry never used words like that towards her. Mary knew that if she spent any time unaccompanied with the Spaniard, her defences would collapse, and she would give in to the lust smouldering within her, an emotion she had never experienced before, and its intensity frightened her. Then Henry's threats would appear in her mind and she knew she must resist and simply fantasise. Already he had begun to hit her again since his return and she knew it would continue and only intensify if he discovered her deep feelings for Rafael.

The festivities of Christmas and twelfth night were loud and jolly. Everyone feasted on too much food, there was dancing and games that Mary appreciatively sat out of as she grew tired easily these days. There were gifts exchanged; Rafael gave Mary a ring set with an attractive blue opaque stone. He told her the stone was a turquoise and that it came from the New World. Mary and Henry's gift in return was an elaborate dagger with a jewelled scabbard and handle.

Regretfully and, equally, thankfully for Mary, Rafael announced that he would depart after twelfth night. He had enjoyed his stay immeasurably, Eleanor and William had been exceptional hosts, but business called him back, and he needed to return home as soon as he was able to. He had also left his wife alone for too long and wanted to get back to her.

The day before Rafael left, he cornered Mary in the gallery.

'You cannot evade me any longer, Maria. You still have your opportunity to escape with me. We can go tonight while everyone is asleep,' Rafael urged, kissing Mary's hands. She shook her head.

'I have told you, I cannot, I will not. I thought you loved your wife. We are both married, and I have this,' she said, pointing at her stomach.

'I shall divorce Pilar, Henry will divorce you for the infidelity you will commit with me now, and we shall live in France where no one will know us,' Rafael explained. 'As for the child, I shall care for him as though he is my own son. He shall want for nothing.' That sounded so appealing, Mary wanted to accept his proposition, and however, she knew she had to decline him.

'Your daughter is your heir. You may have children by your second wife. You know I can't, sorry, I must stay,' she said making excuses and shaking her head. Rafael sighed despondently.

'You yearn for me; do not deny what you know to be true. I know you love me, Maria. I have seen the way you look at me when you think I do not notice. Pilar can never give me a child. I need a son; your son will be mine. I want to spend my life with you. I knew it the instant I set eyes on you,' he said keenly. Then, catching Mary entirely by surprise, Rafael pulled her forcefully to his body and brought his mouth down on hers in a fierce kiss. At first, she ineffectively struggled and feebly thumped his back. Then, intuitively, though she knew it was wrong, Mary relaxed her fists, and she held him close as their lips locked simultaneously. Henry had never kissed her with such fervour, he hardly kissed her at all, and this felt very right. Rafael pulled his head away, though they remained in each other's arms. 'I shall never forget you, Maria. Remember, when Henry is abusing you, when he lays an angry hand on you, you could have lived a life as a desired woman with me.' He released her and stood back, regarding the bewildered, wavering young woman before him breathing intensely,. Then bowing, Rafael turned on his heel and left her.

Mary stood like a statue, abruptly feeling very alone, watching Rafael walk down the gallery until he turned through a doorway and was gone. She knew she was in love with the Spaniard, this was no infatuation. She would not have allowed what had just happened to persist if otherwise. Mary wanted to call him back and tell him she would leave with him right there and then. He was right, telling her he would desire and love her. She had only known Rafael for such a short time, yet she had known deep down it would be right to be with him. Henry would bring her wretchedness. He would find her and bring her home. He would ensure she would be sorry she thought that for even a moment she could escape his clutches.

With a mixture of melancholy and relief, Mary said goodbye to the Spaniard when he made his departure in the new year of 1514, with William. They were to travel to London together to settle a deal struck on their last visit, then Rafael would return home to Spain, and Mary knew she would never see him again. She was to have only reminiscences of a passionate man who would have changed her world completely. She glanced at Henry, as she recalled Rafael's words and that stolen moment of ardour. Henry would abuse her again; she knew it would happen once her child was born. He would beat her throughout their married life regardless of how many sons she bore him.

Life returned to normal quickly afterwards. Markham seemed dreary and insensible now Rafael was gone. Mary spent most of her days in the solarium, gazing out of the window at the garden, watching Henry practice his archery and she would recall in every detail that kiss in the gallery. Now, all her thoughts were turning towards the impending birth.

Mary awoke one night realising the birth was impending. Henry, who had been sleeping elsewhere, appeared. It was the first time she had seen him looking so disconcerted, he was feeling ineffectual. Eleanor and Margaret, who had arrived to be with her daughter a month earlier, along with the midwife pushed past him, and slammed the door in his face, leaving him to pace up and down while his father attempted to keep him calm.

All the pain and hurt Henry had caused Mary paled into irrelevance to what she now experienced. The midwife coaxed Mary through labour, with Margaret sitting on the bed, holding her shoulders, and Eleanor dabbed scented water on Mary's brow. For hours, all the women urged and encouraged Mary. With the midwife's directions, she gave a scream of agony and one final push.

'Bless the little one,' the midwife cooed, wrapping the bawling newborn in a blanket. Margaret helped Mary into a sitting position. For a moment, she listened to the crying of the baby with wonder. That was her baby.

'What is it?' she asked holding out her arms to receive the infant. The midwife, beaming with satisfaction, handed the bundle to Mary.

'You have a daughter, a lovely healthy daughter,' she said. Mary's heart lurched; Henry had wanted a son, how would he feel? She looked into the face of her daughter, and smiled with elation.

'She is beautiful,' Mary said, looking between Margaret and Eleanor. The midwife washed and dressed Mary in a clean nightshift before Eleanor flung the door open. Henry nearly fell in; he hurried to Mary's bedside and he peered into the blanket. She had never seen her husband look so animated and happy.

'My son?' he asked eagerly.

'This is your daughter,' she answered. Henry straightened up.

'Not a son,' he said flatly. Mary held the baby girl out towards her father. Unenthusiastically, Henry uncomfortably took the baby in his arms. He looked intently at his daughter. 'I wanted a son,' he said impassively.

'What can we call her?' Mary asked, hoping to ignite a spark of affection in Henry for his daughter. He looked at his father.

'My first son shall be called William. The girl shall be called Cecily,' he announced.

'Cecily,' Mary echoed. Henry handed Cecily to his mother, leant over and indifferently kissed Mary on the forehead, though there was no sentiment in his action, it was what was expected of him.

'Get well, we must try for my son as soon as you are able to.' He then left the bedchamber, without even looking back at his exhausted wife.

Eleanor laid the baby in her crib then left with Margaret, leaving the midwife and Lettie to bustle around the bedchamber. Mary settled down and quickly fell into an exhausted and very welcomed sleep.

Henry immediately rode to Bastelden, and to the tavern. Nellie was sitting at a table, plying her trade with a potential client, but the man seemed unresponsive to her wanton charms. Seeing Henry made Nellie give up on the man and approach him, loosening the ribbons on her bodice.

'Harry, why are you here? Surely you wife needs you more right now. How is she? Any sign of the baby yet?' She played with a lock of his hair.

'The baby is born,' Henry said gloomily, ordering ale.

'And you are here! You bastard, get you back home and to her side,' Nellie spat furiously. Married men like Henry came to her and the other whores to liven up their uninteresting lives, and give the thrills their wives were incapable or reluctant to offer. Nellie was a good woman with a kind heart; she had said countless times that a husband's place was beside his wife, she merely provided entertainment.

'It's a girl. I wanted a son,' Henry said as he swallowed his ale.

'So? Is that a cause to be here?' Nellie questioned.

'A girl is worthless to me. A girl can't maintain the family name or learn a trade.'

'I am happy with my girls; Annie and Maggie are a joy to me,' she said proudly. Henry snorted his aversion.

'Bastards of a whore,' he sneered. She slapped him hard across his face.

'Just because my girls don't know who their fathers are matters little to me. If you feel like that, don't bother coming back.' She turned her back on Henry. He looked at Nellie's long hair flowing wildly over her bare shoulders; he felt regretful for his remark and an intensifying desire.

'Nellie, forgive me, I am sorry,' he pleaded. 'Let us go to your room, now.' Nellie turned back to face him and regarded him sceptically, and she relented.

'Come on then, Harry, just a quickie, and then back home.' Nellie led the way with Henry following like a faithful dog.

Henry returned home and went immediately to Mary who was cradling Cecily in her arms, talking quietly to her. She looked up, anxious as he closed the door behind him. He leant briefly on the closed door, then walked over to the bed and sat on the edge, looking at his daughter, then at Mary.

'I do still want a son, I never want daughters, but we can't undo what is done. A daughter can be married to bring prosperity into a family, even if her uses are limited,' he said awkwardly, looking again at Cecily. 'She is fair of face, and healthy, she will do for now,' he conceded.

'Henry, she is our beautiful daughter, our precious gift from God, do not speak of marrying her off, and the poor mite not even one day old yet. Let's take pleasure in her growing up.'

'Don't think you can avoid me forever, I must have a son.' He stood up. 'Get well, wife.' He then left the room. After closing the door behind him, Henry leant back on it. He felt no attraction for Mary, and never would, but he knew he could grow to tolerate her if she gave him the sons he desired.

Henry visited his new family regularly and began to accept Cecily, now taking her cheerfully on his knee and talking to her about the pony he would buy for her, when she was older, and that she would be the sister of many brothers. Mary herself began to warm towards Henry, seeing for the first time his gentler side, and liking this.

Gradually, Mary resumed her usual life. This also meant that Henry would return to her bed. She now felt comfortable enough in his presence to feel little trepidation at this thought.

The evening passed contentedly enough, and Mary, along with Henry, retired to their chamber. He locked the door behind him and turned to face Mary, who now felt nervous.

'It has been a year since intimacies between us,' Henry began, taking Mary into his arms. 'How shall we recommence?'

'I have seen you with Cecily, you are a gentle father to her, and will you be gentle to me now?' Mary asked. Henry snorted a laugh and stroked her hair, feeling the thick tresses run through his fingers. He took her face in his hands and he kissed her full on the lips ardently. Was this the Henry Mary had always but never dared wanted?

'You have proven your fertility, now give me a son' he swept her into his arms and laid her on the bed. This encounter was like a light radiating through the shadows. He was changing; perhaps with fatherhood, he would grow to love her after all.

# 5

Everyone saw how contented both Mary and Henry had become, their daughter had brought them closer, and it was a delight to see the young couple walking arm in arm in the gardens, like any couple should. Mary was happy; the beatings had ceased, and Henry appeared to dote on her and she grew confident that they would have as happy a marriage as his parents. Nevertheless, there was still no indication of a second pregnancy. Henry became downcast, and Mary would try to explain that it had only been a short time since Cecily's birth. She began to notice he was becoming aggravated and angry about her lack of conception. The walks in the garden ceased, he started to find faults, real or imaginary with her, and he would lock himself away for hours or take long visits to the town.

Everything came to a head on the night of Christmas. Henry had drunk too much wine and had become irritable with everyone. Mary tried to find a pretext not to spend the night with him, fearing their newly found affection had crumbled away. However, he insisted she accompany him to their chambers. Unwillingly, Mary followed her husband; the old feelings of fear were creeping back, but she obeyed him submissively.

'If I cannot get a son out of you with compassion; I shall get a son out of you by might,' Henry demanded. Mary begged him to reconsider and remember the new love they had found together, the words were usless and once finished; Henry left the chamber warning Mary that he would be back again, so she must be ready for him.

She sat on the edge of the bed. She felt betrayed. Irrationally, she had thought the new man Henry had become would last, she had known in the back of her mind that in reality, it would not, and now she would have to suffer the degradation yet again.

'God, please let me get pregnant with a son,' Mary whispered, as she curled up on the bed to await his next next visit.

By January 1515, news arrived from London to the cities, towns and villages in England that Queen Catherine was with child again. This news was customary as she seemed to find no difficulty in becoming pregnant, but every pregnancy ended with the infant being stillborn, or dying shortly after birth. Within days of the proclamation of the royal pregnancy, came the usual news that the queen had lost yet another child.

Mary felt pity for the queen, how sad it must be to go through so many pregnancies to end with nothing. King Henry must be desperate to secure the Tudor claim to the throne. If she never had another child, Mary would not feel sorry for that. Henry's nightly visits to her bed still brought pain and humiliation. Now, she just let him get on with the loathsome undertaking, the more she protested and tried to fight back, the longer the sex lasted.

News reached Markham that the queen once again was pregnant. She had retired from court life, and had shut herself away with her closest attendants and the best physicians to wait for a successful confinement. Letters from Robert spoke of all going well, the queen seemed to be progressing fine with her pregnancy. The king had taken several casual mistresses during this time, he wrote to say that if Mary had been at court, the king would have commanded her to attend him personally, and she would have to obey the order. She hoped one day to go to court. Would the king, having laid eyes on her, desire her? It was a tantalising thought, she would muse of what she would do and say in front of the king. Would he be an exciting lover? Being the king gave an aura that made him stimulating to the imagination. She had to look to her own marriage to see that this was, in all probability, not true.

# 6

Mary lived in permanent fear of her husband. The beatings never ceased, the assaults continued, the ridicule was constant. All this chipped away at her self-esteem. She felt worthless and incapable of performing anything to his satisfaction. He instructed her to relate to him her actions every day. He wanted to know what she done, where she went, to whom she spoke. She would sit meekly in his presence, eyes downcast. The control over her was absolute. His parents had spoken to their son about his treatment to his wife, but he failed to listen or heed their advice. Mary would assure them that all was well; theirs was a marriage that would always be tempestuous, she dared not confide in them the true nature of this violent union, Henry threatened if he found out that she had spoken out of line, he would silence her forever. Could he be capable of the ultimate act of violence? Whether he meant this or not, Mary did not want to know. Therefore, she endured this sad life, knowing the only balm to sooth her was Cecily.

In February of the New Year, bells across England rang out to proclaim the birth at last of a healthy child to the king and queen. She had given birth to a princess, baptised Mary. This was a good omen for the country; now that the queen had produced one healthy child, unquestionably, more would follow. The country would become prosperous and good times would reign once again.

As if the queen's successful confinement had ignited a light of sanguinity countrywide, Mary discovered that she was pregnant herself. Henry with his disregard for his wife's condition still took her to bed, leaving her sore and bruised when he had finished. Yet over the subsequent months, the child developed and quickened. He was energetic, kicking often. She pleaded with her husband to leave her alone, for the sake of the unborn child. The words were ignored.

Mary began to feel unwell, and there appeared on her gowns small spots of blood. Nothing to be worried about she was advised, just a malady that would pass quickly. The physician did not comment on the bruising on her body. How Henry treated his wife was no concern to the physician. She had also become aware that the child had ceased moving in her womb; again, she was reassured that all would be well 'ere long. He was gaining strength for the birth. She awoke one night to excruciating pains and blood flooding her bed. While screaming for help, Mary miscarried a son. The stillborn wrapped in sheets was hurried away before she could even see it, despite her wretched cries to look upon the face of her dead son just once. He was gone. She fell back onto the pillows exhausted, desolate and inconsolable, pushing away attempts to hold her and to comfort her.

Henry had been waiting outside the door and had seen the bloodied bundle, with a small limp arm dangling from the sheet carried past him. The woman uttered one word: 'Boy.' He threw himself into his father's arms and sobbed bitterly, not for his wife, not for the pain and torment she had suffered by his hand, but for her failure to give him his son.

That unhappy year ended with subdued festivities. A cloud of misery hung heavily over Markham. With no concern for her feelings, Henry returned to the marital bed. When he had finished with her, he would toss himself to the other side of the bed, soon to be sleeping noisily. She would turn to the other side and lay there, her arms wrapped around her body, sleep eluding her as she thought of her lost son, wishing him back with her, and resigning herself to a married life of loveless, aggressive despondency.

# 7

Mary soon noticed her regular flow had ceased. The thought that she may be pregnant crept into her brain, and it was confirmed by the physician that she would be in childbed by October.

Henry was euphoric; Mary elated and immediately took to her bed to make certain that this time there would be no chance of miscarriage. It had worked for the queen, it ought to work for her. Henry had been advised not to sleep in the same bed as his pregnant wife to ensure a successful conclusion. He agreed reluctantly to the condition. Gertrude sent her more medication to aid throughout the pregnancy. As the months passed, Mary began to get a good sensation about the pregnancy again. She felt uncomfortable in Henry's presence, either preferring to be with any person from the hall, or having someone with her when he was close by. She pretended to be content in his company, together, they watched her stomach grow, and occasionally, they saw the little kicks from the baby. Henry was positive that this was his son William. Mary kept silent.

September arrived, by now she was becoming prickly with her husband as she reached the concluding weeks of this pregnancy.

'I am going hunting with my companions; will you be alright if I leave you unaccompanied for a day?' Henry asked.

'I shall be fine. It is only for a day, messengers will be dispatched if aught happens while you are gone,' She replied sourly, feeling thankful to be alone for a few hours.

'I feel this is a new beginning for us, Mary, we can set the bad times behind us once William is born, and I guarantee you will not fear my presence any longer.'

'What if this is not William, but another girl? Shall the beating resume?' Mary inquired tartly. Henry showed no remorse.

'It is a boy, I just know,' he assured, patting her stomach. Mary hoped he was right, if this baby was a girl, would he be so considerate? He would surely return to his aggressive ways. For now, she could think of nothing but the birth of this child.

Henry left the hall with his companions, clattering noisily out of the stables early on that September morning and into the Essex countryside. The hunting trip had been planned for weeks in advance, and the four young men were fervent to ride to hound. The baying hounds ran adjacent to the horses, sensing a good days' sport ahead of them. The runners who would beat the prey from woods ran behind. Mary, unable to sleep watched from the window of her bedchamber. She put her hands on her hips and stretched, uncomfortable with her body. The baby was restless today.

The hunt had not been as successful as Henry would have hoped; the deer and boar were illusive even with the hounds bounding through woodlands and the beaters roaring their way ahead. The single doe brought down was too small to divide between the four of them and was left where she had fallen. There had been sport of a more contemptible kind. The hunters, after stopping at a tavern to rest, had seen a young maid, overloaded with purchases from the local market walking home; they had given chase on foot and caught the frightened girl. Encompassing her, they had taunted her with vulgar suggestions, grabbing at her skirts, pulling at her long plaited hair and throwing aside the products she had been carrying home. Between them, the men pulled the struggling girl off the road into a shallow ditch. There each man had raped her, with Henry being the first to rob the girl of her maidenhood, urged on by his companions as they held the struggling girl down, and subsequently took their turn, laughing at her pitiful beseeching, and then distraught silence. When the deed was complete, they left the girl, lying traumatised in her own blood and strode back to the tavern, clapping each other on the back, laughing and congratulating each other on a job well done.

Back on their horses, they rode past the spot of the assault, the girl was still there, trying to collect her spoilt purchases, her face tear streaked, and the bloodstains on her skirts drying in the warm autumn sun. One of the men called out to the girl, saying he was ready to shaft her again. The others laughed and cheered at the girl's reaction. It was good to inspire fear in the local peasants.

Henry was jubilant. He had a wife who was fertile, a mistress who was exciting, companions who shared with him a lust for life. He felt invincible, heedlessly urging his horse on to jump a fallen tree. As the horse neared the fallen trunk, a rabbit, startled by the noise, ran from its hiding place, surprising his mount. It reared up, Henry struggled to regain control, but it reared up for a second time, throwing him from the saddle. He shouted as he fell from the horse and landed across the tree trunk, his leg twisted, and he felt bone splinter. He cried out for help. As the companions turned, the horse now panicked by disturbed birds that flapped and squawked noisily across its vision, reared up yet again and this time overbalancing fell backwards onto Henry. He screamed as the heavy body of the horse came down onto him, hooves flailing, bones cracking. He was immediately aware of an overwhelming hurt searing from his chest. He could hear voices calling his name, an injured horse whinnying. The world turned red, then black, noises began to grow fainter into a perpetual remoteness, and all pain vanished. The companions turned away sickened, the hunt instantly forgotten.

The late afternoon sun was casting long shadows when the three remaining hunters returned slowly back to Markham with Henry's body thrown over the back of one of their horses. William had seen the party return from his window, and seeing only three, none of them being Henry, knew something terrible had happened. He commanded the women, and in particular Mary, to remain inside until he could discover what had happened. Mary disobeyed, also sensing something wrong. She pushed past William and looked at the desolate expressions that greeted her. Mutely, she looked at the bloodied and broken corpse over the horse, and though knowing it was Henry, she lifted up his head to see his face, eyes shut, mouth open, and blood dripping. William took Mary by the shoulders and tried to lead her away, but she had already pulled back, her shoulders beginning to shake, small sobs, turning into louder and longer cries. Margaret and Eleanor appeared in the doorway; Eleanor's legs gave way under her when she saw her only son, lifeless in front of her eyes. Mary began to screech frantically,

45

grasping at her stomach, staggering back as a small trickle of blood ran down her legs.

'Get her back inside, fetch the midwife, the baby is coming!' William shouted, catching Mary in his arms and barking instructions to every person standing about as she doubled over in pain. The women led Mary into the hall. There, all three collapsed onto the floor, leaving William demanding explanations about the catastrophe that had taken his son so cruelly away. Inside the entrance, on the floor, Mary gave birth. The newborn was alive yet puny; there was no vigorous bawling, just feeble bleating. The midwife handed the small baby to Mary, as Margaret cradled her daughter in her arms.

'Henry has a son, and he shall never see the boy,' Eleanor gasped. Mary looked at the baby.

'Henry wanted to call him William,' she whispered touching the tiny face. The baby instinctivly turned his face towards the gentle pressure on his soft cheek. 'William he shall be.'

'Amen,' was the response.

'We must get you to bed,' Margaret said, trying to help Mary to her feet. Lettie took the baby from his mother and wrapped her apron around to keep him warm. Mary tried to stand, but collapsed yet again. Someone found a chair to carry her to bed.

# 8

Mary spent time looking after her new son, and trying to come to terms with the reality that she was unexpectedly a widow; her emotions veered from hopelessness to an irregular exultation, and trepidation for the future of her young family. Both William and Eleanor assured Mary that she could stay for as long as she wanted, and as the boy was now heir to Markham he could live there whatever she decided to do with her future. Before decisions, there was Henry's funeral to take place.

While Eleanor sat sobbing, Mary remained dry eyed. She felt she should be obliged to try to act sad in front of the congregation, but it would be difficult to invent an emotion she did not feel. The mourners surmised that her lack of tears were an indication of shock from losing her husband so suddenly and so violently.

Mary stood motionless at the side of the open grave. She looked around at the people drifting away, and then she looked up at the church. Only four years earlier, she had entered as a nervous bride, hopeful Henry would grow to love her. More fool her for believing she could be contented in marriage. The four years had been full with pain and fear. However, through all the despair, there had been beacons of radiance, beautiful Cecily and now fragile, small, William. Mary sighed, and turned back to look into the grave.

'I can't cry for you, Henry, and I can't ever forgive you. Your death is my release.' She removed her wedding ring and tossed it into the grave. The ring spun on the the coffin, and then rolled from the lid to fall beside it into soil.

Looking up she saw, standing alone, a flame-haired woman with a shawl pulled around her shoulders, holding a single stemmed flower. She was Henry's mistress. Mary glared unemotionally at Nellie, who in return gave a weak smile.

'I know who you are,' Mary called. 'I can't grieve for Henry; you are welcome to do so.'

'Thank you, mistress,' Nellie called back and stepped nearer.

'Wait until I am gone before you come near,' Mary replied tersely. She looked down again at the grave. 'Your slut is here. At least she is sad to see you gone.' Mary turned away in the direction of the waiting carriage. Nellie waited in the shadow of the church until the graveyard was empty before she approached. Kneeling, she placed the flower on the newly turned earth.

'Darling, this is for you.' Nellie's voice began to break. 'Oh, my love, I'm missing you, God look after you in heaven. I'll visit from time to time if that's alright?' She kissed her fingers, then touched the soil, getting to her feet, blew one final kiss at the grave and turned around to take the long walk back to the tavern.

Once the funeral was over, Mary began to recoup her strength. William was thriving; his chances of survival grew more heartening with every day. There were now decisions to make about her future. She was still only young, being twenty years old. Young enough to make a good second marriage, but at this instant, Mary wanted to remain single, the preceding four years had clouded her ideas of marriage being happy, she was contented enough for now to stay a widow.

# 9

Eleanor had taken the loss of her only child badly, and had noticeably aged since Henry's death. William kept trying to insist to his wife that life goes on even when loved ones have died, but Eleanor refused to listen, saying that there was nothing left on earth for her any longer.

When Mary suggested returning to Yardeley Chase with her children, Eleanor was distraught. This however seemed to jolt the sad woman back to reality. Gradually, she began to recover. When Mary next suggested that she would visit her parents while deciding on her future and that of her children, then to return, Eleanor was calm and agreed.

Eleanor began visiting Henry's grave daily, not returning until the evenings drew in, and the cold wind blew. Christmas was approaching; she had left all the arrangements of Christmas and Twelfth Night to Mary, not feeling like celebrating this year. Possibly next year, she assured.

Before it was light on Christmas morning, she left and rode in silence towards the church.

When he awoke to find his wife absent, William searched his home to find her; the grooms in the stable related to their master that Lady Eleanor had ridden out before daybreak, not telling him where she was going. Mary and William exchanged glances; they knew at once where she had gone. They rode at full speed to the church.

Candle light glowed through the windows, welcoming parishioners to attend early services. Torches in their sconces either side of the porch flared and dipped in the cold wind blowing, but Mary and William ignored the worshippers inward bound, and they made their way behind the church where they saw Eleanor's horse grazing. In the bleak, winter light, what appeared to be a pile of rags lay on Henry's grave. As they approached, William cried out in distress. The rags were Eleanor, her wrists cut, the bloodied knife still in her hand, blood pooling around her motionless form.

The cries brought the congregation out. The priest, pushing his way through the small crowd to the front said a prayer for Eleanor's anguished soul. Willing hands took Mary and William into the church for warmth after the shock. Messages dispatched to Markham to inform what had happened, and to bring a carriage to take the stunned couple back.

William locked himself away once he and Mary had returned home. She dismissed the musicians, inviting them before they left to eat their fill and paying them in full for their short stay. Then, unaccompanied, she sat at one end of the long table looking at the remanents of the food set out before her. In the space of three months, she had lost her husband and her mother-in-law. Eleanor's death distressed her more. She had been affectionate and loving, treating Mary as her own child. Her thoughts then turned to her father-in-law, his bewilderment and pain must be immense. What would he do now? For all his faults, Henry had been an only child both parents had loved. Markham was a big house for a lonely man to live in, and would he suppose Mary and her children stay there, they were his only family now. The future would have to be decided, but not today.

Eleanor's burial was beside Henry, the small group of mourners watching soberly as William said a tearful goodbye to the love of his life.

'Return home, Mary, I shall spend some time here,' he insisted, tenderly pushing her toward the waiting carriage. He saw the apprehension on her face. 'Do not worry, my dear, I will return before dark.'

Mary done as she was bade and returned home unaccompanied, where she went to the nursery to spend time with her children and felt comforted in their innocent presence.

It was late when William returned looking tired and exhausted. He told Mary that he had talked over the future with Eleanor, but said no more, preferring to go to his room after eating a little food and visiting his grandchildren, now both asleep. The sight of them sleeping so serenely was more than he could bear, and he left them. Mary watched his hunched figure walk heavily down the corridor, his stooped shoulders heaving.

Markham became a depressing, forlorn place. William resumed his business trips, but they were brief and he always returned home sad and alone. He scarcely spoke to anyone, preferring to take his meals in his chambers and spending little time with Mary, who herself had now taken over the administration of Markham. She began to feel trapped and more like a housekeeper, trying to commiserate with him, she did not want to waste the rest of her life in this indeterminate state. Each time Mary attempted to speak to William, he would say once the mourning was over all was to be arranged.

One day, without notice, William took Mary into the solarium; he looked more relaxed than he had done for a long while. Sitting Mary down, he positioned himself by the window.

'It is time for change,' he began. 'I have decided to sell this place to a cousin of mine and move on with my life. I am buying a town house at Bishopsgate in London; I shall be close to Bankside for foreign trade and close to court and will make connections there. I will take some of the servants with me, as it is a smaller property, and I shall not need so many. You, Mary, said you were thinking of returning to your home, that you will be able to do now. I shall make provisions for Cecily. William shall become heir to the house in London after my own death. It is the only and best way forward. Markham is too big for me now I am a lonely old man and I need this new start. What thinks you?'

'When will all this happen?' she asked, stunned. He smiled broadly.

'Six months. I have written to my cousin and he is prepared to take Markham on and give me a significant quantity of money to set me up for the future.'

Six months, not much, time to organise anything. Mary wrote to her parents telling of her return home soon, explaining why this was all so unexpected. Then she had to supervise the packing up of the hall and the selling of items not needed. Lettie, Mary's own maid, was to return with her mistress to Yardeley Chase.

The months passed quickly and Markham was soon ready for its new occupants, only the retained servants to attend their new master remained. The hall echoed as Mary walked through the rooms for the last time, saying her own goodbye to the place that had been her home. She stopped and looked around in the bedchamber she shared with Henry, remembering the pain that had filled that room. Then she entered the solarium. She walked slowly down the gallery to the spot where she had shared that fervent kiss with Rafael. How altered would her life have been if she had taken up his offer to run away with him? Mary sighed; her life was shifting now, heading on a different course.

Descending the stairs, Mary saw William, dressed for travelling, standing in the hall, looking around, recalling his own memories of a life spent with Eleanor. He smiled when he saw Mary and held out his arms to her. For the final time, she allowed him to gather her to his chest.

'Well, this is the end of an era for us both,' he began, in his voice a hint of a quaver, 'You will be fine travelling to Yardeley Chase?'

'Yes, I shall.'

'Good. I'm leaving now.' William looked around for the concluding time, and Mary saw the tears shimmering in his eyes. 'Goodbye Eleanor, goodbye Henry. Watch over me from heaven.'

'I'm sure they will,' Mary comforted, putting a reassuring hand on his arm. William nodded, now not being able to converse. 'Thank you for looking after me, you have been as a father to me.'

He nodded quickly. 'Let's go,' he said. William opened the heavy oak door and walked out of the hall for the last time. 'God speed and find contentment. Look after Cecily and William, I shall write to them often.'

Mary mounted her grey mare; Lettie mounted her small pony, the nurse with the children settled into the carriage. She turned to look at William for the last time, waving to her, standing amid wagons that now held all his worldly possessions. She waved and blew him a kiss, and then she rode away from Markham.

# 10

The reassuring red brick and timber walls of Yardeley Chase were welcoming sights when Mary arrived home. Margaret and Anthony were waiting at the open door to greet their daughter back. Mary dismounted and ran into her parents' open arms and hugged them sincerely. The nurse helped Cecily out of the carriage, while balancing William on her hip. Margaret approached Cecily and held out a hand for her granddaughter to take. The girl looked gravely at the grandparents she hardly knew, and hid behind her nurse's skirts.

'Come in, Mary and rest from your journey,' Margaret said, standing aside to let her daughter through. She passed under the arch of the doorway and it suddenly felt as though she had never been away. Little had changed since she had left. As Mary walked into that familiar, family home where she had known nothing but happiness, a short attention-grabbing cough made her look to her left. Her eyes widened and shone with animation and the happiest of smiles lit her face. There, leaning in a stone doorway, arms folded and smiling back was Robert.

'Darling brother, how glad I am to see you!' she trilled, running to him and leaping into his now stretched out arms. Robert kissed his young sister affectionately on the cheek. 'How is court? Do you see the king and queen?' This and a dozen more questions tumbled off Mary's tongue in between kisses. Robert disentangled himself laughing.

'Court is exciting and yes, I do see the king and queen.' He took Mary by the hand and led her into a small room just off from the hall to be alone with her. 'I have had an audience with her majesty, and she wishes you good cheer from your sadness. She has said that when a satisfactory period of mourning has passed, you will be presented at court and may attend the queen.' Robert watched his sister almost faint with exhilaration. 'Your position will be humble, but it is a start to court life, and who knows what adventures lay ahead for you there.'

Robert chuckled as Mary showered kisses over his face, thanking him endlessly on his generosity. He was an ambitious man who cared little for whom he trod upon to reach his goals in life and his name to be remembered through history. His inane little sister would be a valuable instrument. He knew that if the juncture arose, Mary would be malleable and innocent enough to do his command without question. He would not permit her to forget that it was he who had dared to advocate to the queen to consider his sister for the modest position she would hold. For now, he would bathe in her adulation. For now, he was the finest brother in the world. For now, let her imagine that.

The next day, Robert walked arm in arm with Mary in the gardens' telling her stories of intrigue at court. The king had a wandering eye, as Queen Catherine was pregnant yet again, but there was little hope for a healthy delivery as the queen was reaching the end of her childbearing years and apart from the Princess Mary, there had been no child that had lived longer than two months. She had spent hours on her knees praying to God for a healthy son. Some had quietly considered the queen spent too much time praying which could not be good for any unborn child to tolerate. Mary listened, fascinated by all Robert told.

'Do you think the king would ever marry again if the queen bears another girl?' Mary asked. Robert laughed.

'I wouldn't think so; he's still fond of Catherine in his own way even with all her failed pregnancies. It would have to be a very extraordinary woman to make Henry consider divorce.'

'But if the king needs a son, certainly for the country, he would have to do his Royal duty,' Mary argued.

'I have a politician for a sister,' Robert laughed.

'The country can't be ruled by Princess Mary alone. She must marry and give England a king to rule us,' she reasoned. They continued their walk and the subject of conversation changed to lighter themes.

News arrived at Yardeley Chase that the queen had again lost yet another child; a girl, dying only days after birth. What would the king do? The royal families of Europe would be turning their covetous eyes on England now, planning unions with Princess Mary to get their claws into the misty island off Europe's coast.

Robert departed Yardeley Chase promising to return in due course to conduct his sister to London. Margaret waved a heartbreaking farewell to her son, watching him ride away yet again. Now the planning would begin for Mary's future life at court.

# 11

*Greenwich*

Robert's arrival later that year with the summons to attend court heralded Mary's departure from her quiet, pastoral life. The night before Mary left she could scarcely sleep, she tossed and turned, and finally before it was light, she rose from bed and sat at the window seat of her bedchamber, looking out as dawn unhurriedly crept over the courtyard in front of her window.

Lettie, apart from speaking when essential, was uncommonly quiet that morning. She was to stay behind; Mary would have no need for her at court.

'Dear Lettie, I shall miss you,' Mary said. Lettie smiled barely.

'You are fortunate to have this opportunity, mistress,' she replied. 'I shall take pleasure in looking after your children. You may need my services another time.' Lettie laced Mary into her bodice and helped her into a comfortable skirt for riding. Finally ready, Mary went down to the hall to breakfast with her parents and Robert.

Robert was eating heartily, washing the food down with a tankard of ale. He looked up and smiled at Mary. 'Are you ready, sister?' he asked. She nodded and sat down to eat. She kept picking at the food in front of her. 'I'd eat more than that; we have a long ride ahead of us,' Robert warned. Mary tried to eat more, but her stomach felt tight with worry. Now the moment of departure had almost arrived, she felt fearful of the unknown.

'Well, it's time we left; you can't keep the Queen of England waiting,' he chided. The four walked out to the courtyard. Grooms stood waiting with the saddled horses along with a groom and packhorse. Mary turned to her parents and hugged her father.

'I never dreamt that both my children would go to court,'

Anthony said, kissing Mary's cheek.

'Look after yourself, my love,' Margaret added, gathering Mary into her arms. 'Robert, look after your sister.'

'Of course, Mother,' he answered, kissing his mother on the cheek. He then resolutely shook hands with his father and swung into his saddle. Lettie appeared in the doorway with Cecily and William. Mary cried out and ran to her children, sweeping them both into her arms.

'Oh, my darlings, I hate the thought of leaving you. I'll write and visit when I can.' She kissed both children; Cecily threw her arms around her mother.

'Don't leave, Mama.' she said simply. Mary began to cry. If she were able to, she would have remained with her darling children.

'Mary,' Robert called impatiently. She stood up, went to her horse, and mounted it. She looked down at her family standing before her.

'Goodbye, everyone, wish me luck,' she called. Robert turned his horse towards the gate, and Mary done similar. With a shout of goodbye to his parents, Robert trotted away, Mary following with the groom riding the packhorse behind. Anthony returned inside the house, he had complained of feeling unwell lately, and felt the need to rest, leaving Margaret standing unaccompanied and melancholy in the courtyard. She was worried for her husband's health, though she said nothing. No need to concern her children, they were off to lead their own lives now at court.

The small party took the London road, riding through villages and hamlets, stopping at inns and taverns to rest. In her protected life, Mary had never stepped into a tavern before. She gazed around intrigued by the sight and smell of the drinking house. Wizened old men sat in huddles swallowing strong ale in loud gulps, belching and spitting as they supped their tankards dry. Younger men sat swaying in time to vulgar songs, cheering as young women sat on their laps, kissing them. Women expertly carried overflowing tankards of ale, swinging their hips, avoiding groping hands. Briefly, Mary thought back to Henry and his whore, this scene must have been similar between him and Nellie. All these women had rosy complexions with rounded hips and full breasts bearly contained in their bodices. They all appeared to have long curly hair, spilling over bare shoulders, and small caps pinned to the back of their heads. They all looked merry, answering the crude suggestions with language that made Mary blush.

Once the meal was finished, they continued, riding through Blackwall and the Stepney Marsh pastureland towards the River Thames where the ferry would take them to the Palace of Greenwich.

At the jetty opposite Greenwich, one of two ferrymen was waiting for customers. Robert greeted him and paid the toll to be carried across the river. Mary had dismounted and stood regarding the scene before her. There were barges steered by lightermen and small crafts all plying their trade up and down the river and crossing the Thames with speed, skilfully avoiding other crafts. Opposite stood the Palace of Greenwich. There were towers, turrets, high walls and tall chimneys. Robert saw the amazed look on his sister's face and laughed.

'I was like that when I first saw Greenwich,' he said, leading his horse onto the ferry and beckoned Mary to follow. Tentatively, she boarded the ferry, this being the first time she had travelled on water. Robert assured that it was only a short ride to the other landing stage, and the ferryman had never lost a paying customer yet. However, she kept one hand tightly holding the bar that ran alongside the ferry, and the other holding the reins of her horse. She watched uneasily as the cold, muddy water lapped over the rim of the ferry and splashed her leather shoes. Although the journey did not take very long, to Mary it seemed an eternity and she was grateful to set foot on the boardwalk.

With his sister by his side, Robert led the way to the colossal iron gates, defended by yeomen dressed in royal livery. As they approached the doors, the guards crossed pikes, barring the way in.

'Halt!' One of the guards barked in a hostile voice. 'Stand and be recognised.'

'Robert Hawke,' Robert replied in a clear and balanced voice.

'State your business, Robert Hawke.'

'I am in the service of His Royal Majesty.'

'Who is the woman?'

'Mary Crawford, my sister. She is entering service with the

queen.' He produced the letter explaining Mary's arrival at Greenwich.

The guards regarded Mary with distrust, she felt very inconsequential under such inspection.

'The password?' The guard snapped.

'Tudor Pearl,' Robert replied assertively. The guards stood to attention.

'Pass, Robert Hawke and Mary Crawford.' The great gates swung slowly open and they entered the palace grounds. Mary looked at the guards as she passed them by. Both men kept staring forward, ignoring her.

'What is Tudor Pearl?' Mary whispered.

'The king calls Princess Mary his Tudor Pearl; he adores his daughter,' Robert explained. They passed through large wooden doors studded with brass nails and weighty hinges, and then she then turned her attention to the inside of the palace. 'Come, we will find the woman who will take care of you,' He led Mary along long corridors, bustling with men and women all talking at once. Everything was larger than life. Robert was greeting those he recognised and pointing out different people and what position they held at court. When the pair approached the royal apartments, there were more guards, brandishing pikestaffs; Mary had decided she was very small and unimportant. As before, there was a challenge preventing Mary or Robert from passing.

'This is Mrs Mary Crawford, widow. She is entering the queen's service,' he explained.

'Wait here.' The guard responded abruptly, and the letter was handed to a waiting page that scurried off to convey the communication of Mary's arrival.

Several minutes later, an older woman appeared from behind the door. Mary was a little confused; this was not how she imagined Queen Catherine would look. However, she managed an unsteady curtsey. The woman looked doubtfully at her.

'What are you curtseying for, girl?' she asked frostily. Mary straightened up, feeling foolish, realising she was making a bad first impression. Robert was looking sideways, uncomfortable by his sister's conduct.

'I am sorry; I just thought you were Her Majesty.' Mary said quietly, keeping her eyes downcast. The woman raised thick eyebrows.

'Well, I am not. I am Lady Dunning, Her Majesty's closest attendant.' She pointed at the ring Mary wore. 'Where did you get that?' she snapped. Mary looked at her ring.

'It was given to me,' Mary explained. 'It's a turquoise.'

'I know what it is, Mrs Crawford. Her Majesty wears the same stone. I have never seen any person other than the Spanish wearing turquoise. You would do well not to exhibit it while you are here.'

Mary instantly covered the ring with her hand. 'It was a gift which I like to wear,' she protested. Lady Dunning's eyes narrowed.

'Do not deem yourself my equal with whom you can quarrel. Remove that ring or I shall impound it.'

'Mary, do as bade, you are not doing well,' Robert hissed in her ear. Grudgingly, Mary pulled the ring from her finger and placed it in a small pouch attached to her belt. Lady Dunning straightened up.

'Follow me, Mrs Crawford.'

Mary turned to Robert and kissed his cheek. 'Thank you for getting me here, brother. I'm not confident how long I will last after these opening moments,' she whispered. kissing Robert again.

'Just keep that ring out of sight, and try not to upset Lady Dunning again. She has the queen's ear.' He hugged his sister affectionately. 'We will see each other from time to time and you can tell me all you know.' With that, Robert turned and merged into the crowds milling around.

Lady Dunning passed through the door, with Mary hastening behind. She caught up and fell into step beside her.

'I'm sorry for my manners just now,' she said. Lady Dunning sniffed contemptiously and carried on walking. 'It's just being new here, I was not sure what to do or say to anyone important.' Lady Dunning stopped and regarded Mary with her cold eyes.

'Mrs Crawford, I do not like individuals who crawl to me with their feeble excuses. You will only converse to me when I speak to you, or the queen commands. I have little time for the imprudent young people who seem to be invading court these days. I know His Majesty has an eye for a pretty, young thing to entertain him for a night or so. Expect to go the same way as the others. Bedded and wedded to an appreciative husband.'

Mary stopped walking. 'Lady Dunning, you do not know me. I was married to a cruel man who made my life a living torment. Release only came for me when he died in a hunting accident. I shall not go the way you imagine. If I marry again, it will be for love. As for His Majesty requesting my pleasure, I am a loyal subject. If commanded, I shall obey. But I shall not be farmed off to some old fart because I have out lived my use.'

Lady Dunning turned to stare at Mary, startled at the tenacity of the young woman. Quickly, she regained her poise.

'Well, Mrs Crawford. I may have misjudged you. Most women come here expecting to find a titled husband; it makes a refreshing change to find someone who is not looking to go down that road.' The slightest of smiles played on her thin lips. She then turned to face a closed door. 'In here now.' She turned the handle to the door and swung it open.

The room was large with a high ceiling. Tall glazed windows were set with small individual panes of stained glass decorated with Tudor roses and pomegranates. There was mingling scents of lavender and cinnamon prevailing. Furniture was sparse, but elegant. Five other women of various ages sat in window seats and wooden chairs; all were sewing or reading, one playing a lute. A young woman who looked close to Mary's age looked up from her needlework and smiled at the newcomer.

'This is Mistress Corby who will introduce you to the ways of court life and be your companion,' Lady Dunning said. The young woman stood up and took Mary's hands.

'Welcome,' she said. Lady Dunning indicated to Mary to follow her again.

'Your duties here are to fetch Her Majesty's shoes and hand them to Lady Judith.' She pointed at an elderly woman who was concentrating over a sheet of material trying to sew. 'Mistress Corby will show you where the shoes are kept.' Lady Dunning turned to one of the other older women, squinting into a book of devotions. 'Where is the queen?' she asked.

'Her Majesty is with her confessor,' the woman replied. 'She is still offended over the news of Lady Elizabeth.'

Lady Dunning pursed her lips and made a whistling sound. Mary surmised that whoever Lady Elizabeth was, she was not a popular person in Her Majesty's household. Lady Dunning glanced once more at Mary, and then departed the room by a small door.

'While we are in the attendance of Her Majesty, we call every one by our titles, but otherwise, first names are tolerated, except for the older ladies here,' Mistress Colby said patting the empty seat by her side. Mary came and sat down. 'I am Dorothy, but everybody calls me Dot. Well, tell me all about yourself, I have heard bits about you, you're married?'

'I was married, I'm widowed now, my husband died in an accident, then my brother was wonderful enough to find me this place here,' Mary explained. Dot looked sad. 'What about you?'

'I have been here six months, and my father is bargaining for a rich husband for me.'

'My husband, Henry beat me throughout our marriage.' Mary became conscious that the other women in the room had been listening to her account, as she looked up; they all hurriedly cast down their eyes to continue with their pastimes.

'Nothing is secret for long here, your life shall be general knowledge soon.' Dot guaranteed.

The small door suddenly opened. Everyone, together with Mary, stood up as Queen Catherine swept in with Lady Dunning close behind. All the women curtsied low. Without looking at any of her attendants, the queen walked to the raised chair close to an open fire and sat down, resting her head in the palm of a ringed hand. She gazed unseeing into the flames, Lady Dunning took up her position behind the chair. Catherine raised her eyes to her women, and she signalled for them to sit down.

'Be seated ladies,' she said in a soft voice that still held a hint of her native Spanish. 'Even if I suffer, you should not.' She returned her gaze to the fire, and emitted an extended, profound sigh; Mary felt sure she saw the glisten of tears. Lady Dunning whispered into the queen's ear and she looked towards Mary. Beckoned to approach, she curtsied low. The queen looked at Mary's bowed head for several minutes before speaking.

'I believe you are Mrs Crawford, rise.' Mary straightened up, but kept her eyes lowered. 'I am informed that you are widowed.' The queen sighed once more. 'I know the unhappiness of widowhood. My first husband, Prince Arthur, died before we could consummate our marriage, but I have been privileged to find love with the king.' A weary smile curved up the corners of her mouth. 'A husband who loves his wife is a cherished possession, and I have loved my precious husband in return. We disregard indiscretions because of our devotion.' The queen seemed to be speaking almost to herself. She was not concerned in Mary's past life. 'We usually do not allow women from lower birth into our household, but I understand that your brother is a rising star in court circles.'

Mary felt offended by the remark. Her family were not ennobled, but they were of respectable good stock. Nevertheless, she kept unspoken; the queen had more things on her mind than social position. She waved Mary aside and, curtsying, she stepped back to sit beside Dot who had had picked up her sewing again. Mary, with nothing else to do, watched Queen Catherine and Lady Dunning quietly talk to each other. Mary caught the odd word or two of the conversation, something to do yet again with Lady Elizabeth and the king.

Catherine stood up, and all the women copied their mistress.

'Ladies, I feel fatigued and will rest for a short time. Lady Dunning and Lady Judith will attend me,' she said, and swept past the women with a refined movement. Once the door closed, conversation sprang up in hushed tones.

'Who is Lady Elizabeth?' Mary asked. Dot pursed her lips.

'Well, she is the king's mistress and is pregnant with his child,' she began. 'The baby is due in summer and just the fact that she is with child is causing Her Majesty great suffering.' Dot looked around at the other women. 'Queen Catherine worries the king may cast her aside for a younger, fertile European princess, particularly if Lady Elizabeth bears a son.' Dot saw the intrigued look on Mary's face and continued. 'If Bessie has a healthy son, it will establish that the king is able to father male offspring. The queen's incapability to produce sons may be her ruin,' Dot said. She stood up. 'Come, let me show you where you will sleep and eat.' She led Mary into a large hall. At one end stood a raised dais with a long table on it, behind it was a golden high-backed chair. Adjacent to it were a slightly smaller golden chair and several plain chairs either side. Behind them, colossal, vibrantly coloured tapestries hung. At the other end of the hall, there was a minstrel's gallery that stood on tall, sturdy wooden struts carved with elaborate designs of musical instruments and dancing wood nymphs. A huge fireplace with an elaborated hearth and mantle dominated one sidewall, with a blazing fire emitting a warm and pleasing glow. Four large hounds lolled languidly in front of the fire. Enormous candelabras lit the hall, and long trestle tables ran the length of both sides of the hall. Dot explained that the king and queen obviously sat on the best chairs, besides them sat the significant members of court, or privileged guests. At the trestle tables sat the courtiers on benches. The nearer to the high table courtiers sat indicated their prominence at court.

'Come along, I will show you the dormitory.' Dot pulled Mary along a different corridor and up several flights of stairs until they came to a quiet, narrow passageway. There were hardly any people around now. 'Their Majesties don't see this part of the palace; it's where us lesser beings sleep,' she giggled. Stopping outside a door, Dot turned the handle, and entered with Mary following.

The room was average sized, bare-walled with shuttered windows, and lined with single beds; a small chest stood by the side of each bed. Dot ran to one of the beds and sat on it with a bounce. She patted the mattress inviting Mary to sit.

'My own private world is here in this little bed of mine,' Dot said, smoothing the coverlet affectionately. 'In here, I can pretend to be anyone I want to be. I'm sometimes the Queen of England, or a heroic English sea captain, discovering new worlds.' She pointed to one of the other beds. 'That is to be yours. We rise at seven and go to the chapel before breakfast. The queen rises at eight and breakfasts alone, or with the king if they have spent the night together. At nine, we attend the queen and remain with her until dismissed. That can be any period from midday to midnight. It depends on Her Majesty's disposition on the day. Take today; she has dismissed us for this short while. We will assemble in about an hour, and then see what happens after that.' Dot threw herself back onto her bed.

'Will I fit in here?' Mary asked. Dot sat up and shrugged her shoulders.

'Keep quiet; comply with her majesty, even if you think she is mistaken. If the king enters, do not look directly at him, even if he talks to you. Only lift your eyes to him on command.' Dot's face wrinkled into a smile. 'And if the king asks for you, do not refuse whatever the time of day or night it is. It can be quite an experience.'

'Has the king ever asked for you?'

'Once, not long after I arrived. He took my virginity and gave me this.' From under the straw-filled pillow, she produced a silk purse with several gold coins. 'He said it was for the gratification I gave him. I shall not spend this until I am old and grey and need a pension.' Dot held the purse to her breast and sighed blissfully before replacing it under the pillow once more.

'I feel a little overwhelmed by it all,' Mary said. Dot hugged her affectionately.

'Don't be. It scares us all at first, but you will settle in quickly. We surprisingly have a lot of free time these days. Her Majesty spends most of her time praying to God to give her a healthy son. The indignity of Bessie Blount's pregnancy sends the queen almost running to the chapel and her confessor.'

'She's a very sad lady,' Mary said. Dot nodded.

'She risks her life daily to produce an heir to the throne. She takes all kinds of potions to increase fertility.'

Mary's first meal in the large hall was quiet. She sat at one of the long tables. Both the king and queen were absent, leaving the two gold chairs unoccupied, though members of the Privy Council sat at the high table. Along with them sat Cardinal Wolsey, who was also the Chancellor. He was a large man in both stature and girth. Wolsey stood up to bless the meal, and gave thanks to God for providing the food. By now, Mary was very hungry and concentrated on the food in front of her, as she did not have the self-assurance yet to start a conversation with people sitting either side.

Once the meal was completed, musicians performed from the gallery and dancing began. Some men gathered in little knots to gamble with dice, women played cards or gossiped. Lovers sat close together, whispering to each other. Mary preferred to sit alone, watching. Then she saw Robert heading her way and felt appreciative for a friendly face. Hanging onto his arm was an attractive young woman. He sat next to Mary and the young woman flounced down alongside him, he beamed a welcoming smile at his sister.

'How goes your first day?' he asked. Mary looked around at all the activities going on.

'It's all very new and exciting,' she replied. Robert laughed.

'Today is an ordinary day, wait until there is a banquet, and then you'll see real excitement,' he assured, patting her hand, and then he stood up, pulling the young woman to her feet. 'I have urgent business to attend to.' He kissed the woman full on the lips, and patted her buttocks making her giggled with delight. 'Look after yourself, and I shall see you anon.' Robert headed off in the direction of an open door. The young woman's laugh overheard as she walked with him. Dot ran up to Mary next and pulled her to her feet.

'Don't sit alone; we're playing cards over there.' She led Mary across the hall, to a number of the women who attended the queen. They shifted along the bench to allow her to sit with them and at once included her in their conversations for the rest of the evening.

Eventually the hall emptied as everyone retired to bed, whether alone, or shared with lovers. Mary, with the other women, climbed the stone stairs to the dormitory and all fell wearily into their beds. She was so tired after such a long day; it took no time before she fell into an exhausted sleep.

It was early morning when Mary was woken up by Dot shaking her. 'Come on, lazy bones, you are not at home being waited on now, you are the one doing the waiting,' she laughed. Sleepily, Mary sat up, rubbing her eyes. Around the dormitory, the women were splashing water on their faces and dressing, chattering together. With the others, Mary went to the chapel to pray. The chapel was icy cold, the priest's voice droned on, and she found her mind wandering to what would happen this day. Once the prayers were over, the women filed silently out and went down to the hall for a breakfast of ale, warm bread and slices of hot meat, before attending to the queen.

With Lady Dunning shadowing her, Queen Catherine appeared from her private chamber looking pale and strained. As usual, she had slept little.

'This morning, I shall walk in the gardens and take the air to try to clear my head of my troubles,' she said softly, glancing out of the window at the frosty morning. Dot grimaced in Mary's direction.

'When it's cold like this, I'd rather spend my day in front of the fire,' she whispered, making Mary smile. Lady Dunning shot a fleeting look in Dot's direction, whether or not she had overheard the remark was not clear, but Lady Dunning would not stand for dissent from any of the women.

The queen led the way out, and walked slowly past small bushes that hung heavy with orange and red berries. The party wandered down to the lawn. Queen Catherine seated herself on a wooden bench and let the small dogs that accompanied her loose so that they could run around on the lawn, yapping excitedly. Mary, along with the other women, stood slightly apart from the queen, waiting for the next command.

'This isn't much fun,' Dot complained slapping her arms against her side in an effort to keep warm.

'How long will this go on for?' Mary asked. Dot's response was a shrug of her shoulders.

'It could be any length of time. I think Her Majesty likes to play the martyr at times. She seems to enjoy suffering; it makes her feel loved by the ordinary people.'

'They love her anyway?' Mary looked towards the queen who was talking with Ladies Dunning and Judith.

'Well, yes, and she knows it. I think suffering makes her feel commendable of their love.'

Mary looked around at the other women, they were predominantly older than either she or Dot, and they had been agreeable towards her the preceding evening, playing cards and gossiping.

The sound of men's voices from close to the palace made everyone look around; Queen Catherine's face immediately lit up with a smile. She rose to her feet, smoothing down her cloak. Mary's mouth dropped open in surprise as King Henry, gesticulating as he talked to Cardinal Wolsey, appeared. Cardinal Wolsey chuckled aloud at the king's commentary. Queen Catherine sank into a deep curtsey, followed by her women. King Henry stopped unexpectedly, seeing his wife. He signalled to the cardinal to stand back, and strode over to the queen, gesturing to the women to rise.

'Madam,' he said, holding out a hand for Queen Catherine to take to help her to her feet. She kissed his hand and looked devotedly at him. King Henry was a fine man to behold, taller than most men were, his build, athletic.

'My Lord,' Queen Catherine replied, reaching up to kiss the king lightly on the cheek.

'Madam not in public if you please,'

'My heart is content to see you as always,' the queen replied. From a short distance away, Cardinal Wolsey gave a slight cough. King Henry looked round at his Cardinal.

'Yes, yes. We will talk more this evening, madam, when we dine. Matters of state to attend to,' the king bowed to his wife and turned, striding off, resuming the conversation with Wolsey, his loud bellowing laugh echoing behind him. Queen Catherine, now looking radiant, sighed gladly having seen her husband.

'"Matters of state" my arse,' Dot whispered into Mary's ear, making her suppress a giggle. Lady Dunning turned and glared at both of them. 'More than likely talking about what women they've shafted,' Dot continued. Mary's expression turned from amusement to disbelief at Dot's forthright words.

'I shall return indoors now, I feel refreshed after this energising walk,' the queen announced brightly.

'Yes, because she saw her husband. She thinks that the king may bed with her tonight if they dine together.' Dot hissed from the side of her mouth as the women filed back to the warm palace.

That evening, Queen Catherine carefully selected a stunning gown of crimson velvet to wear. Lady Dunning combed her hair until it shone, and then dressed it with a diamond and pearl diadem. The queen picked garnet earrings and a gold cross, studied with pearls and garnets from her jewellery chest. Mary fetched the shoes that the queen would wear, then handed them to another woman who in turn would help Catherine step into them. The shoes matched the crimson of the gown, with pearls and golden thread stitched into them. They were the most beautiful shoes Mary had ever seen. Tenderly, she stroked her thumb over the soft material of the shoes and wished she could afford such extravagance.

Once dressed, Catherine looked dazzling. Lady Dunning

attached a thin golden chain around the queen's waist, upon the end of the chain hung an aromatic pomander of exotic spices to stimulate the king's passion. She stood there, apprehensively smoothing her gown, and adjusting the necklace so that it hung just right. Seeing the queen like this, Mary could envisage how beautiful Catherine must have looked in her formative years, when she had first arrived in England. It was easy to see why the king had fallen in love and after his brother's death, defied all to marry her.

The door opened and the king entered unaccompanied. He scanned the room to see if there was perhaps someone of interest in there that evening. His awareness then turned to his wife.

'Madam, ladies, arise now,' he said in a calm, authoritative voice. He speedily looked at the faces now that he could see them. There was a new young face, but nothing of interest tonight. With the exception of her most senior ladies, the queen dismissed her women and they filed noiselessly out, passing the king as they went. Even though not allowed to, Mary quickly looked up into King Henry's countenance and saw his sharp blue eyes that could fluctuate from tender to cruel in an instant. His mouth was small, but those lips could be amorous to any woman he desired. In that instant their eyes met, Mary involuntarily gasped and saw his eyebrows rise. Just as swiftly, the moment was over and she left the room, the door shutting behind her.

'Mary, you minx, never look into the king's face like that again!' Dot scolded. 'Or do you want to feel his majestic manliness inside you?'

'I am through with men. I definitely don't want to feel his or any man's manliness inside me for a long time to come." Mary exclaimed crossly.

'Uh-huh,' Dot sniggered. 'We shall see, won't we?' With that, laughing she broke into a run and headed down the corridor toward the hall where the evening meal was about to be served. Mary sighed in exasperation and followed her friend.

# 12

Life settled down for Mary at court. She made friends, her dancing skills improved and she learnt to play the lute. She wrote to her parents to tell them the gossip at court and looked forwards to their replies. Since that moment when she had looked into King Henry's face, he had never looked her way again, and Mary kept her eyes lowered in his attendance, not wanting his interest.

Warm spring turned into hot summer, and the court was buzzing with the news that Bessie Blount was due to give birth imminently. Daily, word swept through the halls and corridors of Greenwich Palace that Bessie had given birth, first to a son, then a daughter, and then the next revelation was twin sons! Queen Catherine had become bad-tempered and the king was on edge. The atmosphere was prickling with anticipation. There was frenzied wagering on the sex of the child, with large amounts of money exchanged hourly. The news arrived from the village of Blackmore in Essex. Elizabeth Blount had given birth to a healthy son with Tudor red hair. The entire court was in pandemonium. Catherine shut herself away feigning infection. Henry roared like a lion announcing his competence of fathering a healthy son. Mary felt sorry for the queen, forced to tolerate the public dishonour of her husband's infidelity. However, she found herself drawn into the excitement of the birth of the royal bastard. The revelry for the birth of Henry Fitzroy carried on with banquets, jousts plays, and masques. To outsiders, it seemed as though the king had fathered a legitimate son and heir. Only the best would do for the infant, he was the treasured offspring of the king.

However, the king by his nature was a lusty man who required sexual indulgence. It did not take long before his consideration fell upon another of Queen Catherine's women. Before Henry Fitzroy was two months old, Bessie Blount's position as royal mistress was over, and his new mistress became Mary Boleyn, one of two daughters of a Kentish merchant.

In the dormitory, there was constant talk of Mary Boleyn's rise to position of king's mistress. She had left the chilly dormitory for more comfortable lodgings close to his private quarters and had staff of her own now. She seemed intimidated by all the attention she now attracted. Ambitious men courted her, hopeful she would be a gateway to the king, and showered gifts of jewels upon her. Yet all she wanted to do was to please her royal lover. Her father encouraged his daughter to ask for royal favours, and endorse the Boleyn family. She yielded to parental pressure, and set about bringing affluence and rank to her family.

There was to be an investiture at court; courtiers were to receive honours for their services to the king and queen. Among them were Mary Boleyn's calculating father Thomas Boleyn, now created a viscount, and Mary's brother, Robert who was to be knighted, an honour for the Hawke family. Their parents were unable to attend, as Anthony, still in poor health, was not fit to travel. Proudly, Mary sat with other courtiers in the throne room of Greenwich, watching as Robert knelt before King Henry. He bowed his head as the king touched his shoulders with his sword, instructing Sir Robert Hawke to rise. Impulsively, Mary burst into applause, laughing happily at her brother's good fortune. Others looked at her, some with disapproving expressions, but Mary did not care. Her dearest brother was getting the recognition he deserved.

Will Somers, the court jester, provided the entertainment later. He was man with a sharp wit who could make the king cry with laughter. Somers would observe other people's behaviour, and then elaborate. The king was not immune from the jester's keen eye. One of his best performances was King Henry being pompous. Somers would strut around, exaggerating the behaviour, acting and sounding precisely like the king. For the jester, this ribbing was permissible; it was enthusiastically encouraged by both king and queen. At the end of his performance, the king threw a bag of coins at Somers, who caught it in one hand. He then retired to a quiet corner of the hall to eat and drink in silent, lonely seclusion.

Dancing followed. Robert swept Mary onto the floor to lead her in a Galliard.

'Did you enjoy watching earlier?' he asked, bowing low as the dance began. Mary curtsied back.

'You looked so handsome, I'm so proud of you,' she replied. Robert chuckled.

'Now that you are firmly settled in the queen's household, you can do something for me.' Robert began as the dance steps took them apart, and then back together again. 'Keep an ear open for any news you may hear.'

'What kind of news? Surely you must hear the same as I do.'

'Aye, I do. But from a woman's perspective, you may learn things a man is not privy to.' Robert and Mary circled each other. She looked quizzically at her brother.

'What do you expect to hear?'

'Oh, I don't know. Any bit of news that could help my advancement.' Robert bowed low for a second time as the dance ended. He led Mary back to her seat. 'Just keep in mind it was I who got you into court. You owe me a debt of gratitude,' he warned in a low voice. He then crossed back across the floor to a group of men and immediately joined their conversation. Mary watched him, shaken. She did owe her position at court to him, but had not thought he would expect recompense for the favour.

The early part of the New Year was routine for the courtiers. There was the customary praying for immortal souls, and wondering whether the queen would fall pregnant again. Mary had told Robert that the king never came to Catherine's bed any more. The highlight for her was the court moving from Greenwich to the Palace of Whitehall, further along the river. The king and queen sailed in opulent splendour on royal barges from palace to palace, apparently unaware of the turmoil the move caused.

Mary sat on a barge with other courtiers for the trip up river to Whitehall. On the north bank of the Thames stood the Tower, with its thick grey fortifications. She shivered at the sight of such a cold looking building. The barges picked up speed on the flood tide and passed with a rush under the arches of the bridge that linked London with Southwark. Mary looked up at the buildings lined up across London Bridge. She saw spikes with the heads of traitors stuck on them. Crossing herself, Mary said an unvoiced prayer for their souls.

If Greenwich had left Mary captivated when first she had seen it, then the Palace of Whitehall mesmerised her. It was more than double the size of Greenwich. There were cockpits, bear baiting arenas, tennis courts, bowling alleys, the longest tiltyard in the country, theatres and halls. Elaborate tall chimneys reaching aloft from red-tiled roofs to the sky blew smoke from fireplaces. Statues of Greek gods and wood nymphs stood in the manicured and well-ordered gardens. *This is what what Camelot must have looked like*, Mary decided.

Within weeks of the court coming to Whitehall, the Spanish Ambassador Eustace Chapuys arrived along with his entourage on a diplomatic visit. As soon as Queen Catherine greeted the ambassador, she changed. Her cheeks glowed and her eyes shone. She would sit for hours talking with him in native Spanish and Catherine would laugh merrily again. It warmed Mary's heart to see her mistress happy. Several of the women began affairs with members of the entourage. These Spaniards were all mystifying and zealous. Their English counterparts were resentful of the effect the visitors had over their women, and tension began to rise. Sporadic fights broke out and the king had to personally intercede and demand the two sides to call an uneasy truce before a serious injury occurred.

At a banquet, Mary had her usual seat; this humble location gave her a good view of the top table where the king, queen and the ambassador sat. Mary scanned the many faces of the Spanish all who sat at the next tables down, and her heart lunged. She could not believe that sitting in conversation was Don Rafael Perez. How had she failed to see him before? Now focusing on him, Mary could hear his melodious laugh. She sighed remembering his visit to Markham, and tried to get his attention by waving her hand vaguely. Would he still remember her if they met?

The banquet ended and a masque performed, celebrating the friendship between England and Spain, followed by tumblers; Will Somers performed his latest act of comedic parody, and a comical play that had the audience roaring with laughter. Then ultimately, the dancing began.

King Henry led his queen in the first dance, followed by the courtiers and guests. Don Rafael led a mysterious woman in a galliard and Mary felt an ache of envy as she watched them traverse the floor gracefully. As he passed near to where she sat, she caught a hint of musk. It lingered in her nostrils and reignited memories.

In the dormitory later, there was animated chatter about the banquet and how superb the Spaniards were.

'Did you see Don Rafael?' Mary asked reflectively.

'I saw how you didn't take your eyes off him, Mary. You wished you were that woman he danced with tonight?' One of the women giggled.

Mary blushed. 'I met him once before, he came to my home,' she sighed. There was a chorus of amusement from the other young women and they all gathered on her bed waiting for her to continue. Mary looked down, self-conscious. 'He asked me to run away with him; he said he would leave his wife to be with me. But I refused; I was pregnant with my daughter at the time.' The chorus from the young women became a combination of excitement and disbelief. One of the other women commented on a different Spaniard and all interest switched from Mary to her.

The next day, the queen took the air in the garden attended by her women. Ambassador Chapuys strolled past with Cardinal Wolsey and Thomas More. Following the men were courtiers and Spaniards, Don Rafael being one of them. The ambassador bowed low, taking the queen's hand in his, and kissing it.

'*Majestad*,' he said. 'The day is fair and all the more for seeing the daughter of Spain looking so well.'

'Ambassador, thank you. I like to walk out on days like this.'

'I would accompany you, *Majestad*, but I have urgent work to attend to.' He indicated to Wolsey and More with a sweep of his hand, 'Please excuse me.' He bowed with a flourish and passed by the queen. Mary stared intently at Don Rafael, eager that he would return her gaze. To her delight, he looked directly at her. His eyes opened wide in surprise as he recognised her, and he smiled. He spoke quietly to the ambassador who nodded; and after bowing to the queen, he turned his attention to Mary.

'Maria, what are you doing here?' he enquired, kissing her hand. Mary flushed scarlet with delight, intensely aware of all watching closely.

'I attend Her Majesty now,' she replied, glancing towards the queen who was still conversing with the ambassador.

'But where are your husband and child?' he asked.

'I am widowed; I now have a daughter and son.'

He kissed her hands again. 'I am sorry for your misfortune, but I am glad that man can no longer hurt you. You still look as beautiful as I remember. Will you dance with me tonight?' he asked. Mary nodded, laughing. 'Then tonight we dance and see where that may lead us.' Don Rafael bowed low to Mary, and the queen; then returned to the ambassador, the women watching him as he strode away. The younger women gathered around Mary. She was glowing with delight as questions about the Spaniard bombarded her.

Back in the warmth of the palace, the queen shut herself into her private chamber with Lady Dunning and her senior women. Eventually, Lady Dunning appeared from the room and called Mary over.

'Her Majesty will speak with you,' she commanded and led Mary into the small chamber. The queen was sitting by a fire in a plain hearth. Mary waited.

'You spoke to Don Rafael Perez, Mrs Crawford. How do you know him?' she asked. Mary curtsied again.

'Majesty, when I was married, Don Rafael came to our home as a guest,' Mary explained. Queen Catherine nodded unhurriedly, and then looked towards Lady Dunning.

'You will leave now,' Lady Dunning ordered, and curtsying, Mary left the chamber to additional questioning by her friends.

She dressed carefully, to look her best for Don Rafael. After preparing the queen for the evening, Mary with the other women fell in line following their mistress.

The king stood at the top of the stairs shifting his weight from one foot to another while he waited for his wife. He felt irritated that he, the King of England had to wait for any woman. Hearing the sound of rustling gowns, Henry turned. Queen Catherine along with her gaggle of women appeared. He took the queen's hand and raised her; casting his eyes proficiently over the young women, and noticed one who was dressed with exceptional good taste. She had been the one who had looked directly at him a while ago, and he made a mental note to entertain himself with her one day. Mary took her seat and looked around for Rafael. She saw him sitting much closer to the high table; he looked around the faces, searching for Mary. Not seeing her, he directly began conversing with the people surrounding him.

Once the dining was over, Will Somers tumbled onto the floor and began his new routine. Ambassador Chapuys stood and applauded the jester, saying there was no man in Europe to compare with Will Somers. The king heartedly agreed and said that nothing would make him part with his Master of Misrule. He then lead the dancing with the queen, Mary became excited as Rafael saw where she was sitting and approached her. He stopped and bowed in front of her. She felt certain he would be able to hear her heart thumping against her ribcage.

'*Senora*, would you honour me with a dance?' he asked holding out a hand.

Mary tried to speak, but the words stuck in her throat and all she could do was nod dumbly as she heard giggling behind her. Rafael smiled reassuringly and led her to the floor. She was intensely aware of many eyes watching and hoped she did not look foolish. It was like a dream as he led her in a dance that seemed to end all too swiftly. His eyes never leaving her face for an instant.

'Maria, I will see you tonight, I will send a page to bring you to my apartments at midnight where I await you with expectation,' he whispered in her ear. Suddenly alarmed by such a presumptuous comment and bewildered by her emotions, Mary stepped back.

'I do not dally with men, sir,' she heard herself say. How idiotic! Here was the man she desired with every fibre of her body, yet she was rejecting him. Rafael's eyes shone with naughtiness, to him this was a game and he liked it. His lips curled into a wicked smile. In front of the king, queen and all the courtiers, he stood back and announced at the top of his voice.

'Milady, I am Don Rafael Perez of Bilbao, in attendance of his grace, ambassador Chapuys. I am your obedient servant.' The entire hall fell silent and all eyes turned to Mary who was shrinking backwards with mortification, wishing the ground would open up and swallow her as he swept an overstated bow. The king, his attention caught, roared with hilarity.

'What ho, Spaniard! Planting your cock in an English garden tonight?' he shouted. Queen Catherine scowled at her husband, and then shot a fierce stare at Mary, whose face was burning with the interest focused on her. Rafael straightened up, faced the royal table and bowed gracefully.

'*Majestad*, you are very perceptive!' he answered. There was cheering from the men and the women laughed.

'Then go and rut with your saucy strumpet, and give her your best one from me!' King Henry laughed, making sexual gestures with his hands.

'If the lady is obliging, *Majestad*, I will gladly do as you command,' was the reply, greeted by whooping from the men. Then quietly, so only Mary could hear, 'There, I am familiar with you now, eh?' He raised her hand to his smiling lips and kissed it. 'Midnight, tonight.' He led Mary back to her seat, bowed elegantly and strode off.

'You *saucy strumpet*! Even I would not dare be so familiar!'

'The queen looked shocked!'

'Oh, I know, I know,' Mary blustered. 'I do not know why I said what I said.'

'You are in for a vigorous night my girl!' giggled one of the women nudging Mary in the ribs, and they all burst into laughter. The rest of the evening, she was "*the saucy strumpet*", and unexpectedly found herself very popular.

At midnight, Mary paced up and down outside the dormitory waiting for the page to arrive. Her mouth was dry and the palms of her hands were damp. She felt like a virgin on her wedding night. Then the thought struck her, what if Rafael was not the virile lover she had imagined, or if she proved a disappointment to him? Now was the time to return inside the dormitory to save embarrassment. Too late, a page clothed in Rafael's livery was approaching and, bowing, beckoned her to follow him in faltering English.

'Oh, my God,' Mary whispered to herself. Taking a deep gulp of air, she followed the page through the quiet corridors, past guards who smirked to each other; they had seen this scenario times before. The page pushed open the door, and bowed low to Mary who steadily walked in.

Large candles secured in heavy iron candelabras bathed the room in a sensuous warm light, the heady scent of sandalwood hung seductively in the air. The furnishing was luxurious. Looking round, she saw him. Rafael, wearing a crimson silk robe, sat in a carved chair; he rose unhurriedly to his feet and poured a crystal glass of wine, handing it to her. He looked even more desirable now he was relaxed. Mary began to calm down and wondered why she worried. He would not dissatisfy tonight.

She crossed to him and took the glass, their fingertips touching, sending an exhilarating thrill through her body.

'Thank you for coming to me tonight, Maria,' Rafael said quietly in her ear. The name Maria sounded exotic and exciting. 'Do not fear me; I will not make you do anything you do not wish to. Tonight is all about us and the love we will make.'

For a moment, Mary drew back, fearful of the charged atmosphere in the room. She took a small sip of the wine, and then looked up at Rafael. He took the glass from her and placed it on the table. Taking Mary in his arms, he tenderly kissed her mouth.

'Let me show you what you have never known possible,' he whispered. His hands pushed the headdress from Mary's hair, letting the tresses cascade over her shoulders. His hands ran over her breasts to the front of the bodice where they slowly pulled the laces through the eyelets, releasing her breasts from their confinement. He loosened her skirt and lifted her lightly clear. She stood there in her chemise, feeling very uncertain of her emotions. With gentle hands, the Spaniard lifted the young English woman into his arms, carried her to the ornately carved bed, and laid her down upon it; Rafael removed the silken wrap that he was wearing, letting it drop to the floor and climbed in beside her. His hands expertly caressed her body, his lips kissed every inch of her flesh, bringing Mary to the edge of ecstasy, a sensation never experienced before, she felt scared, in case this was all an illusion, a dream and she would wake up either lonely in her bed or worse still, with Henry, asleep beside her. However, Rafael was going to do all he could to drive out her fears and make this night unforgettable. Mary gazed into his dark, beautiful eyes and knew everything was going to be fine; there was no need to be frightened. She sighed and let the passion envelope her…

Outside the window, a host of sparrows twittered boisterously in a tree. Mary stirred and listened. Looking over, she saw Rafael still sleeping alongside her and a happy smile crossed her face. She stretched contentedly. The previous night had been amazing, and Mary discovered in herself a passionate nature she had never known before. Closing her eyes, she relived the event, recalling each luscious detail; Rafael awoke and placed a tender kiss upon her cheek. Gasping, Mary opened her eyes and saw his kind face looking down on her.

'*Buenos dias, mi ingles se levanto,*' he said.

'Good morning,' Mary replied and held out her arms to him. The Spaniard took the enticement, and they made love, rediscovering again the delight of each other's bodies.

Regretfully, Mary had to rise, dress and depart Rafael's chamber. She had duties to attend, and her friends would be impatient to find out all the details of the night, and speculate who could be the fortunate girl next. She dressed quickly, left Rafael sitting at his table and hurried to the dormitory, slipping in to a sea of inquisitive faces.

'Well, how was it?'

'Was he gentle?'

'Is he good in bed?'

'You look so happy, Mary.'

The women gathered around questioning her.

'I never realised how happy I could feel until now, he was so amorous and gentle,' Mary explained. Giggling, the women helped Mary wash, change her dress, and brush her hair, and then they went to the chapel to pray before attending the queen.

Catherine was already at her table, eating daintily, attended by Lady Dunning and the senior women. As usual, Catherine scarcely acknowledged them. When she had done eating, and had dabbed at her lips with a linen cloth, she turned to look at Mary.

'Mary Crawford, approach,' she beckoned. Mary stepped forward and waited. Queen Catherine regarded the young woman.

'Last night, there was an occurrence involving you and one of our Spanish guests.' She was referring to Rafael's bold declaration in the middle of the floor that had caught the attention of everyone, including the king.

'Yes, Madam,' Mary replied quietly. The queen grunted.

'I would have thought a widow like yourself would venerate the memory of your dead husband. I did so when the Prince of Wales died.'

'I do, Majesty.'

'Then you show an irregular way of reverence, Mrs Crawford.' Catherine regarded Mary. 'I know some ladies have games at night,' her eyes scanned her women, some who blushed. 'I do not encourage it; I expect decorum. If you must conduct yourself in such a way, please be discrete in the future.' The queen waved a hand in dismissal and Mary backed away. Catherine looked at her women and spoke. 'The king is going to France and I am to accompany him.' She stood up. 'You will all be expected to behave yourselves both day and night. The French have loose morals. We will show them that English women behave precisely.' The queen then swept from the room.

Mary had never travelled so far in her life, and the thought of crossing the English Channel filled her with dread. An advance party had already travelled to France to prepare the site, making it suitable for the two kings to attend, as King Henry wanted this event remembered forever.

# 13

On the first day of June, the royal party set out for France. The king and queen were at the head of the parade. Horses, gaily caparisoned, pranced and pennants fluttered in the summer breeze. On that warm summer day, children ran from their homes, men and women, backs bent from working in the fields, straightened up and watched, shading their eyes as the magnificent parade passed by. Mary, with the other women, smiled and waved at children, who waved back some shyly, some boldly.

The royal procession arrived at Dover Castle in the early evening sunshine. The constable of the castle and his wife waited in the courtyard to greet the king and queen and escort them to the state apartments where they would rest until the crossing could take place. Along with the other women of the household, Mary followed her mistress through the corridors and along a brightly lit gallery to the simple, but elegant chambers.

Once Queen Catherine settled in her rooms, Mary took a chance to look out of the window. The castle stood on the top of the renowned white cliffs. The sea stretched out as far as Mary could see and the setting sun sparkled on the waves. Robert came and stood next to her and enjoyed the same view.

'On a clear day, you can see the coast of France,' he said pointing out to sea. 'If tomorrow dawns clear and bright, see if you can see it.'

Just as Mary had hoped, next morning the air was clear. The queen desired to take her dogs for a walk along the cliff top and her women would accompany her.

Mary looked out across the channel and peered as hard as she was able, and just as Robert said, in the distance was a misty smudge that was confirmed as France.

From the docks, huge ships were commencing towards Calais,

laden with provisions, chests full of clothes jewels, gift and money, all delivered to the site to be ready when the king and queen arrived in splendour.

Guards, preventing onlookers from catching a glimpse of their king and queen and to cheer them, had cordoned off the docks. Uneasily, Mary edged up the gangplank onto the galleon, feeling it gently sway under her feet. She made her unsteady way to the side, and looked out towards the open water, gazing in the direction of France with trepidation. She looked over to the adjacent galleon. The king stood on that deck in discussion with the captain; neither seemed concerned about the crossing. The sea breezes whipped Mary's hair across her face as the galleon moved away from the dock. She shut her eyes and gripped the rail so tight her knuckles went white. Dot saw her tense with fear.

'Mary, the channel is calm; it will be a smooth ride, no mean waves,' she laughed and turned away to flirt with a young courtier waiting for her. Mary swallowed hard and looked in the direction they were heading. In the distance, she could see the misty coast of France, wishing that Rafael were close by to assure her the sickness she felt in the pit of her stomach was normal.

With great relief, Mary disembarked the ship and waited in a huddle of women for the other galleons to dock. There would be a brief respite in Calais, until the entire entourage reassembled, then the ride to the allotted meeting place would resume.

That evening, Rafael found Mary.

'I know Calais and where we can spend time alone,' he said leading Mary from the camp, past the guards and in the direction of the town. 'The last time I was here, an innkeeper befriended me and told me that if I ever needed privacy, he could make available a room.' Mary pulled away shocked. 'Do not look like that. I am a man and I have needs,' he explained puzzled by her reaction.

'Am I someone who you use for your needs?' Mary asked, hurt by his casual comment. Rafael stopped and pulled her to him.

'Maria, you are all I need. No woman can compare to you,' he spoke, his lips pressing into her hair.

'What about your wife? Do you think of her when we are together?' she asked pulling away again still not persuaded. Rafael's face darkened.

'I never wanted to tell you like this, but Pilar is dead. She died after childbirth,' he said despondently. 'She gave birth to twin daughters, they both died within hours of each other. She never recovered.' Tears shone in his eyes, and Mary felt appalled with herself for doubting him. 'I think I have lost interest tonight,' he said turning aside, covering his eyes with a hand. Mary pulled him back, took his face in her hands, and kissed him full on the lips.

'Rafael, my love, I did not know, come here, let us be as one, now,' she urged pulling him towards undergrowth by the roadside. He hesitated. 'I don't care if everybody sees us; others must be doing the same at this very moment.' Rafael smiled barely, and then his face lit up into the familiar smile Mary knew and cherished. The couple hurried behind the undergrowth. She lay down and pulled the Spaniard onto her. They made love on that balmy summer night, under starry skies, until content and satisfied; the couple lay back on the grass looking up at the night sky, watching a waxing moonrise, Rafael pointing out and naming the planets and constellations twinkling high above them.

The next day, the procession continued. Before even seeing the site, a golden glow was discernible over the horizon. The clarification given was that the marquees and pavilions were made of golden fabric. All premeditated to promote to the French king that England was a prosperous country.

When Mary and the others in the party saw for the first time the vision that greeted their eyes, words failed them. It was more than they could have imagined. There were large pavilions, pennants fluttering; all were golden, with Greek gods and fables woven into the cloth. Smaller marquees designed to precisely the same specification bordered the pavilion. Kitchens and stables were erected, gleaming gold in the sunlight. There was a tiltyard with pavilions and stands sparkling with gems. Everything was an ocular feast to the eye.

That night, there was a banquet in the main pavilion with tableware of solid gold and as much wine as everyone could consume. Everyone's frame of mind was excellent, this was going to be a triumph that would be talked of for centuries to come.

The French king and queen arrived the following day to fanfares and celebrations. Francis was genial and approachable; he briefly spoke to everyone, including the most humble servants. The two kings greeted each other with a cordial embrace, while Catherine and Queen Claude kissed warmly. Henry arrogantly gave Francis a tour of the pavilions, ensuring he was intensely aware of the cost to the English exchequer, and assuring the French king that there had been no additional taxes on the people of England to pay for such extravagances.

The day's events took place at the tiltyard, the wrestling arena, and bowling alleys, cockpits and bear pit. The two kings and their councillors spent hours arguing over their treaty before breaking to partake of the amusements on offer.

Night after night, each camp put on entertainment more sumptuous in an attempt to outdo each other. The English were confident that they had provided dazzling recreation; the French argued that they were the best. One night both Henry and Francis, sitting side by side, were watching a wrestling match between their two best athletes. Henry made a comment that he could throw Francis if they fought. Francis rejected this claim. The English king then challenged the French king to a wrestling contest. Mary and Rafael stood with an excited crowd watching as the two kings entered the wrestling arena, stripping to the waist. To the encouragement of the onlookers, they circled each other, before Henry made the first move and grappled Francis. They fought, pushed and tussled, struggling to gain dominance. Defeat would be more than simply a personal disgrace. The match carried on until Francis hooked a leg around Henry's and sent him sprawling onto the floor to loud cheering from the French camp. He lay there winded, looking up into the smirking face of Francis, who stood, hands on hips over the routed English king.

'*Mon Ami,*' he laughed, holding out a hand to help. Henry refused the gesture and scrambled to his feet, glowering irately at his vanquisher. He snatched his shirt up and stormed away, French laughter ringing in his ears.

After seventeen days, the English and French parted, no treaties signed, no changes made. Only Henry's bruised ego and disturbingly empty coffers from the expenditure of the disproportionate event.

The English party camped again at Calais before the passage back to familiar terrain. This time, Mary was able to sail with Rafael on the same ship. They found an empty cabin and spent time sheltered away from the world. All too soon, the ships docked back in Dover and the final leg of the journey back to the Palace of Whitehall began.

# 14

News that new ladies-in-waiting were to arrive at court sparked anticipation, for along with them would be the other daughter of Sir Thomas Boleyn, Anne. Rumours spoke of pressure put upon the queen to take up Lady Anne by the king after he had visited Boleyn at his home in Kent where he had first seen her.

Anne Boleyn's appearance at court caused a stir immediately. Everyone was aware of her due to her sister's previous stay at court. Wagers were set up as to when she would go the same way, bedded by the king, and then cast aside when he grew tired of her. Anne was not fine looking like her sister, but she had a presence about her that gave her a dangerous allure. Her hair was long, straight and black and she had dark brown eyes, made all the more prominent by her ivory complexion. She wore the sleeves of her dresses long to cover her hands, gossip said was to hide a sixth finger on her left hand which again gossips said was a sign of a witch. Lady Anne was a woman to watch.

As always, Queen Catherine was civil, but distant to her new women, she was conscious that Anne was different from all the others, and knew it would only be a matter of time before the king called for her.

However, Anne, for all the mystery that surrounded her, had no interest in climbing into the bed of the king readily or otherwise. She arrived at court already in love and eager for marriage. The man of her dreams was from the nobility. Young Henry Percy, son of the Duke of Northumberland, was in the service of Cardinal Thomas Wolsey. As the cardinal was a favourite of the king, Henry Percy was often accompanying his master, so Anne knew she would see him, and they would try stealing moments together to plan their future. If Northumberland agreed to the match, it would be a greater marriage than Anne could ever have dared. She was merely the daughter of an ambitious merchant from Kent. His other daughter had dissatisfied him by quickly losing the passion of the king. A compliant husband was found to give her unborn child a father; the king never acknowledging that Mary Boleyn's child was his.

Mary, now lonely since Dot had been recalled home to marry was the first to extend the hand of friendship towards Anne, and welcome her into the queen's service. Anne accepted the offer of friendship, as she found life in the English court unexpectedly different from the court of France. When the opportunity would arise, Anne would talk of life in France, the grace and style of the women, the passionate encounters that went on clandestinely everywhere. Anne insisted that she kept herself pure and uncorrupted; she wanted to go to her husband a virgin, a virtue that Queen Catherine admired, saying too many young women were ready to fall into any man's bed, referring to Mary and Rafael's affair.

Robert detained his sister one day when she had an hour to herself while the queen prayed. He looked astonishingly happy.

'Mary, how well do you know the queen's new woman?' he asked, drawing Mary in a window seat that looked out at a group of archers.

'You mean Lady Anne? I know her, we prattle when we get the time, why?'

'She is the most beautiful woman in the world, I think I love her,' Robert said. 'I would court her if she permits me to.'

'Robert,' Mary laughed laying a hand on his arm, 'she has eyes only for Henry Percy. Why would she even look at you?'

Robert looked wounded. 'I know I do not own much wealth, and my prospects are not as good as Percy's. Yardeley Chase will be mine one day. Besides, true love can conquer all, and when she sees I am true and honest, she will see me for who I am.'

'Get in line, brother; many men have fallen for the Lady Anne, and she is indifferent to all,' Mary warned with a smile. Robert made an intolerant gesture with his hands. 'Good luck, dear Robert, if you can find happiness with Anne as I have with Rafael, then we shall both be happy for the rest of our lives.'

Robert watched his sister depart along the gallery, and then he turned back to the window to continue watching the archers, though his mind was seeing the vision of himself and Anne happy on their wedding day, then surrounded by many children. As soon as he could, he would speak with her.

On one evening's dancing, Robert manoeuvred himself around the floor to allow him to dance with Anne. The young woman scarcely regarded her dancing partner, so many men clamoured to be with her. One more made little difference.

'Milady,' Robert began. Anne looked at him and smiled politely, 'I would speak in confidence with you.'

'Really, what do you have to say?' she asked coolly.

'It is private and I would not wish others to hear,' Robert exclaimed.

Once the dance finished, Robert led her out into the garden and she sat upon a bench. Uneasily, Robert paced up and down, attempting to find the exact words to say. She wordlessly watched his pacing.

'Lady Anne, I have admired you since the first day you arrived at court and would like to know you more,' he claimed. Anne remained silent. She had an idea where this was leading. 'You would do me the utmost honour if you would concur to become my betrothed and to marry me,' he announced. She pursued her lips.

'Why would I agree to marry you?' she enquired unfeelingly. He did not expect her to fall into his arms appreciatively, but he had hoped for a more optimistic response.

'I love you and would want you for my wife,' Robert pleaded like a lovesick fool. Anne stood up.

'I love Henry Percy and will marry only him. I will be his duchess.' She looked Robert up and down and sneered. 'What makes you think I would give up Percy to marry a man like you?'

'You do not know me at all, Anne. I will have you willingly or not. You shall be my bride,' Robert fumed as a sudden and unexpected fury swept through him. He lunged at Anne, wrestling with her in an endeavour to force himself upon her. She fought back and slapped Robert hard across his face.

'If you lay a hand on me again, I shall tell my father. He has the king's ear!' she shouted and ran from the scene.

'I will converse with your father first, Anne. If he orders you to marry me, then you will comply and call me husband!' Robert yelled back to the woman he would marry. He glared at the people staring at the scene. 'What are you gawping at?' he furiously shouted.

Sir Thomas Boleyn sat behind a table, writing paper and quills were set ready for use. He stared seriously at Robert, who in turn stood awkwardly before him, hat held tightly in sweating hands as he waited for the order to speak. He was beginning to think this was not such a good idea. Boleyn lacked humour, and if it was not for the love for Anne, Robert wished he were anywhere else but here right now.

'I am a very busy man, speak your piece,' Boleyn said brusquely. Robert took a deep breath.

'First of all, I...' he began. Boleyn waved an impatient hand.

'Yes, yes, enough of this, you have something to say, say it.'

'Sir Thomas, I love your daughter, Lady Anne, and I would ask your permission to court her with intent of marriage,' Robert said in a single breath. Boleyn sat back in his chair and tapped his fingers against each other as he regarded Robert.

'Do you now. What can you offer my daughter?'

'I shall give her love and undying loyalty.'

'Love and loyalty will not feed or keep my daughter,' Boleyn said slowly. 'When Anne marries, she will be kept in a state befitting her, not as the wife of a pauper.'

'I am not a pauper, when my father dies, I shall inherit an estate in Essex...'

'Do not interrupt me. Do you know whom my daughter loves right now? She is infatuated to a man who one day will be the Duke of Northumberland. Do you think I would allow my dearest daughter to walk away from a match like that to marry any love sick fool with no prospects whatsoever?'

'Sir Thomas. I love Lady Anne,' Robert pleaded.

'What does love have to do with marriage? Anne is fortunate enough to be loved by Percy and she loves him in return.'

'Lady Anne is a virago who will love me one day,' Robert retorted resentfully, anger mounting at Boleyn. Sir Thomas waved a hand towards the door.

'Good day, sir, leave my presence, do not speak of my daughter in that tone,' Boleyn spat, then picked up a quill, thrust it into an inkwell and began to write swiftly on the paper. Robert remained there, watching him.

'Sir Thomas, before I leave, hear this. I love Anne, one day you will call me son. If not, I shall do all in my power to ruin her and your family.'

'Do not make empty threats in an attempt to alarm me, I can squash you like a fly. Leave before I call the guards to remove you.' Boleyn did not look up from his writing. Robert turned and departed. He was feeling rage building up inside him. Anne was the only woman for him, no other would do. She had rejected him and he would not take rejection. If that woman refused his love, then she would receive his hate, and one day, Anne Boleyn would be sorry.

# 15

Rafael frequently received communications from his home. Usually, the correspondences were nothing more than information about how his estate was running during his absence. Upon reading his latest document, he locked himself away in his apartment and refused to see or speak to everyone, alarming Mary. When he did emerge, he looked pallid and anxious.

'A situation has arisen at home, and I must return as soon as possible,' he said abruptly. Mary was devastated at the notion of her lover's departure. Although she had known their affair would not last forever and that one day Rafael would leave England, she had always kept that thought locked away in the back of her mind.

'Is there anything the king or queen could do?' she asked desperately. Rafael shook his head.

'No, thank you, Maria, but I must attend to it personally. I shall speak with Ambassador Chapuys and make arrangements to leave without delay.'

'Then, we are over, finished?' Mary asked, feeling the pit of her stomach turn with anguish. Rafael shrugged his shoulders in what appeared a careless manner. His face was unemotional. She did not know whether he had tired of her, or whether the sentiment was genuine. He left Mary alone in the great hall, standing there. Although the milling, noisy crowds that seemed to congregate daily surrounded her, she felt as if she was the only person in a room full of silence. No one or nothing seemed to matter anymore. The man she loved was abandoning her.

Her friends noticed her behaviour and asked where Rafael had gone, seeing that he was absent from the hall that evening. Broken hearted, she began to cry and the story of his imminent departure came out between great sobs. Anne hugged her friend.

'Worry not, Mary, we are all your friends and will help you through this. Thank God I have my darling Henry to rely upon.' Then realising what she had said, she hugged Mary once again. 'I am sorry, dear friend. I did not mean for it to sound like that. I am sure there is a beau out there, just waiting for you who will never desert you.'

Mary kissed Anne on the cheek. 'Thank you, I love Rafael and want to be with him.' She forced a weak smile, trying to lighten her mood. 'When you and your Henry are married and have your first child, let me be god mother to the babe, I should like that very much.'

'There may be some great earl or duke demanding god-parentage. However, you will be my child's favourite Aunt Mary,' Anne announced and everyone laughed. Mary began to feel better, even though she still ached with desire lost. He was going and nothing would be able to take away the pain.

Rafael sought Mary out and begged to speak with her. She agreed to this, saying that they would meet in the great hall. There would be no chance for an altercation to transpire. When they met to speak, Mary felt detached from her emotions; she did not want her Spaniard to see the misery he had caused her, or the tears she had shed. At this meeting, Anne and a small group of her closest friends stayed close behind, ready to offer their support. Rafael looked uncertainly at the group huddled behind Mary.

'Why are they here, Maria?' he complained. Mary glanced behind her. The women smiled reassuringly, and then they all glared angrily at Rafael.

'I desire for them to be here. They are all my dearest friends. Speak to me what you wish to say. I will tell them your words after you were gone,' she replied, feeling in control of the situation. Rafael cleared his throat, shuffled his feet and looked uncomfortable. With a big sigh, he began to speak.

'Maria, when I first met you I knew then that I loved you, and you stayed in my heart from that day on. My life was complete when we met again and became as one. Your love for me made me happy, you gave me a reason to live and love after Pilar died.'

'But you are leaving me now,' Mary reminded. 'I have served my purpose for you?'

'Maria, do not twist my words, let me finish what I have to say,' Rafael was irritated at the interruption. He regained his composure and appeared to hesitate for a moment, running a hand through his hair. With a fluid movement, the Spaniard dropped to one knee before Mary and took her hand in his. A gasp rose from the women standing behind. 'Maria, I ask you, would you agree to become my wife?'

There were squeals of delight from behind Mary. She herself opened her mouth and shut it again like a fish. Rafael, still on one knee looked up at her, expectant.

'I...I do not know what to say,' Mary stalled. Rafael nodded eagerly, kissing her hand.

'Then say yes, *mi querido*,' he urged.

'But you are so much older than I am.'

'So you would have me as a lover, not as a husband?'

'Where would we live?' Mary said. 'Would you stay here?'

'No, you would come home with me to *Espana*.' Rafael kissed her hand again. 'I still have to return home, I cannot alter that. When I return, we shall marry.'

'But will you return?' Mary became cynical. She did not want to agree to marriage, then to spend the rest of her life waiting. In a dramatic move, Rafael drew his jewelled dagger from its sheath. Mary recognised it as the Christmas gift given to him by her and Henry years before.

'I shall cut my hand and yours, our blood will mingle, and then we will be one by blood. This will give surety to you of my love and commitment to return.'

The women behind now gasped at his threatened deed. Rafael pressed the blade into his palm.

'No, do not do that, you have no need to, Rafael,' Mary cried. She smiled at him. 'Yes, I will marry you.' The women behind cheered joyfully. Rafael sprang to his feet and, pulling Mary to him, kissed her with fervour. Mary freed herself, looking perturbed.

'I can't marry without the queen's consent,' she said. The familiar wicked twinkle glinted in Rafael's eyes.

'Let me speak to Catherine. We are both Spanish, she cannot refuse me anything,' he assured, pulling Mary close again. 'I shall seek an audience with her and beg her permission.' Rafael bowed low to Mary and her companions and strode off briskly in the direction of the royal apartments. Mary turned to her friends; collectively they laughed and hugged each other, chattering like little birds chirruping animatedly.

'We have a wedding to arrange, and it'll be the grandest ever,' Anne announced. 'Well,' she added with mock importance, 'the second grandest after mine.' Everyone laughed again.

In Queen Catherine's private chamber, Rafael bowed to the queen in reverence. Catherine indicated to Lady Dunning and she beckoned him forward. The Spaniard approached slowly and bowed again.

'What is so imperative that you disturb my meditation, Don Rafael?' she asked, regarding her compatriot haughtily.

'*Majestad,*' Rafael began. 'I request a favour from you.'

Catherine looked bemused and replied in Spanish. 'What favour? Why should I grant you a favour?'

'Because, *Majestad*, you are compassionate and kind,' he replied. Catherine looked sceptical; she was use to sycophantic courtiers. With a wave of her hand at him, Rafael continued. 'I ask your permission to marry one of your women.'

'Mary Crawford.' The queen finished the sentence. He nodded and flashed a dazzling smile at the monarch. 'What about your wife back in *Espana*? What does she have to say in all this?' Catherine sat back in her chair and regarded him with a frown.

'My wife is dead. She died in childbirth. I love Maria, *Majestad,* and would make her my wife if you give your assent.' Rafael bowed low again and stayed down until the queen permitted him to stand.

'I did not know you had been widowed, Don Rafael, my sympathy goes to you.'

'She has agreed to come home with me after our wedding…if you allow it to happen. She makes me happy again.'

'When will this marriage occur?'

'When I return as I have had urgent business to attend to at home.'

'Then if Mrs Crawford is prepared to wait for you, I grant her permission to the marriage. God bless you, Don Rafael, take care of my young woman, she deserves a good man to cherish her,'

Catherine said, smiling kindly. 'True love is so rare these days, I was truly loved once, prehaps, he will love me again one day,' she became reflective, remembering happier times. She turned her gaze to the window and stared forlornly out.

'*Gracias, Majestad*. I shall tell her immediately.' Rafael bowed out of the chamber and ran down the corridors to find Mary to tell her the news, knocking into courtiers in his keenness.

He found Mary and her friends sitting chatting together in a corner of the hall. When Mary saw him hurrying towards her, she stood up; her heart thumping wildly, her friends remained seated.

Rafael took Mary in his arms and swung her around, laughing.

'She has given her permission to us to marry!' he shouted. Others in the hall turned to see what the clamour was. Mary could scarcely believe what he was saying. She would marry her handsome Spaniard. 'While I am away, Maria, you must plan the wedding down to every detail. On my return, we shall marry.' Rafael looked around at Mary's companions, bright eyed with pleasure and excitement for their friend. Then he turned his attention back to Mary, 'I shall write to tell you how my business at home fares, and how much I love and miss you.' Rafael then bowed low to Mary and kissed her hand. He then turned and left to prepare for his departure.

Like clucking hens, Mary was surrounded by her friends all offering suggestions to make her wedding a magnificent success. Yet Mary barely heard a single word, she was thrilling to the wonderful thoughts whirling around in her mind.

The day for Rafael's leaving arrived. Mary stood in the courtyard at Whitehall with him. He was adjusting Zachariah's saddle, and checking the saddlebags. His small retinue waited, standing aside from their master. They had been ready since sunrise for him. Impatiently, they watched him, wanting to be on the road to Bankside and the voyage home to warm Spain.

Mary dabbed at her eyes with a kerchief and sniffled, finding it impossible to hold back the tears. Rafael patted Zachariah's neck, and then turned to look at his betrothed. With a gentle finger, he brushed away a tear from her cheek, and then kissed his finger, moist with the teardrop. Mary sighed, her inhalation catching as a sob in her throat. Rafael smiled and cupped her chin in a hand. Raising her face, he caringly kissed her lips.

'Do not cry *mi querido*, I shall return, you know I will,' Rafael assured. Mary nodded and dabbed at her eyes again.

'I'll be lost without you, Rafael.'

'You have Anne your special friend; she will look after you while I am gone.' Rafael stepped back and took the reins in his hands. Zachariah's ears pricked sharply, instantly alert. With an agile movement, he swung into the saddle. Mary began to sob quietly. The Spaniard bowed in the saddle to her.

'Be safe, Rafael, write often,' she cried.

'*Adios*, Maria, I miss you already.' Rafael blew a kiss to Mary and, with a shout to his men; Rafael rode swiftly from the courtyard and out of Mary's life.

She stood there after he had vanished from sight. There was an empty feeling in her body and a sense of wretchedness that she may never see him again. Anne, who had been watching from the shadows, emerged and put a supportive arm over Mary's shoulders, and with a few words of reassurence, led her back inside the palace. The queen needed attention, and she still had her duties to perform in spite of her feelings.

# 16

The king dallied with women of the court, though none of them held his attention or desires. Mary was not immune to the royal advances. She had been reading quietly in a window seat, taking advantage of a warm afternoon when the call of the king interrupted her leisure. She set down her book and curtsied as King Henry strode past talking to Sir Thomas More. He stopped abruptly, his attention caught and noticing her breasts held firm in the bodice of her gown.

'Pippins, juicy and ripe,' the king murmered appreciatively, dismissing More and his attendants he turned to Mary, inviting her to stand so that he could see the pretty face above such a charming cleavage. His lust began to rise and he quickly desired this young woman before him. Her demure pose and flushed cheeks pleased him and he knew he must have her there and then. Putting an arm about her shoulders, the king ushered Mary into a nearby antechamber. She wanted to refuse and get away, but she knew she was unable to flee. His fingers pressed tightly into her shoulders preventing any escape. The king had singled her out for his gratification and she had no option but to submit to his advances. He was amused at her hesitation this shy demeanour became her. His hands explored expertly, and Mary behaved, as she knew he would wish her to. His voice was thick with desire, his lips hot upon her flesh. She shut her eyes tight and bit her tongue trying to imagine this was Rafael whispering words of passion in her ear, these were his elegant manicured fingers caressing, exploring, and keeping these thoughts in her mind, Mary was able to endure this distasteful incident until finished. King Henry shrugging his surcoat back on, turned hardly glancing back and departed the antechamber, his lusts sated leaving Mary to quickly dress and return to the book still upon the seat. She sat down and gazed out of the window, her mind racing, no longer interested in the book. She quietly said a prayer asking for the king not to notice her again and for Rafael to return soon so that they could marry and leave this court far behind.

Then after a hunting expedition took the royal party to Kent, the king appeared to lose interest in all of his female courtiers, except one…

Anne took Mary aside. Her face pale and she looked anxious.

'Have you seen Henry Percy lately? When the good cardinal was at court the other day, I couldn't see my Henry,' she asked. Mary shook her head.

'No, Anne, I noticed his absence also,' she replied. Anne looked upset.

'I've tried sending messages to him, but there is no reply. No one seems to know where he went. I have written to his father, the duke, but I doubt he will reply. He is against our union. Do you think he's trying to stop us marrying?' Anne lent against a wall, and tears shone in her brown eyes. 'I love him, Mary and can't think of life without him. Henry said he loves me, why doesn't he come to me?'

News filtered throughout court, Cardinal Wolsey had dismissed Henry Percy from his service and the young man had returned to Northumberland and into marriage with Mary Talbot, who loathed Henry as much as he did her. Anne was distraught and took to her bed complaining of sickness. Mary tried to comfort her friend, but Anne would not listen. She wept into her pillow, wishing that she were dead, saying that she would never love again. She sat up in bed vowing to bring Cardinal Wolsey down for ruining her life and robbing her of her one true love. The ferocity of Anne's vows alarmed Mary. She tried to make her friend see sense that the cardinal was a very powerful man and Anne herself was only a young maiden with very little connections, and would make no impact on Wolsey's life or position at court. Anne refused to listen to her friend's wise words. She had now become a woman with a mission and no one would stop her from attaining her goal.

Mary received a letter from Rafael. He wrote to say the important business at home was in order and progressing well. He hoped to be returning to England soon. He also wrote of his love for Mary and explained in intimate detail what they would do on his return. The letter made her blush with both embarrassment and happiness. She hid it away, not wishing anyone to read such private details; also, she kept the letter hidden from Anne, who was still melancholy from losing Henry Percy. On the days when Mary was feeling sad or unhappy, she would retrieve the letter from its secret place to read it and feel closer to Rafael, still so many miles away.

# 17

Anne cornered Mary in the great hall, as she wanted a private conversation with her close friend that would not be overheard. They huddled under an arch where they could be alone. She looked around to make sure no one was listening. None seemed to be interested in the two young women outwardly engaged in tittle-tattle.

'Mary, the king is showing an interest in me, and I am afraid,' she confided. Mary looked surprised. Anne took her hands. 'He has offered me jewels if I allow him to bed me.'

'"If you allow him to bed you"? Anne, he is the king and commands us all. What stops him from forcing you?'

'He has said I am unlike others and would not wish to take me by force. If the king grows tired of my avoiding him, he may ravish me and have done. I value my virginity and shall surrender it only to my husband.'

The king never requested anything. What he wanted, he took. Anne's dark eyes all of a sudden grew wide as an idea began to formulate inside her brain.

'It was the king's doing,' she announced. 'He ordered Wolsey to remove my Henry to make me his.'

'Hush, Anne, speak softly, people listen, and you speak treason,' Mary warned, glancing around the hall. Anne made an impatient gesture.

'So what if I do? I can get to Wolsey through the king and make his life hell. I can also punish the king by denying him my body. If he truly wants me, he will do anything to get inside me. He will have me when I am ready to give myself.' An impious giggle rose from Anne's throat. 'I may be able to hold him off for months if I am clever.'

Mary shook her head in doubt, 'Be careful, please, you are dear to me, Anne and I would not want to see you get hurt in anyway,' she implored. Anne kissed her friend on the cheek.

'What is the most terrible thing that could happen? Would the king have my head lopped from my shoulders?' Anne laughed. Yet Mary could not see anything to laugh about in her audacious plan.

# 18

Twice Mary had to read the words dancing before her eyes. Rafael was returning within the month. The letter dispatched before he had left Spain and had reached her with the news she had been longing to read. He would be at sea, now, as she read the letter, returning to England, returning to her. Then they would marry. The news sent the queen's women into a flood of excitement. The preparations for the wedding swung into action.

Mary's father was ill and incapable of travel to Whitehall to give his daughter away, so she approached Robert. He was sprawled in a chair; a glass of wine stood half drunk on a table beside him. He regarded his sister without a smile.

'What do you want so as to disturb my recreation?' he complained indolently.

'Will you give me away at my wedding?' she asked.

Robert looked surly. 'Still marrying that ancient fart?' he said, shifting his position in the chair. Mary looked annoyed.

'I am marrying Rafael, yes,' she corrected. Robert snorted in revulsion.

'It's wrong, you marrying him, Mary. He is nearly as old as our father. He will die leaving you stuck in Spain. You can't even speak the language, how will you manage?'

'I love him and want to spend my life with him, and he will not die for a very long time, Robert,' she said feeling livid with her brother. He stood up and stretched.

'I decline your request. Who will be my informant when you are gone? I rely on you, and you alone.'

'I haven't told you much, Robert, and all I ask you to do is one thing for me,' Mary said. Robert gripped Mary's hand, squeezing it until she cried out.

'You are letting me down, Mary. You are letting me down. Do not fail to remember who got you here in the first place. You owe me a debt of gratitude,' he snapped irritably, releasing his hold. She rubbed her painful hand.

'Forget about giving me away, Robert. I don't need you,' she retorted, feeling betrayed.

'Go off and let him prang you. You will be a widow again in a few short years, trapped in Spain and all on your own. If you do get back to England, don't be expecting a welcome from me,' Robert spat and left. Mary watched his departure.

'Who needs a brother anyway? I'm better off without him,' she said furiously to herself.

At the very same courtyard where Mary saw Rafael leave for Spain, she now stood waiting for his impending return. She waited throughout the day, chatting with passing courtiers and grooms, watching attentively as visitors arrived and others departed. As shadows, lengthened, lit torches flooded the courtyard; and the evening temperature began to drop. Anne brought out a tray of food for Mary and a fur-lined wrap to keep her warm. A fire blazed in a brazier, she stood close, now feeling the cold. Conversations petered out. The night watchmen arrived and Mary watched the changing of the guards. For the whole day, she had waited for Rafael's return and was beginning to feel despondent that he would not be arriving now. Almost as Mary had begun to give up hope for the day, she heard the noise of horses' hooves clattering on the cobblestones outside the closed gates. A familiar voice called for the gates to open. Mary could hardly breathe with excitement as Rafael rode into the courtyard.

'Maria! *Mi querido!*' he shouted as he saw her.

'Rafael, Rafael!' Mary shouted back. He leapt from Zachariah and gathered Mary into his sturdy arms, pulling her to his body and kissing her with a fierce passion, leaving her breathless. There was a low cheer from the night watchmen and bawdy comments on the night to come for the couple.

'I wondered whether I would ever see you again,' Mary breathed, pulling back her head. Rafael chuckled and kissed her forehead.

'Nothing would keep me away from you, Maria,' he answered. Mary smiled joyfully. 'Now, I must go and pay respects to your king and you must go back inside to warm up.'

Arm in arm, they entered the palace and both went straight to the great hall where dancing was in progress.

Rafael strode up to the dais where the king and queen sat. Mary hung back towards the rear of the hall. With his usual flourish, he bowed low to the monarchs and waited for permission to straighten up.

'Spaniard, how was your journey?' the king asked.

'*Majestad*, I hastened my return to see you and your glorious queen.'

'Don't lie to me, Perez. I am surrounded by syncopates who tell me what they think I want to hear. Do not insult my intelligence. You have returned to marry one of our English roses.'

Rafael laughed in return. 'Indeed I have, *Majestad*.' he admitted. The king nodded amused.

'Was your urgent business attended to, Don Rafael?' Catherine asked, leaning forward in her gilded chair.

'Yes *Majestad*. It was a success and all is well.'

'Your betrothed must be waiting for you, Perez, go and satisfy her,' the king said dismissing Rafael. Bowing, he backed away and turned, looking for Mary. The couple were aware of many eyes watching them as they left the hall to find a place to be alone together.

A small antechamber was unlocked and vacant. They slipped into the room, locking the door behind them. Stumbling towards a table, they were kissing and pulling at each other's clothes with flaming emotions. Rafael swept the table clear and, picking Mary up, laid her on the table. The months of abstinence over, they allowed their passions to rule as they made love as though it was the first time they had come together. In the corridor, passers-by stopped and listened at the door, sniggering and nudging each other.

When Mary and Rafael left the antechamber, they noticed numerous people hanging around watching them. They called a greeting with a chortle in their voices. The couple exchanged glances, not realising that their lovemaking had engrossed an audience. Rafael went to find accommodation for the night, and Mary returned to the great hall where her friends surrounded her, all who had known where she had been and they questioned her on what had happened during her absence.

# 19

Robert approached Rafael and asked to speak with him in private. The two men sat either side of a table. Robert offered Rafael wine that he accepted coolly, waiting until Robert had taken the first swallow. They watched each other cautiously. The younger man leaned forward.

'You still intend to marry my sister,' he began. Rafael took a deep draught of wine and smiled.

'I am. She is the most beautiful woman I have ever known,' he said. Robert grunted, sitting back.

'You have enchanted her. That is why she thinks she loves you. You know Henry Crawford abused her.'

'I do know, and now Maria deserves only the best and I can give her that,' Rafael replied scowling. 'And she does love me.'

'Mary doesn't know what love is. She is too young for you.'

'Maria is old enough to make her own decisions.'

'What do I have to say to make you understand that you are not wanted here? Leave my sister alone. She would be happier without an old wreck like you. Go back to Spain.'

'It is you who does not want her to go. I am marrying Maria and we will live in Spain far away from you. This useless conversation is over.' Rafael stood up to leave. Robert sprang to his feet, knocking his chair over, his hand going to the grip of his sword.

'I am not finished Perez. Do not turn your back on me!' he shouted angrily.

Rafael spun rapidly, drawing his sword, letting the blade catch the light as the point depressed into Robert's throat. He swallowed hard, his heart hammering as he felt the metal on his flesh.

'Do not even try it,' Rafael hissed. 'I shall not kill you this time as that would make Maria sad, God knows why. But it would make me very, very happy to dispatch you.' Rafael lowered his sword, keeping it unsheathed. 'Just do not be on your own in a room with me, my friend; I may not be so merciful next time.' He sheathed his sword and turned to leave the room. Stopping, Rafael turned once more to look back at Robert and pointed a warning finger at him. 'One more thing, Senor Hawke, Maria has asked you to give her away at our wedding. Do not dishearten her, eh?' He departed the room, leaving Robert alone, breathing heavily. He put his hand to his throat. Looking at his fingers, he saw a small spot of blood. Glancing up at the closed door, he cursed the Spaniard for interfering in his life and ambition.

The wedding was to take place as soon as arrangements were made. Rafael had already booked two passages on a ship bound for Santurlzi, leaving from Bankside. Even though he assured Mary that he would never leave her side, she was not convinced that the crossing would be safe. However, the wedding was now imminent and Mary's attention turned to one of the most important days in her life.

She stood in the centre of a brightly lit room in just her chemise. Around her, Anne and her friends helped Mary into the gown of gold taffeta over her head and a veil of sparkling gold thread was pinned to the back of the fashionable French hood. Anne stood back and clasped her hands together.

'Mary, you look beautiful!' she exclaimed and murmurs of agreement swept around the room.

There was a sharp rap at the door, and Anne answered it. Robert glared at her, she stiffened and she returned the stony stare.

'What do you want?' she asked frostily. Robert looked over Anne's shoulder at Mary.

'I will speak with my sister,' he replied, pushing past Anne and ignoring the protests. Mary looked up.

'Have you come to ruin my wedding day, Robert?' she said crossly. Robert bowed to his sister.

'No, Mary. Quite the contrary I hope.' He crossed the room to stand before her. 'You know I do not agree to this match of yours, I still think he is wrong for you. Nevertheless, this is your wedding day and you need somebody to give you away. If you still allow it, permit me.' Robert stood there watching Mary's expression change from annoyance to bewilderment.

'What gave you this change of heart?' she asked. Robert shrugged his shoulders, Rafael's warning still echoed in his mind.

'I only have one sister, and we should not fight,' he murmured. Mary regarded her brother warily.

'How do I know you mean this?' she asked suspiciously. Robert stood back.

'Father cannot be here, our parents would want us to be united on this day, and I cannot think of you leaving for Spain hating me,' Robert lied convincingly.

'Don't trust him, Mary,' Anne warned from the other side of the room. Robert glared impatiently at her. Mary smiled joyfully.

'Dearest brother, I am so pleased that this is how you feel. Thank you for doing this for me.' She kissed him on the cheek and laughed lightly. Robert held out an arm, ignoring Anne's complaining.

'Let us away to chapel,' he said. Mary picked up a small nosegay of fragrant herbs, and together they led the procession.

The chapel at Whitehall was an intimate place, holding only a small congregation. Robert, along with Mary, stood at the doorway. He looked at his sister, and saw how happy she was looking. His face clouded when he saw Anne seating herself with her friends, vibrant with happiness as she talked with them. For this instant, he would hide his loathing. Mary's departure to Spain not only deprived him of his spy in the queen's household, it was going to be a big mistake for his sister, if only she realised it.

'My groom waits,' Mary breathed. On Robert's arm, she entered the chapel. Rafael turned and gasped at how beautiful his bride looked as she approached.

Rain beat relentlessly against the leaded windows, and rumbles of thunder rolled outside as Rafael slipped the band of Spanish gold onto Mary's finger.

Once the service was over, the wedding party made their jubilant way, led by Mary and Rafael to a small hall. Robert had absented himself directly after giving the bride away, not able to tolerate being in the same room as Anne or his sister's Spanish husband. He had fulfilled the promise made under duress to Rafael, his presence was no longer obligatory.

Mary lay on the matrimonial bed, watching her new husband undress. The riotous crowd of well-wishers had gone back to the hall to continue celebrating, and now the room was still. She could feel her heart hammering. Rafael turned to Mary and smiled at her.

'Nothing or no one stands in my way; I always get what I want every time, and I want you, Maria. You are no coy virgin, or I a callow youth,' he said. Mary sighed with satisfaction.

'I love the way you say my name,' she sighed. Rafael knelt upon the bed. His hands caressed Mary's bare feet, and he pushed her silk shift up, exposing her legs.

'Maria,' he breathed and kissed her toes. 'Maria.' His lips kissed her knees. 'Maria.' Now, his lips kissed the inside of her thighs. He moved slowly up Mary's body, pushing the silk shift further up, then over her head, leaving her defenceless to his rising desires. He kissed her belly, her breasts, her neck and her closed eyes. Then he softly kissed her lips, Mary drew him close. They came together as husband and wife.

Being married did not exempt Mary from her royal duties, and the following day she was back, only this time she was the hub of attention. The queen did not mind this, her lady-in-waiting had married a fellow Spaniard, and that was acceptable. It took her mind off the king's latest obsession. He was courting Anne Boleyn, but the young woman was resisting him. What bewildered the queen most was that, generally, women would fall over themselves to become a royal mistress, so why had she appeared to dismiss the prospect of receiving the king into her bed with repugnance? What perplexed the queen more was that her husband appeared to be prepared to wait for Lady Anne? This could develop into something more serious. For now, Queen Catherine would smile and be happy for the new Lady Perez; she was on the brink of a wonderful life in a wonderful country. She envied Mary going to live in Spain.

Tearfully, Mary said her farewell to her friends. She and Rafael were to depart, first to Yardeley Chase to visit her family before returning to London and the docks at Bankside. Anne hugged her friend warmly.

'Mary, take care of yourself, you have been such a dear friend to me since I arrived,' Anne stated, hugging Mary again.

'Be careful playing against the king, you can't hold him off forever,' Mary warned.

'I know. I will become his mistress when I am ready to, he tries to send me gifts and I send them right back, unopened. He will not buy me, I am no easy ride as my sister was, I have learnt from her silliness. Do you think I could persuade the king to marry me?' Anne questioned, a mischievous spark lighting her dark eyes

'Anne!' Mary exclaimed. 'You speak treason! The king would not divorce a royal princess to marry someone like you. Let him have his way with you and be done with it.' Mary warned. Anne laughed, somewhat maniacally.

'It is going too far for that now, I cannot back down. I'll be his mistress when it suits me and I know I can win more,' Anne replied. Mary was anxious.

'I won't be here to counsel you. Please, Anne, take care, think of what I've said and what you are doing.'

'Enough talk about me. You know all the women wanted Rafael in their beds, even the queen, I wager. You are the lucky one. When you do come back to England to visit, find me and we will talk about our lives. Who knows where I shall be or who I even am by then.' Anne kissed Mary's cheek. 'Now go and take your place by your husband's side and have a long and happy life with him.' The two women embraced again and kissed as friends kiss. Mary still could not help but be concerned over Anne. The game she played was hazardous, her luck could run out, and then where would she be? Her ambitious father would not allow that to happen. He saw an advantageous future in his daughter's association with the king. Thomas Boleyn was not a man to let an excellent chance like this pass his family.

With mixed emotions, Mary rode from the Palace of Whitehall by the side of Rafael. Robert had not attended his sister's departure. He had given the excuse saying he was too busy. Rafael knew the real reason. He was satisfied that Mary was going to be far away from her devious brother, she was just a pawn in his plan to carve a place in history for himself.

When Mary and Rafael rode into the courtyard at Yardeley Chase, she shrieked with delight at the sight of her mother waiting for her. Margaret now looked older than her years. The worry of her husband's infirmity had taken its toll on her health. Unladylike, and without waiting for either her husband or a groom to assist, Mary scrambled from her horse and ran into her mother's waiting arms. Rafael swung down from his horse and stood back, uncomplainingly waiting for them to finish their reunion. Mary turned and pulled him towards her mother.

'This is my mother, Margaret. Mother, here is my wonderful husband, Rafael,' she announced proudly with satisfaction. Rafael took Margaret's hand in his and kissed it.

'*Senora*, you give your daughter her beautiful face,' he said, making Margaret giggle childlike.

'Come inside Mary, your father is waiting for you.' Margaret took Mary's hand and led her back inside the familiar home.

Anthony Hawke sat in a chair by a fire; he had a blanket wrapped around his legs and a shawl pulled over his shoulders. The deaf white cat slept curled up on his lap and his hound stretched out beside the chair.

*He is not the father I remember,* Mary reflected as she saw the sick old man, hunched in the chair. She remembered him as a loving family man who had taught her and Robert to ride their first ponies and had played games with them both as any loving father would.

'Mary,' Anthony said weakly trying to sit forward in his chair. Emotional tears shone in his eyes as she softly kissed his forehead. He sat heavily back coughing severely. The cat, disturbed from her slumber, leapt from his lap hissing crossly and ran from the room. The hound leapt to his feet, tail wagging furiously.

'Father, this is Rafael,' Mary said, straightening up and moving aside for him to approach. Anthony extended a thin hand for him to shake, and then tucked it back under the blanket.

'Mary has written to us about you. It is good to meet you,' Anthony said. 'I only wish I could have been there to give her away.'

'Robert had the honour,' Rafael confirmed. Anthony's tired eyes brightened at the mention of his son's name. Rafael knew better than to criticise Robert in front of his sick father. Let the old man carry on believing his son was a good and kind man.

'He does well at court and is in favour with the king.' he proudly said. Anthony looked around the hall. 'One day soon, all this will be his.'

'Not for a long time yet, father,' Mary cried. Anthony shook his head.

'It will be soon, Mary. I am dying. My physician says there is a cancer in my lungs. Our grandchildren keep me happy. Have you seen Cecily or William yet?' Anthony began coughing violently again. Margaret hurried to his side and patted him on his back until the racking cough eased.

'Not yet, I'll see them soon,' Mary replied. Anthony nodded panting breathless.

'Leave your father in peace for now,' Margaret excused. 'He will see you later.'

Tearfully, Mary led Rafael from the hall and up to the nursery where her two children lived. Cecily was now eight years old and William a small five years old. They greeted their mother cautiously at first, but soon, both children were clamouring to climb upon her lap and to have stories read to them.

Cecily was a beautiful child. William did not have the healthy constitution of his sister; he was sickly and prone to illness. Rafael exclaimed how such a brute like Henry could have fathered such handsome children. His natural affability quickly won the shy children over, soon he was sitting on the floor with both children either side of him listening attentively as he told stories of his adventures.

Mary insisted that Lettie was to go with her to Spain. This left the children distraught with the prospect of losing the woman who had helped raise them since their mother's departure. Margaret arranged for a local goodwife from a nearby manor house to be their nurse. Rafael was a little perturbed, as the passage had been booked only for two people. However, he was desperately in love with Mary and could refuse her nothing. There would always be ways around any problems that arose.

That night, Mary and Rafael retired to her old bedchamber she had slept in as a child. The room brought back happy memories for her. She sat in the window seat looking out at a scene that had never changed. Rafael lay in bed and threw back the coverlets inviting Mary into bed, wanting to make love to her. She shook her head.

'No, Rafael, not here,' she refused. He sat up, mystified.

'But why, *mi querido?*' he asked. Mary shook her head again.

'This is my old bed where I slept as a girl. I just can't, not here.' Mary saw her husband look hurt. 'My parents are here too, I just can't,' she repeated for a third time. Rafael fell back against the pillow, annoyed. He had a beautiful young wife who was exciting in bed, and already, so early in their marriage, she was denying him her body.

'They would not hear us, *mi querido,*' Rafael tried to reason, but Mary was obstinate and refused, preferring when she eventually climbed into bed to sleep on the edge of the mattress, not wanting to feel her husband's hands on her body, knowing that if she did, she would relent. Snorting in disgust, Rafael turned over and tried to sleep. She lay there, listening to his breathing become slow and steady as he finally drifted into sleep. Once she and Rafael had departed, all would be well between them again.

They remained for one more day before returning to London. Anthony, leaning heavily on a stick, accompanied his wife to the door to stand and see his daughter leave. He knew he would never see Mary again. He stood puffing in short laboured breaths as Rafael helped Mary onto her horse, and then he swung into his saddle. Briefly, she looked back at her parents, and then seeing her husband, Mary knew she was making the right choice. Her future lay in the direction of Spain. Anthony looked at Rafael, who was becoming impatient with the delay.

'You have your husband to care for you now.' Anthony slowly and with difficulty walked to Mary's side, leaning on his stick, took her hand and kissed it. 'Go now, and God speed,' he finished and waved to his daughter. Rafael smiled to his wife, then saluted Anthony and Margaret. He turned Zachariah towards the gates and rode through towards the open road with Mary and Lettie following behind. Mary kept turning in her saddle to see her parents vanish from view, feeling sick with worry and remorse for leaving her father with his health so frail.

# 20

Mary had passed Bankside when travelling by barge, but had never visited it. It was bustling and hectic, with people coming and going, cargo loaded to and from ships. Alehouses seemed to be on every corner, with fierce, bloody fights commonly bursting out of their doors. Prostitutes plied their trade brazenly up and down the lanes, calling to Rafael the prospect of good times with bad women. There was noise, music, filth and colour everywhere. Mary both loved and abhorred it.

The galleon, the *Santo Philippe* dwarfed other ships. Rafael looked proudly at Spanish ingenuity; this vessel was grander and more imposing than the smaller English ships. He supervised the boarding of Zachariah himself, placing a scarf over the horse's eyes so that it could not see the water through the gangplank. The horse tentatively trod the boards, sensitive of the unusual noises around him, encouraged by his master's gentle words. Soon he was safe in his stall below deck. Rafael returned to Mary. He could scarcely wait to sprint up the gangplank, pulling his young wife behind him. Mary was less sure about boarding the ship. Her husband had demonstrated more care for his horse than her when boarding. The ship may look impressive, but it would still rock and sway. She preferred to keep her feet on solid ground.

'Capitan Humberto has prearranged the best cabin beside his own. We will be fine there until we reach Spain,' Rafael said. His eyes sparkled like a small boy out on an adventure. He took Mary's hand. 'Let us see where it is, and then we can come back on deck to watch as we cast off.'

'When do we go?' Mary asked, holding onto the side of the galleon for support.

'*Senora*, we depart on the evening tide,' Captain Humberto said, coming up to stand beside Rafael. The two men began a conversation in Spanish. Mary, who had started to learn the Spanish language, recognised several words, but still found it difficult to follow the conversation exactly. She turned her interest to preparations to set sail. There was shouting from the sailors and the men on the dock. Men hauled chests and rolled barrels up the gangplank to be stored below deck. Two sailors, each carrying four squawking chickens by their legs, strode up the gangplank taking the protesting fowl down to the galley to where they were stored for their eggs and eventually food for the crew and passengers. Rafael came and stood by her.

'Our cabin is ready, Maria,' he said leading her away from the side of the galleon. He swung a low door open and entered, with Mary following.

'This is the captain's best cabin?' she exclaimed in revulsion looking around the weakly lit cabin.

'The *Santo Philippe* is not built for passengers, it is mainly for trade,' Rafael excused with no trace of regret in his voice. Then he added in a lower, sinister tone. 'And war.'

The cabin where Mary and Rafael were to stay was small and sparse. A bed that was just big enough for them to share stood against one wall. A table with two chairs stood opposite and a small chest was all the furniture. A lantern hung from the beams above them, which, even though the voyage had not yet begun, swung gently. Nothing else, no home comforts. There was an unmistakable smell of dankness and pitch about the cabin. Mary was appreciative that her husband would never leave her side during the voyage. Close by, a moth-eaten curtain separated Lettie's crude bed.

'How long does the captain expect the voyage to take?' Mary asked. Rafael shrugged his shoulders.

'It all depends on the weather, the sea. It can take anything from ten days to three weeks,' he explained. She looked shocked.

'That long!' she exclaimed, looking around in consternation. Rafael chuckled at her distain and pulled her close.

'Enough time for us to *haga el amor,*' he whispered, kissing her ear. She knew what he was proposing and her fears regarding the voyage began to subside. He pulled her on the bed and slid a gloved hand up her legs; she felt the soft kid leather part her thighs. Their coming together was succinct and passionate.

The couple emerged calmly from their cabin. Stepping carefully up the gangplank was a plump woman following behind her husband. She looked as hesitant as Mary had first felt. At least she and Lettie were not the only women onboard. The woman gave Mary a small smile, to which Mary reciprocated with a smile back to her.

Captain Humberto strode over grinning broadly. He was a tall, brawny man with a weather-beaten face and eyes that were alert and missed very little. A golden charm dangled and danced from a ring through his left earlobe. On his right cheek there was an old scar, and both tattooed arms bore scars from altercations during a lifetime spent at sea. His hands were large and square, with stout fingers on which he wore equally large jewelled rings.

'Everything is ready now, Don Rafael. The tide is turning, we shall be away soon.' He turned to Mary. '*Senora*, it is time to say goodbye to your country.'

Mary walked shakily to the side of the galleon and joined the other passengers to watch the final preparations. The woman who had recently boarded the galleon came and stood by her side.

'*Estare alegre salir de esta isle fria y vueltra a mi pais de origen,*' she said. Mary did not understand what the woman had said to her. She pointed to herself.

'*Ingles*' she said. The woman made a small sound of distain, and turned her attention to her grinning husband standing by her side and said something derogatory in Spanish about Mary. Rafael had joined Mary and she looked at him. 'Did you hear what that woman said? Tell me what she said?'

'She said she was glad to leave cold England and return to warm *Espana*,' Rafael translated.

'Well, I like cold England and I am only going to warm Spain because of you,' Mary retorted indignantly. Rafael laughed aloud and waved a greeting to the other woman's husband and they exchanged brief friendly words about their wives.

Men on shore released the lines mooring the galleon to the dock. Sailors onboard caught and stowed away the ropes. At an enormous windlass, hefty Spanish sailors were slowly turning it round, shouting and cursing at the effort of raising the anchor. Fascinated by the scenes, Mary admired the strength these mariners showed. She felt the galleon sway into movement and began to drift slowly away from the jetty. Rafael stood by her, and covered her hand reassuringly with his.

'Goodbye England,' Mary said forlornly. Then she turned to look into Rafael's face and smiled happily. 'Hello Spain.'

The *Santo Philippe* moved slowly out into the Thames and turned eastwards towards the estuary.

Captain Humberto strode around the deck barking orders. Men scrambled up the masts to the rigging, others hauled ropes in, two sailors were at the huge wheel, turning it as commanded. Rafael explained that it was vital to get the galleon in the correct position to avoid shallow waters. The tide would carry them downriver, towards the English Channel, out into the Atlantic Ocean and through the Bay of Biscay. Winds and tides would guide their way, with the captain plotting the best course to steer his vessel so that they could reach their destination safely.

Humberto still shouted commands until he was satisfied that the manoeuvre was successful. He then descended wooden steps to stand beside Rafael and Mary.

'What do you think of my beautiful galleon, *senora*?' He asked Mary, beaming with pride.

'I am, impressed, captain,' she replied. Humberto laughed and ran a hand through his thick, shoulder length black hair.

'We Spanish are proficient at all things marine, *senora*. You English, an island race full of mariners? Bah! We Spanish have brains and discipline,' he boasted tapping his head with a finger. 'We rule the seas and oceans. We command the Caribbean, not your English sailors.'

'I think, Captain Humberto, you say too much now,' Rafael interrupted. Humberto looked aggravated and stopped in full flow. 'You forget my wife has become Spanish, just like you and I.' He took Mary's hand. 'When she married me, she ceased being English.'

She withdrew her hand sharply. 'I may have become Spanish when I married you, but I still have the heart of an English woman, and I always shall,' she replied tersely. Both Spaniards looked surprised at her outburst.

'You let a woman speak to you like that *senor*?' Humberto asked Rafael crossly. 'No women speak to me like that. Spanish women know their place.'

'Captain Humberto, we have a long voyage ahead of us and I have it in mind it to be a good one. Do not insult my wife. She is a good woman and she knows her place. You will be civil towards her.' Rafael then continued in Spanish to the captain. Humberto bowed his head. He turned to Mary, taking her hand and kissed it.

'*Senora*, forgive me, but I love this galleon as your husband loves you.'

'That is fine, captain. You have a right to be proud, she is a fine craft, and I shall enjoy travelling with you.' Mary conceded. Humberto beamed his roguish smile again, a glint of gold shone from his mouth.

'Tonight, you both dine with me in my cabin. I insist,' he said, and then bowing turned to shout angrily at a sailor who had spilt a bucket of water over the deck, and clipped the unfortunate man harshly across the back of his head.

The *Santo Philippe* had traversed the Thames estuary and headed on a brisk breeze south eastwards, ploughing gracefully through the water. Mary stood on deck, attempting to familiarise herself to the movement; Rafael was in a state of high excitement. He had professed to her that when he was a small boy he would go to the docks to watch galleons depart and arrive. He had wanted to run away to sea for a life of adventure. If he fathered a son, then he would make sure the boy went to sea to live out his father's dreams. Mary secretly hoped she would give Rafael the son he wanted. A beautiful, olive-skinned boy, tall and handsome with dark brown eyes and thick black hair. His daughter in Madrid would return home and they would become a happy and loving family.

That evening as promised, Mary and Rafael were entertained in Captain Humberto's cabin. His cabin in comparison to theirs was lavish. There were tables and chairs, a cabinet, a very comfortable looking bed and several large elaborately carved chests. On one of the tables there were several maps, some rolled and tied with ribbon, and others opened, weighted down at corners. Instruments of navigation lay strewn across the table; Mary looked at the open maps with interest. One charted the course between

England and France, and a second showed the Bay of Biscay and the northern coast of Spain. Rafael pointed out Bilbao and the small port of Santurlzi. It did not appear to be so far, Mary did not imagine the journey could take three weeks as Rafael had indicated. Captain Humberto tapped the map of Biscay

'*Senora*, the bay is not to be taken lightly. The seas are rough, we may only achieve four knots an hour, and we could make only eighty nautical miles in twenty four hours.'

'Is that fast?' Mary asked, scarcely understanding the maritime terms of the captain's description. He grinned again, and led Mary to the leaded windows that looked out onto the sea.

'Prevailing winds in Biscay are north west to south east,' he said, indicating the directions with his hands. 'I need to calculate our progress, our position, the weather conditions, the position of the stars and the sun, many factors.' Humberto pointed at the sea. 'The currents flow mostly north to south which slows our progress. But, on the return, it is a quicker passage.'

Rafael, sipping wine, listened to Humberto talk. He came to stand beside Mary.

'So, Maria, what do you think?' he asked. She smiled up at him.

'It is all so fascinating,' she replied. Humberto picked up a large bell and rang it several times. The cabin door opened and the cook came in, followed by several small, barefooted boys, all carrying trays of food. Humberto pointed to the clear table, for the plates of steaming hot food. The cook and his boys departed, Humberto led Mary to a chair and helped her into it.

'Please, *senora*, eat all you can. My cook is the best in the Spanish fleet and can make a banquet out of a herring,' he proudly said. Mary looked at the food, some she recognised, some not so familiar. She smelt the familiar aroma of chicken and decided to eat that.

The meal continued with Rafael and Humberto talking in an animated Spanish conversation. Mary felt isolated each time she tried to join in; with she still did not have a grasp on the language that baffled her, and she began to wonder how she would cope when she was living in Rafael's home.

Once the meal was over, Mary and Rafael left the captain's cabin and returned to their small quarters. Lanterns hung from the rigging and along the sides of the galleon, and ropes creaked gently as it swayed. The sky was cloudy and the moon shone briefly through small gaps in the clouds. The air felt cold and Mary shivered. Rafael put his arm around her shoulders, she felt comforted by this.

Back in their cabin, she quickly climbed into bed and before Rafael could caress her body into lovemaking, she had fallen into a deep sleep. He looked at his sleeping wife, and smiled at her. Placing a light kiss on her brow, he turned over and was soon asleep himself.

The voyage south was mostly uneventful, and Mary found she was enjoying herself on the *Santo Philippe*. She chatted to the other passengers, all who were Spanish and knew enough English to converse with her. Even the plump Sapanish woman was friendly enough now to tutor Mary in her new adopted language. Lettie was having less of a good time. From the moment the galleon has cast off, the young woman had felt nauseous, and spent hours curled up in her bed wishing for death to release her from the misery.

One of the sailors, Carlos, a young man with a round face and a thick mop of straight black hair, had noticed Lettie when she had boarded and brought a potion to her that would cure seasickness. When he had spare time, he would sit with Lettie and talk to her with his limited vocabulary of English. Lettie allowed Carlos to wipe her forehead with a damp cloth, and she took the potion. Gradually, she began to recover. Mary noticed how Lettie's eyes would light up when she saw Carlos. Eventually, she left her bed and went up on deck, holding onto his arm. The young couple conversed with a variety of shouted words and hand signals, and for the first time Mary heard Lettie laughing with happiness. How sad to think this budding romance would not develop and grow, once they had reached Spain, Lettie would leave and Carlos would remain on the *Santo Philippe*.

For several days, the winds had been vigorous, buffeting the galleon about. The clouds hung low in the darkening grey sky, blotting out the sun, waves increased in magnitude and power, a storm was brewing. Flashes of lightning, crackling in their intensity branched aggressively, illuminating the menacing, heavy clouds, followed by ear-splitting thunder that reverberated through the ship, making it shudder and groan. Captain Humberto ordered the passengers to remain locked in their cabins until the storm was over, and not to venture on the deck until permission was granted. The crew tied themselves to lifelines as the storm began to howl, shriek and screeched over the ship, hurling it about like a plaything, attempting to shatter it to tinder wood. Hailstones, like missiles, pummelled the exhausted sailors, water, ice cold, frothing in its vehemence crashed viciously over the deck, dragging souls to their deaths in the angry blackness. Humberto remained at the wheel, bawling commands above the noise of the storm, wrestling with the elements for control over his beloved ship. The shrouds groaned like gostly spectres, rigging creaked agonizingly, canvas sails snapped ferociously, all tested to their limits. Locked in their cabin, Mary, Rafael and Lettie huddled together for safety, though the violent lurches of the *Santo Phillipe* threw them apart, sending them sprawling, then scrambling back together. Water flooded through a gap at the base of the door and spilled across the floor until ankle deep. Furniture rolled from side to side of the cabin, the edge of the table ramming into Rafael's leg, cutting a gash. Mary did her best to bandage the wound and stop the bleeding; the barber surgeon would tend to him in the morning.

Hours later, the wind began to abate, though the rain still lashed the ship like arrows and the waves still knocked it about. The storm was gradually dying and calm was beginning to return. The clouds slowly lifted, as if a monster realised it had not claimed the ship as its own and had given up, now losing interest. As the first slim and misty haze of dawn on the horizon began to show, Humberto invited his passengers to his cabin to drink warmed wine to revive them, leaving his crew to restore order to their battered ship.

Later in the morning, after the sun had risen and the skies were blue and cloudless, the passengers returned to their cabins. Rafael hurried down to the stalls to check upon Zachariah. The stallion, still nervous, was stamping his hooves and swishing his long tail rapidly. Seeing his master, Zachariah's ears pricked forward and he snorted a greeting, pleased to see him, and began to calm down immediatly. Once he knew his horse was fine, Rafael, on Mary's insistence, went to the barber surgeon.

Lettie had found Carlos; his arm bandaged after a rain sodden rope lashed him during the storm, tearing his skin. The barber surgeon, kept busy all through the night, was still tending to the injured sailors. He made Rafael sit and wait his turn before treating the gash on his leg. Mary wanted to help her injured husband back to the cabin, but he insisted on staying on deck to enjoy the sun and watch the daily routine. Mary sat by him, and Lettie wandered over to Carlos as he went about his duties, apparently oblivious to his injured arm, but enjoying the attention, receiving good-natured mockery from his crewmates over the interest shown in him by the English woman.

One night, Mary could not sleep. Leaving Rafael deep in slumber, she carefully climbed from the bed, pulling a wrap over her nightshift, and ventured onto deck. Sailors not lucky enough to have hammocks slept on the deck, so gathering her wrap tightly around her, Mary picked her way cautiously over the slumbering bodies. Everything was still; waves lapped against the side of the ship gently. Above her, the sails billowed out, catching a breeze. At the top of the main mast, a solitary sailor in the crow's nest kept a look out, a lantern beside him flickering. A second sailor was at the wheel; he glanced at her and beamed a toothless smile as the iridescent lanterns close by illuminated his weatherbeaten face. She walked slowly over to the side and leant on the rail, gazing up. Stars twinkled down at her, and the full moon was luminous in the night sky. It looked so close, Mary felt she was almost able to reach out and touch it. Its distorted reflection danced silently in the water. Everything felt so peaceful and perfect, for one moment, she wished time would stand still.

'I knew you had come here,' Rafael's voice startled Mary and she turned round to see her husband standing behind her. She sighed contentedly.

'I've never seen so many stars, they're like diamonds,' she said, turning back to gaze up at the sky again. Rafael leant against her, his arms sliding around her waist and inside her wrap to cup her breasts in his hands. He kissed the nape of her neck, and they watched silently as a shooting star flashed across the night sky. The intense passion they shared that night would remain a cherished memory. After, they stood watching as the rays of the sun from below the horizon began to streak upwards, chasing the moon and stars away, turning the sky from the dark night to a pink dawn and then the brilliant day. Mary felt loved, safe and secure just standing there with her husband. They watched the sunrise until its light grew too bright. The crew already began stirring for another day. The sailor from the crow's nest stiffly climbed down, replaced by the day watch who energetically ran up the rigging with incredible agility. The sailor at the wheel told his replacement of the night's entertainment provided by the amorous passengers. The habitual noise and bustle of daily life aboard the *Santo Philippe* resumed.

Mary became aware that the temperature was getting warmer, and that the end of the voyage was drawing near. Seagulls had begun to appear in the sky, some bold birds landed on the rigging and sat there, screeching at anyone that came too close to them.

A cry of '*Terre ho!*' brought all on to the deck to look portside where the crow's nest was pointing. Captain Humberto pulled a telescope from inside his doublet and peered through it. Mary strained her eyes, and could barely make out a faint outline. He snapped his telescope shut.

'*Espana!*' he announced proudly. 'It will be another day before landfall,' he added. Mary peered again at the faint outline. Not long now, and her new home would be revealed to her.

She spent the following hours watching the distant coastline draw nearer, and she began to see detail appearing. Steeples and towers of churches were the first to become noticeable. Then the buildings along the coastline came into focus, small crafts sailed out to greet them, or scudded past, heading for fishing grounds.

Mary had left the packing of her personal effects to Lettie while she remained on deck. When Lettie did emerge from the cabin, Carlos was close behind. She looked at Mary and blushed.

'Mistress, Carlos and I shall not see each other again after today. We just wanted to…' she cast down her eyes. Mary did not know whether to be cross with her maid, or to congratulate her on finding a lover. Rafael looked amused as Captain Humberto stormed towards Carolos, shouting and swearing at him for deserting his post, and threatening him with a beating. Lettie, bemused, watched as Carlos hurried away shouting crossly back at his captain. She had not even the chance to kiss her lover goodbye.

'Everything is packed away, mistress,' she said. Then her face clouded over. 'I will miss Carlos so much when we are gone. I don't want to lose him, but I know he can't come with us, and I can't stay here.' Mary put a comforting arm around Lettie's shoulders.

'It doesn't matter what station in life we women hold, we do, and we go as we are told without question. We leave those we love behind and we find new love in a new place.'

The *Santo Philippe* docked in the harbour and Captain Humberto came to say goodbye to his passengers. He warmly planted two kisses on Mary's cheeks.

'*Senora*, your beauty has enhanced this voyage. *Gracias,* may you find happiness in my beautiful country,' he said. Then he turned to Rafael and they spoke Spanish, finishing with a hearty handshake. Sailors were unloading the chests that belonged to the passengers. Mary, following Rafael, descended the gangplank and she took her first step onto Spanish soil. Lettie brought up the rear, hoping for a final sighting of Carlos. He shouted her name, making everyone turn to look. Then, in front of Captain Humberto, and risking his rage a second time, Carlos grabbed a rope from the rigging and swung onto the quay, landing firmly on his feet directly in front of her. Everyone gasped and laughed at the tenacity of the young Spaniard. He pulled Lettie to him, swinging her downwards as they kissed. Spontaneous applause broke out over the quayside as Carlos straightened up.

'*Adios*, Lettie,' he said touching her face and turning to sprint up the gangplank. Captain Humberto stood glaring at Carlos, and then he burst out laughing and clapped him hard across the back, almost knocking the young sailor off his feet. He turned to look once more at Lettie and blew her an enormous kiss, which she returned with a euphoric smile.

# 21

*Spain*

As Mary rode beside Rafael along the cobbled roads towards his hacienda, she marvelled at the brilliance surrounding her. Flowers bloomed in a frenzy of colour, along the roadside and from window boxes. Looking at the ordinary townsfolk and peasants, she remembered riding to Greenwich, and the people in the fields of England. How drab they appeared now that she was seeing the tanned faces of the people here. She glanced over to Rafael. He looked so illustrious astride Zachariah. The stallion pranced like a colt, delighted to feel solid ground under his elegant legs. She wanted to pinch herself again to believe this was all true.

Rafael's estate was large and extensive; he lived in a huge brick built home with whitewashed walls that sparkled in the hot Spanish sunshine. Slatted wooden shutters opened outwards from the windows to allow the sun into all rooms. The window boxes were a riot of colour. Roof tiles were warm red, adding character. There was a pasture nearby where a small herd of cattle grazed. A bakery and a buttery were among the outhouses behind the hacienda from which delicious aromas floated on the air. In the middle of the large cobbled courtyard stood a magnificent oval fountain featuring a sculpture of Poseidon, wrestling a sea monster with water gushing upwards from its mouth. Smaller sea creatures spouting water gathered at Poseidon's feet. Water splashed constantly into the bowl surrounding the statue creating vibrant rainbows, and coolness from the intense heat. This was a small town enclosed within the walls, safe and secluded from the outside world.

Rafael proudly showed Mary around his home. The luxurious bedroom with a large ornate bed made from African ebony made

Mary linger there a moment longer than any other room. The solarium excelled the one in Markham. There were cushions made with silk from the East, and Persian rugs covering the floor. They wandered along a gallery lined with portraits of ancestors, and he pointed out the images of his two dead wives. Manuela was a thin, plain looking woman with sallow skin and unemotional eyes. However, the child who stood beside her was beautiful. She was Isabel. She had the fortune to inherit her father's good looks and looked a happy child. The second portrait showed Pilar as a very alluring, beautiful and sensual woman, with thick long black hair, wearing a vibrant deep blue velvet dress cut low, exposing a voluptuous bosom. Mary could easily see why Rafael had fallen so deeply in love with her. He sighed sadly, as he gazed at Pilar's likeness.

'You still love her, don't you?' Mary softly said. Rafael touched the painting lovingly and moved on, unable to speak, the emotions welling up inside him were still painful. Quickly, he composed himself and took Mary to introduce his trusted servants to her.

'I have many servants; and they are all loyal. However, I must introduce you to the two I trust without question. They have been with me since my first marriage. They know their master very well. Better than I know myself, I think.' Rafael laughed in self-deprecation pointing to himself. The two in question had entered the solarium while he was showing Mary around, and were standing side by side. She was convinced she could feel coldness from the two people waiting for her. Rafael first spoke Spanish to the servants and they both bowed their heads. 'Maria, this is my *Administrador*, Wilfredo and my *Ama de casa*, Sarita.'

'*Hola senora*,' Sarita said.

Mary tried her limited use of Spanish to thank the couple for their welcome, but both just looked at her with unresponsive faces, making her feel uncomfortable.

'Do not worry, Maria. Wilfredo and Sarita adored Pilar. It will take time for them to accept you,' Rafael said.

'I do not like the way they look at me,' Mary replied. Rafael looked uncomfortable for a moment. He shot a glance at the two servants and Wilfredo audaciously returned his stare. He was also aware of their unfriendly manner towards his new young wife.

'Give them time, I will speak with them,' he promised. 'You have full access to my entire home; go wherever you wish, Maria.' Rafael added in an effort to lessen the atmosphere. He then turned to Wilfredo and Sarita and spoke severely to them. Mary could not understand entirely what he said, but she was surprised by the way Wilfredo replied. A servant should never speak to his master in such a manner; he used a belligerent voice to Rafael, and Sarita nodded in accord. Rafael replied more potent and Mary recognised the names of Pilar and Isabel in the conversation. The two servants bowed and retired from his presence. Both swept past Mary without a second glance.

'What did you tell them, Rafael?' Mary asked. He shook his head.

'Maria, it is nothing to concern you. They resent you because you are English and not Spanish,' Rafael explained. 'They will have to accept the fact that you are their mistress now. Pilar is dead, nothing can change that. I have business to attend to.' Bowing, Rafael excused himself and departed, leaving Mary standing in the centre of the room, suddenly feeling very alone and afraid. Remembering where the bedroom was, Mary hurried through the corridors and up an elaborate staircase to find it. Lettie was there unpacking the chests.

'This is a fine place, mistress,' Lettie remarked. Mary nodded as she crossed to the window and gazed around the room.

'I never imagined I'd have a husband who was so affluent,' she said with a sigh. Lettie noticed the slight hint of sadness in her voice.

'What is wrong, mistress?' she asked, stopping what she was doing and coming to stand before Mary. She looked out in the direction of the garden laid out below her. She was unspoken, trying to find the precise words to say. Her brow furrowed.

'I love Rafael; he is a man any woman would dream of marrying.'

'Are you full of regret already?' Lettie asked. Mary nodded and then shook her head.

'I do not know, Lettie. It is one thing marrying an Englishman and going to live somewhere in England, but I have left everything and everyone I know to come here,' Mary blurted out. 'Have I done the right thing?'

'It's not my place to say,' Lettie conceded.

'For once, act as if you are my equal, not my servant,' she snapped irritably.

'Then as if I were your equal. You are a dutiful wife, you follow your husband and live in the home he lives in, where ever it is,' Lettie began. 'Give it time, mistress. You will become accustomed to living here, as shall I.'

Mary leant over and kissed Lettie on the cheek.

'We are two English women alone in a foreign land; we will stay together, a little piece of England in Spain. As for those servants, they will be reconciled to me eventually,' Mary commented, feeling happier now. Lettie curtsied and returned to unpacking Mary's belongings.

That evening, Mary and Rafael sat outside in the warm Spanish evening. She felt relaxed and enjoyed this undisturbed moment with her husband. He sat close by with his eyes shut, listening to the sounds of the night. In his hand, he held several sheets of written paper.

'What is written there?' Mary asked. Rafael awoke with a start.

'Not for you to concern yourself about, Maria. Accounts, that is all,' he replied too quickly, she thought. 'I shall go and file them away. Not to worry about,' he said standing up and hurrying back into the home, leaving Mary puzzled by his response.

Later, as they lay in bed, Mary brought up the matter of the papers again.

'Why did you not want me to see your papers?' she asked. She felt Rafael uneasily shift position in the bed.

'You are a woman and do not have the brain capability to deal with accounts and finances concerning this place. Leave it to me,' he replied brusquely, but Mary was not going to let the subject go that easily.

'I helped my mother-in-law run Markham, what is so different here?'

'My estate is large and there are…' Rafael paused, apparently reluctant to continue. 'Complications you would not comprehend.'

'But…' she began

'No more, be quiet. Enough has been said,' he pulled Mary to him and kissed her resolutely on the mouth, silencing her in a prelude to lovemaking. Yet, while he caressed and stroked her body, she kept thinking there was something he was hiding, a secret, and this perturbed Mary. One way or another, she decided to try to find out what he kept from her. For now, a wave of ecstasy was pulsating through her again. Tomorrow she would begin her investigations.

The next morning, Mary sat at the side of the long table as Sarita coordinated the servants serving breakfast. She tried to talk with the woman, but as the day before, Sarita was distant and regarded Mary with distain. Rafael strode in, rubbing his hands together with keenness. He came round the table and kissed Mary affectionately. He spoke briefly to Sarita; she curtsied and replied to him. She glanced at Mary, and then departed the solarium.

'I have business to attend to today and shall be gone until late tonight,' Rafael announced. Mary's face dropped. She was to be by herself already.

'Can't I come with you? I would like to see the countryside,' she asked optimistic of an answer to the affirmative. Rafael shook his head.

'No, *mi querido*, you can stay here and practice your adopted language. I have instructed Wilfredo to assist you.'

'But he dislikes me!' Mary complained. Rafael huffed and dropped his spoon noisily.

'That is all in your head, Maria. I have engaged my two most dependable servants for many years. They obey my command. I have told him to help you with our language,' he replied. Mary pouted. He pretended not to notice and continued to eat. 'When you are not learning, stroll around the grounds, there are many outhouses and buildings to be investigated. Since Pilar's death, this place has lacked a woman's touch. You can bring beauty back to my empty home.' The look he gave Mary was a warning to be quiet. She knew it would be ineffective to maintain protesting.

Shortly after breakfast, Rafael left. Mary spent some time trying to read a book in the Spanish language. Yet after an hour, gave that up. By then, Wilfredo had appeared in the door, ready to begin tuition. Just as Sarita, he was distant and seemingly judgmental of Mary. Finally, she put down the book she had been studying and looked directly at the servant.

'Wilfredo, why are you like this towards me?' she asked in

English, expecting the man not to understand her. He replied in English.

'The *Senora* was goodness and light. Everything she touched and said she made beautiful,' he said.

'You speak English!' Mary exclaimed. Wilfredo nodded.

'Yes, my lady. *Senora* Pilar did not have to suffer,' he answered enigmatically.

'My husband has told me what happened,' Mary remarked. Wilfredo raised his eyebrows.

'I do not think so. *Senora*, I am to teach you my language, and I will do just that. We will begin with that book you have been studying,' he said taking the book from Mary's hands and thumbing through it.

For the rest of the morning, Mary practiced simple Spanish phrases and sentences, with Wilfredo correcting her mispronunciations with cold authority.

'Enough lessons for today. I have duties to perform,' he eventually excused himself abruptly. He gathered up the books and departed leaving Mary alone again. She felt confused about her adopted language, but she would pick up the basics and learn from those around her.

In the afternoon, Mary wandered through the scented gardens, admiring the flowers. She walked over to the dairy and introduced herself to the men and women there. Their reactions were akin to that of Wilfredo and Saritas. The workers in the bakery were friendlier, but she still could not help but feel wholly welcomed here. Everyone spoke about Pilar with adored veneration, saying how sad the master was when she had died. Mary tried to insist that she would not try to imitate their former mistress, but wanted acceptance for herself.

Thankfully, Rafael returned home as night fell. He was tired from a long and productive day and was very pleased by the welcome Mary gave him. She was thankful to see him back. He told her where he went and what he did, and presented a gift of crimson satin shoes, with pearls and golden thread stitched into them. Mary could not believe the generosity of her husband, recalling she had told him only once of Queen Catherine's crimson, pearl and gold thread shoes she had held in her early days at court.

'I should like to accompany you, my lord,' Mary requested simply, choosing her words cautiously. Rafael shook his head.

'Maria, I have already said, you are to stay here and look after my home while I am away.' He pulled Mary into his lap and kissed her. 'You must get use to your new life. Once you are settled everything will be fine,' he guaranteed yet again, and refused to listen to any more complaints from his wife.

Over the subsequent weeks, Rafael was proved right. Mary began to relax and found her life became easier and more contented. Wilfredo and Sarita were still distant towards her, but she had become familiarised to that. Wilfred's tutoring progressed and Mary used Spanish, though haltingly at first, more than her native English language. She even taught Lettie and insisted that they conversed in Spanish to become fluent in it.

Rafael was frequently away, and Mary now began to appreciate how Eleanor had felt during William's long absences. The lonesomeness enveloped her, she would count the days until her husband returned, and they would have ardent reunions. Although there was plenty to do to occupy the long hours, Mary felt happiest when Rafael was close by. It could have been because of his absence, Mary found herself becoming clumsy and tripping over obstacles. She put this down to her thoughts drifting to her husband.

It was only a matter of time before Mary discovered to her joy that she was pregnant. Rafael was ecstatic.

'Would it be a good time to have your daughter return?' she asked. 'I should like to meet her and you could be a father to her again.'

'Isabel cannot return yet, Maria. Her life is settled in Madrid now; she has been educated there and will live there for the rest of her life.' Rafael refused the appeal. 'She is better off where she is She is my daughter, and I think of her daily. We have been apart for too long now. Too many years have passed between us,' he replied.

Mary smiled and hugged his arm affectionately. 'I may still meet her one day,'

He smiled blankly and stroked her stomach. 'I would rejoice in a son.' He said, 'Isabel will never return,' he added mysteriously, refusing to be drawn any further.

A letter arrived from her mother.With trembling fingers, she broke the seal before reading it; she felt she knew the contents. Her fears were correct. Margaret had written to tell her that her father had died. The cancer finally claimed him. Robert had returned to Yardeley Chase to take control of his inheritance. That was not all the awful news. Mary's son, William was very ill. It was doubtful he would survive the month. She had secretly known from the day he had been born her son would not live to adulthood. Rafael did all he could to console his wife, but she was distraught. She regretted not being with her father at his end, and the thought of her son dying without his mother by his side was more than she felt she could bear. Mary's pregnancy continued its term, and during nighttime hours after a long and difficult labour, she delivered a stillborn daughter.

Hours passed before Sarita, smiling to herself emerged from the room with bloodied sheets gathered in her arms. She passed Rafael without a word. He pushed open the door and peered in to see Mary lying silently in fresh sheets. Her face pallid, her eyes closed, her breathing slow. He uncertainly approached the bed and tenderly took her hand in his, sitting on the edge of the bed, his eyes never leaving her face.

'*Mi querido,*' he whispered. 'I thought I was going to lose you. I cannot lose you as I lost Pilar.'

Mary stirred and groaned inaudibly. Her eyelids fluttered open and she looked vaguely at her husband.

'I am sorry I could not give you a son,' she weakly said. He smiled through his tears.

'It matters not, Maria. You are alive and will recover from this.'

'The baby…' she began slowly. Rafael pressed a finger to her lips.

'Hush *mi amor*. Save your strength and sleep,' the midwife was insisting he left, so Rafael stood and left Mary to rest. Behind the closed door, he covered his eyes with his hands as the emotion of the night, and recollections tore into him like a knife to the heart. He stumbled blindly to the gallery and stopped, staring up at Pilar's portrait.

'I had to marry her, you could not stop me, Pilar, and I would not allow you to,' he said angrily, clenching his fists, then fell heavily into a chair, putting his hands over his ears, trying to shut out the demons laughing, mocking and taunting inside his head.

Progressively, over the weeks, Mary began to recover and her strength returned. Lettie was her constant companion throughout the recuperation. The local wise woman visited daily and prescribed tonics made from roadside herbs until she was well enough to return to her normal routine. Rafael was happy to have his wife back to her usual self.

# 22

Mary was content to return to her explorations when Rafael was away. Her wanderings took her past the buildings that were in use daily and she found herself in a more run-down part of the estate. There was one building Rafael had not shown Mary when they had toured his estate on her arrival. It stood alone, enclosed by a high wall. The only way through the wall was by a solid wooden gate. The top of the rotunda building that Mary could see rising above the wall looked old. However, the lock on the gate appeared to be newer than the rest of its surroundings, signifying use. When Mary questioned the servants, they conveniently managed not to understand. On Rafael's return, she challenged him as to the use of this strange mysterious building. His response was equally puzzling to her.

'That is the *Casa de abeja*. I forbid you to go there again, Maria,' he said crossly, shaking a finger in Mary's direction.

'Why? What is so special inside there?' Mary asked, sensing there was more to the building that Rafael was ready to divulge. He just shook his head and turned away.

'The place has become contaminated; it contains poisons that could harm you. Stay away, please.' He refused to talk any further on the secrets of the building. This only fired Mary's curiosity to discover the secret behind the gate. From then on, she slipped away as often as she dared to watch the gate to see if there was anything that could give her a clue.

Her diligence paid off. Eventually, Mary, hidden behind a log pile, saw Wilfredo and Sarita approach the gate carrying baskets of what appeared to be food and pitchers of wine. Wilfredo took a heavy key from his belt and unlocked the padlock. He pushed the gate open and entered with Sarita, locking the gate behind them. Mary stayed hidden, not wanting to give her position away, waiting for the servants to reappear. When the gate opened, the couple emerged, smiling and waving to someone Mary could not see. She heard a mature woman's voice call goodbye. Then Wilfredo locked the gate behind him. He and Sarita walked past the log pile talking quietly to each other, both unaware of Mary. Once the couple had gone back towards the kitchens, she went and stood in front of the gate and tried to peer through the small gap, and could just see a well-kept lawn. What was a lawn doing in such a rundown place? Mary kept wondering who was inside, and why this was such a secret. The names of his two previous wives kept invading her mind. Surely, neither of them was behind this wooden gate, they were both dead. Then there was Isabel, why was there such reluctance to talk about her? Even so, the explanation Rafael had offered her about his wives and daughter no longer seemed true somehow. Something was not right.

That night in bed, Rafael noticed, Mary seemed diffident; seeing her turn away from him and settling to sleep infuriated him.

'What is wrong tonight, Maria?' he asked impatiently shaking her shoulder. Mary pulled away with a shrug.

'I have a headache that is all,' she replied tersely. He was not satisfied with the reply.

'There is more than that. What is it?'

'Nothing, I feel unwell today, please, let me sleep.' Mary pulled the sheets up over her shoulders and shut her eyes.

Rafael would have none of this and pulled the sheet back. 'There is more, tell me.'

Mary sighed and turned to face her husband. 'When will I get to meet Isabel?' she asked. Rafael looked puzzled, then annoyed.

'I have told you, she lives in Madrid, too far away for us to visit, or for her to come here. Why do you ask?'

'What goes on inside *Casa de abeja*? I saw Wilfredo and Sarita going in there, someone lives there, who?'

Rafael shuddered involuntary 'Why do you disobey me? I told you not to go there. Did your first husband abuse you because you were a disobedient wife?' he shouted. Mary shrank back. 'Is this how you repay my kindness to you?'

'Rafael...' Mary started to speak, but stopped seeing the face that had only ever shown her love now contorted with rage.

135

'If I find out that you go anywhere near that place again, you will be dealt with severely. Understand?' he shouted getting out of bed and pulling his wrap around him. She nodded dumbly for the first time feeling afraid. Rafael left the room, slamming the door behind him. She sat in the bed alone now, not knowing what to do. She wanted to find out who was behind the gate. Had he been lying to her all the time she had known him? If he was lying, what else had he told her was true or false? If her curiosity had not taken her towards the *Casa de abeja*, she would not have known any different and she would not be sitting here alone. Mary knew that now she had gone too far to leave her investigations unresolved. Risking her marriage was a chance Mary had to take. She would return to *Casa de abeja* and find out who lived there, and if so, why?

Relations between Mary and Rafael were cool for several days; he insisted she accompanied him everywhere he went. This he hoped would keep her from slipping away to *Casa de abeja*. She rode with him into Bilbao and had to sit through tiresome meetings he attended with other merchants from the region. They all regarded Mary with mistrust; a woman had no place attending these meetings.

Eventually, Rafael had to go away on one of his trips. Mary would not be able to accompany him this time; it would be impractical for him to take her due to the nature of the business. On the night before he departed, Rafael locked himself and Mary in the bedroom.

'Sarita has been instructed to watch you while I am away. She is to report to me on my return of your activities. If you go anywhere you are not permitted I will personally see to your punishment,' he warned, pulling Mary towards the bed and roughly pushed her onto it. She lay obedient, counting the minutes until he was finished with her.

The next morning, Sarita, as usual, was in the hall waiting for their arrival. Mary ate silently, keeping her gaze upon the plate in front of her while Rafael talked about his trip; it would take him into France and all the way to Paris. If everything went well, he would head for home within four months. If not, he may be gone for at least six. Before, when he had announced his trips away, Mary had been despairing to see him leave, and would count the days and hours before his return. This day, she impassively looked at him, and found herself almost wishing his departure would hasten. She knew this was an appalling thing to desire, however, since the discovery of *Casa de abeja*; their relationship had begun to deteriorate. Mary had decided to avoid going to that place while her husband was away. He had threatened her, yet despite her doubts, she did still love him. *Casa de abeja* would be there, so would its elusive occupant after Rafael returned. If Sarita testified her as the docile wife on his return, she could broach the delicate subject another day?

In the courtyard, Rafael stood by his stallion Zachariah adjusting the girth. The horse was restless and kept pawing the ground, snorting with impatience eager to be gone. Rafael fastened his cloak and pulled his hat on. Mary stood watching him, and remembered that first day she had set eyes upon him. Despite the chill in their relationship, she found herself falling in love with her husband again, as he stood there, giving orders with such panache to the retinue that would accompany him. Now the reality of his departure began to set in, and Mary's heart began to ache at the thought of it.

'Write when you can, Rafael,' she pleaded. He smiled sincerely at his wife. He did not want to see Mary sad, still loving her deeply, and the incident with *Casa de abeja* would be resolved upon his return.

'I shall, Maria. You will never be far from my thoughts,' he guaranteed kissing her. Mary smiled back at him through her tears.

'I'll be lonely without you. I still love you.'

'I know,' Rafael confirmed. He swung into the saddle and Zachariah reared up whinnying. *'Adios!'* he cried waving his hand. He blew a kiss to Mary. *'Les falto ya, mi amor.* I miss you already, my love,' he shouted to Mary. She blew a kiss back to him and watched as he rode through the gates followed by his retinue and then were gone.

Forlornly, she wandered back into the hacienda. The long months that would follow were to be lonely and hard for her to undergo. Mary now had taken over the daily running and accounts of the house. Rafael kept certain documents under lock and key in his study to which no one except him had access. She had given up questioning him about them; guessing they involved *Casa de abeja*.

The servants, except still for Wilfredo and Sarita, now accepted Mary as mistress. They carried out her orders without question, but their manner was still hostile. They would both mention Pilar often, still determined to remind Mary how wonderful her predecessor was, and how awful her death had been. She tried to encourage the pair to tell her about Pilar's last moments, but neither Wilfredo nor Sarita refused to talk. They insisted their master was the one to recount Pilar's last hours to their new mistress. She attempted to draw the other servants to talk to her; they said Pilar's heart had broken after her twin daughters had died and she never recovered.

To keep boredom at bay, Mary would ride into Bilbao weekly with Sarita always close by. The two women would barely converse more than necessary, as this woman was spying on her, keeping records of her movements, who she spoke to, what she saw, where she went. It was aggravating to be watched this closely, yet Mary would not give the housekeeper the satisfaction of knowing this situation infuriated her. She would conduct her business; buy fine materials to make her dresses and quality linen for Rafael's shirts, even juicy ripe fruit for a delicious treat throughout the lonely days.

On one visit, the two women entered the plaza and saw a small crowd gathered, all seemed to be laughing and enjong a spectacle. Mary, curious to know what was happening, dismounted her palfrey, handing the reins to the accompanying groom and walked towards the crowd, pushing through them to see what was causing the laughter. Sarita as always was a step behind.

In the cente of the crowd stood a young man with smooth olive skin and bright black eyes talking incessantly in front of an easel on which stood a thick wad of paper. He was drawing sketches with a stick of charcoal of people gathered around him. Once each sketch was finished, he would hand it to its recipient for payment in return. His eyes fell upon Mary and he stopped talking immediately, gazing open mouthed at her pale English complexion. Quickly, he tore the latest sheet of paper into shreds tossing them into the air and began with rapid strokes drawing Mary's likeness.

'Oh beautiful foreign lady,' he said breathlessly, 'Let me capture you on paper.' He stopped briefly to study the contours of Mary's face; her cheekbones, lips, and the shape of her nose. She laughed as he touched her face to move her head to one side and then the other, leaving a smudge of charcoal on her chin, from behind Sarita tutted and Mary ignored her.

'Who are you? I have not seen you here before?' she asked. The young man returned to his drawing and with flamboyant sweeps finished in lightning speed. He stood back allowing Mary to admire his artwork. For all its haste, the likeness was excellent and she was more than happy to pay for the young man's work. He gave an exaggerated bow and then flinging his arms out he announced loudly:

'I am Guido, the most famous artist in all of Spain and Italy you have never heard of!' he raised a finger and chuckled. 'But one day you will have heard of me!'

There was a round of applause from the onlookers. Guido bowed appreciatively. Mary nodded satisfied, an idea springing into her mind.

'Come to my home tomorrow, I may have a commission for you,' she instructed. Guido's eyes opened wide and his mouth made an O shape.

'The *senor* will not like this,' Sarita hissed in Mary's ear.

'The *senor* is not here and there will be no impropriety,' she replied tartly. The housekeeper muttered under her breath, turning away disgusted.

'I shall be there beautiful foreign lady,' Guido promised, bowing low. Then turning to the people, he continued. '*Senors, senoras* and beautiful *senoritas*, I have finished here today. Have no fears, Guido shall return!' There was cheering and the crowd slowly dispersed, leaving Mary facing him.

'I live…'

'Guido knows where you live; you are the wife of Don Rafael Perez. Everyone in Bilbao knows of his beautiful English wife.'

She watched his lovely young face beam with pleasure. 'Tomorrow morning,' she affirmed and turned away to return to her horse and ride home.

Early the next morning, Lettie shook Mary awake. 'Come and look at this,' she insisted. Rising from her bed and pulling a wrap on, Mary went to the window and looked out to where Lettie pointed. Along the dusty road, approaching the gates of the hacienda was Guido, riding a jenny donkey who's foal trotted by her side. He was holding onto the reins with one hand while with the other hand he held a leash pulling a cantankerous jack donkey laden with his artist equipment. Seeing this made Mary laugh.

'I have instructed the servants to allow him entry,' she said to Lettie and returned to watch the amusing scene. The gates swung open and Guido rode in. He reined in his donkey and slid off her back to admire the fountain. He ran to the second donkey, pulled out sheets of paper and charcoal, and began drawing it, moving around observing all aspects.

Now dressed, Mary came out to greet him; the exuberant Italian bowed low, then showed his drawings, babbling on excitedly about how he had hardly slept the previous night.

'Have you eaten?' Mary interrupted and he shook his head. 'Then come and have breakfast first and we can talk.' She signalled for the groom to take the donkeys to the stables once Guido had unloaded his baggages from the jack donkey, his eyes following the groom as the donkeys were led away. Then he followed Mary as the foal followed its mother instinctively.

Mary watched as the young man ate ravenously; it was obvious he did not eat regularly. He explained that most of the money he earned paid for a single room in an old house in Bilbao, paper and painting equipement. It would all be worth the suffering now as once he was known throughout Europe, he would dine on the finest food money could buy and live in a grand house in Holland.

'I want you to paint my portrait,' Mary announced as two of the servants cleared the remnants of the meal away. 'It shall be a gift for my husband and I shall pay you well for your efforts as long as I think they are worth it.'

'Lady, I shall begin at once. I work fast and I am good.'

Mary could not help but smile at his infectious self-assurance.

'I saw your drawings in the plaza and they were good, but can you paint with oils as well?' she asked. He dived into a large sack, pulled out small oil paintings, and handed each one to her explaining the story behind them all. 'I am convinced. My husband is expected home in five months. Is that enough time?'

'I am the maker of miracles,' Guido boasted proudly. Mary laughed, caught up in his boldness.

'So when will you begin?' she asked. He looked puzzled.

'I thought you wanted me to start at once, *senora*.' he said.

'There is a room at the top of my home; you can use that while you stay. I shall instruct the servants to provide you with victuals.' Mary rang a bell close by and a maid entered. 'Take our guest to the top room and see that everything he needs is accommodated for.'

The Italian rose to his feet and followed the young woman. Mary remained seated after he had gone, thinking about him. Guido was so charming, just to have him in her mind made her smile. He would brighten the lonely days during his stay.

Guido worked late into the night, preparing the canvas for his commission. By the morning, several promising sketches remained on the table and the easel stood ready.

Later that morning, he spoke to Mary about his ideas. The portrait would have her positioned by the fountain, gazing directly out of the canvas to the viewer. The rest of the day Mary spent out in the courtyard bossed around by Guido as he made her stand in one direction, then another, sitting on the edge of the fountain, hand dipped into the water, or hands folded in her lap. With every positioning, he frantically drew ideas on sheet after sheet of paper until, finally pleased, he dismissed her briskly. Bemused, Mary wandered back into the hacienda as he gathered his equipment up into his arms and ran past her to get to his room to begin on the preliminary lines on the canvas.

That night as Mary lay alone in the ebony bed, her mind wandered to Guido and her heart fluttered; she was having a fancy for him. He was nearer in age to her, maybe that was the attraction. He had a passion for his work, which she liked. Secretly she hoped his stay would last for the entire length of Rafael's absence. Nothing would happen; there would be nothing for him to be angry about. An innocent flirtation that was all. Then Mary began to imagin the flirtation going further and she scolded herself for such impure, adulterous thoughts. Yet the thoughts remained and grew in their intensity. She loved Rafael and he loved her. She employed Guido for one purpose: to produce a painting and nothing more than that! Both Wilfredo and Sarita had already made acid remarks to his attendance; she had not expected anything less from these two. They continually threatened to tell Rafael about Guido living in the hacienda with her. She ignored their intimidation, refusing to lower herself to their level and enter into a pointless arugment. Neither was worth the effort.

Over the following weeks, Guido worked tirelessly late into every night. He had now banned everyone from entering his room, demanding the trays of food and wine left outside the locked door. Not even Mary was permitted entry to see how the work was progressing. This lead to fears that perhaps it was not progressing as well as she had hoped, was this idea as good as she had originally thought? She had judged his talent on a few scrawled drawings, it had been an impulse, a way to stave off the solitude while her husband was away. Mary still felt her heart flutter and her stomach turn when she thought of Guido, her cheeks would redden and her eyes sparkle. So what had been the true reason for inviting the charismatic stranger into her home? She tried not to allow herself to carry this thought forward. However, the images in her mind of the two of them locked in a passionate embrace would not go away. She imagined his lips kissing her bare flesh, his fingers caressing and stroking, and an eagerness to possess her body paramount in his own thoughts. So deliciously wicked, Mary revelled in her fantasy.

Eventually, she stood in front of the locked door and hammered onto it. After the initial day, the only sightings of Guido was when he would hurry from his room, locking the door behind him and dash to the stables to see his donkeys. He would stroke them and talk to them in Italian, and then walk them around the courtyard talking aloud to them, gesticulating boldly as though describing his thoughts to them before returning them to the stables and hurrying back to his room. So today, Mary stood there demanding entry. She heard the key turn in the lock and it opened enough for Guido to peer round looking curiously at her. Her heart skipped a beat with pleasure.

'Lady, is there something I can do for you?' he asked.

Mary nodded. 'You can let me in. I want to see your work. Seeing that I am the one who is giving you this room over your head, I should see what is so secretive about you?'

Guido sighed with irritability. 'Guido works alone,' he complained attempting to shut the door. Mary's foot stopped this.

'Let me in,' she commanded. Reluctantly, the Italian pulled the door open allowing her to enter.

The floor was still strewn with paper and the paint splattered walls looked exactly as Mary had imagined. The fleeting, hopeful thought of him pulling her to the floor and taking her there invaded Mary's mind. It did not happen. The easel with the canvas was facing the window for the best light and she went to look at his work.

'It is not complete,' Guido said nervously. She could not believe what she saw. He had captured her likeness with incredible accuracy; she was standing by the fountain, with the water looking so real, Mary felt she could almost feel the spray from the jets spouting upwards. In the distance the hacienda with its white walls and red tiles sparkled.

'It is wonderful,' she gasped. Guido smiled. 'Tonight you must dine with me and we shall talk into the night.'

'I take my meals here, lady,' he said quickly.

'Not tonight, I insist,' she replied, he nodded. 'Tonight,' Mary repeated firmly. Tonight she would declare her attraction to him.

The meal was set in the solarium to make the diners purposely sit close. Mary listened entranced as Guido told her stories of how he had come to Bilbao. He had been the son of impoverished villagers in Italy where he lived with his four brothers and two sisiters. At an early age, realising his parents could not afford to feed their large family; Guido had left home and headed for Venice to seek his fortune. Over the years, he worked for many people, but the one man who had made the biggest impact on his life was an artist in Milan. He talked about this man with such love and affection. After the old man had died, Guido travelled through France and into Spain earning a living the only way that he could. His ambition was to go to Holland and learn from artists there.

Mary drew her chair closer to him and put a hand on his leg. 'I like you, I think I desire you,' she said. Bold words, but she did not care. Guido pulled away.

'Do not talk like this, lady,' he answered. 'You do not know me.'

'I know how I feel about you and I want you, Guido,' she said softly.

'I cannot.'

'Why?'

'You want me to bed you. I just cannot, do this.'

'My husband would not know, he would never know, take me to your room please, just once,' Mary pleaded, not understanding his rejection. He took her hand to his lips and kissed her palm.

'Lady, you have been good to me, trusted me. I shall not concede to your request. You have a husband who you love; I cannot let you betray that love. My choice of life means I am not attracted to women.' They were enigmatic words. He stood up embarrassed and went to the door. 'I shall leave at the end of the week; you do not have to pay me.'

Mary also stood. 'Guido, no, sorry, I did not mean to insult you, I admire your honesty. I've been foolish, let us part as friends, please,' she cried, quickly realising what his comments had meant and how desperate and imprudent she had sounded. Would she really have permitted him to make love to her? He hesitated and then relented.

'I shall leave soon,' he insisted and returned to his room.

That night as Mary lay alone again in bed, she felt ashamed for her behaviour. She had allowed her fantasies to rule her sensible head. Turning and hugging the pillow, she comforted herself with the knowledge that Rafael would be home soon, and smiled at the thought of his strong, protective arms embracing her and the joy of feeling his naked body move against hers again.

For the remaining days of Guido's stay, he kept himself in his room, cleaning it and not allowing any of Mary's servants in. She saw little of him, avoiding him herself still repentant for her thoughtless words.

On the day of his departure, Mary and Guido stood by the fountain that spouted water high into the clear air. They waited as the groom brought the donkeys to them. As Guido packed his equipment onto the jack donkey's back, she rubbed the foal's soft ears and gave its mother an apple to munch. She then fed the other donkey with a second apple as Guido mounted his jenny donkey.

Across his body was a bag that held a purse of money, which he said, was enough to get him nearly to Holland. He sat astride the donkey beaming brightly, then leaned forward and placed a gentle kiss on Mary's lips.

'A kiss for what might have been. *Adios* lovely lady,' he said, then kicking his heels into the flanks of his donkey, rode away from the hacienda, the foal trotting by its mother and the jack donkey led behind, braying noisily. Mary stood and watched until they were out of sight and then returned into the hacienda, glowing inside from that kiss.

# 23

Although Mary attempted to immerse herself in the affairs of the hacienda once Guido had departed, thoughts kept returning to *Casa de abeja*. Sarita absented herself from her duty to watch Mary every afternoon since Rafael had departed; she would make excuses to say it was siesta time, or she had other duties charged to her. Mary knew that she and Wilfredo went to *that* place. She began to ache with curiosity to know what was going on, and Rafael's continuing absence did not help to ease her fertile mind. She would make up stories as to what was going on behind the closed gates. Did Rafael have a secret mistress locked in there? Was it Isabel? Mary even entertained the thoughts that Pilar may still be alive and locked away. These ideas were too absurd. On the other hand, were they?

One occasion, Mary waited until as usual, Sarita left her side, and then after giving her time to go towards *Casa de abeja*, Mary crept from her room and, being careful, she headed for the *casa*, seeing both Sarita and Wilfredo ahead of her. This was going against her husband's express orders, this time Mary was willing to risk his displeasure. As every other time, Wilfredo unlocked the gate and he and Sarita passed through. Mary hid until the couple left before coming out of hiding and went to stand in front of the gates. She peered in through the gap again, and this time Mary was sure she saw a young woman about her own age in the garden. The woman was dancing, and Mary could hear her singing softly. Why was she under lock and key? Mary stepped back and stood on a twig that snapped, giving her presence away. The singing stopped and the young woman peered with deep brown eyes through the small gap back at Mary.

'Who are you?' she inquired with suspicion. Mary moved back a second step, startled at the discovery.

'I am *Senora* Maria Perez. Who are you?' Mary replied confidently in Spanish, trying to sound calm, but the quiver in her voice gave away her emotions. The young woman gasped.

'Where is that whore?' she spat angrily.

'Who do you mean?' Mary asked.

'The whore stole my father!' was the angrier reply, and the young woman hit the gate violently with her fists, making them rattle on their hinges. Mary recoiled back. Rafael had lied to her all the time. Isabel was not in Madrid; this was his own daughter locked in her own prison in his own home.

'Do you mean Pilar?' Mary asked deliberately slowly. The young woman screamed. 'She died after childbirth.'

'That whore!' Isabel screamed maniacally, pummelling the gates. Mary suddenly wished she had not been so curious and was back in the safety of her home. Rafael would find out about this now. There was no way she would be able to keep this revelation secret. She had to ask the young woman the one question even though it was irrelevant now.

'Are you Isabel?'

'Yes,' she replied simply and steadily after the outburst. An older woman's harsh voice from behind Isabel startled her into silence. Mary saw Isabel move away from the gate and the other woman, with a rounded face, looked through the gap.

'I do not know who you think you are, but leave us alone. You are not welcome here,' she snapped viciously.

'I just wanted to…' Mary began hesitantly.

'*Inglaterra*, go away *Inglaterra*!' The older woman shouted, not waiting to hear Mary's defence. She then boxed Isabel's, scolding her in rapid Spanish and pushed her back towards an open door in the building behind the gate. The woman briefly turned to see if Mary was still looking through, and spat at her.

Mary walked slowly back to the house, now not caring if she was seen or not. Her life was changing now because of her own actions. Sarita was overseeing a maid performing a task in the solarium when Mary returned.

'Leave us,' Mary instructed the maid, who after looking to Sarita departed. The housekeeper stared at Mary. 'Why is my husband's daughter locked away?' she asked. Sarita's eyebrows rose.

'So now you know. I knew you could not resist finding out,' she said triumphantly. 'My master will be most displeased when I tell him what you have done.'

'Tell Rafael,' Mary replied tiredly. 'I wouldn't expect you to do anything less.' Sarita swept haughtily past, not disguising her pleasure.

Mary had no appetite for food or drink that night, all she did was to lie on her bed with her face to the wall. She was feeling totally lost. This wonderful marriage would end because of her inquisitiveness. She was happy with her life, which was perfect, and all she had done was to destroy it; Rafael would never forgive her.

The arrival of a letter from Rafael took Mary's mind off her troubles. He wrote to say he was in Paris where he had met with contacts from Germany and had conducted his business to a successful conclusion. News reached him from the English Court. Anne Boleyn was still holding off King Henry's advances and he had not looked at any other woman. Anyone who wanted a royal favour would court Lady Anne as she had the king's ear on all matters. Cardinal Wolsey was gradually falling from grace. Mary wished she could be in London, close to her friend. She knew Anne was an intelligent woman and would not do anything ludicrous, but she remembered Anne had become malicious and wanted to see the great cardinal ruined. It seemed her wishes might be coming true.

# 24

Rafael had been away for six months when news reached Mary that he was heading home and was expected to arrive back within weeks. Her reaction was what both Sarita and Wilfredo knew it would be. She was anxious of his return. He would take her in his arms and kiss her with devotion, expecting a loving welcome home. All he would receive was news that his wife had discovered his secret. She contemplated escaping with Lettie, and head for the port and hopefully a passage home to England where she could seek refuge. Rafael's return days sooner than expected, stopped that plan from reaching fruition.

The sound of horses' hooves in the courtyard heralded his return; Mary knew it was only a matter of time before the truth would be out.

Without stopping to take off his cloak, pull of his riding boots or wash the dirt from his face, Rafael ran into his home, glad to be back, eager to see his beautiful wife after such a long absence. She was fearfully waiting in the solarium for him. Before either Sarita or Wilfredo could say anything, Rafael bounded up the stairs and flung open the door, to see Mary standing modestly there. Crossing the room, he pulled her to him and kissed his wife tremendously, leaving her breathless.

'Maria! *Mi querido* I have missed you! Have you missed me?' he asked brushing away a tear from her pale cheek. She could not bring herself to speak; she nodded, and then shook her head. 'You do not know whether you missed me or not?'

'Oh my love, don't leave me again. I want us to be together forever,' Mary stammered through her tears. Rafael laughed and gathered her close to his chest where she could hear the reassuring sound of his beating heart. The thought that Rafael had lied about

Isabel and her whereabouts suddenly seemed unimportant. There must be a logical reason for her imprisonment.

'Now I shall get out of these stinking riding clothes. Tonight you can tell me what you have done while I was away,' Rafael said. 'Then later tonight, I can make love to you again in our bed where we belong,' he added burying his face in Mary's hair. 'Mmm, I forgot how wonderful you smell.' He strode out of the solarium shouting for Wilfredo. Mary stood alone her body shaking from the reunion. Would Wilfredo tell his master about his wife's indiscretions or would he and Sarita play with her emotions and not tell him yet. She decided to tell Rafael herself, hopefully before the servants could get their moment of victory over her, but not yet. Let him settle back home first, let him enjoy his wife's company for a short while before he found out the truth.

Mary put on a brave face as she and Rafael dined that evening. Sarita and Wilfredo kept giving her frosty looks, yet they did not say anything. Rafael talked continuously about his journey, who he met and what he saw, she listened attentively, ignoring the servants.

'While you were away, were there any other women?' she asked in a small voice. Rafael looked incredulous. He laughed and kissed his wife's hand.

'*Mi querido*, what a question. There are always women, an amusement that is all. I love and desire only one woman, and that is you, my Maria,' he assured. Mary smiled submissively knowing that her husband was a man who could never be satisfied with just one woman. While married to Pilar, he had tried to seduce her at Markham and had succeeded at court.

'I have a gift for you.' Mary said and signalled to a page hovering close by. He left to return with help carrying the painting. 'I commissioned an artist to paint this for you. Do you like it?' she asked. Rafael gazed astounded at the portrait.

'*Mi querido,* it is wonderful, it is beautiful.'

'I wanted to say thank you for making me so happy,' she continued.

'It is I who should thank you, Maria; you have made me love life again,' he assured. She smiled obediently. When the truth about her discovery of Isabel was out, this painting may soften his anger.

Later that evening, they took a stroll arm in arm in the garden. There had been a shower during the day releasing beautiful scents from the flowers. He drew Mary to a bench in the garden and from his pocket took a string of pearls.

'I acquired these in Paris and thought the colour of the pearls would complement your complexion,' he said, fastening the pearls and kissing Mary's neck.

'I don't deserve this, Rafael.' Mary said looking into his eyes. He kissed her neck again, letting his lips slide to her throat.

'Of course you do. You have brought me happiness after Pilar's death. I cannot love anyone more than I love you,' he said tenderly. Mary looked down, unable to speak. Rafael smiled affectionately and lifted her face, kissing her lips firmly, ignoring the tears shining in her eyes. 'No one is watching; make love to me now, here in the garden. I cannot wait for our bed,' he urged looking around. Without question, Mary was very glad to oblige and climbed onto his lap, winding her arms around his neck and kissing him with a loving passion. Could it be one of the last times they were together in their love?

From a window in the top of the hacienda, Sarita and Wilfredo watched their master and his English wife together.

'When shall we tell him?' Sarita asked. Wilfredo licked his lips and manipulated his genitals, panting deeply as he watched the lovemaking below.

'Not just yet. We will make her sweat for a while. Then we can enjoy her downfall,' he replied with a smile and looked fondly at her as a master would look upon his favourite hound. 'My devoted slave, what would you not do for me? What secrets you keep for me.' He stroked her face with his free hand and Sarita laughed, unlacing her bodice and pulling up her dress.

'You lead, I follow, Wilfredo,' she conceded slavishly. He accepted the invitation and they came together.

Mary desperately wanted to tell Rafael about finding Isabel, yet feared his wrath when he found out she had ignored his warning. Sarita and Wilfredo kept up the pressure on her, dropping subtle hints that very soon they would reveal her secret. She began to find it difficult to sleep or eat; growing thin and exhausted with worry, her trips and falls became more frequent. Rafael noticed the changes in his wife and became concerned for her health. Mary knew that very soon she would have to admit she knew, but could not bring herself to confess. She had not visited *Casa de abeja* since her discovery, and now did not want to return. Rafael cancelled all his appointments and stayed at home to be beside Mary while she was ill; he thought his presence would help her recover from the mystery illness.

As she lay in bed, Sarita gloated with pleasure. 'Soon the master will know. Shall you tell him or shall I?' she suggested, pretending to plump up pillows while she hissed the threats into Mary's ear.

'I am dying. Do your worst, I do not care anymore,' Mary replied, turning her face away. Sarita did not like the way she was giving up; there was little fun in taunting her when there was nothing to fight.

Lettie, always loyal to Mary, was not going to let her mistress give up and fetched herbal medicines from local wise women. Reluctantly, Mary allowed the medication administered, and gradually she found she was beginning to gain a little strength back. By the grace of God, Mary would not die and she found recuperation came rapidly thanks to Lettie's constant caring.

Rafael was almost hysterical with delight when he received the news that Mary was going to survive. Sarita and Wilfredo were glad too. This meant that soon they could resume their campaign of terror. Why not carry it on for as long as possible, the English woman was an easy target now. Rafael's physician had found no reason for this strange malady that had afflicted her, and was sceptical at Lettie's traditional medication. Convinced it was a miracle, Rafael travelled to a small church in the countryside and said prayer after prayer to God in thanks for her recovery.

He had abstained from suggestions of sexual relations with his wife, but now as Mary's strength returned, he began to drop subtle hints that he had been patient long enough. At first, Mary was reluctant to receive Rafael back in her bed, but eventually she decided that he had waited long enough and planned a special night for him.

She had excused herself from the table after dinner and had hurried to the bedchamber with Lettie to prepare everything for the night to come.

Lettie had been into town earlier in the day and had purchased dried rose petals and candles infused with musk roses to flood the bedchamber with a sensual aroma. Together, they scattered the rose petals over and in the bed, and Mary lit the candles giving them time to release their fragrances. The two women giggled together knowing what lay ahead. Mary felt happier than she had done for a long while.

She climbed into the bed, and then sent Lettie to find Rafael to tell him his wife requested his presence in the bedchamber. Once Lettie was gone, Mary pinched her cheeks, and bit her lips bringing colour to her face. From outside the closed door, she heard urgent footsteps. He threw open the door and stopped immediately as he saw Mary lying in the bed, inviting him over with a wave of her finger.

'*Mi querido*,' he breathed as he crossed the room in a fluid movement to stand at the foot of the bed, his eyes taking in the visual feast of his wife. Fumbling like an unproved youth, Rafael tried to undress quickly, but managed to get his arms caught in sleeves and legs in hose before finally pulling the clothes from his body and climbing onto the bed. Mary sat up, tossed the coverlet from her body, and held out her arms to receive her husband.

His prowess never failed to amaze Mary, and when he had finished, she lay satisfied. Rafael propped himself up on an arm and regarded Mary with affection.

'I thought I had lost you, Maria,' he said softly. Mary touched his face affectionately.

'You cannot get rid of me that easily,' she replied with a little laugh. Rafael took Mary in his arms and kissed her.

'I would never wish to do that,' he replied.

The couple did not emerge from their room for a day, a happy Lettie served food to them, and a sour-faced Sarita took the empty trays away.

Sarita drew Wilfredo aside, needing to speak urgently with him.

'They are back in love again. It must be time to tell him,' she said. Wilfredo nodded in agreement.

'Yes. We will give her one final chance, if she does not, we will tell him in front of her and watch,' Wilfredo said.

'I shall speak with her tomorrow.' Sarita replied smugly, anticipating the distressed reaction from Mary.

Rafael had been away two nights, and on the day of his return, Sarita requested an audience with Mary. Wary of the topic, Mary agreed reluctantly.

She stood by the fire in the solarium watching emotionless as Sarita entered the room and curtsied.

'*Senora*, Wilfredo and I have decided to tell our master about your secret on his return, unless you confess to him in front of us,' Sarita warned. Mary felt the fear pulsate through her body, but she would not let the evil woman before her know this.

'Why would my husband believe you over me, I am his wife,' Mary bravely said. Sarita raised her chin a little.

'We have been employed by him for many years, he trusts us. There are reasons for the *senorita's* incarceration,' Sarita replied. Mary met her gaze steadily.

'You cannot scare me anymore, Sarita. I shall explain all to Rafael, he will be angry with me, but anger passes,' Mary amazed herself at her calmness. Sarita's eyes narrowed.

'You are not welcome here, *senora*. You will leave once you know the truth about our master and *Senora* Pilar.'

'You may go now,' Mary answered turning her back. The woman mumbled something wicked under her breath and left the solarium. Once alone, Mary began to mull over Sarita's words. What did she mean in "the truth"? Mary decided it was just the ramblings of a mad woman. Neither Sarita nor Wilfredo would be happy until she left. This was something Mary had no intention of doing. Yet she decided to tell Rafael about her secret visits to *Casa de abeja* on his return. She had kept putting it off and knew she would rather tell her husband herself than have the two evil servants twist the story to discredit her.

His homecoming was, as always, a passionate reunion and gifts. Sarita and Wilfredo watched from the side as Mary greeted her husband ecstatically. Bemused with the adoration showered on him as he had only been gone for the two nights, Rafael welcomed the attention. She planned to tell him the next day; the night was not the time to divulge secrets. The admission could wait until tomorrow.

At breakfast, Mary was acutely aware of both Sarita and Wilfredo loitering in the hall while Rafael ate and talked. She felt uneasy and fearful of his reaction. However, if she did not tell him, the two servants were waiting to expose her secret. Mary took a deep breath. Her heart thumped and her throat was dry.

'Please leave, I wish to speak to my husband in private,' she said, attempting to sound calm and controlled. Rafael looked puzzled and turned in his chair to look at the servants expectantly. They remained. 'I said go now,' Mary said resolutely. The couple both bowed and departed obediently, hardly trying to hide their smiles of triumph. Rafael turned back to Mary.

'Maria, what is wrong?' he asked, and then his face lit up excitedly. '*Mi querido*, are you with child?'

'No, Rafael, it is not that. I have a confession to make to you,' Mary began. There was no going back. Rafael sat back in his seat, a scowl now covering his face, and he crossed his arms, waiting. 'When you were in Paris, I disobeyed you and went to *Casa de abeja*. I know that Isabel lives there.'

There was an awful silence. 'You did what?' Rafael growled low. 'You were under strict orders never to go near there. Why did you go? Have you already forgotten the vow you made before God on our wedding day to obey me?'

'Why did you not tell me the truth in the first place? Why is your daughter locked away there?'

'You would not understand. It happened long before I even met you. Is this how you repay my love, with waywardness?' Rafael replied. He stood up slowly and walked around the table to stand in front of Mary. 'You were happy here, I love you because you make my life happy again and now you wish to destroy everything we have. Why?' Rafael's voice rose in ferocity.

'I...' Mary began, standing up. Rafael raised a hand ready to strike her face, and then bellowing with rage, he brought his closed fist down on the table with such force, the plates and cups clattered to the floor, and his knuckles ran red with blood.

'You do not need to know what happened in my past. You are my today and tomorrow.' he shouted. 'Do not think this is the end of this. We shall speak again later. Get out of my sight; you disgust me!'

Mary fled sobbing through the doorway. Sarita and Wilfredo who were both waiting outside looked exultant as she ran past.

155

Wilfredo peered through the doorway at Rafael who was pacing up and down cursing loudly. He glared furiously at Wilfredo, who shrank back to keep his distance at this moment.

Sitting on her bed with Lettie for company, Mary had time to think deeply about the events of the past hours. She had never seen Rafael so angry and had never imagined he could ever strike her at all. Her curiosity was ruining everything. She had a husband whom loved her and she loved in return, and she had ruined it all. The servants had their wish; he would obtain a divorce and instruct her return to England. She would return shamed.

Hours later, Rafael entered the bedroom. Mary looked up at him through lowered lashes and saw his face still like thunder. His expression altered and he looked miserably at her. She looked up, trying to look brave, but felt terrified inside.

'Maria, after all I said, why did you go there?' he asked evenly, sitting on the edge of the bed. She moved away towards the door ready to make a quick escape.

'I was curious, that was all,' she replied quietly. 'Why did you lie to me about Isabel being in Madrid?' Rafael was silent for a while. He ran his bandaged hand over his face before speaking.

'Isabel was not like other children. She kept seeing demons when there was none to see. She accused me of killing her mother,' Rafael explained. 'She knew her mother and I did not like each other. When Manuela died, Isabel thought I had poisoned her.'

'Did you? Would you have hit me, Rafael?' she asked. He sighed looking shame-faced.

'I am no monster. I was very angry with you, Maria. I did not want you to know about Isabel, or meet her; she is dangerous and it is best she is alone. I implore you not to go back there again.' He held out his bandaged hand to Mary, who took it hesitantly. 'I am sorry, can you ever forgive me?' he asked. She looked into his face. He looked so regretful; she could not help but love him. Convincing herself she had caused his violent outburst; she herself was to blame.

'Is there any way Isabel could return to live here with us?' she asked tentatively.

'I should have told you, but I thought that if you knew I had an insane daughter, you would not agree to marry me. Isabel is cared for, she can never lead a normal life. She would try to harm us,' Rafael said, shaking his head and smiling weakly. Mary came and stood in front of him and touched his face.

'I married you, not Isabel,' she said gently. 'But you must know, Sarita and Wilfredo threatened to tell you if I said nothing. They both said I am not welcome here and wanted this to happen to break us apart. They also said to ask you to tell me the truth about Pilar.'

'What!' Rafael exclaimed paling in shock. 'The truth is that Pilar was universally loved by everyone here and whatever you say or do, in their eyes, you will never live up to the paragon everyone has made of her.' Rafael stood up and drew Mary into his arms. 'I am sorry again for what I have done. There will be no more secrets, Maria. I shall never raise a hand in anger to you again. I swear on my life,' Rafael assured placing his hand over his heart. Mary felt comforted and she believed him.

Arm in arm, they left the bedroom. Both Sarita and Wilfredo had been waiting close by, enjoying the prospect of seeing the marriage collapse before their eyes, and to see their master and mistress united was more than either could believe. Mary shot the two servants her own victorious look, and passed by safe in the knowledge that she and her husband were to be as strong together as before and all their scheming was for nothing.

Rafael paused and regarded his two servants coolly. 'I shall speak to you both later,' he warned.

However, Sarita and Wilfredo were resolute not to be defeated that easily. They began to plot again to rid themselves of the English woman, and this time nothing would stop them from succeeding.

# 25

Their marriage grew stronger and more content. Mary never returned to *Casa de abeja*, she felt she had no need to. Rafael's daughter had all the care she needed and would not cause trouble between them again. Sarita and Wilfredo had both received stern reprimands from Rafael. He warned them that they risked dismissal from service if either of them tried to cause a rift again. They apologised grudgingly in front of Rafael to Mary and promised to serve their new mistress dutifully from that day on. Even though they both gave their word, both had planned their next move.

Mary began to notice recognisable changes in her body, and knew the signs were telling her that she was pregnant again. Rafael's reaction was as she expected. He picked her up and swung her around laughing with delight. Then realising his actions may harm his unborn son, he gently lowered her to the ground and backed away apologising for any distress he may have caused her.

'Oh Rafael, you are a lovely man,' Mary laughe, pulling her husband to her. 'You know I am stronger than I look, you cannot hurt me.'

'I shall sleep elsewhere at night,' he said anxiously. Mary looked aghast.

'No, don't do that, I want you in the same bed as me,' she urged kissing his hands. He looked uncertain.

'But I may want to ravish you as you become more beautiful while my son grows inside you,' he said, genuinely worried.

'All I know is that I want you by my side during my time.'

Rafael had limited his trips away and spent no more than one night away before returning home. In the first months of her pregnancy, Mary became obsessed with the thought that Sarita and Wilfredo were trying to harm her. They kept suggesting that she would die in childbirth so would the child. Rafael dismissed her fears as nonsense. However, she did not feel placated by the assurance. He assured his worried wife that it was her condition addling her mind.

The months passed and Mary blossomed as her pregnancy advanced. Rafael was becoming an even more conscientious husband than before. Daily he would talk to her belly and sometimes the baby would respond and kick.

She spent most of her time inside her home, feeling uncomfortable and sheltering from the heat outside as her time drew near. Rafael had ceased his trips away now, wanting to spend as much time as he could with her. He became restless as the day of the birth approached. Mary tried to reassure him, but this seemed to have little impression. He was agitated and became short tempered with everyone in his fear of the oncoming birth.

The local midwife and Lettie assisted Mary throughout the delivery of the child. Rafael sat outside in the garden trying not to think of Pilar. He loved Mary more than he realised and could not bear to think of life without her. He walked through the garden, inspecting the flowers and bushes, but not really seeing them. He could hear Mary's distress from behind the shuttered windows of her bedroom, and he shuddered. Then after hours, there was the sound of a newborn infant crying. The bawling sounded strong and healthy. Rafael stopped and swung round to gaze up to the window, not hearing his gardener congratulate him. Hurriedly he ran back inside the house and sprinted two steps at a time up the stairs, skidding to a halt outside the closed door. He could hear excited talking and laughter. That was good. It meant the child was healthy and his wife had survived. Hesitantly, Rafael tapped on the door.

'Maria, can I come in?' he called. After a moment, Sarita, her face impassive, opened the door and allowed him to enter.

Mary was sittng up in bed holding the baby wrapped in a blanket. She looked exhausted, but happy to see her husband. Rafael was afraid; the scene seemed too perfect. Slowly, he approached the side of the bed.

'Rafael, look, God has given you a son,' Mary said holding the baby out. He took his son into his arms and looking at the small face gazing back at him, he burst out laughing.

'I thought I could only father daughters. He is beautiful, a gift from the angels. We shall call him Angelo,' Rafael announced proudly. He returned to Mary's side and handed Angelo back to his mother. He slid his hand behind her neck, brought her face close to his and they kissed warmly. 'You have made me the happiest man in all *Espana*. Thank you for Angelo.' He bowed to Mary and departed the bedroom. Behind the closed door and in absolute exuberance, he punched the air and danced victoriously down the corridor.

Mary soon recovered after the birth. Angelo became a happy baby who thrived on his parents' love. Rafael doted upon his son and Mary delighted at her life of domestic bliss.

It was now that Wilfredo decided to set his plan in action. He sat Sarita down and explained in detail the plan and its implementation. If all went accordingly, Rafael would throw Mary out of the house. The infant would remain as heir, which was acceptable. Sarita, laughing, threw her arms around Wilfredo's neck and praising his genius at such a simple but effective plan. He returned the kiss as a prelude to sex.

Rafael had left early one morning to travel to Pamplona and would be returning home late the next evening. Mary was happy left alone. She would find things to do to fill the days. Angelo now occupied most of her time, and the household accounts needed attention, Rafael left these for Mary now, though, he conducted the accounts for *Casa de abeja* himself. This he had insisted, and Mary was satisfied to let this continue.

She sat at a bureau calculating outstanding bills from tradesmen and totalling the monthly expenses. A sound from outside made her pause in her work; she looked up and thought she saw a figure moving in the garden, close to the window.

'Who is there?' she called but there was no reply. Standing and going to the window, Mary looked through the glass, but there was nobody visible. 'I must be seeing things,' she muttered to herself, shaking her head and returning to the accounts.

The following day, Rafael returned. The couple were able to spend a gratifying evening in the solarium, making love on the soft rug in front of the fire. They were unaware that, in the shadows, a figure, hidden from their sight was watching every movement with revulsion. The person crouched in the dark corner, not wanting detection just yet. They would wait until the morning. Revenge would be sweeter in the cold light of the day.

# 26

The following day, contentedly, Mary sat in a window seat in the solarium for the best light, sewing a shirt for Rafael; he was sitting by the fire studying documents. Angelo was asleep in his crib by Mary's side. The door slowly began to open and both Mary and Rafael looked up, neither had summoned service, and both were interested as to who was entering.

As a young woman appeared, Rafael drew a sharp intake of breath and his face drained of colour. It took Mary a few moments, and then she recognised the woman. It was Isabel. She closed the door, in her hand was a dagger with a jewelled handle. Rafael had mentioned several days before that the dagger had gone missing, and did Mary know where it could be.

Isabel was clothed in a plain brown gown, her hair hung loose over her shoulders. Eyes that were the same deep brown as Rafael fixed unemotionally on her father, unblinking.

'How did you get out?' Rafael asked slowly, his voice no more than a whisper. Isabel smiled slightly.

'I found this in my garden a few days ago, then the gate had been unlocked by someone yesterday, I pushed it, and it opened, so I decided to visit you, Papa and return this, I think it must be yours.' Isabel held out the knife blade outward, her calm voice sent a shiver of ice down Mary's spine Rafael looked towards her.

'It wasn't me,' she confessed. 'I had no idea where it had gone either.'

'The only person apart from me who has a key is Wilfredo,' Rafael said, ringing a bell that stood on the table Sarita entered the solarium. She appeared shocked seeing Isabel.

'Bring Wilfredo to me,' Rafael ordered. Sarita departed to return shortly with Wilfredo. Isabel greeted both with warm affability.

'Master, what is *Senorita* Isabel doing here?' he asked.

'I thought you might be able to tell me that,' Rafael said firmly. 'Where is your key to *Casa de abeja*?'

Wilfredo looked to his belt. 'It is here, although yesterday after Sarita and I visited the *Senorita,* I noticed it missing. I believed it must have come loose and fell to the ground. I found it again after a long search,' he lied.

Mary in her window seat watched and listened to the conversation with no desire to join in. Instinctively, she put a hand out to touch Angelo who murmured in his sleep.

'Is that your baby?' Isabel asked looking towards the crib.

'This is my son, Angelo,' Rafael replied quietly. Isabel's eyes shone fleetingly.

'I have a brother,' she exclaimed, looking in the crib, and laughed, but the laugh was maniacal, without humour. It disappeared as quickly as it came. 'I hope, Papa that you are not making him heir to your fortune. I am your first born,' Isabel said guardedly.

Rafael looked to Mary. 'Do you know anything about the missing key?' he asked her. She shook her head.

'I've not been back there since you found out,' she answered candidly. Sarita looked across with mock surprise.

'That was not what you told me, *senora,*' she said. Sarita then turned back to Rafael. 'She said she wanted to know *Senorita* Isabel and would find a way to get into *Casa de abeja*.' She said intently.

'That is a lie,' Mary snapped. Since the episode when Mary had exposed to him of Wilfredo and Sarita's deceit, Rafael was not sure whether to believe his housekeeper.

'Stop!' Isabel shouted edgily, putting a hand to her head. 'I want to talk with my father and the English woman.'

Sarita and Wilfredo moved towards the door to exit the solarium, just as Lettie entered, she had heard the noise and wanted to ensure her mistress was safe. Mary made a sign with her hand to keep Lettie at a distance. Sarita and Wilfredo's plan was going precisely the way they had intended, Isabel was behaving the way they wanted. She wandered across the solarium to stand before Mary, and unpredictably gave her a warm embrace.

'She died; and my father married you,' she said brightly, and then turned towards Rafael, her eyes swiftly overflowing with tears, and she spoke innocently as a child. 'Papa, why did you not come for me?'

'You are deranged, and wrong in your head,' he said crossly, tapping at his own head. 'You would have tried to hurt Maria.'

'I would love any woman that replaced that whore,' Isabel said laughing, and then turned back to Mary. 'Maria, did my father tell you how my mother died?'

'No, but death occurs,' Mary replied firmly. Isabel's eyes widened.

'Then you do not know how my mother died at my father's hands.' Isabel looked again at her father, waiting, wanting him to be the one to tell of his first wife's death. 'You killed my mother so you could marry that whore,' she spat maliciously.

'Isabel, you do not understand. Your mother and I never loved each other. I had to…' he stopped talking abruptly, looking quickly between his wife and daughter.

'But you did not have to murder her!' Isabel interrupted. Tears now began to flow, and her voice grew shrill. 'Tell her, tell her everything!'

Rafael looked at Mary's horrified face. From the other side of the solarium, Sarita and Wilfredo watched, eagerly. He breathed a long, heavy sigh and sat on the edge of a table. There was tense hush in the room before he began to speak in a low voice.

'All I told you about Manuela was true. We disliked each other from the very first day of our marriage. But for the sake of the contracts signed, we tried to tolerate each other, but neither of us could.' He looked at Isabel who was breathing hard. 'We consummated our marriage and by God's grace, Manuela conceived that very first coupling. Isabel was the result and we both loved her.' Rafael tried a pathetic smile at his daughter. 'But she did not bring us any closer together, and we stopped sharing a bed. Manuela led her own life, so did I. I took mistresses. They would come and go and mean nothing to me.'

'Get on with it!' Isabel shouted. Rafael looked fleetingly cross.

'Life continued until one of the women became important to me.'

'That whore!' Isabel growled.

'She was not a whore, Pilar was a beautiful and urbane woman who loved life and took an interest in what I liked,' Rafael smiled reflectively at the memory. 'She wanted to be your friend, Isabel, remember?'

Isabel grunted angrily. Rafael continued. 'We became lovers and over the months I began to realise that I was falling in love with her, and wanted to marry her.'

'But you were still married to Manuela,' Mary interjected. Rafael nodded.

'Yes I was. My family is prosperous; Manuela had royal blood in her veins, which gave her family the authority to dictate the terms of the contract. It stated that I could not divorce her. If I did, half of my estate would go to her, and she would reclaim her dowry, leaving me virtually homeless. My love for Pilar was now so strong; I knew I had to do something so that we could be together. I was prepared to risk everything for the woman I knew I loved.'

'You had to remove Manuela?' Mary said gradually, already beginning to know the comeback.

'If one of us died naturally, then the estate would go to the living partner. Manuela had to die,' Rafael explained. Isabel gave a loud sob. 'I sent Sarita to see an old woman who knew about herbs and potions, she gave her a powder. A little of it causes sickness, too much can result in death, Sarita gave me the powder and I sprinkled it onto Manuela's food and a little on mine so that we both became sick.' Rafael lowered his head. 'Isabel saw me administer the powder to the food and threatened to tell her mother of my plans. I grew angry with her and commanded Wilfredo to lock her in her room until I could think of what to do to her.' He looked again at Mary, ignoring Isabel's cursing from under her breath. 'We sat at the table and I watched as Manuela put the food into her mouth. I took a small bite from my meal...' His voice trailed away recalling that significant day. 'We both became violently sick. The plan worked, I retired to my bed with food poisoning, and Manuela retired to hers. She died a wretched death soon after.'

'You murdered Manuela,' Mary gasped, putting a hand over her mouth. Rafael nodded.

'It was the only way I could be with Pilar. Once we married, I thought Pilar and I would be happy for the rest of our lives. We tried to make Isabel see that I was happier than I had ever been, but she refused to acknowledge Pilar as a stepmother.'

'What do you expect?' Isabel interrupted. 'My mother was dead by your hands.'

'Your mother was not happy in our marriage, neither was I,' Rafael explained. Isabel glared in the direction of Mary, and stabbed a finger towards her father.

'This is the man you married, a murderer. There is more, tell her, Papa. Tell her how you came to lock me away for all those years,' Isabel said now turning to Mary.

'Isabel was caught trying to harm Pilar, by poisoning her food.'

'It worked for you!' she retorted unsympathetically.

'She tried to stab Pilar, but I caught her every time, and there were other attempts upon her life. Consequently, the only solution was to lock my daughter away where she could not harm my wife. The uninhabited *casa* was a suitable location. I told everyone that she had gone to live in Madrid with relatives, yet she was here all the time under lock and key. Wilfredo, Sarita, and Consuela were the only ones who knew the truth.'

'So did Pilar actually die because of the twins?' Mary asked slowly, not wanting to hear whether Rafael was telling the whole truth. For what seemed an eternity, he stood silently looking at her before speaking. Isabel lowered the blade, wanting to hear for herself the death of her despised stepmother.

'Pilar and I were deeply in love and very happy together. Everyone accepted the justification of Manuela's death and Isabel's absence without question. Everybody loved Pilar, and Pilar was an angel on earth. Nobody could dislike her.'

'Except for me, remember!' Isabel called. Rafael ignored his daughter.

'My life was to be complete when she became pregnant; the physician told her that she could be carrying twins! Imagine that. With a mother like Pilar, how could any child be anything but perfect?' Rafael's eyes shone brightly. 'Pilar was happy carrying our children,' he held out a hand to Mary, who remained where she now stood.

'Her confinement was early, it was long and complicated, I shall never understand about childbirth, but I listened and waited at the closed door as women came and went. This went on for days. Eventually the midwife came and told me I had two daughters, but they were both small and weak.'

'What happened?' Mary whispered, knowing herself the pain of losing her own infants.

'The girls were both so very small and shared a crib together. Pilar was looking ill, she was crying, we both knew our girls would not live and named them Alta and Amada. I sent for the Padre and we had them baptized immediately.'

'Amada died two days after birth and Alta soon after. Pilar changed from the beautiful, laughing woman I knew; she became despondent and strange. I could not comprehend the state of her mind. Yet I still loved her and was prepared to wait as long as it took until she recovered.' Rafael paused, choosing his words carefully. 'When I came to England and saw you, I realised I no longer loved Pilar, I was fooling myself. She would never become my beautiful wife again. You were so forlorn; I wanted to make you laugh. I wanted to make love to you, to make you happy again.' He laughed briefly, recalling a moment from that visit to Markham. 'Remember, I wanted you to come away with me to France.'

'If I had gone away with you, you would have given up all of this for me? You would have left Pilar on her sick bed?' Mary interrupted. Rafael nodded.

'I would have given everything up in a heartbeat if it meant you would become my woman,' he confirmed. 'When I returned home, I put you out of my mind. You had resisted me, a challenge that had failed; I knew I would never see you again, yet because of you, I began to detest my wretched little wife. She hung onto the past, refusing to realise that life goes on. I moved on and took lovers again.' Rafael poured himself wine and drunk it silently. When he had finished, he continued. 'I moved to Madrid and gained a position at the Spanish court in the service of Ambassador Chaprys and accompanied him to the English court. So imagine how I felt when I saw you. There you were, more beautiful than I remembered. I had to have you. You played the coquette to me; I would have taken you on the floor in front of the king himself if I had the opportunity to.' His short laugh was hollow.

'But Pilar was still alive at this time?' Mary asked. 'You told me in France that she was dead.'

Rafael shrugged. 'To me she already was.' His voice altered and became insensate. 'She had to go.'

'Would you have divorced her?' Mary said quietly. His eyes now became as cold as his voice.

'Divorce would have taken too long. She had to go quickly.'

'Did you mean kill her?' Mary assumed.

'Kill her,' Isabel echoed indistinctly.

'There was no other choice. You accepted my marriage proposal.'

'Because I thought Pilar was dead,' Mary breathed.

'When I told you I had to return home on urgent business, there was no such business. I returned home to rid myself of the unwanted baggage.'

'Is that how you saw Pilar after we met, "unwanted baggage"?' Mary exclaimed. Rafael nodded silently and swallowed more wine.

'How did you do it?' Isabel asked enthusiastically with intensifying excitement.

Rafael shrugged. 'After you kill once, to kill again is easy, but I could not use poison a second time,' he explained grimly. 'I needed her out of the way quickly.' He looked around the solarium. 'She was standing by that window, looking out, I had a cord in my hands, and I came up behind her, I pulled the cord around her throat. She tried to struggle, tried to call for help. I tightened the cord until she stopped breathing.' Rafael re-enacted the actions slowly. 'I carried her to our bed and left her there. During the night, Wilfredo assisted me to dispose of the body. I told everybody that Pilar with her unhinged mind had left me during the night. They believed me, they believe anything I say.' He gasped and looked up at Mary and Isabel, as though seeing them for the first time.

Mary looked between her husband and Wilfredo. 'You murdered her with your own hands?' she uttered, shaken by his admission.

'Yes,' breathed Isabel jubilantly.

Rafael sighed profoundly. 'That is why they never liked you, Maria; Wilfredo knew I killed Pilar to make way for you, and he poisoned Sarita's mind against you.'

It all suddenly made sense to her; the inexplicable trip falls and near misses from falling objects since arriving at the hacienda. Wilfredo and Sarita were attempting to kill her in retribution for Pilar's death. Sarita now hung her head, shamed.

'Everything you have told me has been a lie. Rafael, how could you be the man I thought you were. You are a cold-hearted killer and a liar. Did you every truely love me?' Mary cried.

'I was seduced by you, Maria; you were a woman fertile and ripe for the taking.' Rafael repeated earnestly stepping towards Mary who backed away, staggered by his confession. 'I thought I would never see you again. So when I did, I wanted to be with you for the rest of my life.'

'You said that to Pilar once. What would have happened to me if you found another woman you loved and wanted to marry? Would I have been unwanted baggage to be removed too?'

'Never, Maria, you are my one true love, you gave me Angelo!' Rafael exclaimed moving forward once more. Isabel growled and raised the dagger.

'My mother died because of you, you killed that whore to marry this woman. I can forgive you that, but you killed my mother!' Isabel shouted. 'Why could you not tell me? I would have been your loving daughter again.' Rafael turned to face her.

'Daughter, you do not comprehend anything of life,' he began. Isabel laughed hysterically.

'Of course not, I was thirteen when you locked me away from a world I wanted to be a part of! I have never known the gentleness of a man's touch, felt his tender kiss upon my lips. I never had anyone to talk with, only Consuela that fat old bat.'

'It was for your own good,' Rafael argued.

'For *your* own good you mean. Me out of the way, you and that whore could play at being happy families together while the world forgot me, forgot that I even existed. *Isabel? Who is Isabel? She was Rafael Perez's daughter once.* That is all I became, an afterthought.' Isabel shrieked.

They began vehemently arguing. Mary picked Angelo up from his crib and moved backwards to keep out of their way, sensing this dramatic moment was reaching its culmination.

Wilfredo and Sarita were looking from Rafael to Isabel,

following their argument intensely. The plan was now going wrong, neither had intended to see their master in danger, Wilfredo had planted the jewelled dagger for Isabel to find in order to dishonour Mary, not to harm his master.

Mary felt she would be safer by Lettie's side, so she edged around the solarium to stand beside her maid and the two servants. Sarita smiled faintly at her and held out a supportive hand for her to take. Mary refused the gesture of reconciliation. Standing by the door, she made no movement, terrified that Isabel might turn the knife on her or Angelo. Rafael had dropped his arms to his side, and attempted to talk steadily to mollify his daughter's hysteria. Isabel's shoulders were now heaving with immense sobs, and she began waving the dagger erratically through the air at Rafael.

'You deserve to die, I deserve to be orphaned!' she screamed frenziedly, and then with an ear-splitting scream ran at her father, the blade tearing deep into Rafael's flesh as it penetrated his shoulder. He cried out in pain, staggered back falling, clasping at the wound as blood squeezed between his fingers, and ran down his shirt, staining it violent red. Mary screamed and ran forward to her husband; Wilfredo threw himself onto Isabel, wrestling her to the ground, pinning her down as she thrashed about trying to get free. He shouted to Sarita to get help. Lettie dropped to her knees beside Mary, taking a howling Angelo from her. She began tearing strips of material from her dress to try to stop the bleeding. Rafael lay there groaning in pain, his bloodied hand still holding the jewelled hilt of the knife. From the other side of the solarium, Isabel was screaming at Wilfredo to let her go so she could finish the task she had set out to do, and kill her father. Two grooms ran into the solarium and instantaneously came to a halt at the sight which greeted them.

'Get her out of here! Lock her back in that place; I never want to see her again!' Mary screamed frenziedly pointing towards Isabel. The three men pulled Isabel to her feet and dragged her struggling in the direction of the door. She turned and glared crazy-eyed at her stepmother.

'Just try. This place is mine when he is dead. You and that *mocoso* of yours can go back to your cold island and rot!' Isabel spat she was dragged away still screaming, to wait for her fate to be determined. Mary turned her attention back to Rafael who was trembling, his breath ragged.

'It is not too bad, I think,' he said shakily, Mary stroked his damp forehead affectionately, all memories of his revelations abruptly forgotten in the intensity of the moment.

'I will get you to your bed and the physician shall come and tend to you,' she guaranteed. With help, Rafael got slowly to his feet, and with care was carried to his bedroom. He fell heavily onto the white sheets, splattering blood, and lay there, now incapable to speak while Mary cleaned the wound with water brought to her in a bowl. The physician seemed to take a long time to arrive, and when he did, she waited outside the closed door, pacing up and down. He finally appeared and closed the door behind him so he could speak to Mary.

'Your husband should make good recovery. I have applied a poultice, and secured the wound. He sleeps now, let him rest.' The physician bowed and departed. She carefully pushed open the door and peered in to see Rafael, as the physician had said, sleeping. Finally she was able to relax, and she felt herself begin to shudder and a vast sorrow begin to engulf her as she realised their life together had been a lie. Tears rolled down her cheeks and she began to sob, her shoulders heaving to every raw intake of breath. He had survived the attack; yet her feelings for him could never be the same again. Slowly sinking to the floor, incapable now to stand, she cried realising just how much she had loved him. Sarita, now disgraced by her actions, assisted Lettie and they took Mary to her own bed where she lay, until at length exhausted, she fell into a troubled sleep.

The next day, Mary awoke feeling ready to tend to her wounded husband. In his bed, Rafael was propped in a sitting position. He looked sallow, yet his face lit up when Mary with Angelo came to his bedside.

'Maria, *mi querido,* you need to keep yourself strong, I shall be fine,' he urged. Mary, shaking her head, sat on the edge of the bed.

'Whatever your say, I am caring for you until you are well again,' she insisted and refused to listen to Rafael's protests. She enjoyed the responsibility of nurse and spent hours in his company, changing his bandage, bathing the wound and talking about their future. The

171

revelations disclosed never mentioned. By the end of each day, Mary retired to bed exhausted. Rafael's resurgence would take a long time, but as a dutiful wife, she cared for him with no complaint.

It had been a week since the attack, and Rafael had contracted a fever. He lay in his bed perspiring, trembling as the fever took grip, and he became recurrently delirious. When Mary was able to remove the bandage to clean the wound, the area around the puncture was swelling and changing colour. His skin felt cold to the touch. In lucid moments, Rafael complained of a great pain to his shoulder, scorching through his upper torso and travelling down his arm. The wound still was not healing. Worried, she sent for the physician to see what his diagnosis was.

He examined Rafael in one of his lucid moments, applying leeches to drain the poison from his blood.

Once alone with Mary, the physician indicated to a chair for her to sit down as the news he was to share was not good.

'*Senora*, your husband's blood has become poisoned and it is spreading through his body. I have bled him and I shall return to do so again.' He took a phial from the bag he carried and handed it to Mary. 'This is poppy juice; it dulls the pain and will keep him comfortable. I will do everything I can for him. Pray for a miracle, *senora*, God sometimes listens,' he said unhappily.

After his departure, Mary went into Rafael's bedroom, sat on his bed, and looked at him. The man who lay before her was a pale shadow of what he once had been. He was looking old and feeble now as he lay there, drifting in and out of consciousness.

Mary tucked the coverlet of the bed. 'I shall stay by your side, Rafael. You will not be alone and I shall pray for a miracle. If I pray hard enough, God may hear me.'

Over the subsequent days, and true to her word, Mary sat by her husband. Occasionally, he would recognise her and the old Rafael she had once fallen in love with would briefly appear. Most of the time, he would throw himself restively about in his bed, swearing and cursing. Mary continued her vigil, through her husband's fever induced behaviour.

The physician tried everything in his knowledge to save Rafael's life, though he knew all of his efforts would end in failure. The end would be soon now.

It arrived. Mary summoned the servants to assemble around the bed and with her quietly wait for death to come.

Rafael gave a sigh and opened his eyes to look for the last time upon his English wife and child.

'Mi *querido*.' he whispered faintly and raised a trembling hand to touch her face. Grasping at his hand, Mary, blinded by tears, kissed it and tried to smile at him. She placed Angelo in the crook of his arm. The small boy cooed contentedly and smiled. Rafael looked at his son, and smiled barely, his misty eyes shut. He gave one gasp and was still.

'Rafael,' Mary whispered lifting Angelo back up. 'Go and be with God now.'

From the gathered servants, there were prayers spoken for their master's departed soul. Gradually, they all left while Wilfredo hung back, wanting to speak to Mary.

'We wanted our master to cast you aside because you were the reason he murdered *Senora* Pilar, but we did not wish this to happen,' he said quietly. Mary looked at him. Her eyes void of emotion.

'At this moment, I could not care less. Just get out of my sight, Wilfredo,' she said frostily. Bowing, Wilfredo backed out, leaving Mary alone to pray silently until Lettie led her away and put her to bed, giving her a sleeping draught.

Mary awoke the next day confused and sat up calling for Rafael before remembering his death. Lettie, who had slept in a chair, came and sat on the bed beside Mary and gathered her mistress to her, crooning quietly. She felt too numb to cry, she just allowed herself to stay in Lettie's arms, listening to the regular heartbeat.

'What is to become of us, Lettie?' Mary asked, looking up into Lettie's face. Lettie smiled gently at her mistress.

'Do not worry about that yet, mistress. We can think about things like that on the morrow.'

Mary pulled away sharply. 'Angelo!' she cried looking around.

'He is safe in the nursery,' Lettie assured.

'Bring him to me now. I want to see him.'

Lettie called out and requested that the child to be brought to Mary. The waiting servant departed and returned soon after with the nurse. Mary held out her arms to receive her son and looked lovingly into the face of the child.

'Sweetness, your father loved you dearly from the moment you were born, I shall not let you forget him,' Mary whispered in English. 'I want my son to sleep in the same room as me tonight,' she said louder in Spanish. Servants fetched the crib into the bedroom and Mary settled down again to try to sleep, knowing her child was close by.

Later in the day, the realisation of what had happened began to dawn upon Mary, she locked herself in the room with Rafael's body, and stayed there with him, crying wildly, venting her fury to him for the passion and the deception he took to their marriage. She did not allow anyone to enter to bring her either food or comfort. He looked serene in the freshly made bed, dressed in a crisp white nightshirt, hiding the ugly scar on his shoulder where the dagger had penetrated. Although she knew it would not happen, her husband looked as if he might open his eyes at any moment, sit up, smile with delight, and welcome his wife.

Exhausted, Mary left her dead husband's side as night fell. She strangly felt at peace now, accepting Rafael's death and had cried all the tears she would shed. Now would be time to arrange the funeral and to think about her future.

On a chilly and wet morning, a sad procession left the hacienda and wound its way towards the old church in the hills for the funeral service. Mary followed the coffin on her horse and the servants, who had requested to attend, followed behind on mules and foot. As Mary dismounted, she looked up, feeling the rainfall on her face.

'It was raining on the day we married,' she observed almost to herself.

The Padre stood in the doorway, waiting for the party, when everyone was ready he led the way into the cold church.

As the Padre's voice droned on and the scent of insence filled the church, Mary sat thinking. Two starkly contrasting marriages and widowed for a second time. Why had providence been this cruel towards her? What had she done so wrong to receive punishment like this? Her mind wandered to Henry's funeral. She had been glad of his demise. Now, her emotions were in shreds, and inside she was screaming. It would not be easy to live in Spain, no longer protected by her husband.

# 27

Mary's life settled down to routine after the funeral. She had quickly decided upon the future for herself and summoned Wilfredo and Sarita to speak with them. They came sheepishly into the solarium. Mary stood in front of the fireplace looking calm and composed. She made them wait uncomfortably for several minutes before speaking.

'In light of the recent events, I have come to the decision about this hacienda, my future, and the future of my son. I shall grant you your wish and leave as soon as I am able to. I cannot live here anymore.'

Wilfredo gasped and Mary continued. 'I shall not sell this place to anyone, but I will leave it to Isabel, though Angelo is the rightful heir and should inherit it. I do not want my son growing up where there has been murder, lies and treachery. So, Wilfredo, I want you to take me to *Casa de abeja* so I can speak directly to Isabel herself.'

'Mistress, *Senorita* Isabel knows nothing about estate management,' Sarita exclaimed. Mary shrugged her shoulders.

'When I am gone, I shall not care. You wanted me out of the way; it will be up to everyone here to cope. My Angelo will come with me, as I shall be returning to England. I have sold much of the furniture which is to be collected before my departure; I am taking with me back to England mementos of a husband, who I once loved more than life itself.'

Wilfredo and Sarita exchanged incredulous glances. Mary made a gesture to depart the solarium. 'Take me to Isabel now,' she commanded.

The servants led the way past the out buildings towards the *Casa de abeja*. Wilfredo unlocked the gate and pushed it slowly open. For the first time, Mary was able to get an unhindered view of where Isabel lived.

The painted white rotund walls and a red tiled roof stood solidly surrounded by a beautiful garden of luscious grass and vibrant flowers. It looked very tranquil.

'There were bee hives in the fields nearby. The honey was collected and taken here. We had our share and the rest sold to villagers. That is how it got its name, *Casa de abeja*. The bee house,' Sarita explained. Mary ignored her, walking up to the door and rapping firmly on it. After a short wait, the door opened and a plump, middle-aged woman with black hair streaked with grey pulled tightly back into a bun stood glaring irritably at her. Mary recognised her as that malicious, angry woman who had shouted at her the first time she had spoke to Isabel.

'Who are you and what do you want?' she demanded. Wilfredo stepped forward.

'Consuela, this is *Senora* Maria. She is Don Rafael's widow,' he said. Consuela looked Mary up and down disdainfully.

'His widow? He is dead?' she echoed. 'I know you; you are the one who has snooped around before,' Consuela added, now recognising Mary.

'Rafael was murdered by the hand of his daughter,' Mary replied steadily. Consuela narrowed her eyes. 'I want to speak with her immediately,' she continued. Consuela grudgingly stepped aside to allow Mary to enter. The *casa's* interior was cool. Furnishings were simple but comfortable. Consuela indicated to a table and chairs.

'Wait there, I shall get the *Senorita*,' she said and vanished through a doorway. Her stern voice and Isabel's animated reply was heard answering. Running footsteps came down the stairs and Isabel burst into the room as she looked towards Mary.

'Is it true? Is he dead? Why was I not told?' Isabel rattled off questions in one breath.

'He died from a stab wound.' Mary said emphatically. Isabel giggled with rising hysteria.

'Finally I am rid of him,' she abruptly turned serious. 'So what are you doing here, I thought I would be the last person you would want to see.'

'You are, Isabel. There is not a single person in the world I would rather see less of than you. But there is something I am going to do for you.' Mary sat on the chair looking up at Isabel. Consuela had now descended the stairs and was looking distrusting at Mary over Isabel's shoulder. 'Soon, I shall be taking my son and returning home to England. From that day, this estate will be yours. My child shall know about his Spanish ancestry. I will tell him that an insane woman murdered his father. May God give him vengeance on you.' Mary stood up and met Isabel's gaze unblinking. 'I loved Rafael and your madness has taken him from me.

'He killed two wives and locked me away in here,' Isabel reminded. 'If he found another woman he claimed to love, he would have killed you as well.'

'Then I should thank you for probably saving my life, we shall never know.' Mary turned to leave the room. 'The place is to be yours. Do with it as you will. Until the day I depart, you shall remain locked in here.' She glanced at Wilfredo and Sarita. 'Come,' she commanded calmly.

'You cannot keep me in here now! Papa is dead and I am free!' Isabel shouted. She ran towards Mary and grabbed her shoulder. Mary swung round on a heel and brought her hand across Isabel's face with a vicious smack, sending her stepdaughter crashing on to the chair, then the floor.

'I am mistress here and you will obey me, Isabel. You stay. When I leave, you are released.' With dignity, she departed *Casa de abeja,* ensuring Wilfredo locked the gate behind them. Isabel and Consuela, from behind the gate, could be heard screaming obscenities, yet she walked undaunted and with assurance back to the hacienda.

Preparations were under way to leave. Clothes were packed in chests; the valuables Mary was to take with her were loaded onto carts for the journey to the docks. The galleon they were to return to England had the name *The Ignite,* captained by Howard Foyle, an Englishman with many years experience at sea.

A neighbouring landowner purchased Zachariah, Rafael's black stallion, as Mary wanted to ensure the magnificent Andulusian would be cared for, and not left at the mercy of Isabel.

Mixed emotions swirled around inside Mary on the day of departure. Slowly, she walked through the hacienda, reliving the happy days spent with Rafael. The bed they had shared passionate nights in the rug in front of the fire in the solarium where again they had made love. Every room seemed to have a memory of intimacy.

With a sad sigh, she walked through the door. The deal for transfer of tenure to Isabel was underway. When Mary reached the docks and Wilfredo returned with the horses and carts, he would then release her.

Lettie was already on her horse, with Angelo in her crooked arm. Mary looked back one last time and mounted her horse. The gathered servants watched her silently. She smiled at their upturned faces.

'Good luck for the future. Thank you for accepting me into your home, most of you,' she said and looked toward Wilfredo then Sarita who lowered her gaze. 'Goodbye to everyone.' She turned her horse and rode past the fountain and out of the gate, Wilfredo driving the horse and cart following close behind. She kept looking directly ahead, not wanting to look back, the reminiscences were still fresh and painful in her mind. Another phase of her life was ending. In two, maybe three weeks time, she would be back home in England, safe within the walls of Yardeley Chase, cocooned from pain and suffering. A quiet rural life now waited for her, and Mary was eager to return.

The party reached Santurlzi and it was easy to spot *The Ignite;* stoutly built and fast by reputation, it was small next to the elegant, large Spanish galleons. The first mate was seeing to the loading of provisions onboard and greeted Mary with a well-mannered bow.

'Captains apologies, ma'am, he is detained on business before we depart. I am Dalton.' He looked at Wilfredo who was unloading the cart. 'I'll get the crew to help bring your cargo aboard.' He turned back to face *The Ignite* and gave a loud whistle. Men hurried down the gangway and began to take Mary's belonging and stowed them away where they would be safe.

She looked at Wilfredo and sighed. 'I am sorry to be leaving Spain, it is a beautiful country, but circumstances prevail and I cannot stay here any longer,' she said. Wilfredo met Mary's gaze with a churlish expression, remaining defiant to the end.

'Your inquisitiveness put into motion events that led to the death of my master. He would still be alive today if it was not for you,' he replied indifferently. Mary knew Wilfredo's intimidation could no longer harm her.

'Think what you want to. I loved being married to Rafael and he loved me in return, whatever had happened.' Mary signalled to Lettie to follow her up the gangplank onto the ship's deck. She turned to look once more at Wilfredo. He was already was on road that led out of Santurlzi. She turned her gaze towards the city of Bilbao and the hills that lay further on. The last four years spent in Spain had predominantly been happy for her. That was the same number of years her marriage to Henry had lasted. Two short and blatantly contrasting marriages, filled with terror, fear and intense passion. No more, Mary decided, marriage was to be a past tense for her now.

Dalton came and stood behind Mary. 'Ma'am, we will set sail on the morning tide, I'll show you to your sleeping quarters, if you'll follow me, please,' he said. Mary and Lettie followed him below deck, down steep steps to a dark, small cabin. It was nothing like the cabin on their voyage from England. Dalton saw Mary's distain and shrugged his shoulders. '*The Ignite* is not built for lady passengers; it's the best that I can offer you. You both are the only women on board, so keep yourself to yourselves. If the captain is inclined, he may let you share his quarters,' he said, and then with a bow, left Mary to become familiar to her quarters.

'Well, the Spanish knew how to treat their guests.' Mary ultimately said as she gazed around the dingy cabin that stank of brine and pitch. There were no beds, only hammocks strung from side to side, and an ancient table with two stools.

'I think I shall spend as much time up on deck with Angelo to keep him in the fresh air. It'll be a long voyage,' Mary said, taking him from Lettie. 'I wonder how disciplined the crew are here? Captain Humberto kept his crew under control.'

Lettie began to giggle a little, remembering her clandestine meetings with Carlos. Mary regarded Lettie with a wry smile.

'It's a shame Carlos can't be here to look after us,' she remarked knowing what her maid was thinking.

'We must converse in English again; we are returning home and I hope the captain will engage in civil conversation,' Mary contemplated.

Dalton rapped sharply on the closed door.

'Ma'am, Captain Foyle is on deck and will speak with you at your earliest convenience,' he said. Mary turned to Lettie and nodded.

'See, we shall speak and I will try to get a more equitable accommodation for us,' Mary announced and ascended the steps to reach the deck.

Captain Foyle was standing watching two busty women edge their way down the gangplank. Hearing Mary approaching, he looked round and he smiled broadly.

'Mary Perez, I've been expecting you,' Foyle said heartily. 'You married a Spanish gent. What's he done to make you up and leave him?'

'He died,' Mary replied flatly. Foyle looked fleetingly shocked.

'Blow me, that's not a good start, is it? Sorry missy,' his humour quickly returned. 'So, you are going back home now. I expect to make landfall at Portsmouth in about two weeks.'

'Portsmouth!' Mary exclaimed. 'I thought we were going to Tilbury, I need to go to Tilbury.'

'Not going near Tilbury this time. It is Portsmouth or you stay here, your choice.'

'I was told you were going to Tilbury,' Mary argued impatiently. Aggravated, Foyle looked sternly into her eyes.

'Then you believe wrong missy,' he retorted. Mary could do nothing about the situation; she had nowhere to stay in Santurlzi, and could not return to the hacienda.

'Then its Portsmouth,' she said with a small voice. Foyle rocked with an explosion of laughter at his victory.

'While you are onboard, you will have the same rations as my crew. There will be nothing more, and nothing less. No mollycoddling on my ship,' he added, and then bowled away down the gangplank to argue with a merchant who was counting barrels that stood on the quayside waiting to be stowed.

'Obviously not,' Mary mumbled resentfully under her breath.

After an uncomfortable night spent in the hammocks, Mary

ventured on deck at first light to watch *The Ignite*, on the morning tide, pull slowly away from the dock. She watched silently as the coastline began to recede before her eyes. A jumble of memories tumbled around in her mind. Rafael had been a lover, a delighted father to Angelo, a liar, a wife killer, a feeble man dying in his bed, the corpse now cold in his grave. Mary was leaving Spain a stronger woman because of him.

From the moment *The Ignite* left Spain, Mary was aware of the crew regarding her and Lettie with dour expressions; she felt her presence onboard was not welcomed. Captain Foyle had threatened his crew if any of them even considered vulgar thoughts about either of the female passengers. Mary had paid well for the passage to England, she and her attendant were to have the respect shown at all times. This gave her some small comfort, but she still did not feel completely secure. Most women sailors knew were whores and doxies, not women of breeding. Nevertheless, she spent time on deck with her son.

The first week of the voyage was quiet, as Captain Foyle had expected, small squalls rocked and drenched *The Ignite* as the galleon traversed the Bay of Biscay. Carried along by the tides and buffeted by strong winds, making the sails swell out, straining against each blast of air. Still, Mary remained on deck for as long as it was safe even when she was soaked to the skin by the waves crashing over the side of the ship; she kept a tight hold of Angelo, who appeared to be enjoying the experience. He chortled and clapped his baby hands together. One of the sailors observed that he seemed to be a born sailor.

*The Ignite* was now heading north west, on course for Portsmouth and a day in advance than its captain had anticipated. Before long, they would see land for the first time, and then navigate the Solent and into Portsmouth harbour.

Foyle summoned Mary to his quarters. At the appointed hour and with trepidation, she stood before the closed door. Captain Foyle, although appearing to be a man who stood no nonsense had until now behaved impeccably towards her. Would he make a move now? She tapped lightly on the door and a shout to enter came from inside.

Mary pulled up the latch and stepped into the captain's cabin. The cabin looked familiar with instruments and charts Mary had seen on board the *Santo Philippe* on the outward voyage, except that Captain Humberto had good taste. Captain Foyle's cabin was austere in contrast, only practical furniture was available. Foyle was standing at his desk; compass in his hand plotting the course for the following hours. Without looking up, he pointed silently to a chair. Mary went and sat down, waiting for what would happen next. When Foyle finished, he straightened up and stretched his arms above his head, yawning widely.

'This has been an easy voyage; you brought good weather with you,' he observed glancing out of the window at the fading light, and scratching his bearded chin. Mary remained silent. 'Wondering why I'd sent for you?' She nodded, still keeping silent. Foyle looked hard at Mary's face and an unhurried smile began to spread across his own. He now rubbed his beard and a chuckle caught in his throat. 'You think I'm going to ravish you?' He inquired.

'I don't know,' Mary replied quietly. She felt uncomfortable in his company. The captain was tall and broad, a man no one would dare cross. If he was going to assault her, there was nothing she would be able to do to stop him. He could easily overpower a woman like herself. Foyle sat back in his chair and linked his fingers behind his head staring sombrely at Mary before speaking.

'It's true I like the feel of a woman's flesh against my own. It is something I do not enjoy often, being at sea. My wife satisfies me in the marriage bed.' He saw Mary tense. 'But don't worry, missy, I have no intention of shafting you, I prefer my women to be willing, you wouldn't be, would you?' His eyes twinkled with the thoughts invading his mind of a tussle with a woman fighting to protect her virtue.

'No,' Mary said in a small voice. Captain Foyle spoke again.

'I have a proposition to put to you, missy.' He began, standing up. 'I don't know whether he ever told you, but your first husband Henry Crawford was my cousin. My mother was sister to his father.' Mary sat back in her chair surprised at this disclosure. William or Henry had never mentioned this in all the time she had known them. 'William would write to my mother to tell her about

Henry, his marriage to a sweet young girl, and the birth of your daughter. See, I know all about your earlier life.'

Mary felt confused. 'But how do you know it was me buying passages home?' she then asked.

'William wrote to say how both Eleanor and you were smitten by a Spaniard called Perez who visited. It was a long shot, but when an English maid came to the docks to book passages home from Spain for two women in the name of Perez, I took a chance it could be you, and you were you! Your maid expressed Tilbury as your port of destination. I had to get you onboard somehow, so I said, *"Aye, I am bound for Tilbury,"* It worked.' Foyle announced exultantly. 'You are almost exactly as William described, he was very fond of you and worried about the treatment you received from his son.'

'So why didn't you tell me this earlier?' Mary asked, Foyle strode around his cabin.

'I ramble now. To business: your daughter, what was her name?' He continued, ignoring Mary's question.

'Cecily.' she answered.

'She must be approaching marriageable age now, how old is she?'

'My daughter is twelve.'

'I have a son, Ambrose, about fifteen. What say you to our children becoming betrothed?' Foyle suggested. Mary was speechless. He began to pace the floor. 'What dowry would she bring with her?'

'Wait, wait, captain, this is all too much for me,' Mary said. 'I have not considered Cecily's future. Why would she have to marry? Why could she not do whatever she desired with her life?'

'A woman cannot be expected to make her own way in life alone,' Foyle argued.

'What if Cecily does not want marriage?'

'Women are born to obey and pleasure men and bear their sprogs. Your girl and my son, nothing could be better.' He was unwavering in his argument. Mary refused the bullying into submission. She stood up and looked Captain Foyle straight in the eye.

'Please, captain, do not expect me to give you an answer immediately. I must think this over,' she said firmly. Foyle inclined his head.

'Very well, missy. When we reach Portsmouth, I insist you stay at my home before you journey home. My wife and children will be pleased to provide lodgings for you. You can give me your decision then,' the captain conceded.

'How many children do you have?' Mary asked.

'Ambrose is my only son. I have five daughters for my sins. I named my girls after treasures I have relieved from the Spanish and French. The eldest two are married. The others live at home still, so your girl would not want for female company.'

Mary crossed to the door and looked back.

'Please, Captain Foyle, let me think this over,' she said again and departed the cabin to walk across the deck, pausing to look out to sea. In the distance, she thought she could see a thin, grey smudge on the horizon that would be the coastline of England. Looking up, she watched the darkening, moonless evening sky and the first stars appear. This was so much information for her to take in. Throughout her stay in Spain, Mary had not given Cecily or her future not much thought, to her shame. The last time she had spent time with her daughter, the little girl had expressed a desire to one day marry; girls either married or became nuns. There had to be much thought about Cecily and Ambrose. Mary decided to hold back on a decision until she met Ambrose and his sisters.

The thin grey smudge grew bigger and began to change as the coastline came more into view. Ahead the sharp jagged rocks that jutted out into the sea from the west tip of the Isle of Wight were an imposing sight as *The Ignite* sailed past. Mary watched as the island to the starboard and the mainland to portside revealed more and more detail. Small fishing boats sailed past, reminding her of her arrival in Santurlzi. Mary, holding Angelo, stood at the side of the ship as they sailed efficiently towards the dock. Moored close by were galleons of the English fleet. Two seemed to command notice. Foyle informed Mary that they were *The Great Harry* and *Mary Rose*.

'They are fine looking vessels,' Mary observed approvingly. Foyle nodded and looked admiringly around his own galleon.

'*The Ignite* is a fine craft, and I have earned the position to captain her. However, I desire to captain one of those.'

*The Ignite* moved slowly alongside the dock and gently bumped against the wooden boons. Foyle ordered Mary's luggage brought on deck. On the dockside, there were women waiting, waving and calling out names. Some of the crew shouted back. Mary looked to see if any of them could possibly have been Captain Foyle's family, but he seemed too busy to notice whether his wife or any of his daughters were present. As requested, Mary and Lettie followed him down the gangplank back onto English soil. Someone found a barrow and waited with it laden for the captain and his guests.

'We'll walk,' Foyle said. 'It feels good to have solid ground under your feet, doesn't it?' he added, stamping away the weeks at sea. Mary was not so sure about this, she had expected at least some kind of carriage for her to ride in, but said nothing. He was lodging her in his home and she had to be grateful for that.

They walked through the town until they came to a narrow street with large town houses erected along it with gables leaning over and almost touching, blocking out much of the sunlight. Women leant from the open widows in the gables gossiping to each other in loud voices, complaining about the price of bread from the local baker and how much the vintner and brewers was now charging for barrels of wine and ale. Children played noisily up and down the filthy street; excited dogs ran alongside the children, barking loudly. From a windowsill, a cat sat haughtily watching the children and dogs. This sight of chaos made Captain Foyle's face break into a wide grin.

'Here we are, missy, home,' he announced, stopping in front of a closed door. Taking a key from a pocket in his jerkin, Foyle unlocked the door and pushed it open, shouting out a greeting as he stepped over the threshold. Excited voices came from deep inside the house and the sound of feet running.

A slim woman cradling an infant, followed by two young girls appeared from the other side of an internal door and all three threw themselves at Foyle. He disentangled himself and turned towards Mary and Lettie.

'Susannah, this woman is our guest, newly arrived from Spain,' Captain Foyle announced. Susannah Foyle pushed past her husband and took Mary in her free arm.

'Welcome, dear, come in.' She ushered Mary into the house. The two girls instructed the sailor where the barrow and luggage were to be stowed, and then followed their parents back inside the house, boisterously questioning their father whether he had brought them back any gifts.

The room they entered was large and comfortably furnished and had a welcoming feel about it. Pictures hung on all the walls and a blazing fire burned in a hearth. The two daughters had now run back upstairs, one carrying the baby and the other carrying a sack their father had given them. Susannah was trying to be the genial host to her visitor; all Mary began to wish for was a soft and comfortable bed where she could sleep deeply and recover from the voyage home. Captain Foyle, familiar with the rigours of sea life recognised the signs Mary was silently sending out and he interrupted his wife.

'Susannah, there is plenty of time to talk with missy later. Let's eat first,' he urged. He then groped Susannah's breasts in front of Mary. 'Then get you up to bed, wife, I have a need to sow my seeds in a wet trench and you look good to me,' he announced. Mary tried conveniently to disregard his crude talk. Susannah's cheeks flushed with pleasure, having missed her husband's company the months he had been away.

Mary's first meal back on land was a simple affair, the meat pie tasted well after the hard biscuits and salty beef she ate while aboard *The Ignite*. After dining, and when the room was prepared, Mary, with Lettie's help, quickly disrobed and fell into a soft duck down bed and quickly fell asleep. Angelo slept fitfully that first night back on land. He had become accustom to the ship's movement and found the stillness of the crib restricting.

The following morning, Mary awoke refreshed and feeling good. She went down to the room where the Foyle family dined and ate a hearty breakfast.

'I do not wish to impose on you for long; I need to return to my family home as soon as I am able,' Mary explained. Foyle laughed.

'Not until you have met Ambrose. Where is the boy?' he asked his wife across the table.

'He told me he was going to the dockside yesterday, I haven't seen him since,' Susannah replied.

'I didn't see him yesterday as we came in,' Foyle mused. 'He follows in his father to sea. He has the makings of a fine captain,' he added proudly.

'With you as his father, he will,' Susannah added with blatant adulation.

As the day progressed, Mary relaxed. She scripted a letter addressed to her mother announcing her arrival back in England and that she hoped to be returning home shortly. A local merchant who was travelling to London took the message. He promised to find someone who would carry the letter onwards to Yardeley Chase. Captain Foyle had locked himself in his study preparing already for his next voyage.

Finally, in the afternoon, Ambrose returned home. Susannah welcomed him as though he had been absent for weeks. He greeted Mary with courtesy and appeared a genuine and pleasant young man. His father appeared from his study roaring a welcome to his only son and they instantly fell into a lively conversation about the sea and captaining English ships that would rule the waves and defeat any French, Dutch or Spanish galleon that dared to cross their bow. Mary found herself liking Ambrose and she began to agree to the prospect of a union between Cecily and this young man.

She spent the rest of the week preparing for her journey. A group of travellers were planning to go to London and were willing to allow Mary to join them. They guaranteed safety in numbers along England's perilous roads. Once in London, Mary would be able to hire someone to accompany her on the final leg of her journey. This was agreeable and the date was set for her to leave Portsmouth.

# 28

The day of departure arrived, and Mary bade an affectionate farewell to Captain Foyle and his family. She promised to write to let him know of her decision regarding their children; even though she had already decided to agree to the match, she wanted to speak to her daughter first.

In the group of travellers there were two nuns making a pilgrimage to Canterbury, a merchant going to London and several more young men, one with his wife going to seek their fortune.

The travellers departed Portsmouth and Mary made friends with the wife of the fortune seeker who was reluctantly accompanying her husband. She had been happy to remain living on the south coast, but her husband had wanted a better life for his wife and the family they would one day have. So here she was, riding towards a city she never wanted to live in. Mary told her of her adventures at court and in Spain. How she longed for a peaceful life in Essex. The two nuns both expressed consternation at Mary's admission to amusing the king one afternoon and her friend, Lady Anne's revenge on the good, God fearing Cardinal Wolsey. The king and cardinal were Godly paragons of virtue the nuns exclaimed fiercely.

The journey towards London for the travellers was uneventful and thankfully trouble free. They passed through small villages and hamlets, stopping at inns, monasteries and convents to eat, rest and purchase more provisions to sustain them. When they reached the town of Guilford, the nuns split from the company. The group said farewell as they left. A monk from a local monastery accompanied the nuns on to Canterbury. Everyone else stayed for one more night in the local tavern. The next day would see the final leg of their journey towards Southwark, where they would cross the bridge and enter London.

Southwark was noisy, bawdy and colourful. Tall gabled houses crowded the stinking streets. Men and women shouted and swore at each other, children running wild targeted the travellers, trying to steal purses. From ale houses and taverns on every corner came raucous sounds of fighting. Prostitutes brazenly propositioned the men in the group, yet the travellers kept themselves to themselves as they hurried down the filthy street, heading for the bridge.

An enormous gatehouse greeted them as they arrived at the south end of London Bridge. Looking across the bridge, houses, shops and taverns lined both sides, supporting a thriving community. A farmer herding a flock of sheep passed the travellers. He called to his two dogs to keep the flock in check as they began the crossing and onwards to Cheapside Market. The travellers then set out themselves, alongside carriages and riders on horseback. The houses, just like in Southwark, were tall, but these were imposing and elegant, owned by wealthy merchants and tradesmen. Shops selling food, leather goods and household utensils opened onto the bridge with their shopkeepers calling their trades to the shoppers browsing. Taverns served quality wine and ales. At both ends of the bridge stood churches with tall spires, and a second gatehouse leading out into the city. Above the gatehouse were erected spikes on which impailed-severed heads of traitors gazed down with unseeing eyes. To the northwest on Ludgate hill stood the cathedral where the travellers' journey was to end.

Before long, they were standing in front of the heavy oak doors of Saint Pauls.

'Well, this is where we all must part and go our separate ways,' one of the men announced, looking around the small group of travellers standing before him. 'It has been long, and for most of the time pleasant to keep your company. I'm sure you all agree,' he added. Everyone hugged each other and the men shook hands.

'Good luck for the future,' Mary said, kissing her travelling companion on her cheek.

'May you find the peace you are looking for,' she replied.

Once everyone had departed, Mary found the directions to Bishopsgate, remembering Sir William had taken a house there. She walked the length of the thoroughfare asking people if they knew Sir William Crawford. Eventually, a middle-aged goodwife said she knew where he lived and led Mary until they came to a tall gabled house.

'Sir William lives there, mistress,' she said, and carried on walking. Mary slowly walked up to the closed door and uncertainly knocked on it. After a pause, the sounds of locks drawn were heard from the other side a woman dressed in a sensible brown dress and apron opened the door. Mary swallowed hard and spoke.

'Is your master at home?' she began in a dry voice. The housekeeper regarded her.

'Who wishes to know?'

'I am his daughter-in-law, Mary Crawford. I was married to his son, Henry.'

'Wait, I shall see if he is receiving callers,' the housekeeper replied guardedly and closed the door on Mary. She waited until the door opened sharply and the familiar figure of William stood in the doorway.

'Mary! I cannot believe it is you!' he gasped, throwing his arms around her and hugging her tight. He then saw the boy. 'Who is this?' Then remembering his manners invited Mary in.

'This is Angelo, his father was Don Rafael. I married him,' Mary announced brightly. William looked surprised.

'I remember seeing a connection between you and that Spaniard when he came to Markham. So, where is he now? Why is he not here with you?'

Mary recounted her life until the present day. William listened attentively. It had been many years since Mary had left Markham a young widow and here she was widowed again, and again with a young child. She told him the news that his only grandson, William, had died and of her plans for Cecily's future.

'I never mentioned my kinswoman to you, it seemed not necessary, we were never close. I would write occasionally and tell her of my life and she would tell me of hers. When you gave birth to Cecily, I talked with Henry about the prospect of her and Ambrose marrying, I am pleased that Howard remembered our plans. Eleanor would have liked it; I know my sister would have agreed too,' William said.

On his invitation, Mary agreed to stay. He was happy to have her back with him, even if it was only for a short while. Since she had last seen him, his face was now more lined and his hair greyer, but the concern for her welfare was still there. He knew a local merchant who frequently travelled to Suffolk along the old Roman Road. William would ask him if he would accompany Mary back to Yardeley Chase, she accepted that offer gladly. William said he would contact his associate the next day and they could arrange when to leave.

Mary sent a message to let her mother know where she was and that she would be home soon. Until the day of departure, Mary enjoyed William's hospitality and he enjoyed playing with Angelo.

On the evening before Mary was to leave, William led her down into the cellar of his house. There, amongst thick dust-covered barrels of wine, he had a large wooden chest locked with heavy metal padlocks. Slowly, he opened the padlocks with different keys and pushed the lid open with effort. Inside were documents, leather pouches and items of women's jewellery. He picked out a gold necklace studded with diamonds. He rubbed it lovingly over his cheek.

'This belonged to Eleanor. I gave it to her on our wedding day. She wanted it to be given to the daughter she hoped we would have. Give this to Cecily to take with her to Portsmouth, and this too.' He handed the necklace to Mary and then brought out a pouch that was heavy with coins. 'This money will help her dowry. Take it.'

'I can't,' Mary said pushing the pouch back towards William.

'What use of it do I have? I have enough money to run this house and pay my servants. I bring in capital from my business. Please, take it,' he insisted. Once again, there was no use in quarrelling and unwillingly she accepted the money on Cecily's behalf.

Mary retired early to bed that night, as she, Angelo and Lettie would have to leave early the next morning. She found it difficult to sleep, thinking that soon she would be seeing her mother again and be back at her family home to where she had decided to retire. She was still young enough to marry again, but after the history of her two previous marriages, Mary had no desire to enter the state of matrimony ever again.

Mr Allen had arrived early the next morning. He talked for a while with William and they discussed the nature of his trip. His journey would take him to Felixstowe where he would take ownership of goods arriving from Europe.

Tearfully, Mary said goodbye to William again, knowing this time she would never see him again. He embraced his daughter-in-law affectionately, and then helped her onto her horse.

'I wish you God speed and good luck,' he called and stood in the middle of Bishopsgate watching as the small party headed out of London. He watched until Mary had vanished from sight, then sighing, he returned inside his house, now resonant with silence, no more sounds of childish laughter; no more light, nonsensical chat. The silence was so evident suddenly. He looked around the room he now stood in and felt alone. He would become familiar to it again. Pouring wine, William stood at the window gazing out onto Bishopsgate and daily life continuing outside. 'Enough,' he said firmly to himself and turned to his waiting desk.

# 29

*Essex*

As the evening drew in, and the riders felt a chill in the air, excitement was beginning to race through Mary's body, she was nearly home and she kicked her horse into a canter.

The gates to Yardeley Chase were open, ready for Mary to enter. Laughing with delight, she looked around at the familiar buildings, and instantly it felt as though she had never been away. The oak doors opened and her mother ran from the doors to her, calling and crying for joy at the sight of her daughter after so long. Mary dismounted and flung herself into her mother's open arms.

Margaret summoned a servant and instructed to make ready a chamber for Mr Allen to spend the night in. 'Cecily spends much time in her room, reading, she is very reflective for her years. I will request her to join us. I know she is looking forward to your return. A daughter should not be separated from her mother for so long.' Mary inwardly winced at the remark; she knew what her mother said was true. Margaret then turned to Mr Allen and held out a hand to him. 'Thank you, sir for bringing my daughter safely home, please, rest here tonight as my guest,' she said appreciatively.

'I'd be most delighted to, thank you,' he replied, swinging down from his horse. Margaret led the way into the warm environment of Yardeley Chase. Not much had changed Mary thought. Margaret appeared to be bearing the mantle of widowhood extremely well.

When everybody assembled in the hall to dine, a pregnant, small, mouse-like woman already sat waiting. Everything about her appeared to be brown, from her mousy brown hair and pale complexion, to the taupe coloured loose fitting gown she wore. She did not stand up when everyone entered, but smiled amiably.

'Mary, you have not met Alice,' Margaret said, indicating towards the young woman at the table. 'She is Robert's wife, and mother to the sweetest little boy,' she announced proudly. Mary could not believe what she was hearing. Of all the beautiful women at court, he had married such an ordinary looking woman. 'Alice is living here with me. She is good company and my grandson Stephen is a constant source of delight.'

'Hello,' Mary said, stunned by the announcement. Alice finally stood up, placing a hand over her neatly swollen stomach. When she spoke, just as the rest of her, her voice was small.

'Margaret has told me much about you, your adventures in Spain.' she said. 'You have been so unlucky to lose both of your husbands. I hope to be married to my dear Robert for a very long time.' At the mention of Robert's name, Alice seemed to glow with enchantment.

After introductions, Margaret summoned Cecily from her room, and Mary found herself fearful about meeting the daughter she had last seen four years earlier. Would she really be pleased to see her mother?

Cecily descended the stairs and stood before her mother. At twelve, the girl was growing tall and pretty. She curtsied very formally.

'I am pleased to see you again, Mother. I have thought of you often since you went away,' she spoke a rehearsed welcoming and Mary thought the words a little strained. It would take work to bring back the bond again between them.

Once this discomfited moment was over, everyone sat down to dine, while Mary recounted her life in Spain once more. Mr Allen amused his host with tales of his meetings with a variety of characters. Alice was enraptured listening and Cecily remained silent throughout the evening.

'So, Alice, how did you meet my brother?' Mary asked at last.

'My father is very wealthy and brought me to court. I could not believe how beautiful all the women there were. I felt unexciting and plain. Surprisingly the men there found me interesting. It was my father's money they saw, not me. Then Robert appeared from nowhere. He was so charming, so affectionate; everything I had dreamed. He told me he was not concerned for my wealth, he loved me for who I was. My father did not want us to marry; he had his eye on a duke for me,' Alice sighed blissfully. 'Robert and I married secretly. Father threatened to disinherit me even after I told him how I loved my husband. He still refused to speak to Robert. When Stephen was born, my father accepted him as his heir,' Alice turned to Cecily. 'This young woman adores Stephen and helps me to look after him,' she said taking Cecily's hand in hers. Cecily smiled for the first time, Alice had become a replacement mother to her; there was nearness between them, making Mary feel outside the moment. Margaret looked between her daughter and daughter-in-law, noticing Mary's brief look of isolation.

'Tomorrow, Cecily, walk with me in the gardens, I would like us to know each other once more. I shall be here now to be a mother to you again, as I should have while you were growing up,' Mary suggested to her daughter. Cecily looked to Alice, who nodded assent.

'Yes, Mother,' the girl replied quietly. She then turned to Margaret. 'Grandmother, may I retire please?' she asked. Margaret waved her hand in consent. Cecily, rising from the table, kissed both Margaret and Alice on the cheek, and then with slight awkwardness, kissed Mary's cheek, and curtsied towards Mr Allen before leaving the hall. Again, Margaret noticed Mary's look of dismay.

'Don't worry, my dear. Cecily is a little confused at your return, give her time and she will be fine with you.'

'I hope so. I never meant to be such a bad mother to her, or William. Did he suffer at the end?' Mary said miserably, thinking of her son she knew so briefly. Margaret smiled empathetically.

'William would have died even if you had been here. Nothing could have stopped that happening. He was never going to make old bones and he did not suffer.' Margaret's voice became quieter. 'Not like my darling Anthony.' She looked down trying to hide her tears. Alice came round and put a supportive arm over her mother-in-law's shoulders. 'The physician gave Anthony as much help as he could, but he could not take the pain any more.'

Visions of Rafael's own death flashed into Mary's mind, bringing tears to her own eyes and making her catch her breath involuntarily. Mr Allen shuffled uncomfortably in his seat and Margaret looked up at him and smiled slightly.

'We are a bunch of sad women. At least Alice has happiness to look forward to,' Margaret said, patting Alice's hand. She straightened up and ran a hand over her stomach before stretching slowly.

'If you will excuse me now, I will retire to bed,' she said tiredly.

'If you don't mind, I shall retire too; I have an early start in the morning,' Mr Allen also excused himself and stood up. He bowed to Margaret. 'Thank you for a delicious meal, very enjoyable,' He said and departed the hall as well, leaving Margaret and Mary alone at the table.

'I am surprised at Alice's presence,' Mary remarked. 'I never thought Robert would marry.'

'I know, you cannot imagine how I felt. Your father had become gravely ill by then and one day, without warning, Robert arrived home with Alice and announced that they had married at court a month earlier, and he wanted us to meet her,' Margaret exclaimed. 'When you see them together, you will see how in love they are which gladdened my heart. They both returned to Greenwich, only for Robert to return shortly after when your father was close to death. He stayed here until after Anthony died and arranged the funeral and then took over the accounts and ownership.' Margaret pushed a scrap of food around her plate with a spoon in an absent movement. 'When Robert told me that Alice was with child, I insisted she resided here until after her confinement and she has stayed here ever since. Robert returns whenever he can, he is very busy at court and is becoming important now.'

'Does he still want to be on the Privy Council?' Mary asked, smiling at the thought of her brother's burning aspiration. Margaret nodded.

'Oh yes, Mary. He's still working at that,' she replied with a laugh.

Shortly after the conversation, Mary retired to her bedroom and was delighted to find her old room as it was since her last visit and memories flooded back. She quickly settled into the familiar bed for her first night's sleep at home.

By the time Mary came down for breakfast the next day, Mr Allen had already departed. Alice, wearing a loose woollen robe, was picking at her food, eating little. However, Mary felt famished and enjoyed a good serving of meat, wine and crusty fresh bread. Alice departed the hall and returned shortly afterwards with her son, Stephen. Mary's nephew was a cherubic-faced happy boy, healthy and hearty; she fell instantly in love with him. He in turn smiled sweetly at his aunt and willingly sat upon Mary's lap laughing as Alice waved a rattling toy towards him. He was without doubt Robert's son; Mary could see the likeness in the child's face to that of her brother. Lettie brought Angelo, one year younger than his cousin, to Mary and the two boys were sat on the floor by their mothers facing each other and began playing with toys laid out for them. Margaret, who had been quietly sitting at the head of the table, sat back and watched her grandsons playing happily together, laughing at the simple pleasure she was observing. She was unable to resist the urge any longer, got to her knees and joined in their playtime.

Later Mary called for Cecily to walk with her in the garden as she had requested the previous evening. They strolled along and Mary tried to make light chat. Cecily only spoke when necessary, she seemed unwilling to relax and open up to her mother. They sat on a bench and Mary looked around, the low wall now had a large black and white tomcat and his small black and white mother sunning themselves on the warm bricks. *Cats on that wall, some sights never change,* Mary thought.

'I know you feel uncomfortable being here with me, Cecily, but I want to try to make things right between us now I have returned,' Mary began. Cecily remained unspoken. 'Tell me, what have you been doing since last I saw you?'

'Not much really. Grandfather taught me to read and write. He said it is not imperative for a woman to be educated, but he thought it could help me,' Cecily said quietly. 'I am teaching Alice to read and write now.'

'That is very good of you. Alice seems a nice person. I am pleased you have someone to be a companion to you and for your grandmother. I expect she must get lonely sometimes,' Mary said, trying to draw her daughter into conversation. Cecily just shrugged her shoulders.

'Grandmother cried a lot when Grandfather died, Alice made her smile again, especially when Stephen was born. Uncle Robert visits occasionally, and he ignores me when he is here.'

'How do you see your future?' Mary asked shifting the subject. Cecily smiled for the first time during their talk.

'I do want to marry and have children,' she announced and began to blush just a little. 'There is someone who lives not far away; I think he is rather nice, and Grandfather liked him.'

'Who is that?' Mary asked. She wanted to raise the subject of a move to Portsmouth. Cecily giggled like the girl she still was.

'Edward,' she said and giggled again. 'He is fifteen and his family want him to be married by the time he is seventeen. I will be fourteen then, do you think that is too young to marry?' she asked. Mary was suddenly happy at her daughter asking her counsel.

'You don't have to marry the first man you meet,' Mary reasoned, trying to sound composed. Cecily's face dropped.

'You did. Grandmother told me about you marrying Father after only meeting him once,' she retorted.

'That's because our marriage was arranged, I had little say in it, though I did think your father was a very fine-looking man when I did see him,' Mary replied. There was no need for Cecily to know about the misery she had endured at Henry's hand.

'I think I can remember Father shouting at you a lot,' Cecily said slowly, trying to recall the past. 'At least I shall know Edward by the time we marry.'

'I may have other plans for your future, Cecily,' Mary began. 'I met a kinsman who has a son, Ambrose, he is your second cousin, and I think a match between you could be successful.' Mary watched as Cecily's young face registered a look of horror.

'How can you say that, Mother? You only came back yesterday, and already you are trying to run my life, what do you know about me?' she cried. Mary put out a hand toward Cecily. 'You leave me and William to go to London with Uncle Robert only to return with an old man who took you hundreds of miles away again. You could not even return when Grandfather was dying or when William died. How can you tell me what is good for me when you hardly know me!' She stood up and looked at her mother as the tears rolled down her cheeks. 'I like Edward a lot and I want to be with him one day!' she shouted and ran back to the house, leaving Mary sitting alone in the garden. This endeavour at reconciliation had not gone to plan at all; in fact, Mary had only alienated her daughter more. For a twelve year old, Cecily was very single-minded in what she wanted from life. Mary would have to work to win her over to her way of thinking. Slowly, she got to her feet and walked back to the house. She knew Cecily would want nothing to do with her right now, so she would keep quiet until the girl had calmed down enough for her to talk reasonably again.

Later that day, Mary sat with Alice in a sunlit room, both working on their embroidery, talking about light matters, nothing serious until Alice set down her needle and looked directly into Mary's face. Unnerved by her sister-in-law's sudden attention, Mary shifted in her seat.

'Cecily was distressed earlier today,' Alice said. Mary sighed.

'We talked about the future and Cecily told me about a young man called Edward,' Mary said. Alice nodded knowingly.

'Ah yes, Edward. The young man takes her heart already; it would be a good match if his family and my Robert can come to an agreement for their future,' Alice replied smiling. 'He is quite attractive to the eye and his family are up and coming farmers in Essex.'

'What does Robert have to do with my daughter's future?' Mary snapped, suddenly cross. 'Cecily told me he ignores her.'

Alice looked astonished at Mary's reaction. 'You were in Spain, never coming back for all we knew. Someone had to think about Cecily's future, and you weren't here to decide on it,' she retorted back with a sudden harshness.

'Well, I am here now and I have a more suitable match for Cecily than a farmer's son.' Mary tossed her embroidery down in annoyance. 'His name is Ambrose Foyle, and the future captain of *The Great Harry*!'

'That explains Cecily's tears,' Alice said struggling to her feet. 'She will not accept marriage to any other man than Edward; she has her heart set upon him.' Alice, for all her mildness was suddenly resolute.

'What does love have to do with being married?' Mary exclaimed. Alice's eyebrows rose into high arches.

'You married your Spaniard for love,' she answered back tersely, Mary emitted a loud huff of annoyance and stalked from the room.

Maybe coming back was not such a good idea. She had returned to Yardeley Chase for only one day, and already she had upset her daughter and sister-in-law.

She spent the rest of the day avoiding everybody, by visiting the church to see her father's grave. The old church was still standing as solidly as ever. The wooden door was unlocked; Mary stepped inside the small stone building, and looked around, remembering the times she had spent here. Her wedding, when she had felt such hope for her future, and then the funerals. Mary had not been here to say goodbye to her father. He had died without his daughter by his side. Now all she would be able to do was to mourn for him at his graveside. Mary walked out of the porch and began to look, searching for the grave that held her father. She found it and sat beside it.

'Well, Father, I seem to have made a mess of my life, haven't I?' Mary said quietly. 'Cecily despises me, I've upset Robert's wife – who'd have thought Robert married! I let my heart rule my head and ran off to marry Rafael instead of staying here to care for my family.' Mary looked up and around, tears swelling in her eyes. 'Now you are gone, I never even wrote to tell Mother about Angelo. I never even thought how she was feeling caring for you when you were ill and my William was fading away. I just turned up and expected everyone to be fine.' Mary tenderly stroked the grave. 'I shall wait until Robert returns and ask his guidance. When the baby is born, he will return.' Mary got to her feet and brushed away the grass clinging to her skirts. 'I shall come again another day and see you,' Mary promised. She kissed her gloved hand and touched the grave. Then turning, she returned to her waiting horse.

That evening, there was an uncomfortable silence at dinner; Cecily sat as far from her mother as she could and did not speak throughout the entire meal. Alice pretended to be attentively engrossed in her meal; Margaret tried to lighten the tense atmosphere with a strained cheeriness. Mary sat feeling accountable for causing the situation. Thankfully, with the lack of conversation, the meal was quickly over and Mary retired to be alone with her thoughts.

She peered out of the window of her room, straining her eyes in an attempt to see the courtyard in the rapidly dimming light, feeling wretched, her homecoming was not to be like this, it was meant to be a happy occasion, the prodigal daughter returns to the bosom of her family.

Mary slept restlessly that night, fretting over the previous day's events, and awoke early next morning still weary. She dreaded facing her family, but she could not hide indefinitely, so guardedly, she faced her mother and Alice at the table.

Margaret looked up and smiled brightly, Alice, too smiled towards Mary. She returned the smile just a little and sat down quietly.

'About what happened yesterday,' Alice began, wanting to be the first to break the tense atmosphere. Mary looked up, listening. 'I think things were said that we shouldn't have,' she continued. 'I have been used to having Cecily to myself, being almost a mother to her, I meant no malice, I care for your daughter and want to see her happy, and Robert wants to see her settled,' Alice said. Mary sighed a little.

'I know I just somehow expected everything to be as it was when I left. I still had an image of Cecily as a small child, not the budding woman she has become; I should have handled our talk a little more sensitively,' she admitted. From her position at the head of the table, Margaret visibly relaxed at the reconciliation.

'Cecily is on the brink of womanhood and confused about her emotions and her life to come,' Margaret added, joining in the conversation. 'The young man she talks about is kind enough, and a successful match could be made between them both, but I still somehow felt there was someone better out there for her. Who did you have in mind, Mary?'

'When I returned from Spain, the captain of the galleon was the son of William Crawford's sister,' Mary explained. 'His son, Ambrose, was mentioned and I met him in Portsmouth, he is a good young man with excellent prospects.'

The next predicament to overcome was talking Cecily out of her adoration of Edward and extolling the virtues of Ambrose. Margaret took on the task of talking to her granddaughter, keeping Cecily on familiar territory in her own chamber where she sat the twelve-year-old down and gave her a gentle lesson about dutiful daughters and their expectations. By the end of the day, as the light began to fade, Margaret and Cecily emerged arm in arm, tired but happy. Mary stood at the foot of the stairs watching her mother and her daughter descend. Margaret gave Cecily a little nudge forward. The girl took a step towards Mary and looked into her mother's face.

'Grandmother and I have talked about my future and about you and Alice, and lots of things,' Cecily began. 'And I realise that even though you had been away for years, I was still in your thoughts, and what you do is for my best.' Cecily shuffled on the spot sheepishly. 'I am sorry for shouting at you yesterday, Mother.'

'Do not worry, Cecily,' Mary accepted the hesitant apology.

'I do still like Edward, but I would like to meet Ambrose,' Cecily suggested quietly. Mary smiled at her mother who had succeeded where she had failed.

'Once you have met him you will like him. When you become betrothed to Ambrose, you will go and live with his family in Portsmouth,' Mary continued and saw a flicker of alarm cross Cecily's face. 'He has five sisters, three who still live at home, so you would not be alone. I will write to Captain Foyle and tell him of our decision.' Cecily left the hall to wander alone in the garden with her thoughts as the evening began to draw in. Margaret watched after her granddaughter and smiled with satisfaction.

'I told you she would be fine.'

'How did you manage it?' Mary asked. Margaret put an arm over Mary's shoulders.

'I told her all about her grandfather and myself and how happy we had been in our arranged marriage and how happy you and Henry were when she was born. I just told her that daughters rarely marry whom they choose, and love arrives in due course. I also added that her grandfather would approve of the match. When Cecily asked about your second husband, I told her that you had been lonely and he made you happy again. Then we talked about whatever she wanted to.' Margaret smiled placidly. 'Call Cecily in, it is time to eat and I need a good meal,' she added firmly.

After that, life became pleasant for everybody. Mary settled back into her old life quickly, she even found that she was forgetting the Spanish language. She and Alice became close as sisters. Mary had written, as she had promised, to Captain Foyle suggesting he brought Ambrose to meet Cecily and, if agreeable, a betrothal ceremony would take place at the church.

Alice, with Cecily's help, had written to Robert telling him of Mary's arrival home and his reply was that he was too busy at court to be able to return home to greet his sister, although when his child was born, there would be a reunion then.

The child was born with Mary and Margaret assisting the midwife, and the birth progressed easily.

'It is a girl,' the midwife announced jubilantly. Alice laughed, delightedly looking at her baby.

'Roberta,' she said cheerfully. 'Margaret, write to Robert and tell him of his daughter's birth,' she asked.

Mary lay in her bed that night thinking. Cecily was happy again, they were becoming as mother and daughter should be. Angelo was an appealing little boy, adored by all the women of Yardeley Chase, with a sizzling Spanish temper. Already he was eager about what he wanted; it would see him good through his life. For the first time in months, Mary felt at ease with her life.

A week later, Robert arrived home. Alice, still confined to bed after the birth, was unable to rise to greet her husband. Consequently, it fell upon Mary to wait at the open door for her brother's arrival.

Robert had changed little since she had last seen him. He waved and jumped from the saddle, wrapping his sister in a tight embrace.

'God's blood, I never thought to see you again. When Alice wrote to me to tell me of your arrival home, I could not believe it. What happened to that ancient Spaniard of yours? Did he die? Was it old age?' Robert then suddenly remembered the reason for his journey home and, pushing Mary aside before she could answer, he ran in shouting Alice's name at the top of his voice, sprinting up the stairs leaving Mary alone to re-enter her home silently.

Later in the day, Margaret had gone to the kitchens to see the progression of the special meal to celebrate her son's return, leaving Mary and Robert to reacquaint once again. Mary felt ashamed to be in the company of her brother as she sat silently, eyes downcast not wanting to look into his face. She spoke first.

'You were right, Robert. I should have listened to your advice.' Her voice was hushed. 'You said he was wrong for me. Everything Rafael had said was lies. I was just too blindly in love with him to realise,'

'It doesn't matter now,' Robert replied. 'We all make mistakes and you are home safe and sound now. Mother is glad for that.'

'Alice is a lovely woman,' Mary said steering the conversation away from her. Robert beamed with pride.

'Alice, is precious to me.'

'I am happy to hear that. I now intend to stay here for the rest of my life and be a companion for Mother and Alice when you are away. My life will be boringly normal from now on.'

Robert looked surprised at his sister's declaration. He opened up his arms and enveloped Mary in an embrace. 'We shall be the best of friends forever.' As he spoke, he was already formulating a plan to get Mary back to court life and into Anne Boleyn's household. His plans had been on hold while his simpering sister had been away. Robert had considered using Alice as his informant, but delightful as she was, his wife was a shy, retiring woman and would never become close to Anne Boleyn and he trusted no one else to work for him, but now they could restart. He did not want to hear this admission of retirement from his sister. He had to get her back to Anne Boleyn's side again.

Mary was sitting in Alice's bedroom, reading a book to her while she cradled Roberta fondly. Robert entered to pay court to his wife. Mary looked on as her brother and his wife kissed devotedly. The love they shared was apparent. She then enviously watched as he joyfully took Roberta in his arms and kissed her with gentle affection. She remembered Henry's reaction when he had first seen Cecily after her birth. Robert was showing himself a good and caring father to his children. Mary had also seen his interaction with Stephen, crawling around the floor with his son on his back riding his father as though he was a horse, making neighing sounds, causing Stephen to shriek with laughter. With God's grace, Robert and Alice would go on to have many children, and Yardeley Chase would echo with the sound of children's voices for many years to come.

Brother and sister sat in the hall discussing the future of Mary's daughter.

'Ambrose would be an ideal match with Cecily, and his future is assured as the son of a captain, already he follows his father to sea,' Mary explained.

Robert sat back in his seat and folded his arms, sighing. 'I would not let Cecily just loiter around here as my own family grew. So I made it my business to find a husband for her, but if you think the Foyle's are a better family for your daughter to enter, I shall not stand in the way.' Robert's mind had been working fast. If Cecily did marry the Foyle son, she would leave Essex. There would be no chance of her and an ambitious local husband claiming Yardeley Chase while Stephen was still only a boy.

'I am glad you see it like that, Robert. Mother has talked Cecily round to our way of thinking and she is waiting for the Foyle's to come here so she and Ambrose can become betrothed,' Mary said appreciatively. Robert smiled and stood up.

'We are all family and we look to each other for strength,' he said plainly and departed. Happily, Mary gazed out of the window and saw Cecily playing with Stephen and Angelo, laughing and shouting while the nurse cradled Roberta. One day, if God were merciful, Cecily would be playing with her own children in the garden of her own home.

The following day, Robert walked with his mother in the garden while Stephen ran on ahead laughing, throwing a thick piece of rope for his small dog to chase and fetch back.

'It is good to see Mary again after all she has endured while in Spain,' Robert said, attempting to sound casual to fool his mother. Margaret nodded in accord.

'She wants to stay here now for the rest of her life.'

'So she has said,' Robert replied. 'She is still young enough to find favour at court again,' he added. Margaret smiled and shook her head.

'You won't get her to return with you, Robert,' Margaret warned smiling. Robert gritted his teeth. What he was to say made him feel physically sick, but it had to be, if he wanted his plan to resume. He forced a smile.

'Her friend, Lady Anne desires to rekindle their friendship.

When she learnt that I was returning home, and of Mary's misfortune with her husband, she asked I recommend her to come back with me. I cannot return to say Mary refuses to see such a dear friend again.' Robert paused in his walking and pretended to have an idea. 'Why don't you write to Lady Anne, Mother and ask her to command Mary to return. Her power grows these days.'

'I enjoy having Mary's company again and there is Cecily's betrothal coming up soon. I could not begin to think of writing just yet,' Margaret replied. Robert hid his consternation.

'But Mother, you must do it soon,' he urged, nd then fell silent not wanting to raise suspicion. Margaret looked at her son through narrow eyes.

'You may be the master of Yardeley Chase now, Robert, but I am still your mother, so do not presume to instruct me,' she warned. Robert realised he was going too far. Quickly, he picked up Margaret's hand and kissed it.

'I am sorry, Mother. But I think Mary may grow tired of country life, I care for her well-being as much as yours and my family,' Robert said trying to sound repentant. Margaret smiled again and stroked his hair.

'You are always thinking of others rather than yourself, my son. It is a fault of yours and you are loved for it,' she conceded. Robert bowed his head in compromise. He had waited this long, a month or two would matter little. With Anne Boleyn's star rising fast at court, her disgrace would be even more spectacular when it occurred. Stephen was now boisterously demanding his father's attention, he had seen the tomcat pounce, catch and kill a small bird, and the boy was anxious to point out the killing to his father. Robert knelt to be at the same height as his son and, putting a protective arm around the boy's slim waist, they watched with morbid interest as the cat devoured the unfortunate sparrow.

Robert stayed for one more week before duty called, he had to return to the Palace of Whitehall, leaving his mother, wife and sister saddened at his departure. Yet Alice, by nature was content to spend the hours caring for her children, or at her needlework and pottering around in the herb garden.

# 30

A messernger arrived with a letter from Captain Foyle. He, along with his wife and Ambrose were on their way. Their arrival would be within the week, sending Margaret into a panic. She had the dirty rushes from all the rooms swept away and replaced with clean, sweet smelling rushes infused with herbs to please the senses. The cook dispatched her minions to Bastelden to buy more produce so she could offer enough food for their guests.

Cecily became withdrawn and spent her time alone; pondering over the young man she was about to meet and the family she would be joining. Then there was the prospect of leaving all she knew and going to live with no one she yet knew. Whether she would be happy or not did not seem to matter to her mother. This was just a contract as so many arranged marriages were. It was a daughter's duty to obey her family. Therefore, Cecily knew whatever she or Ambrose thought of each other, they would marry for both families' mutual gain.

Mary entered Cecily's room and sat on the edge of the bed. 'You asked to see me?' she asked, guessing where the following conversation would lead. Cecily sat silently in her chair, trying to find the suitable words to begin.

'Mother, how did you feel when you first met Father?' she asked slowly. Mary smiled.

'The very first time I saw him, I thought him the most handsome man in the kingdom with his blue eyes and blond hair,' Mary replied, remembering the occasion. 'I fell in love with him that very moment.'

'Were you happy being married to Father?' Cecily then asked. Mary thought the response over before speaking. She knew not to tell her uneasy daughter how Henry had beaten and violated her.

'All marriages have good and bad times. Sometimes we argued, but that is natural. However, there were times we were very happy together.'

'Will I like Ambrose?' Cecily then asked hesitantly.

'He has a kind face and disposition. I think you will not find him distasteful. He is sure to like you. You are so sweet in everything you say and do he, cannot fail not to love you in return.'

Mary left her daughter to her thoughts and returned to help Margaret prepare for the visitors.

Captain Foyle arrived with Susannah riding in a carriage. He and Ambrose rode at the head of the small procession. Margaret, Mary and Alice stood in the courtyard waiting to greet their guests on their arrival. Cecily remained in her chamber, not allowed to meet Ambrose until later.

'Thank you for receiving us, Lady Margaret,' Foyle said, and then turning to the carriage, indicated with a wave for Susannah to join. She climbed from the carriage and Ambrose swung down from his horse.

'This is my wife, Susannah,' Captain Foyle introduced. Susannah and Margaret embraced lightly. 'And this is my son and heir, Ambrose,' Captain Foyle announced proudly pulling him forward. The young man bowed politely.

'Please come in everyone and take refreshments, you must all be tired after such a long journey,' Margaret said, taking the captain's arm and leading the party in. Mary watched the captain as he walked with a roll to his stride that she found rather amusing.

Inside the hall, the table laden with food, fruit, wine and ale stood waiting for the guests. They would eat their fill, then in the gallery, Ambrose would meet Cecily for the first time. He talked little, letting his father, with his dynamic style, do all the conversing while Susannah picked daintily at her food. Everything appeared to be over polite and uncomfortable. Mary wanted to get this meal over with so that the important matter of the terms of the betrothal and future marriage could get under way.

Eventually, and finally to everyone's relief, Margaret suggested the group congregate in the gallery. Mary went to fetch Cecily. The young girl was already standing outside her door. She looked even younger than her thirteen years. The gown made especially for the occasion was green velvet to accentuate the green flecks in her eyes. The skirt and sleeves were slashed to reveal the golden underskirt and chemise, and small pearls sewn into the headdress she wore.

'You look exquisite, my darling,' Mary whispered. Cecily looked down at the skirts billowing out from her petite waist.

'What if he doesn't like me?' Cecily asked fretfully. Mary kissed her cheek.

'Let us go and see, shall we?' she tucked Cecily's hand in her arm and led her down the stairs.

When they entered the gallery, both Captain Foyle and Ambrose stood up. Cecily kept her gaze fixed safely on her feet. It felt as if time was standing still, and everyone held his or her breath. Not needing prompting from his father, Ambrose slowly walked over to Cecily. She kept looking down, and then slowly she looked up into Ambrose's face, her cheeks flushed pink. In turn, the young man was blushing with his own anxiety.

'Hello,' Ambrose said in a trembling voice.

'Hello.,' Cecily echoed in a voice so small. Then remembering what his father had said, Ambrose slid an arm around Cecily's waist, pulled her gently towards him, and kissed her soft cheek. There was an audible sigh from everyone; this awkward first meeting was over.

'Come and sit here, girl!' Captain Foyle called, patting the seat next to him. Led by Ambrose, she sat beside her future father-in-law and he turned to her. 'Your mother was right, you are a beauty,' he said boldly. Cecily blushed at the compliment.

'My father is right, Cecily,' Ambrose added a little more boldly. She looked up into his face and smiled.

'Why don't you two take a walk while we talk about your future?' Margaret suggested. Mary had a sudden flashback to the day she had met Henry. They had taken a walk themselves while their parents had the very same conversation she was about to have. Ambrose extended and hand that Cecily took and the young couple left the gallery.

'Well, that went to plan,' Foyle announced. 'Your granddaughter is a fine girl, Lady Margaret. We should get the betrothal performed as soon as possible so that I can get back to Portsmouth; I am due to take *The Ignite* to North Africa, plenty of trading to be done with those natives down there, and I don't mean just jewels or furs either.' He guffawed and tapped his nose in a knowing way.

'We had hoped you would stay a while,' Mary suggested. Captain Foyle laughed again.

'Time and tide wait for no man, not even me!' he said boldly. 'Get it arranged soon and we can be on our way again.' the captain was adamant, this was a business transaction, and delay was money wasted. 'Right, bring those children back in here, cannot keep them together too long in case Ambrose get any ideas.' The captain laughed. 'After all, he is his father's son!'

Mary and Alice went to find Cecily and Ambrose.

The young couple were sitting on a bench hand in hand, talking heads close together. Flushing, Ambrose stood up quickly babbling an apology for no apparent reason. Mary smiled at him; he really seemed a nice young man.

'Were we interrupting anything?' she asked gently. Ambrose blushed and Cecily giggled. 'It is time to come back in.'

Ambrose looked back at Cecily, and with his cheeks still glowing, hurried towards the house, muttering some kind of fond farewell, a lovesick fool already. Leaving Cecily to walk slowly back with her mother and aunt, the young girl's face animated with pleasure.

'So?' Mary asked in an attempt the draw Cecily into talking.

'Ambrose has said he wants to marry me. Ambrose is very nice; Ambrose already goes to sea and wants to be the Admiral of the fleet one day,' Cecily said breathlessly. Mary and Alice exchanged pleased glances; this match already seemed to be heading for success.

After the betrothal, Cecily would be departing with her new family to live with them. Mary dreaded that day's approach; even though she had not been present raising her daughter, she had always known Cecily was safe with her grandmother.

For the following days, the young couple spent as much time together as they could while Mary organised the packing of her belongings and the hiring of a personal maid to accompany her.

Captain Foyle was now impatient to be on his way, the business transaction successfully concluded and he needed to get back to sea.

Emotionally, the three women stood in a row in the courtyard watching Cecily step from Yardeley Chase for the last time, on the arm of her betrothed. Her eyes were red from the tears she could not hold back. The door of the carriage was open with Susannah already seated inside waiting for the newest member of their family. Captain Foyle was in the saddle, holding the reins of Ambrose's horse. Cecily paused in front her family, Ambrose stepped back to permit her to hug all three tightly. The captain sighed, wanting to be off. They all whispered words to each other and kisses were exchanged until Ambrose touched Cecily's arm, reminding her it was time to go. He led her to the carriage and helped her in. The door was locked shut and she leant out of the window.

'Goodbye,' she called waving a kerchief. The women waved back as Captain Foyle shouted the command to move, the carriage rattled into movement and departed the courtyard, Cecily kept leaning out of the window until she was unable to see anymore.

'Our baby is gone,' Margaret muttered sadly, Mary and Alice watched Margaret, head bowed, walk slowly back into the house. She would be the one who would miss Cecily the most.

'We must make sure our children cheer her up,' Alice observed to Mary. 'I have never seen Margaret look so sad.'

'I'll fetch Angelo and Stephen,' Mary added. 'Bring Roberta, too, and I'll ask Mother to tell them a story.'

Margaret was sitting at the table, absently toying with a flower stem pulled from the floral display. Her expression was blank, her mind was blank, and she felt empty. For all the years she and Anthony had cared for Cecily, she had loved the child. Now the girl was gone, Anthony was gone, who would go next? She had already sent a letter to Anne Boleyn. Robert had been right to suggest Mary should return to court. After the life she had led, settling down to become a matron of a country home would not suit her daughter at all. Interrupted from her thoughts, Margaret then looked up as she heard the door opening. Mary and Alice were coming in with enforced happy faces, with their children. An attempt, she assumed; to make her feel happier after Cecily's departure. Margaret felt she did not need this. She wanted to be alone with her emotions and would come out of this melancholia in her own time. Her daughter and daughter-in-law meant well, Margaret conceded that. Therefore, for their sakes, she attempted a smile, gathered her grandsons in her arms, and pulled them onto her lap, Roberta, in her mother's arms was gurgling happily, stretching out her arms.

A messenger arrived with a sealed letter for Mary. Looking at the seal, she was vaguely aware of the crest of a falcon imprinted on it. It looked familiar, but surely, it could not be… Mary was cautious as she broke the seal and read the contents of the letter

Running through the rooms, Mary called out for her mother; Margaret was in conversation with the cook about the cost of meat from the nearby livestock market.

'Mother, you will not guess who this is from!' she cried waving the letter in the air, before Margaret could reply, she continued. 'Lady Anne has written to me from Greenwich! Word had reached her I am widowed. She commands me to attend upon her soon. *Commands me,* Anne has never been in the position to command me… unless. No, she couldn't have given into the king's desire, she must have done.' Mary paced the floor talking to herself, forgetting her mother's presence. 'Oh my God, I must go as soon as I can.' Mary scanned the rest of the letter. 'She is sending an escort. Robert will be back here soon; I am to be ready to leave at short notice.'

'You must go, Mary, you belong there at the centre of life, not stuck here in the countryside,' Margaret urged.

'But I like being back here, how can I leave you and the children?' Mary argued. Margaret dismissed the cook and turned to Mary.

'You like being here now, but I know you would get bored eventually. I have Alice for companionship, she is happiest here with her children, keeping a home for her husband. Do not worry about me,' Margaret assured, stroking Mary's face affectionately. Already, she could see the returning flash of exhilaration twinkling in her daughter's eyes.

'I must tell Alice of Robert's return, she'll be pleased to see him again,' Mary said, hurrying from her mother's side to find her sister-in-law and tell her the good news.

Robert came home to an ecstatic welcome from Alice. Mary stood back watching their reunion, and she found herself jealous of Alice. She had the fortune of love from a man she so evidently adored, and Mary began again to desire feeling secure in the arms of an ardent man who loved her and her alone.

Robert greeted Mary and his mother warmly, then surrounded by the women who loved him, entered Yardeley Chase.

'My stay is to be brief; His Majesty has given me leave to collect you, Mary, and return within the week.' He looked at Alice at his side. 'So we must make the most of our time together.' He squeezed Alice's hand warmly and she gasped at his touch.

'Mary and I shall arrange everything.' Margaret said. The couple both giggled with delight and hurried from the hall, hand in hand like young lovers. Mary knew to where they were heading with such haste, and again a twinge of jealously fluttered through her body.

At their evening meal, Robert and Alice appeared both wearing wraps and looking very content, they sat close, whispering secrets that made them both laugh. It made Margaret glad to see her son so happy in his life. Everything was right for him. His life was successful at court, he had a lovely wife and two beautiful children, Anthony would have been proud of his son had he been here to see him. She felt a lump rise in her throat and she swallowed hard. Her becoming emotional must not spoil their perfect moment. She would hide her tears of joy and sorrow for when she was alone in her bed where no one would see them.

As he had said, Robert's stay was brief and all too soon he was ready to leave for Greenwich with Mary by his side. Lettie had requested to stay behind to help look after Angelo while she was away. Emotionally, she took her son in her arms.

'I am leaving you as I left Cecily. But I'll be back soon, Lady Anne only wants to see me, I shall not take up residency at Greenwich, so be brave for your grandmother and Aunt Alice and I shall return to you, my angel,' Mary said, kissing his thick black hair. Not understanding, Angelo laughed and pulled at her hood. Reluctantly, Mary handed him to Lettie and with a groom's help mounted her horse. Alice was wiping her eyes as she stood by Robert, who was already astride his horse. He lent down and kissed Alice tenderly on the lips.

'I'll write when I can,' He said tenderly. Alice nodded and held his hand until the very last moment. Robert looked at Mary. 'Let's go,' he said briskly. Alice gave a cry of anguish as she watched Mary and her husband ride out of the courtyard. Margaret waved, putting on a cheerful face, though her heart was breaking once more. Both her darling children were riding out of her life again. Again, she had Alice to keep the loneliness at bay, and this time Angelo along with Stephen and Roberta would keep her amused on her darker days. Together, Margaret and Alice walked back into their home arm in arm, not knowing when they would see their loved ones again.

# 31

*Royal Court*

Just as the first ride to Greenwich, Mary and Robert took the same route, stopping at the same taverns. Hardly anything had changed. When they came to cross the Thames, Mary confidently boarded the ferry this time. This narrow strip of water held no fear for her now. Guards in royal livery barred their entrance and demanded the password.

'La Boleyna,' Robert said, gaining admittance.

Immediately Mary was aware that court life had noticeably changed as she entered the palace. There was a certain atmosphere about the place, she detected that the courtiers seemed to split into two factions. You supported either the queen or Anne Boleyn.

'Make a good impression on Lady Anne and win her trust again,' Robert said. Mary hugged her brother.

'I am nervous, Robert, so much has happened since last I was here,' she answered, in a faltering voice.

'Be yourself, Mary. Good luck,' Robert kissed Mary's cheek and disappeared into the bustling crowds. He smiled with satisfaction as he strode along the corridor. That detested woman would demand that Mary's return to court life be permanent, and then he would re-employ her into his services and this time, his quest to destroy Anne Boleyn would not fail.

Mary followed a page through corridors towards the royal apartments. Anne must have finally conceded her virginity and allowed the king to bed her.

The guards protecting the doors to the royal chambers blocked Mary's way. After reading the document, the guards pushed the door open, allowing Mary to pass through into the opulent rooms.

Lady Anne was steated by the fire, surrounded by her ladies-in-waiting. The woman had lost none of her mystic charm. Her complexion was as pale as ever, though her cheeks slightly flushed. Her long black hair fastened in a silver thread net, studded with pearls and diamonds. The gown she wore was scarlet and gold, colours that suited her best. Her sleeves hung bell shaped, hiding the deformity on her left hand. As soon as Anne saw Mary, she gave a cry of joy and hurried towards her, arms outstretched. Mary sank into a curtsey. Tutting, Anne pulled her into a standing position and hugged her old friend warmly.

'Mary. How it pleases me to see you again after all these years,' she cried happily. 'No ceremony between us. Tell me everything that happened to that gorgeous Spaniard you married. No one thought you would ever return to England,' she added and led Mary towards the fire and indicated an empty chair to Mary. 'Bring us wine, and then leave us,' Anne commanded. She sat back in her chair and smiled broadly. 'So tell me about Rafael. You know we all had a fancy for him and were all jealous of you for capturing him for yourself.' She sat forward and placed her chin in her hands. Yet again, Mary recounted her Spanish adventure, omitting nothing to her friend.

'Who would have thought of him a wife murderer?' Anne exclaimed when Mary finally finished.

'You have come a long way, Anne,' Mary observed, looking around at the portraits hanging on the wall and sumptuous furniture.

'The sweating sickness came to England and it came to court, My Lord sent me to Hever and the queen to Ludlow to prevent us both from catching it. Henry still seemed to have a soft spot for Catherine and that did make me cross. Nevertheless, I still caught the sweat and nearly died. The king sent his best physician to tend to me, and here I am, stronger than ever. It made me rethink everything about my life, I could have so easily been another one of the thousands dead. I now intend to live my life to the full.'

'So you became the king's mistress?'

'Yes, I held out until I knew I could get my revenge on Wolsey,' Anne giggled. 'He is still in the king's favour, but I can see little chinks in his armour, and I work on it. Bit by bit. You know, he

217

gave the king his palace at Hampton with no objection or anything, he just said, *"If your majesty wants it, then take it."* I told Henry that I wanted it, so he got it for me. Simple.' Anne swallowed the last of her wine and smiled broadly again. 'I held the king off until he was going mad with desire for me, then I told him something very important before I allowed him to invade me. That spoilt little half-Spanish brat will never become queen, and do you know why?' Anne's eyes shone with excitement. 'I told Henry: *Your wife I cannot be. Your mistress I will not be.*'

'What!' Mary exclaimed in horror. 'What do you mean?'

'My noble lord, King Henry is going to divorce his frumpy old queen and marry a new one.' Anne paused for dramatic effect. 'Me!' She pointed at herself and fell back in her seat laughing. 'Little Anne Boleyn, not important enough to marry a duke, will marry a king!'

'Anne, be careful. Married men promise anything to get the woman they lust after into bed, and then fail to deliver,' Mary warned. Anne pulled a face.

'In return, I have promised the king a palace full of sons. The Tudors will reign for centuries because of me.'

Mary was concerned at her friend's foolhardy promises. 'How can you assure the king you will give him sons?' she asked. 'You may be barren or have only girls.'

'I am young and healthy, my monthly course occurs and I *will* produce princes, maybe a princess or two as well. It makes sense, of all the children I bear; at least one will have to be male.'

'What happened to that promise to the king for a palace full of princes?' Mary retorted. Anne laughed her friends warning off, and changed the subject.

'Enough prattle. I have asked you to come here to command you – no request you – to become my senior lady-in-waiting. We shall rule court together as friends.'

Mary stood up and curtsied low. 'If you command it then I can only obey, Lady Anne, but I had intended to retire to a quiet life in Essex,' she said formally. Anne sat back in surprise; she had imagined her friend would be grateful for the chance to return to court.

'I do not want to actually command you, I would rather you accept the position because you love me. As for your son, he can come and live in the nursery with the other children,' Anne reasoned. Mary knew she would not be able to talk her way out of this command, for all her insisting it was a request, Anne was now in a position to command anything.

'When you put it like that, how can I refuse?' Mary replied. Anne clapped her hand with joy.

'Good. Return home and prepare to come to me and take up residence. I shall expect you soon.' This was the dismissal, so taking the cue, Mary left her friend.

While returning home, Mary thought over the conversation with Anne. Her friend was playing a dangerous game. Those who displeased him knew the king as cruel and brutal. If Anne failed to give him the sons he wanted, would he dispose of her as he hoped to dispose of Catherine? Queen Catherine had done nothing wrong in her life; her downfall was not to provide a living prince. Would she be able to succeed where Catherine had failed? Mary liked Anne for her vivacity and love of life. She only hoped that Anne would not live to regret the words that may come back to haunt her. To be divorced or retired into a convent would be more than Anne could tolerate. She had to be the centre of everything and everyone, basking in adoration of their glorious mistress.

'I have a bad feeling about this,' Mary said to herself.

Mary's return home was short. Angelo was to remain with her mother and Alice, he had settled and it would be unfair to take him away from his adopted home.

Robert was unable to escort Mary again to Greenwich; she made her own arrangements to travel to London with a group of travellers heading from a nearby village. Mary brought Lettie along with her as her maidservant.

She quickly resumed life back at court and, within weeks, felt she had never been away. It was like old times again, Mary and Anne would sit together gossiping. They spent their days walking in the garden, or if the weather were inclement, they would stroll down the long gallery, arm in arm while the other women followed at a respectable distance.

It was only a matter of time before she came into contact once again with King Henry. He had changed in the five years since Mary

219

had last seen the monarch. He seemed more relaxed when he was near his beloved Anne. His blue eyes were softer when he looked upon her, his voice gentler. The king showed all the signs of being a man absolutely smitten. In return, Anne's face would brighten when he was in the same room, Mary noticed.

King Henry indicated to Mary to rise to her feet, this she did and he looked her up and down, his expression uncertain.

'You seem somewhat familiar, madam. Have we met before?' he asked, beckoning Mary to approach him. She stood in front of him and curtsied again.

'Majesty, I served under the old Queen Catherine,' she replied, keeping her eyes downcast. Henry sat back in his chair and rubbed his beard thoughtfully.

'Did you now,' he muttered trying to remember. 'Refresh my mind, madam.'

'I married a Spaniard and returned to Spain with him until his death.'

'No man could compare to you, my lord, which is why Lady Mary returned,' Anne added. The king chuckled.

'Nevertheless, we are pleased to have you in our court. Your friendship with my dear heart will be a boon for her while I attend to the drudgery of royal business,' the king said. Mary stepped back, took up her position by a window, and gazed out, leaving Anne and the king to share a private moment together.

# 32

The royal divorce was not progressing as smoothly as King Henry would have wished. Queen Catherine refused to grant her husband a divorce, as in the eyes of God and the Pope; they were married until death. Henry tried to cajole her into an agreement, yet she refused to comply. Wolsey put all his efforts into finding a way for the king to be free of his useless queen. He charged his secretary Thomas Cromwell to find a legal way out of the king's marriage. Cromwell brought together top lawyers to help resolve the "secret matter". Among them was a rising star in legal circles, and Cromwell's close friend, Gregory Paxton.

Gregory was the youngest of three sons. His mother had died in childbirth. The grieving father rejected the baby, telling everyone the child was a superfluous error who should have died instead of his wife. He showed little interest in his youngest child, investing all his time in his older sons. Consequently, the lonely boy retracted into his own safe world where no one could touch or hurt him. The steward of the house and his wife took Gregory in and taught him to read, write and find solace and all the friendship needed in books.

He left home at the age of fourteen and arrived in London impoverished, finding service in a lawyer's house in Lincolns Inn and earned his keep running errands for his master. On occasions when he had spare time, his master, who recognised in this young man a raw, natural talent, would permit the young lad to read legal documents. He would explain their connotation and what actions to take to resolve problems and disputes. Gregory was fascinated and decided to become a lawyer. His master, having no children of his own, sponsored the young student to attend university at Cambridge where he met Thomas Cromwell and they forged a lasting friendship.

Gregory proved to be a gifted and assiduous student with the predicted instinctive talent and, despite never having a formal education, it was heralded a great future lay ahead for him. Cromwell left Lincolns Inn, and joined the household of Cardinal Wolsey as an advisor, while Gregory preferred to remain and practice his profession. He quickly gained a reputation for excellence and, to his astonishment, he had also caught the attention more than once of Cardinal Wolsey. Thanks to Cromwell who had used Gregory's services himself, Wolsey in turn recommended him to the king who admired inquiring minds in the men who surrounded him. King Henry had commanded Gregory took up residency in the royal household, and for this he was knighted and in receipt of a healthy pension, comfortable lodgings and servants of his own. His services were always in demand. He was the man who could accomplish the impossible. For all of this, he habitually put in long hours of work alone in his apartments.

Gregory no longer cared what his family thought of him. He did not propose to crow to his father or brothers about his prominence at court. Yet even though people regularly surrounded him feigning friendship, he was in truth, a lonely man, and Cromwell remained his only true friend. By building an emotional wall, he kept out pain, hurt, and kept loneliness locked in. He would not be in the banqueting hall swigging ale and womanising, but in his study pouring over documents, or ardently reading legal books by candlelight late into the night. This, he felt, gave him all the contentment and stimulation he needed. People considered him as boring, peculiar, but this did not trouble him, what did they know? Gregory ostracised gossips for having nothing more positive to do than to spread rumours and counterfeit lies about people and situations they knew nothing about.

Yet one of the women of Lady Anne's household caught his attention. She was the senior lady-in-waiting, an attractive woman with thick brown hair and hazel-green eyes. He could not comprehend why he felt drawn to her and wanted to know more. He had asked surreptitious questions about her life, claiming to be researching information. Livid with himself for becoming sentimental, Gregory tried to put the thoughts of this woman out of his mind. A silly infatuation that was all. He engrossed himself even more in his work, but that only brought him into contact more with this enigmatic woman. She appeared affable to all, and greeted Gregory courteously when escorting him into Lady Anne's company, but that was all. She scarcely looked at him.

Now, instead of hiding away in his books and documents, Gregory found himself thinking about this woman continually, and his work was beginning to falter because of it. He felt he should ask advice from his colleagues about how to make the first move and to introduce himself to her. However, for once, the thought of his fellow lawyers openly laughing at him for this unusual emotion deterred him from speaking to anyone and he continued to watch Mary from afar, hiding deeper behind his emotional wall.

Anne herself had noticed Sir Gregory gazing at Mary when he thought no one would see. She made discreet investigations about the lawyer. What was his marital status? Was his income substantial? Did he have any unnatural habits? Always on the lookout for love interests for her women, Anne sent unsigned messages to both Mary and Gregory requesting them to go to the palace herb garden one afternoon.

Mary received a curious unsigned message that somebody wanted to talk with her in the herb garden. She wanted to ignore the message, but Anne, not revealing that the message was from her, urged her to go, just out of curiosity. Therefore, at the time stated, Mary stood surrounded by the fragrant herbs waiting for the mystery person to reveal himself or herself. She was unsure about this assignation, and was curious to know who wanted to speak with her, and why. It was not Robert; he always signed his communications. There was no one else around who she could think it could be.

From the palace, Gregory walked briskly, his cloak billowing out behind him, and books held tightly under one arm. The strange message he had received said that there was information from a reliable source that could assist with the "secret matter". The lawyer, also turned up at the herb garden. He came to an abrupt halt at the sight of Mary. She looked cautiously at him. He snatched the hat from his head, looking confused and his cheeks flared red.

'You arranged this meeting?' she asked carefully. Gregory shook his head.

'No, I was told someone wanted to speak to me privately and to meet here,' he replied, producing the message and showing it to Mary. He could hardly believe he was in the presence of the woman he secretly adored. He began to shake with fear and consternation and hoped this delightful woman did not notice. Mary showed him her message. They read their messages and looked at each other, then looked around to see if anyone was watching. Apart from a gardener, they were alone. 'I did not arrange this meeting,' Gregory said. His mouth had suddenly become dry as a nervous tension threatened to overcome him.

'Neither did I,' Mary replied, not seeming to notice the lawyer's faltering voice. They looked at each other again, and both began to laugh simultaneously. 'Someone has arranged this, and I may know who,' Mary said, smiling. The lawyer still smiling managed to look confused again.

'Then I must thank them, I have wanted to speak to you for some time now. But have never had the courage,' he admitted. Mary raised her eyebrows in surprise.

'I have seen you when you have come to talk with Lady Anne. I paid little attention to you, sorry,' she apologised. Gregory fumbled with his books and eventually held out his hand for Mary to take, which he shook firmly instead of the kiss she was expecting.

'I am Gregory Paxton; I am a friend of Master Secretary Cromwell, and I am helping with the…' he stopped talking suddenly. 'I think you know why I am employed,' he added in a quieter voice. Mary nodded her head. He continued. 'I know you are Lady Mary, I have watched you for a long time.'

'I wasn't aware of that,' she replied, surprised again at the disclosure.

Gregory indicated to a bench nearby. There they talked, both relaxing and becoming comfortable with each other's company.

From a window in the palace, Anne watched the scene playing out below. She smiled to herself and nodded with satisfaction. The lawyer had a gentle push in the right direction. It was now up to him to follow this opportunity through. Mary had said she never wanted a liaison with another man again, but Gregory Paxton could become an interesting interlude, and who knew where it would all end?

That evening in his apartment, Gregory sat at his desk and laid documents and books out before him. From a pouch attached to his belt, he took out a pair of round framed spectacles and put them on. Many years of working with the only light coming from candles had weakened his eyesight. He picked up his quill. Instead of settling down to business, Gregory sat there, quill poised, his mind wandering back through the hours to that encounter in the herb garden. He hardly dared to speak to Mary before, yet he had sat close to her, smelt the fragrance she wore, or was it the lavender that surrounded them? He had talked with her in a natural way, they laughed together, something he never expected to be able to do with any woman. He looked over to the closed door, then back to the paper, still blank in front of him. He put the quill down and put away his spectacles, pushing back his chair as he stood up. Pulling on and buttoning up his doublet, Gregory walked to the door and pulled it open. He could hear the sounds of voices and music coming from the great hall where the courtiers were enjoying the evening's entertainment of dancing, card playing and love making. Taking a deep breath and feeling an overwhelming sense of panic, he walked slowly towards the sounds. For the first time, he was going to join in the revels, and if Mary was there, perhaps he could talk with her again.

He stood in the doorway observing the scene before him. The musicians in the gallery were playing merry tunes to which several couples were dancing. Knots of people stood or sat huddled together conversing or gaming, couples sat in window seats engrossed in talk of love. He looked around, scanning for that one familiar face to lift his heart. He felt uncomfortable being here, he wanted to turn and go back to the secure cocoon of his apartment, but he knew he had to find her. Slowly, Gregory entered the hall and began to circulate. One or two people saw him and professed surprise at his presence; he just smiled nervously and walked on. Then he saw her! Mary was sitting with a small group of women; they were talking and laughing together, drinking wine and playing cards. He stood still suddenly terrified of approaching her. He began sweating again and his heart raced. Almost instinctively, Mary looked up and saw the lawyer rooted to the spot. In what appeared to be a deliberately slow movement, she stood and began to walk towards him.

'Sir Gregory. How good it is to see you again,' she said, holding out her hands to him. He swallowed hard and found a timid smile came easily.

'Lady Mary, I hoped to see you. I wanted to thank you for a very pleasant time in the herb garden,' his voice was scarcely audible above the noise in the hall. Mary saw how uncomfortable the lawyer felt and tucked her arm in his.

'Come on; let us take a walk in the evening air. It's hot and stuffy in here,' she suggested. Relieved to be away from the crowd, Gregory gladly led Mary towards the door and the short walk to the garden. Her friends looking on began speculating on whether a romance was beginning between Lady Mary and the boring lawyer.

Outside, the evensong of blackbirds floated in the clear air. In quiet, secret gardens, lovers met. The general buzz of conversation and music from inside the great hall carried out on a soft breeze. Mary and Gregory were just content to walk along the paths talking and they found they were heading towards the herb garden.

'This will be our special place from now on,' she said softly, drawing Gregory down onto the bench they had sat upon earlier in the day. Without analysing his actions, or thinking about what was happening, he instinctively drew close to Mary and her to him. Their lips touched lightly, he drew back sharply, acutely aware of what he had just done, and Mary looked at him. 'Do not be afraid, Gregory,' she whispered.

'I'm not,' he answered quickly. 'I have watched you for months and I didn't know how to begin to speak to you, now I am here by your side. I cannot believe it.' He did not know why, but this felt right. Their lips touched again and the kiss was lingering. The couple held each other tightly in a loving embrace. When they finally parted, Mary was smiling and Gregory was trembling. He was shaking his head as he slid away on the bench from her, with an awful realisation of what he was doing.

'Was it that bad?' she asked, not sure how to interpret his action.

'I've never done that before. I think it is moving too fast. I must go. Sorry.' He stood up and hurried away, confused by sensations never felt before, leaving Mary sitting alone on the bench equally confused. She did not intend to "move too fast". This could have developed into a harmless flirtation, nothing more; she had not expected him to be the one who ran away.

Gregory slammed the door shut behind him and leant on it, panting hard. His mind was in a whirl and his body was behaving in ways he had never experienced. No woman had ever made him feel like this. He talked to women professionally; that was his work, that was what he did with no problem. Yet this woman without realising it had instantly played games with his emotions and he could never feel the same again. Then he realised he had acted like an idiot when he had turned and fled, what would she think of him now? He paced the floor angrily berating himself for his inexcusable behaviour. Then he began to form the excuse he would use when he saw her again – if he saw her again. By the time Gregory climbed into his bed, he felt wretched and worthless. Who would want to employ him for his services after word had spread through court of his foolish behaviour in the company of a woman? He would be a laughing stock. His title stripped, the position he held at court taken from him. He would probably have to leave court, London! England! His life would be over.

He slept little that night, and the following day, ignored the looks he was receiving as he hurried along corridors. He reported to Master Secretary Cromwell, with documents he had been working on. From behind his desk, Cromwell observed Gregory solemnly.

'I do not tell those I regard as friends how to lead their lives. I expect them to be truthful and not to lie to me ever. You look like shit, Paxton. I have heard certain talk circulating this morning. Is it true? Let me tell you women have only three uses in this world, to spread their legs for our entertainment whenever, wherever and however we desire; to obey our every command without question and to bear our children,' Cromwell said counting on his fingers. Gregory sat heavily in a chair, and ran a hand through his uncombed hair.

'I panicked, Thomas. I have never felt attracted to a woman before and I realised I did not know what to do,' he admitted, not meeting Cromwell's unyielding gaze. Cromwell allowed a smirk to spread over his face.

'Are you telling me you've never been with a woman before?'

he asked, amused at the confession. Gregory shook his head still avoiding looking at Cromwell. 'I thought you were just intent with your work, too involved to be out sewing your oats. I knew you were dedicated to your cause, but not at the cost of all else.'

'I felt I always had to prove myself at Cambridge. I never found time for that side of life,' Gregory muttered shamefully. Cromwell raised his eyebrows in astonishment.

'I can find a doxy or two to educate you, so when the time comes for you to breach your fair lady you'll know what to do.'

Gregory grimaced at the thought of physical contact with any woman. 'If she talks to me again,' he mumbled to himself. Cromwell shook his head, now irritated with the delay and held out a hand.

'Enough talk, we have business to attend to. Show me your latest reports.'

It was late afternoon when Gregory finally emerged from Cromwell's privy chamber, exhausted and drained from little sleep and intense work. As he walked slowly down the corridors, he was aware of eyes burning into his back. He was the topic of the day and the sniggering hardly suppressed as he passed by.

Once in the privacy of his apartment, Gregory despondently threw the books and rolled up documents onto the desk and he went to stand in front of the window to gaze out at the people strolling in the gardens in the late sunshine. How was it all those men and women seemed to be interacting with such ease. Why did he find it so difficult to be close to a woman? A solitary tear rolled down his cheek. He was destined to be a lonely man for the rest of his life, shunned by all, ruled by his own lack of confidence; his only true friend would be his work. That would never let him down or laugh at him. His work would always be there to welcome him. A light tap on the door interrupted his wallowing in self-pity. *People come to make fun*, Gregory thought miserably.

'Go away!' he shouted without turning round. His servant emerged from an antechamber and went to open the door. Without saying a word, Gregory shook his head, and dismissed him. The tapping sounded again. 'I said go away, leave me alone!' he called out again angered at the intrusion.

'Gregory, it is me, Mary Perez, can I come in,' called the voice from the other side of the door, he spun round. Surely, she was not going to add her voice to the ridicule.

'Of everybody else, I thought you would have stayed away,' Gregory shouted painfully.

'Why should I? Let me in, please,' Mary called urgently. Sighing, feeling it would be a big mistake to allow her in, he crossed the floor and slowly opened the door. Mary hurried in and closed the door behind her. She looked up into his face and smiled.

'Go on then, say your piece, and be off,' Gregory said sourly turning away.

'Alright, I will. I realised you were unsure about being in my presence from what you had told me yesterday. Moreover, I realised you were unsure about what might follow our kiss. I will tell you this: I did not intend to have sex with you last night,' Mary said firmly. Gregory slowly turned round, still listening. 'I would like to be your friend if you will let me. We do not have to kiss; we certainly do not have to have sex, unless you wish to. I have buried two husbands, I know about that side of a relationship. I am in no hurry to skip into bed with any man, so do not feel pressurised into anything. There,' Mary finished crossing her arms. Gregory was silent, taking in all she had spoken.

'So you are not laughing at me like all the others?' he asked timorously.

'No. It is nice to find a man who doesn't want to plunge inside a woman.'

'But they're all laughing at me.' Gregory pointed towards the closed door; beginning to feel foolish.

'Let them. We will step out together and show that lot there is nothing for them to laugh at. There will be another poor soul to torment next week, you know what court life is like.'

Gregory hesitantly indicated to a chair that Mary sat in, then after sighing heavily, he spoke. 'Until I saw you, I had no time for women. I never thought I would ever find anyone who could like me. Learning to become a lawyer gave me no time to go out womanising, unlike the other students; they seemed to manage, bedding countless women, drinking themselves into stupors and still study. I was as always too shy. So I just studied my trade to become the best lawyer in the land,' he said quietly.

'Were you not lonely?' Mary asked.

'My father and brothers blamed me for the death of my mother. Loneliness is just there, it is consistent, I am use to being alone, and it is the way of life I chose.'

'While I am here, you never need to be lonely again,' Mary promised gently, standing and crossing to Gregory's side, she noticed him tense slightly. She stretched up on tiptoe and softly kissed his cheek. He flushed scarlet and touched where the kiss had placed. 'Do you want to escort me back to my apartment?' she asked carefully. He looked worriedly towards the closed door, then to Mary.

'I don't think so, this time. I am very tired, I hardly slept last night, there is much work for me to do and I need to think over that you have just said,' he excused himself. Mary laughed low.

'That is fine for now, but you cannot avoid me. We'll just see what happens to us,' she said and opened the door. In a loud voice certainly overheard by the inquisitive courtiers, Mary said, 'Thank you, Gregory, you are a very dear man, and I shall see you again very soon.' She then closed the door leaving him standing alone, confused and emotional once again.

As Mary wandered towards her apartments, she allowed herself a content smile. Sir Gregory Paxton was complex man with an unhappy past. He would prove a challenge, and she had found a liking for him. There would be nothing sexual, or basic like that. He would be a good friend to have on one's side. Mary knew she could do no worse than this lonely lawyer.

She went to see Anne to see whether she had any tasks that needed attention. Anne looked up from her book she was reading and smiled mischievously.

'Someone saw you going into that lawyer's chamber, Mary, what have you been up to?' she looked around at her other attendants and they all giggled. Mary scowled.

'What I do in my free time is my business, madam; Sir Gregory is shy around women,' she replied in his defence. Anne raised her fine eyebrows.

'I had seen him looking at you so I arranged that meeting in the herb garden for you both.'

'Well, madam, Gregory, and I had a long talk earlier and we are together now,' Mary answered with triumph, she enjoyed watching Anne and the other women gawp. 'Are you dining in the hall tonight, madam? Or are you staying in your privy apartments?'

Anne quickly regained her poise and smiled gracefully at her friend.

'I am expecting the king to join me tonight,' she said. 'Ladies, you are excused for the evening and Mary, go to your lawyer and make a man of him.'

By the evening, the news of her visit to Gregory's apartment had swept through the court and as she expected, Robert approached her. He pulled his sister to her feet and, ignoring her complaining, dragged her aside to speak privately.

'You know how to pick them, don't you?' he exclaimed angrily. 'This'll make you a laughing stock, Mary. You can do better than that waste of space.'

'Oh, Robert, what is your problem? We had all this when I married Rafael,' Mary complained.

'Yes, and I was right about him!' Robert countered quickly, stabbing the air with a finger.

'Yes,' Mary conceded, and then the spirit rose in her again. 'However, Gregory is not Rafael and I do not intend to marry him. I am dedicating my life to my children and to Lady Anne.'

'Filthy bitch.' Robert swore under his breath and spat on the floor.

'Do not speak about Lady Anne like that! She is good to me and may become our queen one day, so curb your tongue,' Mary stormed. Robert looked truculent, and then regained control of his temper.

'That'll never happen; he's just promising her the crown, once he's got her sprogged up he'll lose interest. Anyway, this isn't about that woman, it is about you, Mary, you can find a better man than mister dull and boring; let me find you a man who will treat you the way a woman should be treated.'

'What, beat and violate me?'

'Crawford did that to you, and if you deserve it, yes.'

'So, do you beat and rape Alice?' Mary hissed. Robert raised a hand to strike his sister, and then thought otherwise and let his hand drop to his side.

'Alice is obedient and compliant. She loves me,' he answered coldly. 'I have great affection for her and our children. When I visit Alice, she is grateful for the attention she receives from me. Stop twisting this conversation, Mary. Ditch that peculiar man; he will only bring ridicule upon you and our family. Any information I should know about that woman?' Robert continued changing the subject. Mary sighed heavily and passed on unimportant news to her brother. Anne had shared secrets with Mary, trusting her friend not to recount anything to anyone. The most crucial information Mary kept back. Her mistress trusted her, and Mary would not break that trust.

After Robert had departed, Mary returned to her friends and told them about her brother and how despicable he was becoming as his stature grew at court.

The following day, Mary was attending Anne while the king paid court to her, and she was delighted to see Gregory enter to speak with him. Gregory's eyes immediately fell upon Mary and a nervous smile played on his lips. He would have spoken with her, but the king took presidence and they began a conversation with Gregory spreading documents on the table for him to read. He took his spectacles from their pouch and put them on. Mary looked amused and suppressed a small laugh. Even though he had been in Anne's chamber at the same time as Mary over the last weeks, she had paid little attention, and had never really noticed the spectacles before. Gregory looked up and squinted at her through the lens.

'Why do you laugh?' he asked, hurt by her mirth.

Mary, unable to speak, pointed towards his spectacles. 'Why do you wear them?' she finally asked. Gregory took the spectacles off and looked at them.

'When I read documents, I find the script blurred. These help me to focus and understand the written word. I wear them to assist me in my work, not for any other use I can assure you,' he replied unusually sharply. Mary fell silent.

'Lady Mary,' the king warned irritated at the delay.

'I am sorry, Your Majesty.' she apologised. The king grunted, Gregory nodded in satisfaction and replaced the spectacles back on and, picking the document up, returned to the discussion with the king.

Mary sat by Anne and talked quietly. Then they began considering whom would look good wearing spectacles, and laughed together.

'Madam if you must talk consistently, Paxton and I shall go elsewhere where there is golden silence. Remember, I do this for you and for England,' Henry complained angrily. Anne pouted.

'Come, ladies, let us take the air. The men here are being busy and important,' Anne said in mock seriousness. The king glared at his mistress. She was a vixen who could raise his blood in an instant to both lust and hatred. The women filed out to walk in the garden and exercise the lap dogs bounding around the hems of their dresses. Once finally alone, the king straightened up.

'Lawyer, you are wise not to involve yourself with women. More trouble than they are worth,' he said. Gregory smiled.

'I think I am involved with a woman, Mary Perez,' he said happily.

'You think? Either you are or you are not, Paxton,' the king exclaimed with surprise.

'I never thought I'd find a woman who would want me.' Gregory took off his spectacles and absently cleaned the lens with the edge of his shirt. The king smiled warmly and nodded in satisfaction.

'Aye, they are harridans every one of them, yet this world would be a dull place without them,' he replied.

# 33

Queen Catherine was refusing to comply with the king and grant him the divorce he wanted. To his annoyance, her nephew was Emperor Charles V who reigned over most of Europe, and held sway with the Pope in Rome. She declared she would have her case heard only in Rome itself, knowing the Pope would be influenced by the emperor. Cardinal Wolsey, anxious to please his royal master in these challenging times, prepared to depart London and travel to Rome to plead the king's case directly to Pope Clement. Tangled up inexplicably with the royal divorce, Wolsey knew that if he failed, he would be disgraced, giving his enemies the fodder needed to attack and destroy him. Already, he had seen how Thomas Cromwell was enviously eyeing his position of chancellor. Cromwell had a great future ahead of him, but not at Wolsey's expense. Not if the current chancellor could help it.

Sir Thomas More was also making life difficult for King Henry. Sir Thomas was an old friend, going back to the days when Henry was merely the second son, and expected to enter the church. Henry trusted Sir Thomas, knowing that the man was wise and only spoke the truth. Sir Thomas's refusal to endorse the divorce rattled the king immensely. Henry wanted his father figure to indulge him and deny him nothing. More had spoken honestly to him, saying to split from his wife would cause the king great angst and give his country nothing but trouble. Henry did not want to hear this. He wanted More to be of an accord to this union, to see Anne as his wife and the mother of his sons, where was the problem in that?

Eventually, Wolsey returned from Rome along with Cardinal Lorenzo Campeggio, who was representing Pope Clement at an English trial.

Campeggio was frail and old; and walked heavily with the aid of a stick. The long journey from Rome to London had left him exhausted. He immediately took to bed on arrival, claiming himself too ill to sit in judgement at a trial of such magnitude. Incensed by this, the king was powerless. He had to curb his annoyance and wait. Although the cardinal was suffering exhaustion, he also intended to delay the proceedings for as long as possible, not wanting to anger Emperor Charles or the Pope. Campeggio received money, jewels, lands and titles in an attempt to hurry him on. Eventually, he could not delay any longer and ordered the trial to begin at Westminster.

The king swung Anne round with joy. 'Sweetheart, the waiting is over. Soon, the Pope will grant an annulment and I shall be free to wed thee and you shall give me the sons you promised,' he cried happily. Anne laughed joyfully. Henry continued, 'All Catherine has to do is attend the trial and admit that she and my brother consummated their marriage and was not a virgin when she came to my bed as my wife. I was duped into believing her purity and that she was uncorrupted. I will see that she is cared for with all the honour given to a Dowager Princess of Wales.'

'But what if she refuses to admit to this?' Anne asked.

'Catherine shall not if she knows what is best for her,' Henry answered grimly, sensing Anne's fear and uncertainty.

The hall at Westminster was full. On one side behind Cromwell sat the lawyers, talking inaudibly together. At the front sat the earls and barons in full ceremonial dress. On a raised dais sat the cardinals and on raised thrones, in front of a magnificent stained glass window, sat Wolsey and Campeggio. From a balcony, high in the hall, Anne and Mary stood looking down at the scene below. Anne's eyes were sparkling with excitement, knowing that in a few short hours, there would be nothing to stop the king marrying her. Mary was feeling more reserved, wanting to hear the affirmation before celebrating. From his throne, Wolsey nodded to a herald who shouted above the noise in the hall:

'Enter, Henry, King of England.'

To a grand fanfare, King Henry strode resolutely into the hall and bowed to the cardinals. He sat on a throne to await the queen. Wolsey nodded again to the herald.

'Enter, Catherine, Queen of England.'

All eyes turned to the doorway. Catherine did not appear. Wolsey nodded brusquely again to the herald who repeated the call. Still the queen failed to appear. Murmuring began to increase from the audience gathered. The king looked around at Wolsey, then to Cromwell and the lawyers, now gathered in a knot and whispering urgently to each other. The herald gave one more call for the queen to appear. To a fanfare, Catherine swept in and dropped a deep curtsey to the king, then to the cardinals. Wolsey sat back in his throne, thankful to see her. Before either Wolsey or Campeggio could speak, Catherine walked up to the cardinals. She dropped to her knees and clasped her hands to her breast.

'I do not recognise this court. I shall obey the decision from Rome. None other than the Pope himself shall hear my petition,' she said in a ringing voice. 'I shall concede only to the decision of his Holiness,' she elegantly stood, curtsied once again to the king and cardinals, and swept from the hall leaving pandemonium in her wake. She would fight to defend her position as queen to both the king and country.

'Catherine! I demand you return immediately!' Wolsey shouted standing up. King Henry sprung to his feet, glaring at Wolsey and Campeggio with ferociousness, Campeggio, visibly shaking and sitting back in his throne, took his kerchief from his sleeve and wiped his perspiring brow. This was not what he had expected. Wolsey looked at the king and turned ashen. 'Your – Your Majesty... ' He began above the melee.

'Explain this, Wolsey!' the king roared. He then looked up to the gallery where Anne and Mary were standing and gave a shrug of great exasperation. Mary looked over to Anne and saw the large tears shining on her cheeks.

'How could she? How could she do that to us?' she sobbed. 'Why fight us? Why can't she give in gracefully and accept her providence?'

'Would you let the man you love go just like that?' Mary tried reasoning with her friend. Anne shook her head and wiped the tears away with the back of her hand, as her shoulders heaved with great sobs.

'He's not divorcing Catherine for us, or our lust, it's for

England. It is to give England an English prince. He is sacrificing his happiness for England,' Anne argued through the tears. Mary remained tactfully silent.

King Henry stormed out of the hall; Anne, followed by Mary, hurried from the gallery, and they met in the corridor. She ran into the king's arms, crying bitterly.

'If she thinks she can make a cuckold of me, then that woman's got another thing coming,' Henry swore, clenching his fists in anger. 'Too long I have conceded to her whims, giving her everything she desired and all she gave me was a useless daughter. Anne, sweetheart, be of good cheer, we will marry 'ere long, this is a minor setback, that is all.'

'But, Henry, if her case will only be heard in Rome, it'll take months before we can marry,' Anne argued.

'Madam, you can afford to wait, it will be worth it when you hold England's prince in your arms,' Mary soothed allowing Anne to hear what she wanted to hear. The king took Mary's hand and kissed it.

'Lady Mary, if only everyone was as loyal as you,' he said sincerely.

'Sire, Lady Anne is my dearest friend; she has been there for me when I needed a friend, and I shall be here for her now,' Mary answered. With permission granted, she left the couple, hurried back towards the hall, and pushed past the vigorous crowds streaming out to get in, looking for Gregory. The seats where the lawyers had sat were now vacant, Mary asked a cleric who was gathering up documents and heavy books where they had gone and he directed her to a smaller door to the side of the hall.

Taking a deep breath, Mary tapped upon the door and waited. A squire answered. She asked to speak to Gregory. He disappeared inside, pulling the door shut, leaving Mary waiting. Gregory eventually emerged. He smiled, pleased to see Mary waiting for him.

'Did you see it all?' he asked, closing the door behind him.

'Anne was in tears, she was so sure everything would go the way she wanted.'

'The king is furious, we have much work to do to try and find some loophole in all this, it will not be easy, the queen has a good case to send to Rome as it was the Pope who granted special dispensation for them to marry. We only have her word that she was still a virgin when Prince Arthur died.'

'I shall not keep you then,' Mary said.

'I will come and find you in the hall tonight,' he replied. Smiling, Mary waved goodbye as she departed, already planning a night he would never forget.


That evening, although it was late, Gregory entered the great hall and directly found Mary playing cards. The women all greeted him brightly; Gregory flushed; he had learnt to relax in company with her guidance. He returned their greeting with a self-conscious wave of the hand. Mary stood up and took his outstretched hand. As the couple departed, there were hoots and calls following them, she laughed and Gregory smiled uneasily. Mary squeezed his arm affectionately.

'No walking tonight, I have plans,' she giggled. Gregory's face drained of colour.

'Plans?' he echoed fearfully. 'What plans?'

'You shall see,' she added cryptically and led him away from the hall towards her private apartments.

Once the door was pushed shut, Mary kicked off her shoes gratefully. Gregory stood alone, wringing his hands, his heart thumping wildly, knowing what was going to occur. He wanted to turn and run back to the security of his own rooms, but by doing this, he knew Mary would never forgive him and their friendship would be ruined.

She turned to him and, flinging her arms around his neck, hugged him tight. He felt soft and warm, the bristles on his unshaven chin prickled her cheek, but she cared not. Gregory gradually let his arms slide around her slim waist and she kissed him full on the lips. When they parted, Mary pulled him further into the room towards her bed. The drapes were secured open, revealing the counterpane turned back, and plump pillows, all waiting, inviting use.

'We have known each other for a while now, Gregory, it is time to know each other better,' Mary said in a low voice.

'I…I,' Gregory stammered, feeling panic rising. 'You said not until I was ready,' he tried to say. She laughed and pushed the doublet from his body.

'I am ready,' she stood back and, in front of Gregory, undressed to stand in a chemise of soft silk. 'Come here, you do not have to do anything.' She took his hand and led him to the bed. Making him sit on the edge, Mary purposely took her time disrobing him, aware of his curious gaze fixed on the soft swelling of her breasts under the chemise. She pushed him gently back onto the bed and sat astride him. Untying the drapes around the bed, she drew them together, keeping the world out. Mary pulled Gregory's shirt over his head and threw it outside the drapes.

'Tonight we will be one, my love,' she cooed, running her hands over his body. She pulled the chemise over her head, hearing him omit a small gasp, before taking him into a warm and loving embrace. 'Do what you feel right; let your instincts rule you tonight.'

Gregory stirred. It was still dark, he had no idea what time it was. Looking over, he saw Mary sleeping beside him, and he smiled. Last night she had introduced him to a world he had never dared he would be privy to. She had instructed him in the art of lovemaking. His first attempt had been clumsy; and Gregory had been alarmed and apologetic at his naivety. His second attempt had been more satisfactory, and he felt a new self-assurance rousing in him. He could take on the world with Mary by his side.

Silently, and still naked, Gregory slipped out of the bed and, in the yellow flickering candlelight, found the table, pouring himself wine that he drank in one swallow. From the bed, Mary murmured and slowly awoke. She sat up and looked around for him. He parted the drapes and smiling sat on the bed. Giggling, Mary came and sat beside him and took his hand in hers.

'What will all your lawyer friends say when they find out you spent the night with me?' she asked. Not being able to stop smiling, he shook his head.

'Who knows, they've always regarded me as a weird and dreary old fart.'

'Not any longer. Come on. Let's give all those gossips out there more to talk about,' she happily said, falling back onto the bed. Laughing, Gregory obliged.

In the morning, he was hoping that he and Mary were to be

seen leaving her apartment together, and they were. As she had predicted, the gossips could hardly restrain themselves and the latest news soon spread around court. She found herself encircled and bombarded with questions on how Gregory had performed the previous night. Anne waited while the women took their chance to question Mary, and once they were finished, she drew her to a window seat to hear for herself all the intimate details.

'Well, tell me everything you did not tell the others,' Anne urged. Mary sighed blissfully and gazed happily out of the window reminiscing the nighttime hours.

'What is there to say? How did you feel when you first lay with the king? Did he treat you as though you were made of the most fragile silk and was eager to learn from you and…?' Mary replied.

'Enough indeed,' Anne laughed, holding up her hand. 'Will there be more tonight?'

'I do hope so, Anne,' Mary wished, smiling reflectively.

'Then make sure you do not get pregnant before I do, Mary. I cannot have you steal my thunder and produce a child first,' Anne warned affably. Both women laughed.

'I do not want any more children; I am content with Cecily and Angelo,' Mary affirmed.

'Your Gregory and the other lawyers will be conversing with my lord, Wolsey and Cromwell about what next to do. Why did not Catherine just concede yesterday? She could have gone to a convent, which would suit her for all the praying she does. Henry and I would have been planning our wedding today.'

'It will still happen, madam, do not fret. Everything comes to those who wait.'

Anne stood up and returned to her women. 'Ladies, let us go riding today, I feel the urge to let the wind blow through my hair and blow all my sadness away. I have had enough of sitting around waiting for Catherine to relinquish her title. Let us have a day full of laughter and fun, and go hunting. Who knows, Lady Mary will regale us with more details of last night if we ask her to?'

The women all laughed, a day in the country would gladden all spirits. Together, they went to the stables and rode out of Greenwich leaving despondency behind. The king, shut in his privy chamber with his councillors, glanced out of the window when he heard the laughing. He saw Anne at the head of the group leaving the palace. For a moment, he wanted to join them and ride through the woods and fields, but State business and the "secret matter" detained him. Wolsey, Cromwell and his lawyers were waiting for him to return to the table. Leisure would have to wait until the divorce was finalised and he would have Anne to himself for evermore.

On one of their regular constitutions, Anne walked through the gardens with Mary beside her. Anne looked around, to make sure no one could overhear the conversation.

'Hear this, Mary. My Uncle Norfolk has unexpectedly taken more than a passing interest in me. He never showed any of my family affection, believing his sister had married below her station when she wed my father. Now I have the king's love, I have suddenly become his beloved niece. He thinks he hopes to further his fortunes by siding with me,' Anne said quietly.

'It appears so, madam,' Mary replied. The two women giggled, heads close together.

'If the king should ever tire of me once we are wed and substitute me with another wife, would this new found love of the Boleyn family suddenly vanish as quickly as it came?'

'Never, madam, the duke loves his niece as though she was his own daughter!' Mary announced with mock sincerity. Anne laughed aloud, making the accompanying women look at her with surprise.

'Oh, Mary, you never lie to me, you are the one person in the world I can trust.' Anne's expression suddenly darkened and she abruptly became serious. 'But in all honesty, if I fail to give the king the son he wants, would he do to me as he is doing to Catherine?' Anne took Mary's hands. 'Tell me the truth, not what I want to hear.'

Mary was quiet, her mind working to find the words to please her friend and royal mistress.

'Anne, what the king wants is to leave the country to princes who will reign wisely after he is gone. If you do only produce daughters, for the sake of the country he may look to another for the prince he needs.' As requested, Mary gave a frank answer. Anne withdrew her hands and her face darkened.

'Then pray to God I give the king what he wants. Sometimes, Mary, when I am alone, I think about what Catherine must be going through, I sometimes think that could be me.'

'Madam, you are young and healthy and will have many children,' Mary assured. Anne smiled bleakly, disconsolate.

'Look at you, you have children you adore, and a new man who makes you happy, is there nothing else you want in life?'

'I do not have the pressure to produce a son as you will have once the king weds you. All I want now is for Cecily to marry Ambrose and for Angelo to follow his heart and be happy, and if God grants it, many years with Gregory,' Mary said, smiling brightly, in an attempt to raise Anne's mood. In the distance, she saw the Duke of Norfolk approaching. 'Talking of the devil as we were earlier, madam, look yonder, here comes your favourite uncle, look how happy he is to see his favourite niece.'

'Lady Anne, dearest niece, flower of our family,' Norfolk began, sweeping a bow, then taking Anne in his arms he kissed her cheek lightly. 'I was told you were taking the air,' he continued. 'May I accompany you?'

Anne looked through narrow eyes at Mary, and a mischievous twinkle shone. 'Tell me, kind uncle, would your welcome be this warm if I remained only a royal whore with no desire of a wedding ring?' she asked. Norfolk, taken aback at the question, regained his equanimity hastily.

'You have brought more to our family than any Howard or Boleyn has ever Done,' he said quickly. Anne raised her chin slightly to look down on him. Mary took a step back to allow her friend space to bait the duke and enjoyed the scene playing out before her.

'Strange, how you vocally slated the Boleyn's at my parents' wedding,' Anne continued. 'Had your sister not wed my father, I would not be here to advance either family.'

'I was hasty in my review of the occasion, niece. Thomas has proven a good husband for my sister.'

'Yes,' Anne replied slowly, not believing a word her uncle spoke. 'Anyway, Uncle Norfolk, you wanted to walk with me, please do so and we will talk more.'

She turned to her women. 'Leave us now. Mary, please remain.'

'By your command, madam,' Mary said, dropping back to give her mistress privacy with her uncle.

Mary was content with her life. Her friendship with Anne grew stronger the more the "secret matter" continued. Her relationship with Gregory was blossoming into a deep bond of love for the both of them. His work became more in demand as his confidence grew, although he spent most of his time now with his fellow lawyers, he would always find time for private clients with their own petitions. The only thing to mar Mary's complete happiness was her brother, Robert, who still tried to find ways of discrediting Anne to the court. He was not the only one; there were others who wanted to see King Henry remain married to his legal wife and those who still called Anne a witch and a whore. There were powerful and influential men who publically did not show their true feelings. It was too risky to talk openly against Lady Anne Boleyn while she held such a strong hold over the king.

# 34

It was inevitable Mary was pregnant. It was something she had naievly never thought might occur. After the initial shock had worn away, she knew her lover would have to know. Gregory's reaction to the news stunned her tremendously. Instead of joyfully taking her in his arms and professing undying love, he fled the scene distressed, and was later observed riding furiously away from the palace.

He was missing for several days with no notification as to his whereabouts. Lady Anne and Cromwell assumed Mary would know, but she was as mystified. Clients were angry with him for deserting their cases. It seemed he had purely vanished.

Then as suddenly has he had disappeared, Gregory returned unannounced, his horse exhausted, he himself travel weary, unshaven and filthy from little sleep and living rough. Mary was very pleased to see him alive and unharmed.

Later that day, he sat in a tub of hot water, while Mary gladly washed him.

'I am sorry for my behaviour, I was scared. The idea of becoming a father frightened me,' he apologised sheepishly. Mary smiled and said nothing. 'I thought and thought over what you had said and our future together. We are united forever by this child, so marry me for love and give this child its legitimacy and not to be named a bastard.'

Mary rubbed the soap-filled sponge across his shoulders, watching the suds trickle down his back. She had sworn once never to marry again, but she had not counted on the love she had discovered for this man and now, there was no doubt in her mind to her decision. 'Yes,' she replied simply. Laughing, Gregory turned and pulled her, fully clothed into the tub with him.

'We'll be wed this time next week,' he promised.

The wedding was a simple affair; the only two witnesses were Lady Anne and Thomas Cromwell. Anne felt satisfied in playing a pivotal role in bringing these two people together; Cromwell was relieved that his friend and lawyer was back to his professional best and his work could resume unhindered once again.

Mary enjoyed a smooth, trouble free pregnancy and when her time arrived, went into her confinement. The labour and the delivery were easy. By the end of that day, she was able to savour the delightful picture of Gregory holding his newborn son. The child was healthy and gifted with strong lungs. He sat on the edge of the bed, not giving up his son even when Mary held her arms out to take him.

'He will be called Edmund, after the steward of my family home who cared more for me than my own father,' Gregory said. Mary laughed and touched his face gently.

'A lovely choice, Edmund he is,' she replied, finally taking her son from his father.

'Edmund Paxton, son of Gregory,' Gregory affirmed proudly. '*Son of Gregory*. My son,' he repeated again, his eyes shining with pride. Reluctantly, he allowed himself to be ushered from Mary's side to give her time to sleep and recuperate.

Edmund took his place in the nursery and was the most contented baby there. At his baptism, as promised, Anne was god mother, Thomas Cromwell god father and, to Mary and Gregory's amazement, the king attended and insisted on being Edmund's god father too as a thank you for all the services they had both performed for him and his beloved mistress.

After this brief interlude from all the problems of the world, the king resumed his desire for a solution to his "secret matter" and began to put pressure on Cardinal Wolsey to conclude the events. In turn, Wolsey pressurised Secretary Thomas Cromwell. He gathered his lawyers together threatening severe repercussions if the divorce lingered any longer. The king and Anne were getting impatient waiting for their marriage to occur. She was beginning to worry that if the delay carried on much longer, the king may begin to lose interest in her and seek solace elsewhere. Ambitious fathers presented their daughters at court, to bargain for titled and rich husbands. Recently, there had been two young women inducted into the royal household: Madge Sheldon, Anne's cousin, and from Wiltshire, Lady Jane, a blonde-haired, pale-faced demure girl, sister to the ambitious Seymour brothers. Mary had the task of instructing the two new women in their duties. She doubted Lady Jane would come to much; she scarcely spoke louder than a whisper and kept her blue eyes downcast. She would make an obedient wife to a domineering husband eventually.

Anne still regarded Cardinal Wolsey as her enemy, preventing her destiny from being realised and she found every opportunity to discredit him in front of the king, or to whisper gossip about the cardinal in Henry's ear. He knew of the plotting against him. He was intelligent enough to put his case forward and often convinced the king to his way of thinking. The king would ask advice on ruling England and act on what his good cardinal advised. Once he had said to Cromwell in passing, that if the king ever found out that he did not need to ask and was to act on his own instincts on ruling, England and all who knew the king should beware.

There had been an outbreak of the sweating sickness, infecting the poor and impoverished that lived in London's crowded streets. The court moved to the clean air at Hampton. For the cardinal, it was a peculiar homecoming. He knew all the rooms, halls and galleries and had to watch Anne holding court in her own throne room. She and the king had the state apartments for their lovemaking and privy court while Wolsey found himself in apartments not worthy of his status. He did not complain, he knew his position at court was precarious and he did not want to risk raising the king's anger.

Holding court in the throne room, King Henry sat with Anne beside him. He received visitors and listened to petitions, but really wanted to be out hunting in the woods and parks. He requested Wolsey, who had been standing to the side along with Master Secretary Cromwell, to conduct the mundane business on his behalf. Bowing, the cardinal, as always agreed to take over. Anne got to her feet to join the king on his hunt, but he told her to stay behind at the palace, he wanted for once to go with his lords and knights, no women permitted this time. Anne slouched back into her seat, a petulant pout on her face and watched sullenly as her royal lover strode from the room calling his companions to join him. Now was the cardinal's chance to speak with her alone. To Anne's fury, he dismissed the lingering courtiers, behaving as though she was not present, saying he would deal with their pertitions later in the day.

Once the heavy doors slammed shut, and the courtiers left behind had dispersed, only Cardinal Wolsey stood in front of Anne. Cromwell, permitted to remain, moved back into the shadows from the two enemies. He stood silently watching and absorbing any information that may be of use to him in the future. The two adversaries watched each other, neither blinking in a soundless battle of wills. Wolsey eventually spoke first.

'We all live and die for the king. You madam, More, Cromwell and I, we all orbit that bright sun, trying to please him, cajole him to our way of thinking, keeping him from venting his anger upon us all, basking in his glory. Just bear in mind this, Mistress Boleyn. The whole episode that you conspired is bringing me down, and it may kill me eventually. Fail him and he will drop you like a stone and you shall have further to fall than any of us. The king loved me once as his dependable friend and Thomas More is almost a father to him. Look at us now, we all live in fear of our lives because of you and your fancies. I tell you, I may not be there to see your fall from grace, but one day, be forewarned, it will come and history will remember you for that fall more than your rise.' Wolsey stiffly bowed to Anne and, leaning on his stick, departed, Cromwell following behind as a faithful dog, leaving Anne thoughtful of his words. She began to tremble and tears rolled from her eyes. Her bitter bawling turned into hysterical laughter, bringing her women running, including Mary. She was inconsolable and slid from the throne to the stone floor. She lay there sobbing as if her heart would break, refusing aid from everyone surrounding her.

'I cannot carry on like this,' she sobbed. 'Why won't Catherine just give in? Why won't Wolsey leave me alone?'

'My Lady, you must not let the cardinal affect you like this. If word reaches him that you are becoming weak, he will fight you with every fibre in his body,' Mary soothed. Anne looked red-eyed at her friend.

'Sometimes, I wonder whether this is all worthwhile, should I just be happy to be his mistress and not his wife,' Anne pondered sitting up and stretching her legs out before her. Mary shook her head.

'Dearest friend, you have come this far, you cannot stop now. You will be queen ultimately, just be strong for a while longer,' Mary said. Anne nodded and eventually, with Mary's support, she struggled to her feet, and was lead like a small child to her bed, remaining there the rest of the day until the king returned.

Secretary Cromwell had heard about Anne's outburst and, with Gregory, rode with all haste back to Whitehall, risking contamination from the sweating sickness as he recalled a document he had once seen that could possibly help the king and Anne. Mary was afraid for her husband's health when she heard he was returning to London before the all clear. Despite his promise to take care with his health, Mary could not help but worry that history would repeat itself and she would be widowed for a third time, again with a small child to care for.

With conical masks filled with herbs to prevent inhaling the contaminated air, Cromwell and Gregory rode through the gates at Whitehall, guarded by a small garrison, and hurried to the archives kept deep within the vaults.

Without breaking to rest or eat, the two men searched for the rolled parchment Cromwell remembered. They went back through centuries of laws and legal scripts, until the master secretary finally found it and called his colleague over so they could both read the fragile parchment and faded contents. Eventually, they were sure the law still stood and would relate to their king's predicament.

The two men returned to Hampton so Cromwell could divulge his discovery in a private audience with the king. It would be worth the berating he would receive from Wolsey for deserting him without notice.

In their privy chamber, the king and Anne sat one end of a long table while Cromwell stood at the other end, the fragile parchment rolled up underneath his arm. He was beginning to perspire with expectation of the information he was about to disclose. He spread the document out on the table and showed it to the king.

'There is a law Paxton and I found that states that the King of England rules absolute and his word is the law. He does not need advisors to tell him how to reign or what law to make,' Cromwell said, pointing at the script. The king read to contents himself.

'So, master secretary, what are you saying?' he asked slowly. Cromwell wiped the sweat from his forehead and swallowed hard.

'It means, sire, that if you desire to marry Lady Anne, what is stopping you?'

'But His Majesty is still married,' Anne put in. 'If he marries me, he will be named a bigamist, and our marriage will be a sham. The sons I bear him will never be in the line of succession, they will be bastards.'

'Under the current law today, yes. But if His Majesty breaks with Rome and rules England and its church as he should, he will in all essence be a bachelor and free to wed who he pleases,' Cromwell explained. The king scowled, not totally convinced.

'So you say I should cut all communications with Rome and the Pope and become the true ruler of my country?'

'Yes, Sire. You rule England now, but you have to answer to a foreigner in Italy. What interest does he really have in our country? This way, you will be an absolute monarch and can make the laws you see fit to govern your realm. Your name will go down in history, in the future, schoolboys at their desks will learn of the revolutionary reign of King Henry VIII,' Cromwell said, feeling his confidence increasing. 'You would become the head of the new Church of England!'

'The Church of England, no longer the Church of Rome. What happens to the souls of my subjects? I will be excommunicated and go to Hell for doing this,' the king argued. Anne looked between the two men, listening attentively; beginning to see the prospect of Cromwell's convincing logic.

'No, Sire, forgive me. You will not go to Hell because you will be the head of your own church and accountable to no one but God Himself.'

Henry began to pace the floor, deep in thought. Anne came round the table to read the document for herself.

'I would be a bachelor and my marriage to Catherine would never have taken place. Princess Mary would become Lady Mary and a bastard, the product of a brief liaison I had with the widow of my dead brother.' Henry mulled the thoughts round in his mind. 'Master Secretary Cromwell, where do you see yourself in one year's time?'

'Sire, I see myself serving the true King and Queen of England.' Cromwell answered bowing. The king looked at his mistress and began to smile.

'I like this line of thought. I must give it some more time to study this, to be sure that there will be no way we could be stopped from attaining that which is so near to our reach. Cromwell, inform the court that we shall be advancing to Greenwich. Once we are there, tell Cardinal Wolsey I would have words with him, and send to Thomas More to attend me,' the king commanded, laying a hand on Cromwell's shoulder. Cromwell bowed and backed out of the royal chamber, relieved the audience was over. From the way the king had spoken, Wolsey's fall from grace was accelerating, and who would be there to step into his shoes? Thomas Cromwell.

Mary was thankful to have Gregory back with her; he had suffered no ill effects from his return to Whitehall. They talked into the early hours about the implications of what could happen to their own lives if their royal master decided to proceed with the break from Rome.

The following day the move from Hampton to Greenwich began. Messengers had already ridden ahead to reach Greenwich to inform of the arrival of their royal master and his retinue. The king and Anne had set out on a hunt that would end at Greenwich. The remaining courtiers and servants made their own way by either horse or barge.

There was a feast to welcome the king and Anne back to Greenwich Palace; Cardinal Wolsey, as usual, took his place at the high table, not aware of Cromwell, from his lower position, watching him. Thomas More had arrived soon after the king's arrival. He took his seat at the opposite end of the table to Wolsey, greeting him as a friend. The king looked between Wolsey and More and in his mind planned all he would say to both men when he spoke with them the next day. His eyes turned to Cromwell. The master secretary boldly met his stare and a slender smile widened his lips. Cromwell's star was rising; his loyalty to the king to be rewarded in due course.

The following morning, Anne sat in her chamber while Mary brushed her hair. Her royal lover advised her to dress fabulously this day, although he refused to explain why. Mary had chosen for her mistress a gown of scarlet to emphasise both the colour of her hair and complexion. Upon Anne's head, Mary placed a small coronet of diamonds and rubies.

'To look at you, madam, anyone would think you were already the queen,' Mary exclaimed. Anne laughed as she admired her reflection in a polished mirror.

'I shall be soon, His Majesty spoke more last night about this ancient law Cromwell and your husband had uncovered. This time next year, prehaps sooner, I will be Queen Anne.'

'Don't speak too hastily, madam,' Mary warned.

Anne stood up and waved an impatient hand towards her friend. 'Pish, Mary, the end of our plight is nigh and you will be the lady-in-waiting to the queen again.'

Followed by her women, with Mary by her side, Anne swept from her apartments for the throne room and appointment with the king.

King Henry had already arrived and, seated on his gilded throne. Anne and her women took their places. Thomas Cromwell, with his most reliable lawyers, stood the other side of the king. Everyone waited, although only a few knew the reason.

A bell somewhere chimed the hour, and at that exact time, Cardinal Wolsey entered. He bowed low to the king and approached his royal master slowly, glancing at the impassive Cromwell. The king watched his cardinal with unblinking eyes. He had rehearsed in his mind precisely what he wanted to say to Wolsey, and waited until the cardinal was only a few feet from the raised thrones. Wolsey bowed again and looked from the king to Anne. What was behind this witch? He saw the hatred in her dark eyes, he wanted to go up to Anne and slap her face, and wring her mole-infested neck for the trouble she caused everyone she met.

'Thomas, good cardinal, how long have you served me?' the

king asked benevolently. Wolsey smiled and relaxed, the king was not angry with him.

'I served your royal father before you, so many years, Sire,' he replied. Henry nodded.

'True, you have always looked after our interests and your own, am I right?'

Henry leant forward in his throne. Wolsey chuckled, a little uneasily.

'My lord, I have my own household expenses to cater for, would you not begrudge a little money to come my way?' he said guardedly. Henry nodded.

'Aye, the upkeep of Hampton Court must have strained your coffers, it does strain mine now.' The king looked around and everyone laughed. 'Yet you still seem to live more royally than I, Thomas.'

'When I entertain ecclesiastical emissaries or princes visiting from Europe, I do not want them to think your English cardinal is a pauper,' Wolsey explained, feeling the first stirrings of fear, was this was a trap for him to fall in?

'Nevertheless, you live better than I, I repeat, cardinal. How is this so?' the king now said unsympathetically. Wolsey opened his mouth to reply, but King Henry spoke again. 'Because you take a cut from all the churches and monasteries in my realm and you are in the pay of your Catholic Pope. You do not want my divorce from Catherine or my marriage to Lady Anne to occur because that would mean your link to Rome would be severed…like a head from its shoulders.'

'My lord, Sire, I would never dream of preventing your desires,' Wolsey stammered. Henry stood up.

'Eminence, you have lied and cheated your way through my reign, abusing my benison and friendship, you entertain treacherous thoughts against my royal person,' he shouted. The cardinal shook his head and stiffly got to his knees.

'Never in a hundred years, my lord,' he cried. The king would not listen. He sat back in his seat.

'You are to resign as Lord Chancellor and return the Royal Seal. They will be given to a man I know I can trust,' Henry said. Wolsey struggled to his feet, shaking his head in doubt.

'Can I not dissuade you, Sire? I am loyal and true to you,' he entreated.

'You are loyal and true to Rome and your own purse, not to England. Have them returned immediately, Wolsey. Cromwell, step forward.'

Thomas Cromwell felt his stomach turn. He had worked and waited for this moment; the king was going to pronounce him Lord Chancellor and keeper of the Royal Seal. Outwardly calm, but inwardly churning, Cromwell stood beside a trembling Wolsey and bowed low.

'Master secretary, collect from the cardinal his chain of office and the Royal Seal and bring them to me,' King Henry said steadily. Cromwell turned to his old master and held out his hands.

'If you please, my lord cardinal,' Cromwell said evenly. Wolsey looked directly into the face of the man he had taught and encouraged over the years.

'Thomas Cromwell, I knew you would go far, you have no principles,' the cardinal said so only Cromwell could hear as he lifted the chain of office from his shoulders and handed it to him, then unbuckling the Royal Seal from his belt placed it in the outstretched hand.

'I watched my master, good cardinal,' Cromwell replied quietly. He then turned to the waiting king and held them out for Henry. A squire took the items.

'Cromwell, I have another task for you to perform,' the king said, looking into Cromwell's expectant face. *This was it.* The promotion to Lord Chancellor was imminent. 'Go forth and bring Sir Thomas More to me. He is the only man I can think of admirable enough to wear these emblems of state.'

Cromwell's face visibly dropped, as did his stomach. Wolsey sniggered, heard only by the master secretary.

'Yes Sire,' Cromwell said, forcing himself to remain composed. He was aware of all the eyes in the throne room on him. Backing out he was glad to shut the door behind him. It was to be More and not him! Cromwell shook himself, gathering his senses, and hurried to find Thomas More. His time would come; he just had to be tolerant a little longer.

Back in the throne room, Cardinal Wolsey still stood in front of the king and Anne. He waited in an uncomfortable silence while the courtiers began to talk quietly amongst themselves. Anne beckoned Mary to approach her.

'So, what do you think then?' she asked. Mary shrugged her shoulders.

'I suspected His Majesty was going to do something like that, Gregory and I spoke of it last night.'

'With Wolsey out of the way, I can start preparing for my wedding. It will be an event to go down in history,' Anne said.

'Please, madam, do not be so hasty, the king cannot marry you immediately, and he must be seen to do everything precisely,' Mary said. Anne scowled.

'Are you now against my marriage? I thought you would rejoice with me. Yet you always tell me to keep my caution,' Anne complained in a spiky whisper. Mary curtsied.

'Apologies, madam, I just want to see everything done right. There are still many out there who wish you harm and would jump at the chance to bring you down even now,' Mary explained, thinking of Robert. Anne's face relaxed.

'I have waited this long, I can wait a few months more, I suppose,' Anne said forlornly. 'But, look at the cardinal, how troubled he is.'

Before Mary could answer, Cromwell entered the throne room with Sir Thomas More close behind. More looked confused when he saw Cardinal Wolsey's pallid face, and his shoulders vacant of the Chain of Office. King Henry stood up smiling broadly.

'Sir Thomas, come hither and let us speak before these people present,' Henry said brightly. The two men approached and both bowed. More greeted the cardinal.

The king descended from the raised dais and put an arm around More's shoulders in a premeditated show of friendliness.

'We have decided to reward your loyalty, Sir Thomas, for many years given us good counsel with your wise words.'

'I am humbled in your presence, Sire,' More replied. Henry laughed and returned to his throne. From one of the squires standing close by, he took the regalia. More breathed in sharply.

'Sir Thomas More, you are now created the Lord Chancellor. Kneel before your king,' he commanded. More threw a glance at

Wolsey, and then done as bade and knelt at the king's feet. With great ceremony, King Henry placed the Chancellor's Chain of Office over More's shoulders and held out the Royal Seal, which he took silently. The courtiers began to applaud the new chancellor, who slowly stood up.

'Your Majesty, I am speechless to this honour, but why me?' More asked. The king laughed with good humour.

'There is no one I trust more, More.' The king burst out laughing. 'More more!' He guffawed at his own play on words. The laughter rippled around the room. 'Good chancellor, we shall set to work immediately, come with me to my privy chamber and we shall talk.' Henry chuckled again and strode from the throne room with his arm thrown again over the new chancellor's shoulders.

Once the king was gone, the level of talk rose. Wolsey still stood in front of Anne. Mary was alert to the scene that was playing out in the midst of the noise, yet surreptitiously between Anne and Wolsey.

'So, Lady Anne, you have brought me down as I predicted, I hope you are happy with your actions. To be truthful, the burden lifted from me is a relief. I hope His Majesty will allow me to live out the rest of my days in solitude at a monastery, away from politics and court life. More is the one who will have to tread warily on seashells now,' he said jadedly. Anne regarded him solemnly.

'I almost have to thank you for where I am today, eminence. Had you not sent Henry Percy away, I would have been the Duchess of Northumberland by now. Your actions have brought me to the edge of queenship,' she replied. Wolsey grunted.

'Huh, had you been just his mistress, you would have become the duchess and I would still be the chancellor.' Wolsey bowed his head at Anne. 'Do not think that because having your arse on England's throne and the king's cock in your fanny you will be safe. Good luck with the rest of your life, madam, you will need it.' With solemnity, Wolsey turned and walked jadedly from the throne room, his stick tapping on the flagstones. Mary watching after him felt suddenly sorry for the old cardinal, he had been a powerful enemy to her mistress, but he was also an old man humbled in public. No one deserved that, not even an enemy.

'You will have to be careful of Thomas More, madam; he is a

Christian family man who opposes your marriage with the king also, but in a quieter fashion than the cardinal does,' Mary warned.

'He loves the king as a son and wants to see him happy, which is for him to be married to me,' Anne argued. 'Anyway, we have Thomas Cromwell on our side now, he will find a way to make the marriage happen, and I trust him.'

Mary frowned at the mention of Cromwell's name. She did not like him though he and Gregory were friends, but Anne seemed to think Cromwell was able to solve every predicament set before her and the king. He was invaluable to her.

# 35

Everyone assumed, after Thomas Wolsey's downfall, the king's wedding to Anne would occur with haste, yet Christmas came and went and Anne was still no closer to being queen. She began to get disconcerted of her marriage ever taking place, and began to doubt the king really did want to make her his queen. She had decided that it was all a ruse just to bed her. He remained married to Queen Catherine, and Anne was to stay the mistress. Mary had tried to reason with Anne, to make her see sense that the king would not have gone through all he had if his intention to marry Anne were nothing. Even Mary could not understand when, in February, the king pardoned Cardinal Wolsey and confirmed on him the Archbishopric of York.

Anne stormed when she heard the news, claiming the king no longer loved her and this only proved it. No one was able to placate her, she refused to sleep anywhere near him, saying she would share his bed once again when Wolsey was dead, and not a moment sooner!

Henry felt forced into action to win back his sweetheart's love, and he made a proclamation that England would break from Rome and no longer answer to the Pope, but the reigning monarch would become the head of the newly created Church of England. All sermons would be in English so that the common people would understand the Word of God. The church would surrender their buildings and lands and hand them over to the crown, if not voluntary, then by force. If they did not comply, their churches, convents and monasteries would be destroyed, the monks and nuns evicted onto the streets and anyone found taking pity on these unfortunates would suffer for their actions.

Cromwell sent armies across England to enforce the king's word. Money poured into the royal coffers, swelling them. Even the king could not believe how prosperous the church had been, and none had indicated the extent of their wealth. Anne regarded his actions with approval. She allowed him back into her bed again. Wolsey was far away in York and could no longer cause her trouble, Cromwell had now become irreplaceable, and Anne liked this. He was a man it was wise to have on one's side.

The year progressed slowly, Anne still was the mistress, Catherine still the thorn in her side, and she still refused to give up her title. Her health was beginning to fail and now living in cold damp houses did not improve her constitution. King Henry still thought about Catherine, he would force her submission, with no violence, but simple subtle pressure applied. The decision for him to take a new wife would be difficult for his subjects to understand. A European princess would be endured as a new queen, but a commoner like Anne Boleyn was not a popular choice. Faithful catholics and supporters of the queen could unite and rebel. He knew to eliminate the threat, Wolsey would have to go, and not into exile either.

Guards rode to York to arrest the old cardinal, to escort him to London and imprisonment in the Tower to await his fate, which he knew would be execution.

By now, Wolsey was frail, the long trek from York was gruelling; he had to break the journey to rest frequently, knowing to where this journey would lead to and what he could expect once the gates of the Tower swung shut behind him. At Leicester, Wolsey retired to bed, too sick to travel. On a cold November day, he drew his last breath and died.

When the news of the cardinal's death reached King Henry, he locked himself in his privy chamber and dismissed everyone. Sitting alone, he gazed unseeing, his thoughts remembering the times spent with Wolsey; how they had worked together, the advice he alway sought and adhered to from his wise cardinal. He had been content in the early days to leave the running of his kingdom to Wolsey. By his command, the king had demanded his arrest. He hated himself at this moment. That night, Henry spent the night alone, not wishing to speak or look at Anne. She had been the one to force his hand in this sorry event and he could not forgive her just now.

While all this was going on, Mary was able to tell Gregory that she was pregnant again and both could not be happier.

Anne was pleased for her friend and watched as Mary's waist thickened and expanded. She took comfort in placing her hands on Mary's body to feel the baby move. On one of her melancholy days, Anne was holding Mary's belly and she sighed.

'How is it that you are able to conceive when I find it so difficult? Is it that husband of yours? All those years of abstinence, from a good woman's love have made his seed all the stronger when they finally found a use.'

'Your time will come, madam,' Mary assured. Anne sighed again dispondently.

'I sometimes wonder whether I shall ever produce a child fathered by the king,' she smiled vaguely. 'Other men can father sons. Someone like your Gregory seems capable of making sons so easily.'

'Lady Anne, do not speak so carelessly, people might hear and spread gossip,' Mary warned, looking around at the other women in the room.

'I am amongst friends here, Mary, who would wish me harm.' Anne took her hands from Mary's belly and sat in a cushioned chair. 'One day, I shall have a child, pray God it is male and all the trouble that surrounds me will fade away.'

'Madam, whatever happens to you; nothing or no one will come between us. We shall be friends for life.' She then looked around and whispered close to Anne's ear. 'Not even the king or my husband will keep us apart.' Anne giggled and nodded. Mary straightened up and, looking around, saw the simpering Jane Seymour sitting so demurely in a corner concentrating intently on her needlework. *What an unimportant little creature,* she thought to herself.

Robert had begun a very public affair with one of the younger women at court who despite her age was already gaining a reputation as having the morals of an ally cat. He was aware of this, but it did not deter him from seeking pleasure between her thighs.

Mary sought out Robert to try to dissuade him from his adulterous behaviour, but he was adamant to continue his liaison.

'I thought you loved Alice and your children, why do you hurt them by continuing this affair?' Mary tried to reason with him.

'Alice does not know, so why should it hurt her?' he asked. 'Alice is a good woman; she has given me healthy children and what man could ask for more? But she is not here and I need sport to entertain me.'

'What is it with you men? Why can you not be satisfied with one woman? Why do you have to be unfaithful?' Mary exclaimed.

'Is that husband of yours unfaithful?' Robert countered back. Seeing her expression, he laughed. 'Of course he isn't unfaithful to you, the fool, couldn't get a woman before he met you. No sensible woman would look at him twice,' he sneered. Incensed, Mary slapped Robert across the face with venom. He caught her wrist in his hand and held her tight. 'If I want to, I can destroy your happy little life with that peculiar little husband of yours, so treat me with more respect, sister, or I shall spread the word about saintly Gregory Paxton and the way he looks at your mistress with an animal's lust. You know I will, Mary,' he whispered maliciously in her ear.

'You are perverted, Robert,' Mary retorted furiously. He snorted a laugh and patted Mary's face, making her shrink back with fear.

'But you love me, admit it,' he laughed and winked. 'How about you and me one day share a bed? That would be fascinating; you could not deny that. We would be good in bed together, a brother and a sister sharing sibling love; and you must like a good trenching Mary; you seem to get pregnant easy enough. I never imagined that dreary husband of yours having it in him.'

'Gregory is a good man, more than you can ever be! God will strike you down one day for everything you are saying, Robert and I hope I am there to see it happen,' Mary cried, appalled at even the thought of such a suggestion and turned to leave, but he pulled her back and slammed her into the wall, knocking the air from her body. The baby in Mary's womb jumped, startled by the sudden act of aggression to its mother. Robert's face contorted with anger.

'Until that day happens, dear sister of mine, forget you not of your obligation to me. The king grows impatient. I have heard that he wishes to spread the legs of any wench who catches his eye now, why not you? He'd like a randy little hooch like you,' Robert hissed into Mary's ear.

'The king and Lady Anne are still very much in love. They share the one same bed every night,' Mary gasped as the air returned to her lungs.

'And it must be a cosy place to be. Two bodies, naked and close together. Oh, can you imagine it, Mary? Can you?' Robert's voice turned silky soft and ominous as he rubbed his body up against hers and his lips brushed her cheek, making her catch her breath in revulsion. Then he slowly licked the side of her face. She struggled trying to get free, but Robert roughly pulled her round and kissed her savagely on the mouth. With a triumphant laugh, he released her and watched in amusement as she fled from him. Mary ran as fast as she could towards a door that led into a courtyard where she vomited. In her mind, she kept seeing and sensing Robert's invasion of her person, his hold over her was as strong as ever.

Then Mary wondered what good it would do if she told Gregory of Robert's influence on her life. She had managed to keep the two separate sides of her life apart. He knew Robert was devious, and had little to do with him, knowing he was intellectually superior. However, if Mary had related to her husband about her brother's behaviour, Gregory would want retribution, but he was not a physical man. With words and the law, he was the master who none could equal. However, with a sword, or his fists, he lacked the skills. Mary knew that Robert would make short work of her husband if there were an altercation. Therefore, for now, Mary would keep her peace, and smile sweetly to Gregory, insisting that all was well.

Weeks later, Mary gave birth to her third son, who thrived and brought with him a love to sooth her troubled heart. She named him Simon.

A letter arrived from Portsmouth; Captain Foyle had decided that Cecily and Ambrose should marry soon as the couple's friendship was developing into something more intimate.

Mary and Robert arrived home to a euphoric welcome from their mother and Alice. Margaret greeted Gregory as if he was her own son, much to Robert's vexation. The two men had spoken little on the ride from London. Stephen was, as always, thrilled to see his father and rode gleefully on his shoulders back into his home. Roberta ran alongside her father, squealing with delight and the two youngest children clung to their nurses.

The party set out for Portsmouth. After days of travelling, Mary began to recognise familiar landmarks as they neared their destination and began to feel the excitement rising at the thought of meeting her daughter again. She tried to recollect the route from the docks when she had first arrived back from Spain. Eventually, a fisher wife, broad hipped using language as broad, pointed the direction, she now knew where she was going and led the way to the familiar door. Susannah screamed in delight and pulled Mary to her, hugging her as though wanting to squeeze the breath from her body. With loud swearing, Captain Foyle pushed past his wife, roaring his approval at seeing the travellers. He led the way into his home, heartily clapping a bemused Robert and Gregory on their backs.

In a private room, Mary and Cecily were reunited. The girl was growing more beautiful than Mary had remembered, having inherited her father's good looks and mother's temperament. Cecily stood up and ran towards Mary. Mother and daughter held each other tightly after such a long separation. She greeted her new stepfather warmly, instantly liking him.

The wedding was to take place at Portsmouth cathedral, nothing but the best for Foyle's only son, though Cecily had confided to her mother that she would have been content with a small church.

As always, Captain Foyle was in a hurry to get business done. 'I sail two days later!' he announced proudly. 'I'm off to Holland.'

'And I am sailing with him too,' Ambrose added enthusiastically. Cecily pouted.

'I do not wish my husband to leave me so soon, but as a sailor's wife, it is something I must accept,' she conceded sullenly.

The wedding went without a hitch, and laughing and happy, Cecily and Ambrose emerged into the sunlight from the cathedral.

After a magnificent feast and dancing, the women ushered

Cecily up the stairs, all laughing and joking together, along the corridor. They all hustled into the small bedchamber, filling the room. After wishes of good luck and prayers for Cecily to have an adveturous night, the women left, leaving only her closest relatives. The coverlet pulled back, with flower petals strewn over the sheets, Cecily disrobed with help and her nightgown was brought to her. Margaret took the brush to pull gently through Cecily's long hair until it shone like a spun gold cloak over her shoulders.

The bed beckoned. Mary laid a hand on Cecily's head and blessed her, wishing her marriage to be fruitful. Cecily sat in the bed looking younger than her seventeen years as she watched the women depart, leaving her alone to ponder on her forthcoming married life.

Seeing the return of the women, Ambrose took the prompt to announce his departure from his guests and go to his bride. Captain Foyle bellowed at the top of his voice for all the men to help the bridegroom to his wife waiting for him. Vociferously, the men ascended the stairs, heading to the bedchamber for Ambrose's riotous bedding.

When they all reappeared, there were loud and lewd jokes shouted about the young couple and what they were up to, followed by guffaws of laughter. Gregory found the event exhilarating, never having participated in such an occasion before. The raucous feasting continued late into the night.

As planned, Captain Foyle and Ambrose boarded *The Ignite*. Cecily stood between Susannah and Mary at the dock, watching her new husband prepare to depart. She would miss Ambrose desperately while he was away, he had assured his new wife that he would also miss her and count the days until they were together again.

The captain strode back down the gangplank and walked directly to Mary. 'How old is that Spanish boy of yours?' he asked.

'Angelo is still young, why?' Mary replied suspiciously.

'When he is older, send him to me. I'll tutor him to sail under an English flag,' he continued. Mary agreed it would be a good future for her son.

'You have my daughter in your family, why not my son,' she replied agreeably.

'Good, that's settled then. Ambrose, say your goodbyes, the tides waits for no man, bridegroom or not,' he yelled turning to his son, before pulling Susannah into his arms and kissing her ardently. Ambrose sprinted down the gangplank and over to Cecily. They embraced and kissed, whispering clandestine words in each other's ears before, with one final kiss, he then turned and ran back up the gangplank.

Cecily, with Susannah by her side, watched as the galleon pulled away from its mooring and steered out of Portsmouth harbour.

Mary and her family remained in Portsmouth several more days before returning home. These days were special for both her and Cecily; spending time together. Cecily liked being with Gregory, and announced she would refer to him as father from now, which elated him beyond words.

The party began their long journey home with Mary promising to write to her daughter often.The journey was long and exhausting. Everyone was feeling depressed after an exciting week. Gregory and Robert argued for most of the way home, even mild Alice became sullen and spent hours staring sulkily out of the carriage window. Mary could not wait to get home to her children again. Only Margaret seemed unaffected by the sour moods, she spent many hours of the journey sleeping.

Yardeley Chase was a welcoming sight when the party finally arrived home.

The sight of the children running out in the courtyard to meet their parents brightened spirits. It felt good to be home and sleep in familiar beds once again.

Mary, Gregory and Robert were unable to stay for long, as they had to return to court. They said their goodbyes and returned once again to London.

# 36

Relations between the king and Chancellor Thomas More were beginning to strain; King Henry still faced barriers preventing his marriage to Anne put up by Sir Thomas.

A devoted Catholic, More continued to attempt to persuade the king to see the error of his ways, return to his wife and cast Anne Boleyn aside. He had never been afraid to speak the truth to his king and continued to do so, much to Henry's chagrin. Yet after Cromwell had told the king that he was capable of ruling the kingdom without advice, More's preaching infuriated Henry to distraction and he could be heard shouting abuse and and cursing his chancellor.

Eventually, seeing that everything he tried the king either rejected or ignored, Sir Thomas decided it was time to retire from the chancellorship and, knowing that Master Secretary Cromwell would take up the mantle, retire from public life.

Disappointedly, the king accepted More's resignation, saying he would miss his old friend. Thankfully, Sir Thomas departed the palace and resumed a more welcomed life with his wife and children.

Thomas Cromwell, now Chancellor of England, could hardly believe his good fortune. He knew he had powerful men as enemies; titled dukes and earls resented the fact that like Wolsey, he had risen from humble beginnings to this exalted position, and he would advise the king faithfully on all matters now. With Wolsey dead and More retired, there was nothing to stop Cromwell, and there was nothing to prevent the king marrying his Anne.

Anne summoned Mary to her apartments with a secret and special request. Suspicious of the reason; Mary arrived at Anne's doorway. She was there waiting and greeted her friend affectionately. Dismissing the other women, Anne threw an arm over Mary's shoulders, closed the door behind both of them, smiling broadly. She had news to tell.

Periodically, there were investitures at court, honours given for service to king and country. Word went around that there was to be a special ceremony, slotted into the calendar. Supposition and wagering ran endemic throughout the court to the theme of this event.

The throne room was full to capacity on the October day. Courtiers present saw and noted that there was only one throne on the dais. The queen still locked away in the country was never in London anymore to attend ceremonies. What was to happen would not involve her, everyone had accepted that now she was gone for good.

The king, looking splendid in his robes, strode up the carpeted aisle, followed by the Dukes of Norfolk, Suffolk and Northumberland, and the Earls of Sussex and Wiltshire, to his throne and sat down, scanning the faces looking expectantly back at him.

As a clock chimed three, the great doors swung open to a magnificent fanfare. All eyes turned to see who was standing there. A collective intake of breath rose from the audience. Anne Boleyn, wearing a simple white gown, her long black hair hanging loose with a circle of white flowers on her head, stood framed in the doorway, her hands holding a single red rose clasped to her breast. Slowly, she began to walk towards the king who watched her slow approach with satisfaction. Behind Anne, Mary followed at a respectful distance. Although she had primarily refused to attend upon her friend at the ceremony, Anne had been convincing in making her eventually agree. No one else had knowledge of this event; the only ones who knew had been the king, Anne, Cromwell and Mary. Cromwell had recommended silence about this in case some demented assassin tried to harm the king or Anne. Sworn to secrecy, Mary was not even able to tell Gregory, and certainly not Robert. Both Gregory and reluctantly Robert would be seated somewhere in the throne room watching with different emotions the event unfolding before them.

Once Anne came to a stop in front of the king, Mary took the circlet of flowers from Anne's head, stepped aside to a vacant chair, and watched with the other courtiers as King Henry rose to his feet and smiled benevolently at everyone assembled.

'My lords, you are invited to share with me one of the happiest days of my life so far. Today, Lady Anne Boleyn is to be invested Marquess of Pembroke.' He looked at his mistress and, taking her hand, helped Anne into a kneeling position and fastened an ermine edged cloak over her shoulders. He recited the oath of featly and honour, which Anne repeated in a clear and ringing voice, ensuring that everybody would hear. The king then turned to Norfolk and took a gold coronet he had carried on a silk cushion and lowered it carefully onto Anne's head. She raised a hand to adjust the fit of the coronet slightly. They looked into each other's eyes and both smiled. Raising Anne to the position of marquess had elevated her to royalty, now she was eligible to marry a king.

Again taking Anne's hand, the king helped her back to her feet, this was the cue for Mary also to stand and retake her position behind her mistress.

On the arm of the king, and with Mary following behind, the new Marquess of Pembroke departed the throne room to a silence mistaken for respect. Once outside, and after the doors had shut, Anne visibly relaxed, and the king kissed her flushed cheek.

'My love, did you see their faces in there? No one could believe it was actually happening. Nothing can stop me from marrying you now,' Anne said, her voice shaking with emotion. Henry patted her hand.

'The preparations for our wedding shall begin immediately, it shall be a summer wedding when we can ride under a blue sky to church and you shall become my queen and your coronation shall occur within the month,' the king promised. Anne laughed, turning to Mary.

'Do you hear that, Mary? I shall be queen,' she trilled.

'You have waited long enough for it, and the people shall finally love you,' Mary replied. Anne's face darkened somewhat. The one thing that marred her happiness was the common people's hatred of her for taking the king from his true wife.

267

'When I give them a prince, they shall forgive me,' Anne answered fiercely. The king nodded.

'And he will be English through and through,' he added.

Back inside the throne room, uproar broke out once the doors shut. A common woman elevated to marquess! Moreover, she being the king's whore as well; it was impossible to believe. Robert had been sitting with like-minded men and cursed the mentality of their king to raise a woman like that so high.

Later, he was playing dice in the great hall, spending some leisure time gambling while the king and Anne were together in private. There were crude jokes swapped about what the king and the marquess were doing. Robert looked up and smiled as he saw his sister passing by.

'Here comes the baby machine, boys,' he scoffed. 'My sister cannot stop getting sprogged up these days.' Robert turned to the other men who were grinning. 'She should be our next queen then Henry would have more sons than he would know what to do with.' He looked directly at Mary. 'Or perhaps the marquess should let Gregory Paxton prang her, and then she's sure to have boys!' he guffawed. Mary regarded her obnoxious brother blankly, waiting until the laughter had stopped.

'One day, brother, you shall say too much and that will be your undoing,' she answered coolly. Robert made a gesture of mock fear.

'Oohh, I am scared.' His face and voice grew cold. 'What will you do? Tell Her Majesty the whore?' he replied, as his companions behind him rocked with laughter.

'You are not worth my breath,' she responded and continued on her way, hearing the malicious laughter behind her.

'That bitch shall never sit easily on the throne! She'll be sorry one day!' he shouted at his sister.

The Christmas revels that year were brighter and jollier than ever seen before. The marquess commissioned new gowns for all her women in dazzling reds and blues, set with rubies and sapphires making them sparkle with every movement. Even the quiet Jane Seymour looked ravishing. Anne was so close to achieving her goal of marriage, she wondered whether she had made her women too attractive. She need not have worried; King Henry had eyes only for his marquess throughout the festivities to Twelfth Night.

Early in January, Anne drew Mary into a quiet room where she knew they would not be disturbed. Her eyes were sparking with excitement and her cheeks flushed. Once she knew no one could possibly overhear, she hugged her bewildered friend.

'Madam, what has happened to make you this happy? Has the king named the day for your wedding?' she asked.

'Things are changing for the better. I am finally pregnant,' Anne whispered elatedly.

'Can you be sure?' Mary asked, trying to remain calm and reasonable.

'I am pregnant, Mary, I carry England's hope, England's prince.'

'Does the king know?'

'I have not told him yet, I want to wait for the right moment, when we are alone, and romance is in the air,' Anne replied wistfully.

Mary curtsied low, but Anne pulled her to her feet.

'No ceremony between us, we are friends forever. I am happy, afraid and excited, I do not think I truly know how I really feel.' Anne clasped her hands together ecstatically. 'You must attend me when my hour comes.'

# 37

*The Palace of Westminster 25th January 1533*

Sitting in a pew in the king's private chapel, Anne was thoughtful. It was early morning on a cold January day and the palace was beginning to stir. She could hear faint, indistinguishable voices from outside. She sniffed, and her nostrils filled with the delicious aroma of freshly baked bread. It reminded her of how hungry she was.

She smiled and put a hand over her belly and whispered a little word of assurance to the baby. For him, this was why she was marrying in secret; it would mean that he would be the legitimate heir to the throne upon his birth; she now stood on the brink of an astounding marriage and future

The door to the chapel flung open noisily and King Henry stood there. He looked ill at ease. His eyes scanned the chapel, coming to a stop at Anne. She had turned to face him. Behind the altar, a priest was standing silently. Startled by the king's loud entrance, he knocked the gold cross making it wobble and almost fall. Quickly, the priest grabbed the cross and steadied it, throwing an uneasy smile towards the king.

'How fare you this morning, Anne?' he asked awkwardly.

'Our prince and I are all the better for seeing you, my lord,' Anne replied confidently.

'Good, good, I would have it no other way,' he replied quickly.

'Sire, my lady, we should hasten before the court awakens,' the priest advised, waving his hands towards the altar.

'Aye, Anne, come hither and let us wed,' he beckoned and, taking her hand, led her to the altar. With shaking hands, the priest opened his Bible and began to recite the wedding service with a quiver in his voice; aware of the momentousness of the service he was performing. King Henry was still legally married to Queen Catherine in the eyes of Rome. This was breaking with all traditions and laws respected in England. The break with Rome had created this new Church of England with the king at its head and this ceremony, however bizarre, was the first performed under the new rules.

On the other side of the chapel, Mary and Gregory watched this strange service. Anne had requested that they both attend as witnesses to her marriage. Mary felt honoured by such a command, and it did not matter that history would not recall her by name, but say that a lady-in-waiting attended this most peculiar of royal weddings. It would be something to tell her grandchildren. Gregory looked perturbed. Always the lawyer, he could see the intricacy this would cause once the news broke.

'It's wrong, it's wrong,' he kept whispering so only Mary could hear. 'All the laws they're both breaking. The king is committing bigamy here.'

'There are no laws being broken here, don't forget, now the king is the head of the Church of England so he is unmarried, there is nothing wrong,' Mary reasoned. He shook his head.

'Lady Anne is a commoner, the king could marry you, or any woman in the land, and he can only marry royalty.'

'Hush, Gregory, he is the king and above the law. Lady Anne is the Marquess of Pembroke; she is royal now. The country needs a male heir and Anne carries that heir now.'

'It's still wrong,' he muttered again from the side of his mouth. Mary put a finger to her lips to silence her doubting husband.

Once the service was over, Mary and Gregory bowed to their new queen and king. Queen Anne now looked radiant, all her planning and plotting for revenge had culminated in this, marriage to the King of England. Wolsey was dead; Sir Thomas More was in his Chelsea home, contentedly being the family man and Thomas Cromwell, her supporter, established as Chancellor.

The king, as he had said many times, had done what was necessary to secure the safety of England, putting aside a woman who could not bear a male child and marrying the woman who promised healthy sons was the right thing to do – for England of course. There was to be no celebration, everyone was to keep silent until the news of the wedding became public knowledge, and that was to be when he decided it was time. The king and his secret queen left the chapel to take their usual breakfast together, before he met with members of the Privy Council to talk about the day to come and what was on the agenda. He knew that the "secret matter" would be a usual topic, and the king had to pretend he was still looking for an escape from Catherine. He enjoyed playing these games with his ministers. He would amuse himself in their presence by goading the exasperated lords with demands for his release from an unhappy marriage. He would see how long he could keep the pretence up before announcing to a stunned world that he was a married man and married to the most alluring woman on the earth, who carried his prince in her womb. What fun he would have watching their faces. Listening to their babbling as they tried to express their surprise and delight.

Gregory thankfully returned to his chambers, there was much work to do. Mary rounded up the other women and shepherded them to the chapel for the early morning prayers.

Anne's thickening waistline confirmed what many had guessed, that she carried the king's child. There was surprise at both their lack of urgency to marry now that she was pregnant. Therefore, King Henry decided to take the opportunity to reveal their secret marriage to his courtiers. Varied reactions greeted the news. There were those who welcomed this revelation, feeling it was ushering in a new age of prosperity for England. Then there were those who were appalled, damming Anne for stealing the king from his true, loyal wife. She was nothing but a jezebel, a whore, a witch who deserved nothing less than burning at the stake at Smithfield for her sins. Yet no one would dare speak out to the king for fear of his or her lives. They would wait patiently to see what sex this child was to be. A female child would give them ammunition to strike at a weakened woman and bring her down. Robert, infuriated at hearing the news, demanded from Mary why she had not told him of the wedding. Mary replied that she was loyal to her queen and had promised not to tell anyone, that included her scheming brother.

Royal barges, brightly decorated with ribbons and flowers, some carrying musicians and poets, others carrying laughing and happy women, cruised up river from Greenwich towards the Tower. On the riverbanks, people stopped to watch, guessing who the important person was and to where she was going. News of the king's new Church of England wedding was spreading from the palaces and into the streets and taverns of London, from where travellers took the news across England. Within weeks, it would be common knowledge that England had a new queen.

From her cushioned seat in the most luxurious barge, Queen Anne sat and laughed with her companions, the music blotting out catcalls from the common people. Anne had decided that she would ignore those rude and dirty people; they were a vexation to her.

In the sunlight, the Tower looked almost agreeable. The cold grey walls appeared to sparkle, adding a sensational backdrop for the barges. They entered through the watergate, where the constable of the Tower met the new queen and escorted her along with her retinue to the Queen's House where they would lodge for the night. The next day, Anne would set out for Westminster.

The evening passed merrily for the women, laughing, dancing and telling stories of previous lovers. Anne sat listening, laughing at the hilarious tales, and refused to reveal any secrets of the king's performance in bed.

The following day dawned bright and cloudless. The sun shone down on a London prevalent with complaint. There was an atmosphere of disgruntlement not felt by the Londoners for many years. Rumours had spread that earlier in the year there was a marriage ceremony between the king and Anne Boleyn. Her presence as mistress was tolerable. While Catherine lived, she was queen consort and wife of the king. Now the rumours were true and today, at six months pregnant, Anne Boleyn was to be taken to Westminster Abbey and crowned Queen of England. The people could forgive their king anything, but many had regarded Anne as a witch with that sixth finger on her left hand and the moles on her neck. She had bewitched their king into marrying her while his lawful wife lived. Their feelings for this woman were steadfast. The pennants of bright colours strung across the streets, jolly musicians, honey-voiced choirs and the fountains running with ruby red wine would not buy their loyalty and fealty.

Anne stood proudly in a magifient chariot covered with silver cloth, waiting behind the closed gates of the Tower. Pennants fluttered in a gentle summer breeze; horses, gaily caparisoned, snorted and pawed the ground impatient to be on their way and guards stood dressed in their finest livery, with the afternoon sunlight glinting on their polished breastplates. Anne stroked her body, feeling movement of the growing prince inside her. Henry had turned his kingdom upside down for her, and she now suddenly felt humbled for this. All she had to do was produce this long awaited heir to prove to the common people that all the havoc caused would be worth the while.

Anne's brother George approached holding two single-stemmed roses, one red and one white. He offered them to his sister.

'The king greets you with love and charges me to relate to you that his gardeners are working on a rose that is both red and white in the same flower,' he said. 'He tells me when they succeed; you shall be the first Tudor queen to hold the single stem. Until then, from His Majesty, receive these.'

'Our son shall be that rose that is both red and white, and I will be the only Tudor queen to hold him,' Anne replied steadily. George nodded with satisfaction.

'Good answer, sister,' he remarked smiling

Bells from the chapel chimed the hour, the gates slowly swung apart and the crowd outside got their first view of the head of the parade. Aldermen and mercers of London were waiting outside the gates to greet the new queen. The heralds played a fanfare and drummers struck a beat. Two knights, dressed in white and silver, on white horses led the parade forward, followed by detachments of guards. Dukes and earls on their mounts rode ahead of one hundred knights. Small girls in brightly coloured dresses scattered flower petals dancing forward. Under a silver canopy held aloft by four knights and pulled by two palfreys dressed in white damask, the new queen in her chariot followed, dressed in cloth of gold, blazing with sparkling jewels. Four richly decorated chariots followed behind full of ladies of the court along with Mary in the first, all dressed in scarlet, decorated with pearls and tiny glass beads that shimmered and sparkled as diamonds. More women, also dressed in scarlet, rode behind the chariots. Many more courtiers followed behind on foot. Guards, with their halberds raised, brought up the rear.

For all the magnificence in front of them, the crowds who had gathered to see this unholy exhibition remained noiseless. This woman feted before them as queen was no such thing while Catherine lived. The people lining the route did so in silence, which the queen observed to her displeasure. At Catherine's coronation, women had jostled their babies to the front of the crowds requesting a blessing for their infants and this impulsive behaviour was missing.

The parade made its way through the streets of London, decorated with colourful tapestries and banners in scarlet and gold. Pagents were performed exaulting Anne and musicians played. At every event, the parade would stop and she was obliged to watch and congratulate the performers. The free wine available to all Londoners in the hope that they would sup enough to make themselves drunk and cheer the royal parade as it passed by had been consumed greedily, they preferred to drink themselves into a stupor and make their own fun.

Anne was beginning to feel tired. Her pregnancy and the heat of the afternoon sun combined to wear her down. She felt fatigued, but intractably carried on. The king had offered the royal barge from the Tower to Whitehall, and then the chariot to Westminster, Anne had refused; she wanted the Londoners to see that she was not afraid of them.

The royal procession came to a halt outside Westminster hall. King Henry, dazzlingly dressed and waiting, came forward and helped his queen down from her chariot. Anne felt stiff and sore, stretched to loosen her aching joints. She smiled at her beaming royal husband and accepted his arm to rest upon. She would stay here tonight and tomorrow would see her triumph as she was crowned Queen of England.

To a glorious fanfare, Henry and Anne entered the abbey. Conspicuous by his absence was Sir Thomas More. He had refused the invitation to attend the coronation. The king had been disappointed and annoyed by his former chancellor's behaviour, yet today he was determined not to allow anything to spoil this day. Anne was centre of attention; all eyes focused on her and all thoughts only of her. Sir Thomas could sit in his Chelsea home and stew. The king would show the world he cared not.

He led Anne up the shallow steps and guided her to the cushioned throne. Kissing her hand, he backed away, leaving her sitting alone.

From her position, Mary sat and watched, wishing Gregory were by her side, he was sitting with the knights. She had a deep fondness for Queen Anne, but knew her friend was straying into perilous territory. If the child were stillborn or not male, even Anne with her quick mind would not be able to explain her way out of this.

Choirs sang, prayers chanted, oaths given, Anne received the royal regalia and the archbishop anointed her on her breast and head. He then held aloft the crown and slowly lowered it onto her head and throughout the abbey echoed: 'God save Queen Anne. God save Queen Anne.' King Henry came forward and helped her to stand, kissing her warmly. Instantaneously, the abbey was resonant with applause and cheering. Above the celebrations, the sounds of voices shouting penetrated in from outside, and not words of salutation. The Londoners were going to make their feelings heard and no matter how loud trumpets sounded, their king was going to know precisely what his subjects thought of his new queen.

The mercifully short ride from Westminster Abbey to the Palace of Whitehall hurried along at a fast pace by order of the king to save his queen facing the gauntlet of angry Londoners. He commanded the heralds to play loudly in an attempt to drown out the shouting and cursing of the people lining the route. Although Anne tried to smile benevolently to her subjects and waved graciously at them, inside she was hurting from their malicious remarks and name-calling. By the time the great gates at Whitehall shut the angry mob out, Anne felt physically sick and emotionally drained. All she wanted to do was retire to bed. The king reminded her that now she was queen, there were royal duties she was required to perform. She had to attend and enjoy the magnificent banquet and masque laid on in celebration for her coronation. Wearily, and looking fatigued, Queen Anne took her place by the king's side at the top table and acknowledged the enthusiastic greeting from her courtiers with a strained smile. Her soft, inviting bed kept calling her, and Anne wanted to go to it, but she had to stay in the great hall, laugh and dance. Sleep would be even more welcoming when she finally was able to fall onto the soft mattress and pull the covers up under her chin.

Mary and Gregory sat side by side, close to the top table. Their conversation was about the coronation and their different views of the ceremony. His view had been partially obscured whereas she had an excellent seat. In addition, while she had assisted the new queen with the preparations for her coronation, they had endured a forced separation. The couple were anxious to slip away and spend intimate time together. Looking around, Mary saw her brother standing by the wall, engaged in conversation with yet another young woman. The girl seemed to have a fancy to him, and he still seemed unconcerned that at home his loyal wife patiently waited for his visits. Alice had no knowledge of his exploits and that suited him. Mary would not be the one to divulge the nature of the husband she blatantly adored. This new woman appeared to hang on every word he spoke and giggled like a foolish girl, pleasing her lover immensely. This one was no fool; she was an intelligent woman, using Robert the way that he used her. They were welcome to each other, Mary decided. She had tried to reason with her brother to encourage him to be a faithful to Alice, yet he chose to disregard her advice. She knew that when the woman grew tired of him she would be off to seek more adventures, so long as it did not include marriage. Good luck to her, she would end up as another court mare all men would eventually ride.

The king led his queen onto the floor as the musicians struck a chord and began to play. Everyone cheered and applauded as the king swung Anne around in time to the melody, no one could remember seeing him look so happy. In September, when he presented his son and heir to the English, all his planning would ripen and the Tudor dynasty would sit more secure on the throne of England.

Finally, Mary and Gregory were able to slip away from the noise of the great hall and hurried to that special bench in the herb garden. The fragrant herbs made the couple reminisce about the early days of their relationship, when Gregory was awkward, reticent and fearful to talk to Mary. They sat side by side, talking quietly. He then looked around to see if anyone was close by.

'Let us make love here, in the garden. No one will catch us,' he courageously suggested. Before Mary could express her surprise, Gregory already had stood up and was pulling Mary towards a thick bed of lemon balm. They pushed knee deep into the herb and together lay down. There, with the faint sounds from the great hall drifting on a breeze towards them, and the fragrant scent of the herb infusing into their clothes, Mary and Gregory made love with quiet, intense passion. After, they lay listening to the distant music and laughter, breathing in the sweet scents around them.

Eventually, a chill in the night air forced the couple to move from their nest and return, arm in arm to their chambers, the aroma of the lemon balm wafting behind them. People they passed were unable to miss the distinct fragrance, and they smiled knowingly, seeing leaves, stems and petals sticking to their clothing.

The next day, the gardener was furious to see his lemon balm flattened and ruined, knowing what tomfoolery had occurred the night before. He vociferously cursed the horny courtier who could not keep his cock in his breeches and did not care what he or his slut ruined to have their fun.

Mary, as usual, attended the queen the next morning and Anne commented on the delicate scent of lemon balm that Mary wore that day. A ripple of giggling ran through the women, the gossips already circulated their stories early that morning about Sir Gregory and his wife's amour in the herb garden.

Gregory also faced ribald comments from his clients who had heard the stories already themselves. He was outwardly mortified to be the centre of such hilarity, and heard about the complaints from the gardener. However, secretly, he was pleased that finally he was like the other men around him who humped a woman purely for satisfaction, even if that woman was his wife.

# 38

In the heat of August, Queen Anne retired from court to await the birth of the prince. Her apartments were prepared by royal tradition for the confinement. The shutters on all windows closed and even though the summer weather was warm, the fires were stoked up giving out stifling heat in the darkened rooms. Only the closest and most trusted companions, royal midwives and wet nurses stayed with her, including Mary. No one could enter or leave the apartments; supplies needed were ready for the long stay. Even the chaplain had to conduct his prayers from behind a screen so that he would not see the pregnant queen.

For the first week, there was talk only of the baby, the queen was anxious at the thought of giving birth and insisted Mary spoke of all her experiences. As usual, to her royal friend, she was open and honest and told the queen every detail of all of the births, including the stillbirth and miscarriage she had experienced.

Gradually, life shut away became arduous for all. The queen was now feeling uncomfortable and large. She spent most of her time lounging on her day bed, complaining of the hot dry air and not having permission to breathe in a lungful of fresh air. The other women tried to keep their queen amused by reading to her or suggesting playing music or cards. However, all Anne wanted to do was get the prince out of her body so that she could return to a life of gaiety, figure hugging gowns and being close to her husband again. A sentiment all the others locked in agreed with wholeheartedly. Being pregnant was all well, the queen stated, but when one was the size of a cow, it lost its appeal somewhat. Now that her time was approaching, Anne was bored to distraction.

September was warm and hazy; fruit hung heavy in the orchards and hedgerows invited foraging for luscious berries and ripe nuts. In fields, the farm labourers toiled, gathering in the harvest. Within the safe walls of Greenwich Palace, courtiers wandered through the immaculate gardens, admiring dazzling autumn colours, and enjoying the warm autumn sunshine. In the repressive apartments, Queen Anne was in labour. The pains were coming repeatedly now, and their intensity was more than she could bear. The midwives assured Her Majesty that all was progressing well and before the day was out, she would be holding a healthy prince in her arms. Mary stayed close to the queen giving support and reassurance. The queen cried out as another wave of intense pain swept through her racked body.

Everyone watched, hardly daring to breathe as Anne gave birth, the infant began to bawl, already strong and healthy; there was no doubt of that.

Anne struggled to sit up; there was a muted silence in the room. She looked wildly from face to face.

'My son, my prince…' her voice trailed off as she saw the midwife's blank expression, and she shook her head in disbelief. 'Please, tell me I have a prince, *please*,' she cried, knowing already the answer.

'Your Majesty is safely delivered of a fair princess,' the midwife said, trying to sound cheerful. Queen Anne fell back onto the pillow.

'I have failed,' she quietly said. 'He will never forgive me.'

Mary sat on the edge of the bed and smoothed back the queen's hair from her damp forehead.

'Listen to me, madam, Anne, listen. You have a daughter who is alive and healthy; she is your first-born. Catherine's first pregnancy ended in stillbirth. The king will expect a son, but when he sees that the baby lives, he will realise more infants will follow and he will get the prince he so desperately wants,' she whispered so only the queen could hear. Anne nodded wordlessly. 'There is nothing that can be done now, put on a brave face for him to see. The king knows you love him and he loves you too. Be of good cheer, anger passes.'

From outside, there was a great commotion, the king's voice

heard above all others, and he was laughing heartily, accepting the congratulation from those surrounding him, already celebrating the birth of his son and heir. The door flung open and King Henry strode in looking elated. Queen Anne, now in a sitting position to greet her husband, brushed her long hair back and stared bravely into his face. He was looking at the baby, held by one of the midwives, and now wrapped in a shawl. He stroked the tiny face, chuckling with elation at the healthy yelling of the infant.

'Listen to my son. Listen to Edward Tudor. He's already shouting his arrival to the King's of France and Spain; they will tremble when they learn of his birth,' he said proudly. Then looking around he spoke. 'Stand, everyone and look upon your Prince Edward.' The king's smile froze on his face. 'Why are you none of you happy?' He turned to his wife, still attempting to look fearless. 'Is this a prince?' He pulled his finger back from the infant's face sharply as if scalded by boiling water.

'Majesty, Henry, my dear husband, we have a daughter,' Queen Anne said unsteadily. The king looked again at the baby.

'You promised me a prince. You promised me a palace full of princes,' he hissed angrily, pulling the shawl back to see for himself the child's sex. The queen signalled to Mary to take the princess from the midwife and to bring her the baby. She took the tiny girl from Mary's arms and inspected her, instantly falling in love with her daughter.

'Look at her hair, Henry, it is Tudor red,' the queen attempted an excuse for the infant's sex. 'Lady Paxton reminded me that Catherine's first child was stillborn, this child is healthy and strong.' The king glanced again at the baby.

'Aye she is,' he said crushed and sighed despondently. 'We are both young, sons will follow,' he continued trying to sound indifferent, as if the importance of the child's gender did not matter. 'She will be named...' King Henry paused; he had never given girls' names a thought. Then he remembered his mother, who he had adored while growing up at Eltham Palace. 'She will be named Elizabeth, after my blessed mother.' Without a second look at either the queen or Princess Elizabeth, Henry departed the bedchamber, the spring in his step gone. Anne handed the baby back to a midwife, and brushed tears from her eyes. This birth would have secured her position as queen. The birth of an heir to the throne would have silenced her enemies; now, as the news spread through the court, through London, throughout the land and eventually to the courts of Europe, those enemies would begin to gloat and plot her downfall. She had to get the king back into her bed soon, become pregnant again, and next time with a son, without fail. A second daughter was not going to be an option. Only a son, only a prince would suffice.

Henry stormed into his private apartments with Cromwell scurrying behind. He tore his doublet from his back, threw it with ferocity on the table, knocking over an inkwell.

'She has failed me, Cromwell, the queen has failed me!' he shouted furiously. 'Why am I surrounded by useless women? I divorced Catherine because God punished me for marrying my dead brother's wife. I have turned my country away from Rome, risking excommunication of my subjects to appease that woman, even when the people yelled obscenities at the both of us for what we were doing. Given her, everything, *everything*, she desired because I was foolish enough to think it would *be* enough to ensure a son. Anne who promised me a son has given me another daughter!'

Cromwell signalled to the guards to leave them, and then stepped forward, wringing his hands.

'Sire, the child is bonny and will survive. Sons will surely follow in the future,' he suggested, trying to humour his king. Henry turned furiously on Cromwell who shrank back.

'Oh, do shut up trying to amuse me, you weasel! She told me she would give me a palace full of sons and I believed her!' he bellowed. Cromwell bowed very low, scrabbling forgiveness. 'But you speak well, the queen still has many childbearing years ahead of her, our sons will follow.' A modicum of humour began to return to the king. 'The sprog does have a good voice already. She'll be sister to many brothers anon,' he chuckled. 'And she is all English, no Spain in her at all, unless we marry her to some Spanish lord, then she will have Spain in her every night, eh, Cromwell!' The king now roared with laughter at his own crude suggestions and nudged Cromwell with his elbow, knocking the chancellor off balance. Cromwell sniggered; relieved he had talked his way out of what could have been a tricky situation. He had found the solution allowing Henry and Anne to marry. If the queen failed to produce sons, the king could easily remember who had bound him to Anne's side. Then whom would he blame? For now, Henry was placated. 'Princess Elizabeth, my daughter, my English Princess,' the king laughed, good humour restored.

The news of the birth of Princess Elizabeth flooded through court. There was varying degrees of surprise from all sides. Some sympathised with the queen, and there were the people who celebrated a daughter's birth as just deserts to a witch like Anne Boleyn.

# 39

Robert had joined a secret group of men all who held a dislike of Anne Boleyn for their own reasons. The group was only small in number, six men, with one of them suspected to be a nobleman of high rank, trusted by the king. However, to protect his identity, the man wore a monk's cowl pulled over his face to hide his features. He refused to eat or drink with his fellow men, not wanting to give away any clues as to who he was. He spoke in hushed tones, with a false accent, an attempt in disguising his natural voice. The group of six met covertly in taverns outside the palaces and made plans to rid the country of the woman they all detested. Scraps of paper, hidden in secret places known only to the six, was the way of relating the location of their clandestine meetings. One of the six, a bright man who was clever with words had come up with a name for them by rearranging the words of their mutual hate: "Remove Anne Boleyn" became "Nobleman Every One". It was their password when they met. It sounded innocuous to anyone who overheard it, yet would hide the true nature of the meetings.

They would sup ale and whisper low to each other, not wanting anyone to hear their plans, however ridiculous they seemed to be for fear of passing comments to the wrong ears could lead to their downfall. They all knew the dangerous and treasonable path they trod, but for their goal of removing Queen Anne before she could produce a male heir, they were all willing to risk their lives, the pact they had made with each other bound them together in life and death.

King Henry had accepted Princess Elizabeth and adored her; Anne was happy again. She enjoyed motherhood and had even expressed a desire to breastfeed the princess herself. The king had to remind her, queens do not suckle their own offspring that was a duty for the ample breasted wet nurses installed. The princess would take her fill of their milk and she thrived, growing strong and bright.

Princess Elizabeth was still second in line to the throne after Princess Mary. This perturbed the king and queen. They had assumed that Elizabeth was now the heir. Princess Mary, declared a bastard, had no right to be in the line of succession. The king wanted his English Princess to be heir, until her brothers were born, this had to be resolved, and a way found to ensure Elizabeth's inheritance.

Cromwell, Gregory and other lawyers gathered to find a solution that would make the young princess heir presumptive. The lawyers came up with a document that would resolve all the king's problems. They took it to the king, begging a private audience with him to explain their plans.

Henry sat in his chair, leaning back as Cromwell held out a folder thick with paper while the other lawyers stood back in a tight knot, hoping their royal master would agree to the result of their long hours of work.

'Sire you have to completely break with Rome now, you have done much so already, but by getting the nobility and everyone to swear to this, you will assure the princess's accession to the throne upon your death, until a prince is born,' Cromwell said confidently. Henry took the documents and slowly read the contents in silence while the lawyers stood waiting nervously.

'So, by swearing to this Act of Succession, the lords of this court and realm will accept Princess Elizabeth as heir and no one else born before her,' The king said slowly. Cromwell nodded.

'Aye, Your Majesty, you will have the loyalty of the men of England and issue from the queen will be legal heirs.'

'Hmm. It is good, Cromwell. Lawyers, I congratulate you all on your collective brainpower. After I am gone, a true blood Englishman will rule England. Good.' Henry stood up and bowing to the men departed the room.

The lawyers visibly relaxed and all sighed as one with relief. Their hard work had paid off, the king was happy.

The dukes and earls signed the document, some reluctantly, pronouncing Elizabeth's claim to the throne of England. Several refused to sign their signatures, but after persuasion, they complied. Only Sir Thomas More remained stubborn. He kept stating that it was against all he held dear in his heart to add his name to the list of kowtows. Chancellor Cromwell attempted to persuade More to sign, but he still turned a deaf ear. The king stormed, frustrated with the refusal. All the man had to do was write his name, nothing difficult to pertain, yet still More would not sign. If he continued to hold out against signing the Act of Succession, he could risk his liberty and even his life. Threats like that still fell upon deaf ears. More's own family pleaded with him to sign, telling him that although his name would be on the document, his heart and conscious would still be clear.

The king finally lost patience with Sir Thomas and ordered his arrest and imprisonment in the Tower. He would be free once he agreed to sign. By now, Sir Thomas felt he had gone too far to back down. He would not sign whatever threats and abuse the king threw at him.

Robert received a summons to attend an audience from someone of great importance at court. There were no details of the agenda, or with whom Robert would be present. At the appointed hour, he knocked upon the door and waited for the command to enter. His mouth and lips felt dry. The door opened, a page in the livery of the Duke of Norfolk stood aside allowing entry into the room.

The room was small and the furniture was sparse: a solid oak table stood central in the room with three equally solid oak chairs lined up behind the table. At these seats sat three harsh faced men. Robert recognised them as the Duke of Norfolk and Edward and Thomas Seymour. He stood in front of the table feeling like an errant student standing before his tutor to await punishment. Norfolk was the first to speak.

'Sir Robert we know of your dislike of the queen,' he began. 'Why else would you have joined Nobleman Every One?'

'What do you mean?' Robert asked dryly. 'I know nothing of this Nobleman Every One.'

'Oh come now, Sir Robert,' the duke said in mock seriousness. He leant behind his high backed chair and pulled out a monk's cowl and, tossing it on the table, spoke in a false dialect. 'The six of us meet in taverns, don't we?'

'You are one of us? You are her uncle, why did you...' Robert gasped in disbelief. Norfolk chuckled humourlessly.

'She may be my niece, she may be the queen, but she is also capable of bringing the ancient line of Howards to destruction. The Boleyns are upstarts who have no right at court. There are no signs of pregnancy and the king grows impatient, he may look elsewhere for a queen to give him his prince.'

'You once had affection for Anne Boleyn, is that true?' Edward Seymour asked. Robert explained how as Lady Anne, she had shunned his advances and proposal of marriage ungraciously. 'You were right, my lord, he could be the one for us,' Edward said, turning to Norfolk.

'Love makes a man do stupid things,' Thomas Seymour sighed reflectively. His brother looked over to him and sighed, irritated at his sentimentality.

'Love is a powerful emotion as is hate,' Norfolk continued. 'A man with a heart full of hate could be useful. You can channel this emotion to your advantage. We know of your ambitions.'

'Your grace, I don't understand,' Robert replied quietly.

'That woman used witchcraft to turn the king's head and heart from the True Faith and cast aside his lawful wife,' Edward Seymour carried on from Norfolk. 'She must be removed and a Catholic queen replace her.'

'You have a sister, Jane,' Robert stated. Both Seymour brothers glared angrily at him.

'Do not presume to tell us what we know, Sir Robert,' Edward growled irritably. Thomas nodded in agreement. 'We have observed King Henry watching our sweet sister and will steer his affections towards her.'

'What has this to do with me?' Robert asked.

'Anne Boleyn must be removed before she can produce a male child and our sister Jane will replace that woman in Henry's affections. You are the man to help us succeed in our plan.' Thomas Seymour took up the explanation. Robert felt himself begin to tremble with both fear and excitement. Norfolk produced from a fold in his coat a simple gold ring set with a cabochon-red stone. He placed it upon the table and indicated to Robert to approach and pick the ring up.

'There is a hinge on the side of the ring. Open it,' Norfolk said coolly. Robert ran a finger over the smooth surface and found the hinge. The red stone opened to reveal a precious drop of yellow liquid. 'The poison there is potent. Get the queen to swallow it. After the first hour, she will feel unwell. After the second hour, she will be dead.' Norfolk sat back in his seat allowing the slightest of smiles to play on his lips.

'How can I do that?' Robert breathed, closing the red stone.

'You have a sister, Mary.' Thomas Seymour echoed Robert's words. Robert began to perspire profusely, and his mouth felt dry again.

'What is in it for me?' he asked slowly. Edward Seymour smiled unemotionally.

'We have a bastard sister, Frances, who is approaching marriageable age. Rid the world of Anne Boleyn and Frances is yours,' he said steadily.

'But I am already married,' Robert replied artlessly. Both Seymour brothers laughed without humour. Norfolk spoke with a quiet, commanding voice.

'You prefer to remain obscure, unknown throughout history? Leave her to us. You will command your wife to attend you at court where you will discover her in the arms of another man,' he indicated to Thomas Seymour, 'seemingly committing adultery. As a heartbroken husband, you will find solace in Frances,' Norfolk continued. 'You will divorce your wife. Frances will be yours,' Norfolk produced a purse of coins that he tossed on the table. He nodded towards the purse for Robert to pick it up. 'Five hundred gold coins as an advance. Another five hundred once that cold bitch is dead.' He then sat back in his chair.

'As a further incentive, once our sister Jane has wedded and bedded the king, you shall receive a further three thousand,' Thomas said, leaning forward. 'Also, once Jane has given the king his son, we shall promote you to King Henry's inner circle, his privy council. We shall persuade him to give you the titles of Earl of Essex and Wiltshire. Thomas Boleyn shall have no need of either once his daughter is dead. You would be brother-in-law to the king himself and uncle to the future King of England. Henry rewards those who please him. We will advance you towards your ambitions.'

Robert felt the trembling in his body begin again. It was an audacious plot that could just work. Alice would be hurt in all this, and he did feel culpable about causing his wife such grief, but what would that matter, once he united with the powerful upcoming Seymours. Robert nodded, slipping the ring onto his little finger and the purse of gold into his coat. Norfolk and the Seymours stood up together.

'This meeting has never taken place. Speak of this to no one. Not even your group members. We shall deny as falsehood anything you say,' Edward warned. Norfolk silently led the way out of the room, leaving Robert standing alone, breathing quickly, his heart pounding loudly in his ears. He felt giddy with the exhilaration and leant heavily on the table to prevent his legs giving way under his body. All he was working for was about to materialise. All his life he had craved power and wealth, and now, it was finally near his grasp.

Mary was passing through the hall on an errand for the queen when Robert appeared from the shadows; he had been watching her and waiting for the opportune moment to approach. With a rough movement, he pulled her against the wall, blocking her escape.

'You will listen to what I have to tell you and you will not question me, understand?' he said quietly.

'What are you saying, Robert?' Mary grumbled, knowing it would only lead to trouble. Robert looked around making sure no one would overhear the conversation.

'I have a task for you which you shall complete for me,' he answered and drew the ring from his finger. He forced it into Mary's hand. She looked at it and then looked back into Robert's face.

'What is this for?' she asked.

'Listen,' Robert growled. 'Inside the stone is a poison, empty it into *her* wine and be sure she drinks deeply.'

Mary dropped the ring in disbelief. Robert quickly swooped down cursing and retrieved the ring from the flagstones. He pushed it again into Mary's palm, and closed his hand around her fist.

'You shall do as I say, or there will be trouble.'

'And what if I refuse?' Mary retorted. Robert let go of her fist and gripped her throat pushing her back against the wall, bringing his face close to hers.

'If you refuse, I shall find that half-caste brat of yours and slit his skinny throat and those simpering sprogs of your lawyer shall not go unharmed either. It is lucky for your daughter that she lives lives far away.'

'Not my children,' Mary cried in alarm. Robert clapped his hand over her mouth.

'Speak not of this to anyone. If that husband of yours learns of this, I will arrange an accident for him. I do not care how you do it, but make it soon. I have others who do not expect me to fail,' he released Mary from his grip.

'Who are they?'

'You do not need to know, do not disappoint me, sister,' Robert tapped her face in warning, then vanished into the sea of courtiers milling around, leaving Mary trembling, all thought of the errand forgotten. The ring lay heavy in her hand. She looked at it. It was simple and attractive enough in design. For now, she would wear the ring and wait, as Robert had demanded for the right moment to administer the poison; she loved her children more than life itself and would do anything to protect them, even at the risk of her own life.

Feigning a headache to allow absence from the queen's presence, Mary hurried through corridors to where Gregory was working. Bursting into his chamber, she disturbed him with his client. He rose to his feet, concerned for this unusual interruption. She knew not to disturb him during his working hours.

'My lord, forgive this intrusion, I must speak with my husband in private immediately,' Mary said to the man seated in the chair as she dropped a curtsey towards him. Gregory looked startled.

'Is it one of our children?' he asked.

'Please, I need to speak to you now, in our apartment, please come, Gregory,' Mary entreated and refused to say any more. After a second apology, she ran to their private apartment to wait for him.

Gregory excused himself, rescheduling the appointment and hurried to see what was concerning his wife enough for this strange outburst.

Mary was pacing the floor, agitated when he entered. She flew into his arms, close to tears, talking rapidly in garbled words and gesticulating wildly about something distressing. He tried to calm her to tell him this clearly disturbing news, but to no avail.

'Be quiet wife!' he said severely. The sudden harshness of his usually benign voice shocked Mary into silence. 'Now slowly, tell me what is wrong? Are Edmund and Simon well? Have either of them been involved in an accident and are hurt or…' Gregory could not bring himself to continue the sentence. Taking a deep breath Mary shook her head.

'Our children are well, but I need you to help me to keep them so,' she finally said, regaining self-control. He looked puzzled.

'You speak in riddles, what are you saying?'

'I cannot tell you everything, do not try to make me, I just cannot. Believe and trust me, please. I am thinking of our children when I tell you this,' Mary said. He stepped back, alarmed, putting a hand to his head as the colour drained from his face.

'Have you found another man and you are leaving me for him?' he asked shakily. Mary shook her head and kissed his lips.

'Never that, you are the only man I desire. Please listen and do not speak until I am finished.

'I have heard that there is a plot to harm the queen and if it fails, there will be destruction to everything held dear by many families. I cannot risk the lives of Edmund or Simon, so I ask you to please without question take the children to my mother's home and remain there with them until all is well again,' she said calmly, and then sighing looked trustingly into Gregory's eyes.

'What is to happen? Are the authorities aware of this plot? Does the king know of this?' he asked. 'Do you have anything to do with this?'

'I cannot say, please Gregory, just listen and believe,' she pleaded. He looked distressed.

'If you are involved in any way, I should know; I am your husband and must know your business. Does that brother of yours have anything you do with this?' He saw a flash of panic register on Mary's face.

'I cannot tell you, please, we waste time. I have instructed Lettie to pack everything you need for your stay. She will go with you to help care for our sons.'

'I cannot just go like that, I have clients to see, work to do and

I have to get permission to leave court,' Gregory argued. Mary had not thought of that. She began to fret and paced the floor fearfully again. 'I shall find an excuse,' he conceded.

'Oh Gregory, what would I do without you. I wish we had met when I was still an innocent girl before Henry or Rafael. We would have been happy forever,' Mary wept.

'Are we not happy forever now?' Gregory asked, still doubtful of Mary's irregular request. He sighed in defeat. 'Tomorrow, I shall speak to Cromwell and make my excuses. If I catch him on a good day, he may sanction my leave of absence.'

She took his hands in hers and kissed them. 'Thank you. Do not speak of this to anyone, I am avowed to confidentiality by those who have spoken to me,' Mary replied. Gregory unwillingly agreed to the peculiar appeal. She took his face in her hands and lovingly kissed his lips. 'I may never kiss you again,' she sighed and quickly left the room. Gregory stood alone and touched his lips, what did she mean, "Never kiss you again"? He returned to his work uneasy Robert had something to do with this, that man was nothing but trouble. Mary seemed intimidated when they were in each other's company. However, because of his love for his wife, Gregory would say nothing; everything would be all right once again once this threat to the queen was over. She would explain all once everything was well again.

After a night of emotional passion and a painful goodbye to the boys that morning, Mary let her family go. She now watched through tear-filled eyes from a window looking out onto the courtyard as Gregory on his horse, with their sons in a carriage, passed through the gates, beginning their journey to Essex. She mouthed a silent "goodbye, I love you" as the small party disappeared from view. Then turning away, to return to her duties, Mary rubbed her stomach; she had not revealed to her husband that once again a new life was growing in her womb, it was better for him not to know. This unborn must be sacrificed for the safety of her family.

The queen had been looking pale for several days, yet her temper was excellent. She had spoken quietly to Mary and confided in her that, at last, she was pregnant again. Try as she might, Mary could not feel elated at the queen's secret; she still felt weighed down with the task set for her to perform. This revelation only made the matter worse to contemplate. Robert was getting impatient; he had been urging her to perform the task set for her.

She was acutely aware of the small ring, running her thumb over the gold band that circled her finger and the smooth red stone seemed to be glaringly evident. The queen was calling for wine, now was the chance to put Robert's contemptible plan into action. She waved aside the attendant and took charge of the request herself. With a simple movement of her thumb, Mary released the tiny catch on the side of the ring and the red stone opened up. She quickly deposited the yellow liquid into the wine. Briefly, it fizzed and bubbles popped to the surface before settling down. With trembling hands, Mary carried the glass over. Queen Anne saw how strangely her friend was behaving.

'Lady Paxton, what ails thee? Has that lusty husband of yours filled your belly with more handsome sons?' she teased gently. Mary paled and shook her head.

'No my lady, I feel unwell today,' Mary lied. Queen Anne smiled benevolently.

'Then I shall summon my physician to attend to you, I cannot have you ill and away from my side,' she smiled happily at Mary and whispered. 'Not while my prince grows in me.' She put the glass to her lips and as she was about to take a sip, Mary panicked. Not only would she be killing the queen, she would be murdering an innocent babe. She knocked the glass to the floor with a shattering smash.

'Don't drink it, madam, it is poisoned!' she cried. The queen put a hand to her mouth.

One of the women ran to the door and throwing it opened shouted. 'Guards, there has been an attempt on the queen's life!'

'Mary, why you? If I cannot trust you, then who can I trust?' the queen asked, her voice quivering. Mary stood still, arms by her side, shaking her head as tears rolling down her cheeks. 'I know there are those who wish me harm, but never in my life would I have expected you.'

The guards burst noisily into the chamber and surrounded Mary. The remaining women all moved away, disassociating themselves from her. When Mary spoke, her voice was scarcely audible.

'Madam, you have always been my friend and I yours. I would never do anything to pain you, but the lives of my children were endangered if I did not comply.'

Queen Anne looked at the guards, still surrounding Mary. 'Remove this woman, and take her to the Tower immediately. I shall speak to the king and take his counsel.' She turned her back, still not believing what had occurred and not wishing to see the guards escort Mary from her presence. With no resistance, Mary allowed herself to be led to the jetty and a waiting barge.

News travelled fast through the corridors of Greenwich Palace, the more gruesome the better for the gossipmongers. It was not long before the hearsay of the murder attempt reached Robert. Immediately he hurried along the corridors and galleries to find out whether Mary had prompted the incident. As he walked at a fast pace, he began to realise that the other courtiers he was passing turned away from him or would not meet his eye. He quickened his pace, his thoughts racing. When Robert reached the royal apartments, guards barred his entry.

'What news of the queen? Was anyone else hurt?' he asked anxiously. The guards eyed him suspiciously and kept their silence. 'Is the queen alright?' the guards ignored his questioning as from further down the corridor, King Henry was shouting furiously as he approached. Robert stood aside and bowed low as he stormed past. The king stopped suddenly and turned back to look at him, still bowing low.

'I speak for all when I wish the queen good health,' Robert said, pretending he did not know what was happening. The king sighed, still frowning. 'Sire, have I offended you in any way?'

'Do not disturb me now.'

'Majesty…' Robert continued.

'Do not bother me with questions. My wife needs me. Do as you please,' the king's interruption prickled with rising anger. Robert bowed lower as he carried on his way to see the queen.

His first instinct was to flee back to Yardeley Chase and hide until everything calmed down. However, thinking the plan further, it could make him appear guilty alongside his sister by running away. Remaining at court, and seen by as many people as possible, Robert would appear as though he had nothing to do with the incident. Therefore, he decided the best thing for him to do right now was to remain at Greenwich, keeping his profile visible.

# 40

## *The Tower*

The impenetrable grey walls of the Tower that had glistened with joy two years earlier for Queen Anne's coronation, now scowled menacingly at the small barge approaching. The heavy gates pushed slowly open through the murky water, lapping lugubriously at the steps as the barge came to a halt with a placid thud. Sir John Gage, constable of the Tower, flanked by two yeomen warders stood waiting for Mary. He held out a hand, which she had no option but to take as he helped her step from the barge onto the flagstones.

'Follow me,' he commanded, as the warders positioned themselves either side of Mary. He led the way until they reached a grim tower that cast ominous shadows in the sunlight. Passing through the heavy door, they continued until they came to a wooden door. Gage unlocked it, pushed it open and passed through followed by Mary. She entered the cold, dark interior. They continued the slow progress up cold, dark steps, along a cold, dark corridor, coming to a stop outside a smaller door. Taking a key from his belt, he unlocked the door and pushed it open; standing aside, he indicated silently for Mary to enter the cell. Once inside, the door shut behind her and the key turned in the lock.

There was a small slit for a window; the only other light came from a single torch on the wall. There was a stool, and a crude-looking bed. The walls of the cell were thick enough to block out any sounds, making the silence almost deafening.

Leaning against the wall, Mary looked from the slit of light to the small metal grille in the door and back again, waiting for what she did not know. As night fell, the cell became more claustrophobic and by the time the sun had risen the following day, Mary felt wretched.

Later that day the door was unlocked, and Sir John stepped in. She backed away as far as she could to keep as much distance between her and the constable. She was at his mercy and feared he might assault her. However, he stood, regarding his prisoner impassivly. Although Mary did not know it, he did not intend to force his attentions on her; this was not in his nature, even if the cowering woman before him probably deserved it for her crimes. If she held back any required information, the mere suggestion of being alone in a cell with the guards was usually enough to make any woman confess to anything.

'Lady Paxton, you will follow me,' he commanded dourly, Mary silently obeyed. With a grim faced guard marching by her side, they came to a large room in which a man, Sir Giles Sneddon, sat at a desk, waiting for her arrival.

In the days of her marriage to Henry, Mary had been terrorised and beaten. That was nothing to the fear pulsating throughout her body as she stood waiting. The two men spoke briefly and quietly, their speech inaudible to her. Sir John moved aside to a dark corner of the room and the guard stationed himself by the door. A low wooden stool stood in the centre of the room. Sneddon pointed towards it silently and she obediently sat down and waited for what would happen. Eventually, he cleared his throat and approached Mary. He began to circle her, watching her constantly.

'Do you know why you have been brought here?' he asked. Mary attempted to return Sneddon's gaze, yet his pale blue eyes were hostile, humourless and unblinking. Mary shrunk down under his scrutiny. 'Answer me now.' His voice was harsh.

'I was told to poison the queen,' she replied in a small voice.

'You admit you had the poison. Who gave you it?' he continued.

'I was threatened that my children would be harmed if I failed to do this,' Mary said, her voice tremulous. Sneddon stopped walking and faced Mary front on.

'So, reveal to me who gave you this poison.'

'He told me he would harm my children if I done wrong or spoke his name,' she replied as the tears welled up in her eyes.

'Lady Paxton,' Sneddon continued, 'you *have* done wrong; you have attempted to murder our anointed queen. Do not think that because you are a woman I would not use stronger methods than this to obtain the information. A traitor is a traitor whatever their sex and you will die the traitors' death for this crime. Tell me who gave you the poison and your sentence may be lenient.'

'Would I ever see my husband or children again?' She asked, her spirits lifting a little.

'Doubtful,' he replied turning away.

'If I tell you, can I go home? I promise never to return to court again and speak of this to no one,' she pleaded. Sneddon rounded back; he brought his enraged face close to Mary's and grabbed a fist of her hair, jerking back her head.

'Do not presume to bargain with me, lady!' he shouted, and threw her aggressively onto the floor signalling to the guard who knew what was required. He fell onto Mary, pulling her skirts up, and forced her thighs apart with his knee as she lay there struggling and screaming hysterically. He looked up at his master, waiting for authorisation to continue.

'All I have to do is say the word and this guard will ram his dick so far up your fanny, semen will erupt from your mouth,' Sneddon threatened, drawing his dagger from its scabbard as the guard sniggered and sat back on his heels. He pushed the blade onto Mary's throat; she flinched as he guided it from breast to breast and down to her abdomen. 'You will split from here to here,' he nodded and the guard slapped Mary violently across her face, stunning her. He pulled down his hose, taunting her, yet still the rape did not ensue.

'It was my brother Robert. He gave me the poison for Queen Anne,' Mary screamed between loud and intense sobs. Sneddon smiled with approval. This pitiable creature was terrified, it was progressing easier than he had imagined.

'I need his full name and title,' he demanded.

'Sir Robert Hawke. He is a gentleman-in-waiting to His Majesty,' Mary's voice was now barely perceptible.

'Who supplied the poison? Who gave your brother the poison, woman!' he shouted leaning down over Mary.

'I don't know,' she sobbed. The guard slapped Mary again; she tasted blood in her mouth.

Sneddon regarded her laying there. 'You will die for this, how you die is up to you. Tell me everything you know and your execution will be quick and easy. Hold back on me and the pain will be beyond your wildest imagination. I have witnessed such executions.' Years of experience told him that she was telling all she knew. He straightened up not entirely satisfied. Robert Hawke would supply the rest of the information needed. 'Get off her. You can have her next,' he ordered the guard who reluctantly stood up, cursing under his breath. Sneddon came and stood over Mary, his eyes devouring her body and he licked his lips with anticipation. He shrugged his doublet off and unbuckling his belt, tossed it aside, dropping to his knees, grabbing a fistful of her dress with one hand, as he forced her legs further apart and the other hand pulling at his hose, he pushed himself onto her; clamping his mouth over hers in a brutal kiss, biting her lip, drawing blood.

'Desist!' Sir John stepped forward. Sneddon looked up at him.

'You deny me my gratification?' he asked, fractious at the intrusion. Sir John kicked him off Mary. 'Do you realise *who* I am?' he spat.

'The woman has told you everything she knows; there is no need for the assault,' he insisted. Sneddon stood and squarely faced the constable, looking directly into Sir John's eyes.

'Want the baggage for yourself do you? Not until I have finished,' he snarled. Sir John met Sneddon's ice blue gaze undaunted.

'You are Giles Sneddon. *I* am the constable of this Tower. Prisoners are under my duriction. You and your henchman will leave her alone; she will be escorted to her cell immediately to await execution,' he replied, purposefully slowly. Sneddon glanced at Mary, who still lay on the floor distressed, unable to move or speak, her terrified eyes darting from man to man. Sneddon snatched up his doublet and belt, returned to his desk and picked up a document. He nodded. The aggrieved guard roughly hauled Mary to her feet.

'This is your confession,' he explained, pushing the paper across the desk without looking up. 'You will sign it now.' He held a quill out to Mary. She hesitated and looked around. The guard, sniggering, made a sexual gesture towards her. Without reading it, she put her name to the written document, tears smudging her signature; then subsequently pulled in the direction of the door. Her ordeal, for now was over.

Sir John silently led the way, as the guard dragged Mary back to the lonely, dark cell, and threw her in unceremoniously. She crawled to the corner and sat hunched against the wall, staring into the dark reliving every recent moment. Sneddon's heartless voice cruel in her ears, feeling his hands groping her body and his hot breath on her face. Crouching throughout the night, she was oblivious to the rats boldly scurrying around her cell, squabbling noisily over the bread thrown in for her.

Robert lazed in bed while his latest conquest slept quietly next to him. The king had been most attentive to his queen since the attempted assassination, and Robert along with others found they had more leisure time. Some gambled their spare time away, playing cards and dice; others like Robert spent happy hours with mistresses and doxies. It had been several days since the incident, and the longer the time passed, Robert felt he was safe. This self-confidence was not to last as guards, breaking down the door, burst into his bedchamber.

The young woman, woke, suddenly by the commotion, sat up screaming, the sheet dropping exposing her bare breasts. Robert tried to scramble from the bed in a futile attempt at escape, realising instantaneously what was happening. A guard floored him with a punch and stood over him, keeping his foot on his back, pinning him down.

'Sir Robert Hawke, you are to be taken to the Tower. You will not resist,' a guard commanded.

'What am I being arrested for?' Robert asked as he stood up, knowing the answer.

'Treason.' Came the one word reply.

'I have done nothing wrong, there must be some mistake,' Robert lied attempting to keep his voice steady. The woman had now pulled the sheets up to her chin and sat looking from Robert to the guards, confused and alarmed. He slowly dressed, deliberately taking his time while the guards silently waited for him, except for one; he began to chat to the young woman, attempting to induce a responce. Her replies were at first coy, but soon, she had relaxed and was talking and smiling back at him.

'What is this?' Robert exclaimed, seeing her flirting with the guard. She tucked her knees up under her chin, wrapping her arms around her legs and looked at Robert.

'I doubt I'll ever see you again, you're off to the Tower,' she giggled coquettishly glancing from her ex-lover, to the new interest in her life.

'I thought you loved me!' Robert cried, genuinely dejected.

'I like you, but there are many more men out there waiting for me to explore their delicious bodies,' she said carelessly, and then dropping the sheet again, she kissed the guard full on the lips to his own surprise. The others all laughed, revelling in Robert's humiliation. He looked around at his desperate situation.

'I am innocent of whatever I am charged,' Robert said, as his captures pulled him towards the open door. Passersby who had overheard the commotion had peered in and were watching in fascination. They divided to allow the departure.

'Please, good people, you know I am the king's loyal and humble servant! I have done nothing wrong!' Robert shouted, as the guards dragged him struggling through the corridors.

In a dark corner of his cell, Robert crouched. The only light came from an open cut window high in the wall. It was too small for an attempted escape, and even if he could squeeze through the small gap, it was a sheer drop down to the murky waters of the moat. There would be no escape; no help. Robert stood and threw himself at the thick oak door, hammering on it and pleading for release. He scratched at the door until his fingers bled, shouting and screaming until his voice became hoarse. Then crumpling into a heap upon the floor, he lay there sobbing.

From outside the door, he could hear the sounds of a key being inserted into the lock, and turning. Slowly, the door creaked open on its ancient hinges, and Robert looked up sharply to see two of the Tower guards entering behind Sir Giles Sneddon. He signalled towards Robert and the guards pulled him from the cell.

'Where are you taking me?' Robert asked, looking from guard to guard. They ignored him and followed Sneddon down dark corridors. They passed doors from which mournful, unholy, inhuman sounds echoed. Robert kept asking where he was going. Sneddon stopped and raised a jewelled hand. He turned to Robert and regarded him solemnly before speaking.

'Robert Hawke, you will ask no questions. You will be silent until you are required to speak.' His voice was monotone. He then turned and with a motion of his hand to the guards continued to march through the corridors.

The small party stopped outside a large door. Sneddon selected a key and unlocked the door. The guards pushed Robert into a large chamber with a high vaulted ceiling. An open fire burnt fiercely, with a large cauldron suspended over the flames. Candles melted into grotesque shapes stood in iron candelabras and lit torches hung on the walls, their flames flickering, casting shadows over apparatus throughout the chamber, and hanging from the walls and ceiling. As Robert's eyes grew accustomed to the dim light, he realised where he was. This was the dreaded torture chamber spoken about in hushed tones. Sneddon had sat behind a table and began writing on a document. The two guards stood back. If this was a scheme to scare Robert, then it had worked. He stood shuddering while Sneddon finished his writing. Then he stood up and came around to the front of the table to stand before Robert.

'Do you know why you have been brought here, Robert Hawke?' he asked calmly. Robert shook his head, now unable to speak. 'I repeat, do you know why you have been brought here? Answer me.'

'No.' Robert could not make his voice steady. Sneddon sighed.

'Come now, Robert Hawke, you must have some idea why you are here. I require information, and you will tell me willingly.' He walked over to a small metal construction and stroked it. 'This can trap a man for five minutes, or five hours, or five days. Someone remained in here for weeks once. A good name, the Little Ease, don't you think?' He paused, glancing over at Robert. 'You see, it is not very big, so a tall man, like you, would find it, shall we say, cramped?' Sneddon then went and stood by a large wooden frame that had windlasses, heavy rope and thick leather strips crossed and attached to the frame by large nails, and rubbed his hand over the wood, smiling, emitting a sigh of almost erotic pleasure. 'This is one of my favourite instruments of persuasion. It stretches it's occupant until joints crack with pain. Exquisite.' His voice almost purred with perverted pleasure. He then walked over to a second table on which lay small instruments, he picked several up, one at a time, and inspected them closely.

'What are they for?' Robert managed to ask. Sneddon glanced at him and smiled coldly.

'This can pull out a tongue.' He held up long handled tongs. 'And this one pulls out fingernails by their roots. We can put out eyes, cut off testicles, slice off a cock. But only if there is no co-operation.'

'I will co-operate,' Robert said quickly. 'What do you want to know?'

'Who told you to poison Queen Anne?' he asked quietly.

'His Grace, the Duke of Norfolk, Sir Edward and Sir Thomas Seymour,' he said truthfully, what use was there in lying? Sneddon laughed, but there was no trace of humour.

'Do you think I would believe that?' Sneddon said. Robert shivered involuntary at the coldness of his voice.

'It is true; the duke gave me poison to administer to the queen as he dislikes the Boleyn family.'

Sneddon pulled a face. He signalled to the guards who pulled Robert towards the table. He tried to resist, but it was useless. Sneddon selected pliers, he gave another signal, and a guard held Robert's hand steady on the table.

'I am one of His Majesty's persuaders, and I am very efficient at my work. I help people remember facts they may have carelessly forgot. Who gave you the poison?' he picked up a set of pliers and snapped the ends together.

'You do not believe me when I tell the truth, so why should I lie to you,' Robert said in a hopeless attempt at defiance. Sneddon clamped the pliers over Robert's left thumb and applied the pressure until he began to whimper, and then cry out as the pain amplified.

'You think this hurts? I have only just begun.' He took the pliers to each finger of Robert's left hand in turn until his thumb and fingers crushed. Pain throbbed throughout his hand. Sneddon tossed the pliers onto the table. 'Who gave you the poison?' he asked again.

'The Duke of Norfolk did,' Robert insisted. Tutting, Sneddon shook his head.

'I am disappointed in you. What do you think you can gain by implicating a nobleman such as the duke in this plot of yours? Your name has been mentioned by others elsewhere in the Tower; they said you gave them the poison, so who gave *you* the poison?' Sneddon stood up and indicated again to the guards to bring Robert to the Little Ease; he opened it up. The guards pushed Robert into the metal cage and Sneddon regarded him solemnly.

'I shall give you some time here to think over what you have told me and what you will tell me. Use the time wisely,' Sneddon explained. Then followed by the guards; he departed the room, locking the door behind him, leaving Robert alone. What had Mary said? He groaned quietly in the silent chamber as the pain grew in his back and his limbs became numb from their constriction. Quickly losing track of time, he had first tried calling out for help, to no avail.

Eventually Sneddon re-entered the chamber, followed by the guards, and he glanced casually over to Robert. Then went straight to the table and began signing the documents left there from earlier.

'You have had time to think over what I have said,' he said offhandedly. Robert gave a small groan.

'I have told you the truth. The duke gave me the poison, he dislikes the queen for who she is and the danger to the Howards and he wants her dead. I gave it to my sister Mary to administer it to the queen,' Robert repeated. 'Will you release me now?'

'You speak treasonable words, but why not, you need to stretch those joints of yours,' Sneddon replied mockingly. The guards unlocked the Little Ease and painfully pulled Robert from its confinement. Every joint cried out in pain as Robert's body moved once more. They hauled him across the floor to the instrument of torture that struck fear into every man's heart. The rack. By now, Sneddon had finished his paperwork and had come to stand by his favourite contraption in the chamber.

'I shall give you one final chance to tell me who gave you the poison?'

'I have told you it was The Duke of Norfolk,' Robert groaned weakly.

'Strip him,' Sneddon commanded. The clothes were torn from Robert's body until he stood naked before his torturer. Sneddon pointed to the rack. They pushed Robert onto the leather strips. His arms were pulled up above his head and fastened to windlasses with thick rope. His legs were stretched out and the ropes tied to his ankles. Sneddon turned the windlasses, pulling the ropes, straining Robert's joints.

'I'll tell you,' Robert said breathlessly, fearing what was about to happen.

'Go on.'

'I belong to a secret group of six. We plotted to kill the queen,' Robert said quickly. Sneddon nodded and Robert continued. 'We knew the risks we took, but took them anyway. We wanted to see the king return to the catholic faith and take a Catholic Queen.'

'Give me their names.'

Robert named the other five men. 'We all belong to "Nobleman Every One".' Sneddon pulled harshly at the windlass; and Robert screamed.

'You continue to lie about his grace. Who is the sixth man?'

'He is the duke!' Robert cried, feeling and hearing the cracking of his joints. He groaned, but the windlasses turned again, and again, pulling harder; joints began to seperate. Robert screamed as pain jolted through his body. Sneddon kept shouting for the name of the sixth man. Robert blacked out as pain consumed his body like a tidal wave.

'Hawke, Hawke.' From darkness, a voice, distorted, drifted into Robert's ears. 'Hawke, Hawke.' There it was again, clearer this time. The stench and bitter taste of vinegar thrown onto his face shocked him into consciousness, coughing and gasping for breath. He could feel nothing but pulsation pain, all there was in his world was pain now. Sneddon snatched up a whip from the table and brought it down across Robert's stomach with a vicious whack.

'Hawke, tell me the name of the sixth man.' He swore pushing his face close to Roberts. 'Or you shall suffer more.'

'Mercy, please, mercy,' Robert wept as the windlasses turned once more. 'Gregory Paxton, he is the other man. Gregory Paxton,' he screamed. Sneddon stood up with a triumphant laugh.

'He's that clever lawyer and the husband of Lady Mary, how

obvious. This has been a family enterprise,' Sneddon said triumphantly to the guards. He turned back to Robert. 'We shall bring Sir Gregory and the others in and see what they have to say. A clever man like him will try to talk his way out by using the law, little use that will do him. Take him away.'

Semi-conscious, the guards carried Robert back to his cell and threw him back into the putrid darkness.

Stephen came running indoors shouting excitedly. There were soldiers on horseback riding towards his home at full gallop. Margaret, Alice and Gregory came out to see for themselves. Immediately, the three felt a combined sense of foreboding: this was no social visit. Gregory instinctively knew it had something to do with Mary, she had been so insistent that he and the children went from court, and something dangerous must have happened.

'Go inside and close the door, I shall speak with their captain,' he said, forcing calmness in his voice. Gently he pushed the women towards the door. Without complaint, they done as they were bade, with Alice calling Stephen in. He followed his mother unwillingly, complaining that he wanted to stay and talk to the soldiers.

The guards rode into the courtyard and circled Gregory, their horses pushing and shoving him. The captain reined his horse in and kicked Gregory in the chest, knocking him down.

'Gregory Paxton. You are arrested for treason and shall be taken to the Tower immediately,' he said gruffly. Gregory had stood up, holding his chest. He met the captain's gaze steadily.

'Who authorised this ridiculous summons? I have been living here with my family.'

'Do not question me, sir. It would bide you ill to resist,' the captain said quietly, leaning forward in the saddle.

'Do I have time to say farewell to my family?' Gregory asked.

'No,' the captain replied.

'Let me say goodbye to my children first, captain, and then I shall come with you with no resistance.'

The captain sat back in his saddle. 'Say your farewell briefly,' he conceded. He signalled one of his men to dismount and accompany Gregory. With the soldier following close behind, he re-entered

Yardeley Chase. Margaret and Alice had been waiting for him and they both ran to him, alarmed for his safety.

'I am to go to the Tower. I am arrested for treason,' Gregory explained bleakly as he ascended the stairs followed by the two women and the guard.

'What about Robert or Mary?' Margaret asked anxiously.

'My husband, is he well?' Alice added, looking back at the soldier. He ignored the women, refusing to speak.

In the nursery, Edmund, Simon and Angelo were at their desks writing on chalkboards with their governess. Roberta sat by the window playing with her younger siblings. The two boys tossed down their writing and ran to their father, shouting happily as he gathered them into his arms.

'Give your father a hug; I need hugs from all my children today. Angelo, you too,' Gregory said, his voice wavering. His stepson silently set down his chalk and joined his half-brothers. There in the nursery, Gregory knelt with his darling sons and stepson, kissing their heads and whispering through his tears words of encouragement to them to be brave and do everything asked of them. Stephen tugged at his mother's skirt and asked why his uncle was crying, Alice could not answer her son as the poignancy of the scene overcame her.

'Enough,' the soldier said. Gregory kissed his children each once more and stood up slowly. He then put a hand on Roberta's head in blessing, and then ruffled Stephens's hair. The boy did not understand why his cousins were looking bewildered and began to cry himself. Margaret and Alice stood in the doorway and Gregory turned to them one last time as a groom led his horse forward.

'Do not worry, I shall try to send word to you both of Mary and Robert,' he assured and swung into the saddle. The captain gave the order and with Gregory surrounded by the soldiers, they rode from the courtyard, towards London and the Tower.

The drawbridge at the Tower slowly lowered, permitting Gregory and the detachment of guards to cross and enter into its confines. Sir John Gage stood waiting for the arrival of his latest prisoner. Silently, he watched as Gregory dismounted, then walked towards him.

'Follow me with no questioning the reason. You will remain here until called upon to give information required,' Sir John said soberly.

'I have done nothing; I have no cause to be here. The law...' Gregory began. Sir John narrowed his eyes and took a step closer to Gregory.

'You were told not to speak. If you value your life, you will obey instructions,' he growled. Gregory nodded wordlessly and followed Sir John. He was led to a communal dungeon. Pushed in the back, Gregory fell heavily down the stone steps. Sir John descended behind. Looking around, Gregory saw along the wall iron rings with chains and manacles. What first looked like bundles of rags heaped against the walls turned out to be men.

'Sit,' Gage commanded, pointing to the foul-smelling floor. Gregory looked at the blackened and rotting reeds and shook his head. 'Do it now.' Sir John pushed him down and fastened the manacles to his wrists.

'How long am I to be kept here?' Gregory asked. The constable glanced at him and did not reply, he pulled the chains tight to restrict movement, and then ascended the steps, pulling the door shut behind him. Men were groaning, some were cursing. One was shouting obscenities to an unseen enemy. The creature next to Gregory looked at him.

'Don't think you'll get out of here anon. We're forgotten here,' he said in a dry voice. 'No food, no drink.'

'I shouldn't be here; I don't know why I'm here,' Gregory said. His companion guffawed bitterly.

'None of us should and we've all forgotten why we were brought here,' he replied. Gregory sat back against the wall and sighed. He did not want to engage in a conversation with the wretch by his side. His thoughts turned to Mary and he hoped her prison in the fortress was less insufferable.

Occasionally, guards would enter the cell and carry a man away. He would go loudly professing his innocence to whatever his crimes were, or in pitiable silence. Those who remained behind would howl and screech until the door slammed shut once again. Only Gregory remained mute.

They eventually came for him. Pulled roughly from the cell, he was marched through corridors until they came to the torture chamber.

Pushed into a low wooden chair, Gregory sat looking around, distressed and bewildered as straps secured his wrists to the arms of the chair. Sir Giles Sneddon emerged from the shadows. The acrid smell of vinegar invaded Gregory's nostrils and he could taste the thick air on the back of his throat, making him cough and retch as bile rose in his throat.

'Word has reached me that you were involved in the plot to assassinate the queen. What say you?' Sneddon asked steadily. Gregory shook his head.

'I know nothing of any plot; Queen Anne has been most charitable to both my wife and me,' he replied, swallowing hard. 'I want to know where Mary is. Is she somewhere in here? Is she safe?'

Sneddon inspected his fingernails before speaking. 'Come now, friend, do not act the innocent with me. Your wife is within the Tower for the crime she committed. She gives good sport to the guards here. Is that right?' Sneddon looked at the guards in amusement, who agreed laughing. 'You have been implicated in attempted murder. Did you not make your escape from court prior to the plot?' He watched Gregory's struggle in the chair and smiled maliciously. 'A fine husband indeed, leaving your wife to face the executioner's axe.'

'I have done nothing,' Gregory insisted. Sneddon called his guard over. He pointed at Gregory. The guard punched him in the stomach, making him double over in pain. His spectacles fell from their pouch. Intrigued, Sneddon picked them up and squinted through the lenses.

'Need these to help you see?' he asked, stating the obvious. He dropped the spectacles to the floor in front of Gregory and crushed them, smashing the lens with the heel of his boot. 'You shall not need them again. What was your role in the plot, Paxton?' Sneddon repeated. Gasping with pain, Gregory shook his head, unable to speak. A second punch landed again in his stomach, this time making him spit blood. 'In what hand do you hold a quill?' Sneddon asked.

'I write with my left hand,' Gregory lied quickly. Sneddon

picked up a mallet from the table and brought it crashing down upon Gregory's right hand, crushing bones.

'With all your fancy learning, do you think I am stupid, Paxton?' Sneddon growled. He slammed the mallet on to Gregory's left hand. 'In case you were telling the truth. Fetch the rope.' The guard went away to return carrying a bucket filled to the brim with water. In the water was a length of thick rope and a wooden slat. On a signal, he took the rope from the water and looped it around Gregory's head, tightening it with the slat until the rope pressed into his skull. 'Before we proceed, I give you one final chance to confess to your crimes.'

'I have done nothing wrong, so I have nothing to confess. False accusations would not stand in a court of law,' Gregory shouted defiantly.

Sneddon slapped his face. 'Don't play the lawyer with me. The only law in here is mine.' He waved a hand and the rope tightened around Gregory's head. He grimaced as the pain grew.

'Confess and it will all stop,' Sneddon said smoothly, bringing his face close to Gregory's. He shook his head and remained silent; blood began to trickle as the rope cut deep. He cried out, but still did not speak. Another slap stung his cheek.

'I see you are going to be difficult. You will only make it worse for yourself, Paxton. Save yourself any more suffering and confess your part in this conspiracy.' Gregory's head throbbed, and any movement intensified the pain, yet he managed to shake his head in denial. Sneddon sighed. 'So be it. I shall leave you to think about what you will tell me.' He picked up the bucket and emptied the water over Gregory's head. 'As the rope dries, it will constrict and cut into your skull. Your brain will feel as though it shall explode.' He dismissed the guards, then went and sat behind his desk to continue his work. Gregory heard the sound of a quill scratching across the paper as Sneddon wrote quickly. The rope began to incise deeper. A door opened and a servant brought in a tray of refreshments.

When he had finished eating, Sneddon belched, wiped his mouth on his sleeve and stood in front of Gregory, regarding him as he drank deeply from the goblet of wine tossing the vessel aside once it was empty.

'Do you have anything to tell me?' he asked.

'No,' Gregory whispered. Sneddon looked up at the guards who had returned to their station.

'More water,' he shouted. The guard poured a second bucket of cold water over Gregory's head. Sneddon leant close. 'Think carefully about this bravado of yours, I get the truth no matter how long it takes.' He straightened up and departed, followed by the guards. Only the crackling from logs in the fire broke the silence in the chamber. Gregory sat alone feeling the rope contracting into his head again, like a thousand needles piercing his skull. He could feel a pulsing in his ears and the hammer sound of blood deep inside his head. He shouted out, any movement sent shards of pain through his head. No one responded to his call. Gregory panted painfully. Would this ever end?

By the time Sneddon returned the next day, Gregory was slumped forward in the chair, unconscious. Dried blood streaked his head and matted hair. Sneddon kicked Gregory's foot, waking him; he jerked his head up, the sudden snap reaction making him cry aloud.

'You have had the night to think Paxton. Do you have anything to tell me?' Sneddon asked. Gregory remained silent, hardly hearing the voice as his head pounded continuously. 'Fetch the boot,' he said with relish. A guard placed a metal cage in the shape of a large single boot, and wooden slats in front of Gregory. The metal boot was calf high and large enough to secure both legs and feet inside by bolts.

'What's that?' Gregory mumbled. The boot looked evil for all its simplicity and it struck fear into his heart. Sneddon gave another signal to have Gregory's legs and feet strapped into the boot.

'Tell me your part in the plot and it shall all end right now.' Sneddon waited, knowing the man before him was not going to deny him the warped pleasure. 'Very well, begin.' Wooden slats were forced between Gregory's knees. Sneddon picked up the mallet and brought it down onto the slats, driving them down between his knees. He screamed as the force split the bones in his legs. Again, a second blow drove the slats deeper down, shattering the already broken bones. The world suddenly reeled away as Gregory fell into unconsciousness. However, the acid aroma and

311

stench of a vinegar-soaked cloth wiped over his face awoke him, his head jerking back as he gasped for breath. A second slat hammered between his legs sent waves of excruciating pain coursing through his body.

'Confess, Paxton!' Sneddon shouted above Gregory's cries of pain. Gregory still managed to shake his head. He hammered one more slat in. 'It is no use being a stubborn fool, Paxton; it shall not end until you confess.'

'Let…Mary…go,' he whimpered in short gasps. Sneddon straightened up.

'So she will be free to poison again?' he mocked and brought the mallet down one more time. Frustrated by his prisoner's resistance, Sneddon threw the mallet across the room and punched his face hard. 'Guards, go to work on him!' he shouted. The two hefty men set into Gregory, their fists pummelling him inhumanly until called to halt the assault. The bolts holding the boot loosened. Gregory's legs fell loose. He sat back in the chair swooning and puffing with exhaustion. Sneddon snatched the already prepared confession from the table and thrust it under Gregory's nose and blood dripped onto the words, making the ink run.

'Sign here,' Sneddon said. 'Of course, you cannot now your hands are destroyed. I shall sign on your behalf,' he mocked and wrote Gregory's name at the bottom of the document. 'Take him back,' Sneddon said turning away. All the information he needed was now gathered. There was no escape for the perpetrators.

'I never confessed' Gregory managed to utter. Sneddon smiled.

'Who's to know what you said?' he smirked. The guards dragged Geregory away as he hurled obscenities at Sneddon. He ignored the abuse; it was nothing he had not heard before.

In the communal cell, chains secured Gregory once again to the wall. He lay there moaning in pain. Any movement brought agony he had never known before.

The wretch next to him was speaking, but not listening; he only turned his head aside and refused to talk.

# 41

Mary was restless in her cell. Sir John had informed her that both Gregory and Robert had admitted to the attempt on Queen Anne's life and they also face execution for treason. Pacing the floor, she began talking to herself, asking why she had listened to her brother in the first place. None of this would have happened if she had been stronger and had just said "no" to him. Possibly the threat to her children had just been that a threat. Surely, Robert would not have been that evil as to harm her sons. As the night passed slowly, and the cold air from the Thames blew in through the slit of a window, her head cleared. By the morning, a seed of an idea had begun to formulate in her mind. It was a small possibility, but it *was* a possibility and Mary was desperate to chance anything. She banged on the door with her fists shouting for attention. Her heart raced with alarm as the guard entered.

'Please may I have paper, quill and ink, I need to write letters,' she said attempting bravado. The guard leered at Mary, his lascivious gaze running over her body. Then he grunted and ambled away to return later with the items required.

Ignoring the rats and stench from the reeds, Mary sat upon the floor and began composing her letter. As she wrote, the words flowed from the quill.

*Gracious Majesty, dearest friend,*

 *I write to you as a loyal friend and subject who truly wishes you no harm.*

 *Forces beyond my control had threatened all I hold dear in my life. My actions were provoked, and I was prepared to take any risk to ensure the safety of my precious sons.*

 *As a mother yourself, would you not willingly kill or die to protect your beautiful daughter?*

*My brother, Robert is the only guilty indivdual. He was the one who threatened to hurt my darling boys if I did not do this evil deed for him.*

*He implicated my husband Gregory into this scheme of his, even though Gregory was ignorant of his terrible plan, and is innocent in every way possible. I had sent my husband and children away in an attempt to protect them; thinking that if he remained at court this may have caused my dearest husband harm. I know now, Robert named Gregory.*

*I plead to you to have pity on your wretched friend languishing within the unforgiving Tower to put my case to his majesty to spare our lives and banish my husband and me from court for the remainder of our lives. This we would do willingly without question or malice.*

*Our lives are in your royal hands.*

*I pray you have not forgotten the bond of friendship we once shared.*

*I remain your humble servant and friend always.*

*Lady Mary Paxton.*

Mary drafted the second letter to her mother.

*Dearest Mother,*

*It is with a heavy heart I must inform you that Robert, my darling husband and I face execution. I assure you that Gregory and I are innocent of the crimes for which we are charged.*

*Robert's obsessive desire for retribution has brought us to these final moments without thought for those innocents he has harmed.*

*Tell Alice she is an honourable woman, blinded by a fool's love.*

*Pray for our souls and pray we go to our Maker bravely.*

*I have always loved you and shall continue to honour you from heaven.*

*Please care for our orphaned children. Nurture them and see them grow to adulthood. Let them not forget their parents and assure them of our love until the very end of our miserable lives.*

*I remain your faithful, obedient and ever loving daughter,*

*Mary.*

She read the letters and felt satisfied with her effort. She shouted once more to the guard. He appeared.

'Again I ask a favour of you. Would you request on my behalf speech with Sir John, I would ask him to forward my letters?' Mary chose her words carefully. The guard was not bothered what Mary had wanted, and carried out his duties without question. This woman wanted to speak to the constable, why not let her. What good it could do hardly bothered him. He walked off again, leaving Mary waiting, re-reading her letters, and feeling hopeful that if the queen received her letter it may do her and Gregory some good.

As the sky darkened into night, Sir John unlocked the door and stepped into the cell. Alarmed, Mary pressed herself against the wall, still fearful of attack. He stood regarding her.

'I do not force myself upon women, nor am I your servant to attend upon you, Lady Paxton,' he said brusquely. In reality, Sir John had been busy with his other duties and had not found time until now to come and see what was required of him.

'Thank you, for saving me from that man,' she began, 'I have a request, which I wish you to carry out for me. I am condemned now. So please, can you see these letters delivered to her majesty, and to my mother,' Mary asked, holding out the letters. He took them and read their contents.

'Your execution day draws near; they may not reach their destinations in time,' he warned.

'While there is life, there is hope,' she said, feeling a wave of emotion beginning to sweep over her. Sir John sighed. He felt sorry for the woman before him and knew it would be folly to become emotionally involved with her. His position required him to be inflexible, cold and to distance himself from the prisoners. Those who came here did so because of their crimes and he had seen women imprisoned before. Somehow, she did not look evil. She had been foolish enough to become implicated in a plot that had been exposed. He turned and left the cell, locking it behind him.

Walking down the corridor, Sir John stopped and looked back. He decided to make Lady Mary more comfortable in her last days. On the following morning, he would have her moved from her cell. Her new lodgings would be a slight enhancement. 'I must be going soft,' he chided himself, shaking his head and continued down the corridor.

Sir John personally attended to Mary's move to the Beauchamp Tower the following day.

'Madam, you will follow me,' he said upon entering Mary's cell. Her face drained of colour and she began to tremble noticeably.

'Is it time already? I am not prepared. What about my husband, can I see Gregory before I die?' she said dreading her time had come for her execution.

'Madam, your day of execution has not yet arrived; you are to be moved to more equitable lodgings.'

'Will I see Gregory?' Mary repeated hopefully. Sir John shook his head.

'No, your husband is elsewhere in the Tower. He is not privileged to this favour,' he replied. At first, Mary considered refusing the offer while Gregory remained in his cell. Then the craving of comfort, however meagre, enticed her into accepting the offer.

The constable led the way through the corridors and out onto the flagstones. Mary stood feeling the spring breeze brush like silk against her cheek. Never before had she been so aware of an English spring day. Looking up, she watched white clouds breezing across the blue sky and heard bird song. It was a perfect moment.

'Lady Paxton, you must follow me now,' Sir John reminded. She looked at her jailor and smiled for the first time in weeks. He realised how attractive she was when she smiled, her face lightened with a moment's pleasure.

'Let me enjoy this a while longer then I shall follow you,' she replied. Sighing, he nodded and stood aside, knowing she would not try to escape; there was nowhere for her to run. Looking around at the buildings surrounding them, Mary's gaze rested upon the Queen's House. She along with Anne and the other women had lodged there the night before the coronation. That had been a merry evening with laughter and dancing, and she smiled at the memory. Sir John touched her arm and she flinched.

'Enough time now, madam,' he said quietly. Obediently, Mary followed him towards the Beauchamp Tower and entered its dark coldness.

They ascended a flight of stairs until they came to a door that the constable opened. Stepping inside, Mary looked around. This was a room instead of a cell. There was a glazed window; simple furniture and a fire in the hearth that would make her stay ambient. The view Mary would be able to look upon was a small patch of lawn, not much to see, but just being able to sit and stare from the window brought some small comfort.

She thanked Sir John as he left and locked the door on his departure. Turning back to the window, Mary pulled the stool over and sat on it, looking across the lawn to the imposing White Tower that dominated her vision. Somewhere in there was Gregory, what was he feeling right now? Was he in pain? Mary knew that he would be thinking of nothing but her and their sons. Robert also lay in a dark dungeon, but she wasted little thought upon her brother now, he was to deserve everything that happened to him.

At all times, when the heavy door slowly opened, all heads turned to see who was coming in to the communal cell, and more significantly, who was being removed. This time, the guard was coming for Gregory, and pulling him to his feet, the guard seemed not to hear Gregory's cries of pain or the howls of contempt from those able to make their voices heard.

'Where am I going? Is it time yet?' Gregory asked as the guard dragged him up the stone steps. 'Where is my wife?'

'You have a visitor,' the guard replied curtly. Surely no one would want to be seen communicating with a traitor, even if the traitor kept professing his innocence. Gregory's mind was full of intrigue, unable to imagine who had come to visit.

Outside a cell, a man wearing a cape and a hat pulled down to hide his face stood waiting. Gregory looked, trying to see who this person was, but the man lowered his head, keeping his features obscured. Once inside, the guard again chained Gregory to the wall. He left, allowing the visitor to enter, dropping several coins into the guard's outstretched hand as they passed. The mysterious man glanced back to make certain no one was watching through the grille in the door, before removing his cloak and hat. Gregory gave a sharp intake of breath when he saw who his visitor was.

Thomas Cromwell regarded his friend's scarred head, face,

body and limbs, bruised and swollen from torture and the beating, with disbelief and repugnance.

'I came prepared,' he said apologetically, holding a pomander of cloves and fragrant herbs to his nose to shut out the stench. 'God's blood, Gregory, what have they done to you? Don't say,' Cromwell muttered quickly, waving a hand outwards.

'What are you doing here?' Gregory spat. 'Come to report to the king that I am despoiled enough for his contentment?' he looked away bitterly. Cromwell shook his head.

'No, I have come here to propose a lifeline, a chance for you to live the rest of your life as a free man,' Cromwell replied, sitting down on an old stool that creaked under his weight. Gregory regarded him dubiously through narrowed eyes.

'How can you do that? I shall die the traitor's death soon.'

'I am an influential man. On the day of your execution, another will take your place. You shall live as my privileged guest at my house in Stepney.' Cromwell's face darkened with a moment's grief, and Gregory was convinced he saw the shimmer of tears in his friend's eyes. 'My home has become lonely and silent since Elizabeth and my daughters died of the sweat. My son is now married and lives his own life.'

'She was a good wife to you, Thomas. Your proposal sounds interesting, and I would like to know more,' Gregory said cautiously, intrigued how Cromwell could arrange such an exploit. He pulled the stool closer.

'You shall leave your cell on the morning of your execution, but instead of going to Tower Hill, guards will have been bribed and you shall be taken to a back entrance and the waiting carriage.'

'What about my wife?' Gregory asked. Cromwell scowled.

'She still will have to die, I cannot save her.' Cromwell paused. 'I had to hand your death warrant to the king for him to sign and be objective about it. I am risking the king's displeasure being here now talking with you. I am doing this because of our friendship of many years,' he continued passionately.

'What about my sons? Will I ever see them?'

'No, you can never see them again. Gregory, stop putting obstacles in the way, I am offering you freedom from this hellhole and a chance of life,' Cromwell urged, annoyed at his friend's insistent questioning. Gregory leant back against the cold wall.

'So, I will be a free man living in Stepney, while my wife grows cold in her grave, and my sons denied their father. Sorry Thomas, that is not freedom for me, it sounds like exchanging one prison for another,' he replied shaking his head. Cromwell sighed exasperated.

'You will be alive,' he argued. 'Living in comfort…'

'Call this broken body of mine alive?' Gregory interrupted angrily. 'I cannot walk. Every movement fills me with hurting, I cannot sleep and when I do, I have nightmares and wake up screaming. Truthfully, Thomas, would you desire my company in your home knowing this?'

'You will have access to the best medicine in the land. My private physician is a genius!' Cromwell argued fervently. Gregory thrust his hands close to Cromwell's face and the chains rattled pitilessly.

'Look Thomas, look at my hands! Can he mend my smashed hands? Can he make my shattered legs strong again? Can he turn back the clock, so I can hold Mary in my arms once more? Can he Thomas?' his voice broke with bitter emotion and Cromwell stood up, knowing he was getting nowhere with his obstinate friend.

'So you would rather have your belly sliced open and your head hacked from your shoulders then?'

'If it means by living I am never to see my wife or children again. Yes,' Gregory answered decisively, turning his face away.

'Then I am sorry for you, my friend. I have tried to help and your refusal saddens me. God speed when your hour arrives. I shall not be there.' Cromwell bent over and kissed Gregory on the cheek. He turned to the door. 'Guard, I am finished here,' he shouted, throwing his cloak over his shoulders and pulling his hat on again, waiting for the door to open. He departed without looking back, leaving Gregory alone, evaluating the conversation. The guard kicked him.

'Get on your feet, shuffler,' he swore. Slowly, in great pain, Gregory struggled to stand. Cursing, the guard pulled him to a standing position, then releasing the chains, took him back to the communal cell. Once again shackled to the wall, Gregory shut his eyes and tried to blot out the clamour and stench, but this time, the noise seemed greater than before, this time he could not hide in his own private world of misery. The harsh realisation of what was now unavoidable became too much for him to bear. He had always attempted to be detached from others, not wanting to show any flaw to be seen as a weakness, but now, having let this final opportunity of freedom go, Gregory knew there would be no second chance. Death was lurking, skulking around the scaffold, patiently waiting for him.

# 42

*Execution day*

Mary woke from a fitful sleep. She had intended to spend her last night alive on her knees praying to God for her family and her soul; she had spent only the first hours of darkness in prayer. Sir John had supplied a brass crucifix to focus her prayers on, but she could not concentrate, and had climbed wearily into her small bed and had laid there. All Mary could think of was that moment when she knelt at the block, stretching her neck on the smooth wood, waiting for the axe to strike.

The sky was leaden grey and rain drummed monotonously against the window. The weather matched her disposition. Today she was to die. What were Gregory and Robert thinking this morning in their cold cells? Mary's thoughts turned to her children. They would grow up without their parents, what would become of them? Cecily had Ambrose to look after her now. Her Spanish son and the boys were the ones who would suffer the most. She had gambled with the life of the unborn child, and the gamble had been lost. This life extinguished before it had a chance to begin and Mary was the only one who briefly knew of its existence. She looked down at her body; her pregnancies had left their marks on her. Her hips were broader now, her waist thicker. This time, her belly would not swell with the growing child blooming inside her. She would not feel that delightful sensation as the infant kicked.

'Little one, you, your father and I shall be a family together in heaven.' She whispered protectively covering her stomach with her hands.

Queen Anne sat in her apartment brooding. She had not been sleeping well recently. The king had not shared her bed since she had announced her pregnancy. He had made excuses that to protect his gift to the English people, he would sleep elsewhere. What he had really meant was that he had taken a mistress. Anne had her suspicions that the slut was Jane Seymour. When Lady Jane had first arrived at court, Anne had dismissed her as a simpering country girl. However, she had two brothers who were seeking to enhance their fortune and status. If Lady Jane became King Henry's mistress, the Seymour brothers would waste no time in currying favour with their sister's royal lover. The young woman was eager to please His Majesty in whatever way possible, and if that meant between the sheets, then there it would be. Anne remembered how her father had done the very same thing, prostituting both his daughters for the king. As they shared his bed, and pleased him, the Boleyn fortunes rose.

Anne held the letter from Mary in her hand. It had arrived two days before. At first she had ignored it; let the traitors go to their deserved deaths. Finally, she opened the letter and read the contents, and then she had read it many times over. The words struck at her conscious. Today, this afternoon, her friend Mary Paxton was due for execution. It was true she had slipped poison into the queen's drink, but Anne already knew Mary was not a person who would do such an evil deed willingly. She knew that if the king could rid himself of one queen, he could do it a second time. Anne would do anything possible to ensure she bore a prince, if by doing a good deed pleased God, he may make the child inside her male, and her position on the throne would be safe. She dismissed her women and walked alone to the king's private apartments.

King Henry was busy at a table reading documents and signing them. Chancellor Cromwell stood with a quantity of papers in his arms, handing them one by one to his royal master. They were talking quietly together, Cromwell leaning over him, pointing out paragraphs on the documents for particular attention. The chancellor looked up surprised and bowed as the queen entered. Henry glanced up, quill poised over a document, and he smiled at his pregnant wife. She curtsied low to her husband and turned to Cromwell.

'Chancellor Cromwell, leave our presence, I would speak with the king alone on a private matter,' Anne commanded. Cromwell looked to the king who nodded and, bowing, he obediently backed out of the chamber.

Anne waited until the door closed, and she was sure Cromwell was not listening from the other side. She wandered round the table, gently pushed the king back in his chair, and sat upon his lap. Henry, intrigued by his wife's actions, stroked her swelling body. She planted a light kiss on his forehead, and ran her fingers through his hair, humming a tune lightly.

'Anne, do you feel well?' Henry asked between light kisses. He sighed with frustration. 'I would take you now on this table were you not carrying England's hope.'

'I would have you take me too, dearest, anywhere, any way and anytime you desired,' Anne purred. 'I have been thinking, Henry.' He now was alert. When a woman talked like this, it usually meant trouble.

'Proceed,' he said quietly.

'The three executions taking place at Tower Hill.'

'What of them?'

'Mary has been a good friend to me over the years; I know she would not do as she done without pressure. Read this letter delivered to me. I cannot sit back any longer without taking action.' Anne handed the letter to the king and fetched him a dish of sugared almonds, which he ate slowly, fed delicately one at a time by the queen. 'Would you be magnanimous and send Mary and her husband a reprieve?'

'I knew you were after something, Anne,' Henry cried, stabbing a finger towards her. 'The death warrants have been signed and sealed. All of them are traitors,' he grumbled pushing the silver dish aside as he turned away in his seat.

'Mary and Gregory witnessed our marriage; she assisted me at the birth of Elizabeth. We are also both godparents to their eldest son,' Anne prompted. Henry turned back to face his wife.

'I cannot undo what has been done, the warrant is signed, and I have already told you so,' he explained earnestly, tossing the letter onto the table.

'But Henry, you are the king, surely you can do what you want, not what you are told,' Anne argued back. 'Rules are made to be broken. Remember, Catherine was still your wife the day we married.' The king shuddered at the reminder. She placed her hands on her stomach and looked saintly towards her husband. 'The guilt of knowing an innocent woman who has been our friend died at my husband's hands, even indirectly could cause harm to *your* prince.'

'Stop it, Anne,' Henry complained. Yet he knew he could not risk the chances of displeasing God and possibly damage the chances of fathering a healthy son. He sorted through the paper and found a blank sheet. Dipping the quill into an inkpot, he began to write rapidly. Anne watched anxiously, hardly daring to breathe. When finished, the king picked up a stick of wax and held it over a lit candle until it melted and dripped onto the parchment. With his ring, the king pressed the wax, indenting his seal. He looked up at his wife, his face registering annoyance. Anne curtsied very low.

'My lord, thank you,' she muttered appreciatively.

'Madam, I only do this so that the child remains unharmed. Your part of the bargain now is to produce a healthy son,' the king warned. 'If you fail, you may live to regret your actions of this day.' Henry stood up. 'Cromwell!' he bellowed. Instantly, Cromwell entered. Anne knew he had been trying to listen to their conversation with an ear pressed against the door.

'Sire,' Cromwell said. The king handed the sealed document to him, not taking his angry eyes from the queen's face.

'Get this to Tower Hill in haste. Be sure it reaches its destination before heads roll, or it'll be yours that will part company from its shoulders,' Henry commanded.

'I shall see to it myself, sire,' Cromwell said bowing low, as he backed away.

Anne dropped to her knees in gratitude, and she kissed the king's ringed fingers.

'Bless you, my lord,' she breathed. The king withdrew his hand slowly.

'Go, I have important documents to study,' he growled. 'Do not disturb me again this day.' Although he still desired his queen with a zealous lust, Henry had long since fallen out of love with her. The birth of Elizabeth had begun the unravelling of his passion for

Anne. He watched silently as she backed out of the apartments, a hand strategically resting on her stomach.

Anne walked slowly back to her own rooms. She hoped the message would reach Tower Hill in time. She felt a small movement. Was it the baby? Was it time already for the quickening? She had thought it too early to feel anything yet. This had to be a sign to tell her that what she had done was right. God would be pleased with her and grant her the son that would bring peace to England and her own security. Anne patted her stomach.

'Precious little prince,' she whispered, 'you are to be such a fortunate boy.'

Meanwhile, Cromwell ran along the corridors, knocking into people, pushing others aside in his haste to carry out his master's command, in his hand, the sealed document that would save his friend and his wife. He would not trust anyone else with this important task. People stopped and looked at the chancellor. Why was he in such a hurry? Cromwell was a man who never ran anywhere, so why this uncharacteristic behaviour? He sprinted to the stables and commandeered the swiftest horse, riding at full speed from the palace, determined to reach the Tower in time.

Lady Gage entered the room carrying a tray laden with a simple meal of bread, cheese and ale, a bowl of hot water scented with lavender, a towel and a brush. Over her arm, she carried a dress.

'I have come to prepare you,' she said. Mary lethargically stood up.

'Thank you,' she replied flatly. Lady Gage placed the tray on the table and showed her the dress. It was a simple gown of black cloth. Mary stripped and washed in the hot water, feeling clean and strangly refreshed. With help, she put the black dress on, then sitting on the stool, Lady Gage brushed through her thick hair until all the tangles were out, and it hung loose down her back. She then caught the hair up in a simple net exposing her neck for the executioner.

'My husband showed me your letters, the king should not send a woman to execution, it is wrong. Life in a convent would be enough punishment,' Lady Gage said. Mary smiled hopelessly.

'Thank you,' she repeated, not desiring to talk anymore.

'My husband must attend the event, but I shall not. Here, take these coins to pay the executioner for his services. God be with you. I shall pray for your children and their safe keeping,' she departed the cold, bleak room. Mary now sat calmly at the table, waiting for the end. There was no escape now from death. It was hours away. Rising, she looked again from her window at the small patch of green. Yesterday, she had watched four broken men taken away to their execution; neither her husband nor brother had been with them. Their executions were today with hers. At least for her and Gregory, they would be together in heaven.

Leaning the side of her face against the cold wall, she felt strangely tranquil. Death was a great leveller; it came to all ultimately, even kings die.

She sat at the table and ate sparingly at the food, having little appetite, what good would eating do her now. Lady Gage had been kind enough to provide victuals for her; Mary knew she should show her appreciation. Even Sir John had not been cruel; he had intervened and saved her from rape. Mary wished she had something to give them as a token of her thanks, but she had nothing left, and hoped they would know of her gratitude towards them that had helped her through the last days.

From outside, Mary heard voices calling to each other. She looked out of the window, chewing on a piece of bread. She watched as two wasted men were led in chains to a waiting a cart. She stopped chewing, and the bread dropped from her mouth as it fell open. She recognised to her consternation Gregory and Robert. Guards insensitively lifted both men up, pushing them roughly onto the cart. Robert was looking around at the guards and seemed to be keeping silent. Gregory was appearing to argue with his capturers, they pushed him harshly for something he was saying, but from behind the window, his words were indistinguishable.

'Why did things have to go so wrong?' she said softly, as tears squeezed from her eyes. Mary watched as Sir John conversed briefly to the man seated at the front of the cart, he then turned and headed for the Beauchamp Tower. He was coming for her.

The sound of a heavy key fitting into the old lock and being turned drew Mary's attention away from the window and she took a deep breath. Sir John entered looking grim.

'Madam, it is time,' he said, attempting to sound definite, but his voice trembled with sentiment. 'You shall face the axe. You shall have a quick merciful execution. The other two traitors shall die befitting their rank,' he continued.

She sighed deeply. 'I am ready. I see my husband and brother are waiting for me.' Mary glanced once more out of the window. Sir John indicated to the open door. She looked around her room one last time, and then began the walk through the dark corridors.

The rain had stopped, the clouds disipated and now the sun was beaming down from a blue sky onto Tower Hill. Although filled with unremitting pain, Gregory's eyes lit up when he saw Mary and a sob caught in his throat. Robert's eyes remained downcast. He could not bring himself to look at his sister. Sir John assisted Mary into the cart, she sat beside Gregory, her heart aching when she looked at his bruised, unshaven face, broken hands and wrists bloody and swollen by the manacles, she reached out to hold his hand to give him support, but a guard pulled her back, ignoring their protests. She tried to throw herself forward, only to fail as the guard circled her waist with his arm and dragged her back onto the wooden board.

'No physical contact between prisoners,' he said determinedly.

'Mary, keep good heart, I love you always!' Gregory insisted.

'Shut it,' the guard growled and threw a punch, hitting Gregory's chin, sending him smashing to the floor of the cart as Mary screamed. Robert now slowly looked up at Mary.

'Can you ever forgive me?' he asked thickly. She returned the look with mounting repugnance. Sisterly love had long since evaporated, and an intensifying hysteria was building up from deep inside her body, filling the pit of her stomach and engulfing her lungs, stifling her as it grew. Screaming, Mary hurled herself on him with such energy, they both fell from the cart, tearing the tailboard from its hinges as they landed on the cobbles. She pounded his chest with her fists, screaming obscenities. Sir John pulled Mary from Robert while she continued to kick wildly at him and thrash her arms about, cursing him violently.

'Enough!' the constable shouted crossly, throwing Mary into the cart, the guards doing similar to Robert. She moved as far along

327

as she could to be away from her brother, her hand groping to find Gregory. He looked at Robert.

'Because of you, I have been tortured for a crime I did not commit, my wife is about to have her head sliced from her neck, and our children orphaned,' he spat, as tears fell down his face. Robert hung his head in degradation as each word cut like a knife into his heart. Sir John mounted his horse and shouted the order to advance. The cart lurched into movement. Mary watched mutely as the heavy gates swung open and the drawbridge lowered. Several inquisitive onlookers strained to see the condemned make their final journey.

The cart ascended the hill towards the permanent scaffold circled by guards. A loud and raucous crowd had gathered and enterprising salesmen were selling crudely made toy scaffolds complete with executioners and victims for exuberant prices. A group of musicians were playing jolly tunes to dance to. Pie men calling loudly sold their warm pies and ale men took payment for clay cups of beer, all creating an atmosphere of a village fair on May Day. The executioner and a priest stood silently on the platform, watching their approach.

By the time the cart drew to a halt, the priest had descended from the platform and helped Mary step down; guards cruelly hauled Robert and Gregory to the ground. Before climbing the wooden steps, Mary looked up at the platform, at the lit brasier, the ominiously large execution block, at the added gibbet and at the table where lay the instruments ready to send her husband and brother to their deaths. Drenched in the earlier rain, the scaffold was now drying out and vapour rose into the air from the wooden construction like noiseless, vanishing spirits. She turned to Gregory who was holding on to the cart for support.

'There are seven steps up, let me help you,' she said compassionately. Trembling visibly, he leant heavily onto her arm and together they slowly took each step one at a time, with Mary giving Gregory soft words of encouragement. Once they were on the scaffold, Robert slowly ascended the steps unaided, followed by the priest and the constable. They stood on the platform, looking out at the expectant faces watching them. There was cursing and expletives shouted and empty clay cups hurled at them. Above the noise, a shout sounded; Mary scanned the faces in the direction of the shout. A hand rose in a wave, and she focused on it, staggering back in disbelief.

'Dear God,' she expressed. 'Robert, look.' Mary pointed in the direction of the raised hand. Robert strained to see, and gasped as his eyes fell upon their mother and his wife. The two women had made the journey to see their loved ones for the final time, hoping their presence would bring small comfort.

'Robert, Mary. God be with you!' Margaret shouted in a tremulous voice.

'I'll always love you, Robert!' Alice shouted towards Robert, blowing kisses at him. He felt scorching tears on his face at the sight of his dearly loved mother and the wife he adored. Mary now found her resolute disintegrating and she began to sob quietly.

The priest opened his Bible and narrated prayers for the three condemned souls. Mary dropped the coins into the executioner's outstretched palm. He looked at the payment and grunted, shoving the coins into a pocket.

'Mary, you must go first. You should not see me suffer the ignominy of execution,' Gregory urged. She shook her head, unable to refuse or protest. He and Robert, for so long enemies, finally in accord, exchanged glances, united for the only time.

'He is right, do this now for pity's sake; I would rather see your head roll than for you to see the death that awaits your husband and I,' Robert insisted.

'I do not want to die. Please don't let me die.' Mary's voice was a small as a church mouse. The executioner nodded in the direction of the large wooden block. She faced the crowd, now hushed with anticipation. 'My husband would say that a person is innocent until proven guilty. I go to my death an innocent woman. Queen Anne is good and kind and wishes no ill upon anyone. God grant King Henry long life and a prince to reign wisely after him. He is a benevolent monarch.' Her voice, thin as thread, was interspersed by sobs. Turning, she looked at Gregory, still ignoring her brother. 'I shall go first to heaven and wait for you to join me soon.' She kissed her husband on the lips. They held each other briefly and he kissed her forehead before Sir John gently pulled them apart and guided her to the block.

'Do you want a blindfold?' he asked. She shook her head and knelt in front of the block, disinclined to lay her neck on it. 'Pray briefly if you wish, then stretch your arms out when you are ready,' he added quietly.

With short gasps, Mary laid her neck on the smooth wooden block and closed her eyes, her lips moving in silent prayer.

From the back of the crowd came a strident shout. 'Stop the execution! Stop I say!' Every person turned to see Thomas Cromwell riding his horse through the crowd. Pushing through the onlookers, in one hand he waved a document. At the base of the scaffold, Cromwell dismounted and ran up the steps.

'I have a royal pardon from His Majesty,' he shouted still waving the document. The crowd gasped in astonishment. He broke the seal. 'It reads thus: *"New evidence has come to light. Robert Hawke coerced his sister into using the poison and that her husband had naught to do with the plan whatsoever".*' There was a second gasp and murmuring from the crowd. Nothing like this had been seen before. 'His Majesty instructs me to tell you that Gregory Paxton and his wife are to be spared and must return to their home, all pensions, titles and monies rescinded to go to the royal exchequer. Not to attend court again.' A single voice cheered from the back of the crowd. Sir John snatched the letter from Cromwell's hand and read the contents for himself, scowling. He looked at Gregory, then Mary, his expression softening.

'You are free to leave, your names are cleared, and you are proved innocent in this affair,' he said quietly.

'My darling, we can go home,' Mary stood slowly, aided by the baffled executioner. Gregory looked at her and shook his head.

'How can I?' he asked. 'Look at me, I am a broken man.'

'I will care for you, my love,' Mary insisted. Again, he shook his head.

'Gregory, the king has absolved you and your wife of guilt, you are free,' Cromwell urged.

'How can I let my children see me like this? I want them to remember their father as he was, not as he is.' Gregory looked at the executioner. 'I ask you, please carry out your duty, and send me to my Maker.'

Both Cromwell and Mary shouted out distressed. 'No, Gregory, please, no,' she cried, taking his hand in hers. She looked at the executioner, tears shining in her eyes. 'Do not listen to him please. If he dies, then my life will be over. You can cut my head off as I do not want to live without my husband.'

'Do you want me to continue?' the executioner asked, confused by the peculiar situation. Cromwell intervened before Gregory could reply,

'No. By order of the king, you are to desist immediately. I shall not permit you to continue,' he said sharply.

'Thomas, how did you manage to convince the king?' Gregory asked as Sir John unlocked the chains at his wrists and ankles, allowing them to rattle to the scaffold boards.

'It was not I, the queen pleaded for your lives and His Majesty conceded to her request,' he answered. Gregory looked at Mary.

'I wrote to Her Majesty, it was a last desperate possibility I took. I dared to hope she would remember our friendship,' she explained. Gregory slowly pushed the tears from his face. He looked between Cromwell and Sir John.

'I am given a second chance; help me to go home to my family,' he said. Mary embraced him and gently kissed his lips, a heartfelt sigh and then a cheer rose from the crowd. Robert had been standing aside, trembling hands covering his strained face.

'What about me?' he asked, his voice quivering as he lowered his hands. Cromwell regarded him grimly.

'The clemency is only for Paxton and his wife. You still must face execution,' he said gruffly.

'No, no, not me, I don't want to die, please, not me,' Robert sobbed stumbling back. 'Mother, help me,' he pleaded turning to look for Margaret in the crowd.

'Die like a man,' the executioner growled, pulling Robert towards the gibbet.

'Please, let me say just one thing,' he pleaded, shaking the executioner's hand from his arm. The executioner grunted a reply and nodded. Robert looked into the crowd and focused on Alice's distraught face. When he spoke, his voice was low with emotion.

'I know I have done many evil things in my life. For that, I am sorry for the pain I have caused. I have always loved my mother, my wife and children.' He turned to face Mary, and in a whisper, only she could hear he concluded. 'For what I forced you to do, I deserve to die.' Mary bit her lower lip, fighting the tears that freely cascaded down her face.

'I can never forget, where your evil has led me and my husband,' she said. 'I shall pray for your soul, and care for your children.' The executioner tightened the chains around Robert's wrists, and led him to stand under the gibbet and over a trap door. He fitted the noose around his neck and tightened it.

'Merciful God, receive me!' he shouted. Mary crossed herself instinctively. The executioner watched Sir John, waiting for the nod, and on the signal pulled the lever, dropping Robert sharply. He hung, suspended, choking; his legs thrashing wildly, body twisting grossly, gurgling as the heavy rope constricted his windpipe. His eyes fluttered shut and his body began to go limp. He was cut down and the executioner threw him onto the wooden table, cutting and pulling his clothes off, pushing his chained arms above his head, securing them to a hook, leaving him semi-concious and naked. He picked up a large knife and, grasping Robert's testicles, sliced them off with one expert movement to the roaring encouragement of the crowd, before showing the bloody, severed flesh close to Roberts's face, a pain beyond torture swam through his body in vicious, ferocious waves now. Mary could not look, she had her eyes squeezed shut, and her face buried in Gregory's chest, her hands clamped over her ears did not shut out her brother's screams of pain, horror and shock. She could feel her husband's heart hammering in terror as he recoiled, his entire body shaking with revulsion watching, and knowing that this would have been his death too had it not been for Cromwell's intervention.

Now the executioner had the blade of the slitting knife stabbing into Robert's chest and slowly, to prolong the grotesque event, pulled the blade down the length of his torso, cutting a second incision across his stomach, then stepped back as Robert's guts spilled out, steaming, pouring blood and fluid onto the table. He picked up a lit torch from the brasier and thrust it into the guts, releasing the stench of burning human intestines as the flames hissed. The crowd were now howling in frenzy, loving the spectacle performed before them. Robert, still kept alive by sponges of vinegar wiped over his face, was now hauled, trailing his own intestines towards the block where the axe took two swings to sever his head, his mutilated body jerked back as blood pumped from his neck, forced out as his heart continued to beat briefly.

Mary screamed as blood flooded the boards, splattered her dress and dripped viscously between the slats. The executioner, laughing snatched up Robert's head by the hair and showed it to the baying crowd.

'Look ye at the face of a traitor!' he roared. His head would be displayed on a spike on London Bridge. His body cut into quarters and sent to the corners of the realm as a warning to those with treasonable thoughts. Mary felt her legs give way under her body as the world swirled away and she crumpled, hearing Gregory's anxious voice calling to her as she disappeared into a black void. Strong arms caught her, cradling her safely. Then the taste of beer on her lips revived her, opening her eyes and looking up she saw her husband looking down on her as she lay in Sir John's arms. He assisted her to her feet, ensuring she was able to walk again.

'No one has walked back down these steps, let me help you,' he said, making certain that she was able to stand before leading Mary slowly back to ground level while Gregory, with Cromwell and the priest's assistance, followed behind. Margaret and Alice pushed their way through the crowd. Mother and daughter ran into each other's arms, encircled by the cheering crowd; Sir John and the priest applauded the poignant scene before them. The guards exchanged bewildered glances; they were use to the mob rushing the scaffold with blood lust, not this frenetic, ecstatic cheering. Alice hung back, watching, her own emotions shredded, having seen her dearest husband so brutally disembowled and put to death.

'Ladies, Sir Gregory we shall return to the Tower, your lodging will be more equitable than before. Then we can make arrangements for your return home,' Sir John insisted, indicating to a waiting page to bring his horse over. He lifted Mary, then Margaret onto the back of the horse, Cromwell's horse was led forward for Alice, and with the cart carrying Gregory with Cromwell sitting by his side following behind, the odd procession made its way back towards the Tower. The cheering crowds parted, allowing passage through. Mary barely noticed the tumult going on around her, she was aware only of desolation and peculiar elation to be alive still. Margaret was talking to her, but she scarcely heard her mother's voice. Everyone and everything was moving slowly around her, voices were distorted and distant.

That night after Cromwell had departed; the three women and Gregory were guests of Sir John and treated to a hearty meal. Margaret dined well, Alice ate little, Gregory, clumsy from his injuries, tenaciously attempted to eat his own food with no assistance. Mary just pushed her food around the plate silently; she had no appetite or heart to eat. Sir John and Lady Gage did everything possible to make their guests comfortable, even giving up their large bed for the night.

In the darkened room, Mary lay wide-eyed, unable to sleep. She lay staring into the darkness, listening to the sound of her mother breathing deeply in her exhausted sleep, and Alice continuously weeping. She could not even find words to comfort her sister-in-law's sorrow; she just waited until the snivelling stopped as Alice fell into an uneasy sleep while slumber still eluded her.

'Have I done right?' Gregory spoke aloud, also incapable of sleep.

'Oh, yes my love. We will go home and watch our sons grow,' she replied. 'And our new child I carry shall bring us joy.' She felt her husband jolt to this disclosure.

'You carry another? Why did you not tell me that day, I would have taken you away and none of this would have happened.' Gregory could not disguise the bitterness in his voice.

'Robert threatened to harm Edmund and Simon if I did not comply with his demands, and I could not risk the lives of our boys. I had to get them away from court for their safety,' she reasoned. Gregory remained silent. Eventually he spoke.

'I would have protected you and my sons,' he conceded quietly. 'I would have gladly died a hundred times to save you,' he added, his voice quavering. Eventually, sleep overcame him. Mary listened to his laboured breathing, her heart aching hearing him muttering words of misery as the nightmares returned to invade his sleep. Gregory began to toss and turn, disturbed and anxious in slumber; the muttering became louder and turned to shouts of terror. She moved to his side and attempted to put a comforting arm about his shoulders, he violently recoiled away at her touch, shaking uncontrollably, pleading tearfully with the devils in his head to leave him be. Mary withdrew from his side, helpless. She tried calling his name gently and, gradually, Gregory began to calm down enough for her to take him in her arms and hold him tenderly, rocking back and forth as a mother would a frightened child. Margaret and Alice, woken by the commotion, added their own words of comfort to the now trembling Gregory. He fell asleep safe in his wife's arms; Mary remained awake, humming soft lullabys to him until the sun rose on the first day of their new life.

They remained as guests for several more days until Gregory felt well enough to travel. A carriage arranged by Sir John carried everyone home. The journey made uncomplicated for Gregory by travelling slowly with frequent stops.

Slowly, methodically, Mary crossed the threshold at Yardeley Chase followed by Alice and Margaret. Everything was welcoming, safe and secure. Nothing seemed to have changed; the reeds on the floor rustled under the hem of her dress, releasing their familiar fragrance. A shout from the stairs made Mary turn her head.

'Mother!' Edmund shouted, running down the stairs followed by Simon and Angelo shouting as loudly. Stephen and Roberta brought up the rear calling to their mother.

Mary, dropping to her knees, gathered her boys into her arms, holding them as though she never wanted to let them go ever again. Alice would have to explain eventually to Stephen and Roberta about their father. The children need not know the manner of their father's death, not yet, not until they were old enough to understand. Their two younger siblings would hardly remember their father as they grew. He would become a misty memory in their past. For now, everyone could feel comforted to be home. Gregory, carried in on a pallet, was set down carefully, exhausted by the ardours journey made slower by constant pain aggrivated by every movement of the carriage.

'Father!' Edmund and Simon both cried in unison, breaking from their mother and hurling themselves onto their father, not realising the pain their jubilant greeting caused him. Gregory did not mind, it was a moment he had never dared dream would occur during the hideous time in the Tower. Openly crying, he reached over to kiss his sons.

Now, Mary would devote her life to the care of her husband and darling children, safe with the understanding that they would grow into adulthood, free of fear, away from the corrupt court life, in quiet seclusion. Then they would go on into the world, with marriage and families of their own. Mary and Gregory would grow old peacefully, together, forever.

# 43

## EPILOGUE

### *Spring 1539*

England on a spring afternoon was an exquisite place. Birds sang from the branches of trees that hung heavy with fragrant blossom, and bumbles hummed around the garden, searching for early nectar. Seated on a bench, Mary Paxton gazed dreamily around this haven of tranquillity. Primroses had flowered, followed by the daffodils and now blue harebells were now beginning to take over. On a low wall nearby, a black and white cat basked in the warm sunshine.

Life went along at a placid, slow pace, which suited her and now, five years since the traumatic events at Tower Hill, she would not have her life any different. Mary was glad not to reside at court anymore; life had become precarious for anyone associated with Queen Anne. Sir Thomas More refused to sign the Act of Supremacy, preferring the martyrdom of execution rather than risking his immortal soul. Queen Anne suffered two miscarriages. The first had been associated but not proven with the failed attempt on her life by the audacious plan. The second occurred in January 1536 after two unconnected incidents. First, the king was unseated from his horse in a joust and feared killed. He regained consciousness, having suffered an injury to his leg, which developed into a painful ulcer that was to trouble him for the rest of his life. The queen had then walked in on her husband flirting openly with Jane Seymour. She had stormed and screamed at her husband and that sly country slut, refusing to calm her temper or think of the well-being of her unborn child. The boy she miscarried would have been her saviour. The events that followed saw the queen and her supporters arrested and imprisoned in the Tower for treason, adultery and incest. The men, including her brother George, were publically executed on Tower Hill. Anne's execution was within the walls of the Tower, with a French executioner hired using an elegant sword to dispatch the royal prisoner.

Within the week, King Henry had married Jane Seymour. Seventeen months later, Queen Jane died, days after giving King Henry the one thing both Catherine and Anne had failed to provide, a living and healthy son, Prince Edward. Even Gregory's friend, Thomas Cromwell, like so many others, once a favourite of the king did not escape his royal master's rage. After orchestrating the disastrous marriage to Anne of Cleves, Cromwell's fall from grace was swift and fatal. Hated by all at court and detested by so many countrywide, Cromwell met his end at the executioner's block, dying a bloody and horrendous death.

Gregory had become reclusive, shunning company, preferring to keep himself locked away in his own room where he sat at the window staring out throughout the day and long into the night. Mary attempted to encourage him to resurrect his profession as a lawyer, even hiring scribes and apprentices to write and work for him. Yet his expierences had a left a profound indentation on his life, unable to cope, he dismissed his employees and reverted into his solitary world, shunning assistance. He led as pain free life as medication could allow. The local apocothary provided potions he took daily that kept the agonies of his broken body and the nightmares at bay. Mary faithfully tended to her husband, allowing his solitude and letting him express all his emotions and tempers. On Christmas Day, despite all that had preceeded in the early months of the pregnancy, she gave birth to a healthy daughter named Christina. The birth of his daughter marked a change in Gregory. Holding this new life brought life back to him. Gradually, watching his daughter grow and with the company of his sons and stepson, he found he was able to rejoice in life once again, and freshly fell in love with his wife once more.

Margaret's health had deteriorated after the events on Tower Hill and she entered a convent soon after their return home, leading a life of prayer and meditation until her death.

Alice had become introvert as she mourned Robert. She was enervated, listless. Mary cared for her children, while she remained in the room she had shared with Robert. A loving husband and father was the memory Alice persistently clung to, and stubbornly refused to acknowledge the evil he had committed. Slowly, she came to terms with realisation to the true nature of her disgraced husband and at length acknowledged her widowhood, and found inner peace, never remarrying.

Cecily was content with her husband and children. Angelo, now a charismatic and handsome young man, became more like his father in looks and self-assurance. When Captain Foyle docked at Tilbury, Mary took Angelo to meet him, and the captain fulfilled the promise to take the lad to sea. He became friendly with Jewel's daughter, Atlanta. The captain had written to Mary about the growing friendship between his granddaughter and her son. Everyone agreed that they would make a good match; as a result, Angelo and Atlanta were betrothed. Gregory's sons Edmund and Simon had gone to live with Essex knights to receive an education and when they were both older, they would become squires to their lords. Roberts's children and Christina remained in the nursery.

Yardeley Chase now belonged to Stephen. Along with Alice and Gregory, Mary took charge of the place until the fifteen-year-old boy reached adulthood. He would eventually marry and produce an heir. Mary and Gregory's destiny was here and they would now grow old and die within the peaceful walls of the home they loved. Her life had come full circle. She was home.